# WINTEr DARK

For Justine,

Hope you enjoy!

Lots of love

Alex

X

BOOKS BY ALEX CALLISTER

*Winter Dark*
*Winter Rising*

# ALEX CALLISTER

# WINTER DARK

bookouture

Published by Bookouture in 2020

An imprint of Storyfire Ltd.
Carmelite House
50 Victoria Embankment
London EC4Y 0DZ

www.bookouture.com

ISBN: 978-1-83888-1-085
eBook ISBN: 978-1-83888-107-8

*For the Other Half*
*who is*
*80% Simon / 20% Alek*

# PROLOGUE

*Sexually omnivorous.*

Erik stared at the words until his eyes crossed and the typeface blurred. He said them in his head, trying them on for size. He rolled them over his tongue, *sex-u-ally om-ni-vo-rous.* Nope. He had nothing. Animal, vegetable, mineral? He had no idea. He looked through the mirrored observation glass at the sexually omnivorous candidate in the GCHQ interrogation room.

The dreadlocked girl lounged, side on to the glass, swinging the cast on her left wrist. She blew a vast pink bubble and surveyed her surroundings.

'Just see what you think. That's all I'm asking,' said Control beside him.

Erik peered closer. *A nose ring.* He already knew what he thought.

The bubble popped and the candidate turned and winked at the mirror.

Erik flinched. Face on, she had the kind of looks that bypass beautiful and go straight to unobtainable: long dark lashes, striking green eyes, sharp angular features. Not pretty. *Spectacular.*

Erik scowled. Never in the history of the cyber intelligence services had they hired non-military for the field.

'Is that a Dalmatian onesie?' he said.

Control shrugged.

Erik looked down at the candidate's biography again, playing for time.

*Boarding school from the age of six.*

So, traumatised or psychotic.

Or both.

*Sexually omnivorous.*

She didn't look old enough to have acquired many sexual preferences, omnivorous or otherwise. He checked her date of birth.

*Seventeen?*

At that age, he was still congratulating himself on getting to last base.

'Where did you find her?' Erik dripped disapproval.

'Pulled her off a mountain,' said Control, unrepentant. He turned to the darkened room. 'Put up the Hahnenkamm footage.'

Max typed a command and YouTube appeared on his monitor. 'Extreme Streif posted by JakeBoardPro,' Erik read.

Erik rolled his eyes. The Streif – the World Championship men's downhill ski course. So, she was a skier. He should have guessed from the onesie. A sexually omnivorous, crazy fast skier. Just what GCHQ didn't need.

On the screen, a figure shuffled forward to the starting gate with a swing of the hips, a distinctive, twisting swing of the hips, a spine contorting flick and curl. *Not a skier, a boarder.* A night boarder. Piste lights glinted off her black visor.

Erik knew the Streif. It opened with the Mausefalle, a blind 260-foot jump onto a vertical sheet of ice. He had never heard of anyone trying it at night. He had never heard of anyone trying it on a board.

The figure leapt, and the image went into free fall. A wall of snow hurtled towards them. With a thud of compression and screech of inside edge, the boarder landed the fall-away turn, banking so hard the camera grazed the snow. Crystals of ice filled the lens.

Erik breathed out.

There was no way he was going to be impressed. He just had to stand firm, sound reasonable and wait for Control to get over this sudden interest in hiring civilians.

'So, she's got some boarding skills,' he said. 'It takes a bit more than that.' *A bit more brainpower, a bit more discipline, a lot more everything.*

'She broke the bank at the Colony Club in Mayfair,' said Control. 'She has a photographic memory.'

*What was she doing in a casino at seventeen?*

'Does she know why she's here?'

Control shook his head.

*Great.*

Control put his hand on Erik's arm. 'See what you think, that's all I'm asking. And watch yourself. Some martial arts.'

Now that was just insulting.

'Yeah, I'll watch myself with the little girl with the broken arm.'

\*

Winter sat in the brilliant white of the interrogation room, her wrist burning. She looked at the bare walls with their black rubber skirtings, at the surveillance cameras in the corners and finally at the mirrored wall.

She hated mirrors – the way they showed your true self. Sometimes, if she looked long and hard enough, she thought she could see an entirely different person behind her eyes. She knew where she was. GCHQ. The Government Communications Headquarters. The snoop police. What the hell was she doing here?

A tall dark figure entered and shut the door carefully behind him. Stance said, military. Highly developed pectoral muscles said, can handle himself in a fight. Scarring along underside of right hand said, martial arts – probably karate. Slight curve on left side said, armed. Lines round corner of eyes said, thirty to thirty-five.

*Old.*

Calm. Bored even. Not the heavy squad then – here to talk. Well, he could stick it.

*How about I give you the finger and you give me my phone call?*

The blow caught the side of her head, knocking her sideways. Her chair skittered out from under her, crashing over.

*He was fast.*

She crouched, hair in face, arms outstretched.

'Hey peace, man.' She waved her hands. 'Aren't you supposed to ask the questions first?'

He smiled and looked towards the mirrored wall.

'Consider it more of a practical.'

He rounded the table and yanked her up by her hair, twisting her good arm hard behind her back. She considered her options. Her broken wrist, in its blue cast, hung useless.

*What the hell. It was only her left hand after all.*

\*

Erik opened his eyes and regretted it. The strip light burnt into his retinas, leaving dancing monkeys of black. He pushed himself onto his elbow, feeling his jaw. His fingers worked their way across his cheekbone and up to his temple. Unbelievable. She had hit him with her cast. He had a lump the size of Mexico.

The teenager was back in her seat, arm stretched out along the table, her complexion grey. *Good.* A medic in green scrubs fussed with the cast. Control sat at the table opposite. Erik couldn't remember ever seeing him in an interview room before.

'I think we can say she passes the practical.'

Erik glared.

Control turned to the mirror. 'Bring in the technical.'

The technical interview with Max, the GCHQ Head of Research, was a programming challenge. Erik watched as Max set up the laptop. A snowboarder taking the programming challenge? Now he had seen it all.

Control's cold eyes turned on him. 'Are you getting up?'

Erik knew he was never, ever going to live this down.

*

Back in the observation room they adjusted the camera angles and waited. The darkness enclosed them, cocooning them in a warm fug of pot noodle and caffeine. Erik fingered his cheekbone. In the interview room, the teenager was considering the laptop.

'How long have I got?' she asked the mirror, holding up her wrist.

'Take as long as you need,' said Max through the overhead speaker.

Erik rolled his eyes. *What a colossal waste of time.* He sat back and glared as the teenager took some bubblegum out of her mouth, teased it with her teeth then plastered it on the laptop camera. Beside him, a screen went blank. She did the same to the wall-mounted camera behind her. They looked at each other.

'This is a closed loop?' Control checked.

Max sighed. 'Yes, sir. The laptop exists on its own with no outside connection. The air gap is watertight.'

Control stared at the blank cameras for a moment then he nodded.

'OK. Leave her be.'

They watched the teenager type for ten minutes, wincing as her wrist came under pressure. Then she pushed back from the screen. She put her feet up on the desk, folded her arms, put her chin on her chest and closed her eyes.

'What is she doing? Has she done it? Has she finished?' asked Control.

'I'm guessing she has written something to test the parameters of the system,' said Max with satisfaction. 'It won't work.'

Control was edgy. 'And she definitely can't get a signal out on that?'

'No,' said Max patiently. 'As I said, it's a closed loop.'

'I'll be in my office. Don't take your eyes off her.'

For an hour or more nothing changed. Max watched a 24-hour news channel, Erik paced, the teenager slept. Then, at some signal from the laptop, she sat up and stretched.

'Now she'll see it hasn't worked,' said Max, leaning forward. 'Let's see what you've got for us, little lady.'

She typed for maybe five minutes, then she stopped as suddenly as she had started. She stared at the two-way mirror and pressed the last key with a theatrical flourish.

*Return.*

What was she up to?

They didn't have to wait long to find out. In the corner of the observation room the main terminal registered a firewall breach. Across the screen ran the words:

WHY USE A SLEDGEHAMMER TO CRACK A NUT? ANSWER:
SOMETIMES YOU NEED A SLEDGEHAMMER

WHY USE A SLEDGEHAMMER TO CRACK A NUT? ANSWER:
SOMETIMES YOU NEED A SLEDGEHAMMER

The message repeated over and over.

The internal phone rang. Erik picked it up on autopilot, staring at the words on the screen. It was Control.

'Why have I taken a call from the NSA asking if I have the hacker, call sign Sledgehammer, in custody? Our American friends couldn't stop laughing.'

Erik caught sight of the news channel. The Sky-copter was hovering over Piccadilly Circus. Someone had hacked the giant electronic billboards:

FREE SLEDGEHAMMER. SAVE THE WHALES. PEACE MAN

The message vanished, replaced by a countdown.

10...
9...
8...
7...
6...
5...
4...
3...
2...
1

Thirty seconds later the GCHQ mainframe collapsed under the weight of the world's hacking community. A targeted DDoS of unprecedented scale. A distributed denial of service attack that flooded every server with malformed requests. It was the largest DDoS ever to be aimed at a government institution. It was going to go down in history.

In the bright white interrogation room, Sledgehammer stood up and took a bow.

*

Twenty-four hours later and a thousand miles away, a boy opened his eyes at the bottom of a well in the courtyard of an Italian castle. Far above his head he could make out a circular glimmer of light.

He lifted a cuffed hand to his cheek. Something was dripping on his face, stinging the cuts. He could feel blood trickling down his neck. It was the third time he had been kidnapped and this time felt like it might be the last.

*Fight*, his brother ordered in his head.

Alek always expected him to fight.

His knuckles burned. There had been too many of them.

Maybe if he wedged his back and feet against the stone walls he might be able to inch his body up the shaft. Then, if he got to the top he could use his head to lift the cover. He gritted his teeth.

After twenty minutes he looked down, he had climbed about as high as a man. His head throbbed. The higher he climbed, the harder he would fall. He shifted, trying to ease the ache in his back and thighs.

A light broke overhead, flooding the well. The boy screwed up his eyes, flinching away from the brightness.

Peter's voice echoed down to him, shaky with panic. If Peter was here, so was his brother.

This time Alek had caught up with them fast.

*

Alek had pulled himself off the streets and been on the way to serious money when he found out he had a baby brother left behind in the gutter. The last thing a teenager on the make needed. Even now, years and millions later, Alek still didn't know what had possessed him to yield to that weakness. Because there was no doubt it was a weakness, a vulnerability. If you cared, your enemies had all the leverage they needed.

He looked around at the castle courtyard. Flaming torch brackets on the walls. A well in the centre, dark green moss circling the rim. A tower on one side, silhouetted against the night sky, squat stone barracks on the others. Medieval. Giant stone hounds with collars of iron stood guard. He could see Peter leaning over the green brick wall of the well and his brother being pulled out, blinking, into the light.

Alek turned back to the figures kneeling at his feet. Twelve kidnappers. Amateurs. They needed twice as many for a job like this. His reputation for mercy had probably decided their surrender. He would keep the castle. He knew nothing about the set up in

Umbria but the local Camorra would fold. People were easy to control. Find their weak spot and press.

There had been too many challenges to his authority recently. He was starting to realise it wasn't enough to control his own region. These days everyone was playing on the global stage. Yesterday, hackers had brought down GCHQ – a UK government institution – without leaving their desks. The internet made a lot of things possible. It made the world small. It brought people within reach. And Alek knew that people within reach could be controlled. The potential was all there just waiting to be exploited. He could imagine a time when everywhere would be within reach and the whole world could be controlled.

Alek crouched down on his haunches until he was on a level with the figures in the dust and spoke to them gently. After a while the conversation came to a natural end. He stared at the dirty floor, then got to his feet. He thought about his reputation for mercy as he took his handgun out of its holster and passed it to one of his men. Then he looked at his brother and he thought about vulnerability.

His hands reached into his pockets. When they came out, his fists were ringed with metal.

*

It takes a really long time to beat someone to death with your fists, a really laboriously long time. But there is a certain science to it if you know what you are doing. The boy stood watching, his knuckles white from the effort of gripping a bottle of water, his ears ringing with the steady *thump, thump* of fists on flesh. Finally, his brother held out an iron-covered hand, palm upwards, asking for his gun. The puckered scar on his wrist was splattered with blood. It was an old scar, wide and white, stretching round the wrist like a giant snake. A boa constrictor or an anaconda.

The boy knew what was coming and nothing he could say would prevent it. Alek called his name and he limped forward, handing his water to Peter. He caught the gun clumsily in his bruised hands. The knuckles burned and his grip was weak. He glanced down: a Smith & Wesson. He cocked it one-handed and looked the question. Alek gave an impatient jerk of the head. The boy limped forward and put a bullet between what was left of his kidnapper's eyes. He was twelve and it was by no means his first kill.

Being the brother of a billionaire crime lord wasn't all silver spoon.

# CHAPTER 1

## Ten years later

## Winter

The internet changed everything. It made the world small. Which was gravy for the intelligence services. Everywhere was accessible. Everything was online. Good news all round for the anoraks (and I include myself here). When we found we could hack vibrators we thought we'd hit nirvana.

Then it turned ugly. Where the intelligence services could go, others could follow.

The ransom attack was born: government departments, the utilities, the National Health Service, and that was just the start. Soon, whole countries were being held to ransom and nuclear arsenals dismantled for fear of cyberattack.

And then it got organised.

The old crime networks – that for centuries had been kept apart by distance and differences – woke up to this age of opportunity and found that there was no distance and that their differences were far fewer than they had previously imagined. It took us a while to realise that the Yakuza, the Bratva, the Mafia, the Triads, the 'Ndrangheta and the Cartels were all connected, all regional divisions of the same organisation, and at the top, holding the power, was a single anonymous man.

For a while, things hung in the balance.

Then Firestorm came along.

*

I remember that day so clearly. It was a morning like any other – we were in the Bunker, our GCHQ London home: Viv fussing over an egg-white omelette for Erik, love in her eyes; Max staring at his screens halfway through his first caramel Crunchie of the day; Simon, my quartermaster, standing in the doorway all Buddy Holly glasses and floppy hair, clutching bags of breakfast sandwiches in his arms. Grease had turned the paper clear. Overhead, the ceiling cooling ducts roared. We had been up all night. Bacon and weariness filled the air.

I remember the bacon and my empty stomach and the hit of saliva and I remember Viv glaring because she thought Simon had brought an evil grease-sandwich for Erik, and then I opened the link.

*Welcome to Firestorm*
*Cheating husband? Bitch wife? Hate your boss?*
*Let Firestorm take care of your problem.*
*Safe. Anonymous. Cheap.*

The primary colours mimicked the old eBay homepage. I saw it was the same idea but with Dutch auctions: the contractor with the cheapest price won. A cyber currency.

eBay for contract killers.

Not a closed peer-to-peer market on the dark web but an ordinary Clearnet site. Murder for the masses.

I clicked on a link.

*Rate your Firestorm Contractor:*
*Speed of comms*
*Delivery of service*
*Efficiency*

And I knew nothing was ever going to be the same again.

'Get ICANN,' I said, my voice overloud in the morning quiet.

Simon glanced at his watch. Bacon sandwiches dangled. 'It is 1 a.m. in Playa Vista.'

Viv looked over my shoulder. 'It is a joke,' she said. 'And even if it isn't, I can't see it taking off. Not that many people are really murderous.'

I had stared at my screen in silence with a bad, bad feeling because if childhood had taught me anything, it was that people are really murderous.

*

By its first birthday, Firestorm had chalked up more than fifty thousand contracts and a whole new industry had been born. It passed a hundred thousand a few months later and we were no closer to tracking the site or its founder. By then its potential for intimidation had been realised. People are easy to control if you are prepared to apply the fear. Everyone has someone they care about, someone they don't want hurt.

And the bad news is, the man at the top of organised crime is prepared to apply the fear. He controls Firestorm and we have no idea who he is. All we have is an artist's impression of the white snake tattoo round his wrist. A boa constrictor, squeezing the life out of the whole world.

What does the internet do? It brings people together. It matches buyers with sellers.

Imagine a world where everyone's life has a price.

Now there is not a politician, judge or policeman safe from Firestorm. As Simon says: *control Firestorm and you can control the world*. When the Democratic presidential nominee resigned, blaming the site, we thought it couldn't get any worse.

And then, last month, they spun out Slashstorm.

# CHAPTER 2

The security centre of the Hôtel Grand in Geneva is in semi-darkness. Wall-to-wall monitors flicker with CCTV images of the ballroom and a gala event. The social whirl plays out on soundless black-and-white screens – politicians, glamorous women, guys in tuxedos, round tables littered with the remains of dinner. Men in black stand in the corners. What Firestorm calls a 'target-rich environment'. Fertile ground for contract killers.

I should be monitoring the surveillance at the gala, looking out for the safety of the captains of industry at the World Economic Forum, instead I am on my laptop logged on to Slashstorm.

It is headline news everywhere:

*Slashstorm is back*

The hottest new internet voting phenomenon just launched its ticking countdown again.

The faces on death row stare out from my screen. Boy, girl, black, white. Twelve faces. Twelve scrolling counters. Two weeks for the viewing public to vote. Who will *you* save?

The Slashstorm website. A popular vote for fourteen days then a live climax. Simple. Effective. Primetime TV meets torture porn. Firestorm repackaged as entertainment.

I stare at the thumbnail pictures. Three rows on the screen, four pictures per row. These days it is easy to disguise the point of origin even from the experts. Cold traces the back of my neck, pricks my hairline. The faces are young. Teenage. Twelve to fifteen years old. A girl with wide brown eyes looks into the camera. There is nothing behind her. Mirrors. Or a green screen.

The concept is simple. Twelve teenagers. Who will you save?

The last Slashstorm vote took us all by surprise. The teenager who lost polled well early on. Floppy-haired and cute, he was too good-looking to be in danger. Then, as the public campaigns got behind the chubby one and the sad one in a hysterical global pandemic of voting, he got left behind. He took three hours to die. Three hours that I have watched and re-watched and analysed, until every time I shut my eyes, I see the lurid, blurring images against my crimson eyelids.

Now it is happening again. An hour ago, Slashstorm announced a new vote and we are nowhere. We can't trace the money, we can't trace the site, we can't trace the kids and we can't trace the man behind it. 'The Prince of Darkness' – Simon calls him – the man at the top of organised crime, the man behind Firestorm and Slashstorm. We've never managed to get near his identity. The white snake tattoo on his right wrist is all we have.

Panic grips me, raising my heart rate, drumming in my ears. Fourteen days to crack a website and I am here on surveillance detail in a Geneva hotel, babysitting a gala dinner.

I need to be back in GCHQ. Not that I have anything left to try against Slashstorm. I pulled every technical trick I know last time, my searches desperate as the deadline approached, and then frantic. The GCHQ incident room froze in horror, analysts unable to believe their eyes as I tried everything. I tried everything and it wasn't enough. The screaming went on and on, his hands clutching at nothing.


Slashstorm got started almost by accident. A Firestorm contract was screened live. A US Senator had refused to bend to the fear.

The contract was called: the Senator's son. A blond student. Very photogenic. The robed and hooded contractor who won the contract screened it live like a reality TV show.

*A voyeur*, said the psych profilers. A psychopath and a voyeur. No response to the boy's mercy signals. Cutting and strangling MO. *Unusual*, said the profilers, leaving me wondering exactly how many precedents they have. He took a while to die. By the end, his hair wasn't very blond.

Public outrage was matched only by public fascination. Mouth-drying, breath-catching, compulsive viewing. It practically broke the net and Slashstorm was born in a wave of public hysteria and blood.

The second time, there was a proper online vote with an untraceable cyber currency payment. Twelve anonymous candidates to choose from. Fourteen days to vote. It tapped right into the human traits of choosing and empathising. We just can't stop ourselves having favourites.

The Hôtel Grand may have five stars but there is nothing high-end about its security suite. Dirty scuffed walls, hairy floor tiles, Chanel Bleu cologne – although that may be Brad, my US National Security Agency opposite number. I shiver in the gloom.

Brad glances across at me. He scowls when he sees the faces on my open laptop.

'How many this time?' he says.

'Twelve. Twelve again.'

He smooths the label back on his bottle of water. He has spent all evening picking it off. 'We've got nothing,' he says finally.

A big admission from the NSA. Hearing it makes the panic rise again. It crawls up my throat. I want to screw up my eyes, pull at my hair, rock back and forth.

*Breathe.*

'I just can't understand why we can't trace the kids,' he says. 'That is the weirdest thing. Where are they getting them from?'

He is right. Facial recognition technology has made the world a very small place. Absolutely everyone can be traced once you know who you are looking for.

I zoom in on a US Senator shiny with postprandial sweat. He knocks back his glass and holds it out for a refill. I move on to John J. Traynor III, millionaire philanthropist, and his grey-haired wife. In an age where image is everything, her grey hair and gentle, lined face are almost declarations of war on social media. Serious philanthropists with the Nobel to prove it.

I wonder what Erik would do if he were still alive. The only time I ever saw him cry was after the live Slashstorm show. Nothing in ten years as Head of Field affected him like it. What would he say if he knew it was back? It has been a month since his death and I still can't believe he is gone.

Beside me, Brad swears. The top left monitor has died.

I grab the comm link to GCHQ and search the hotel systems, my hands working the keyboard. Brad is doing the same. I get there first, I have been drilling security systems since I was a kid.

'Systems breach at the venue,' I tell London.

I can hear Brad warning the protection boys on the floor.

The monitors die one by one. A slow, measured strike. A slick job by somebody. Just before the final screen goes blank, the gala erupts in scurrying panic, chairs rock back, wine glasses crash. If there was sound, there would be screaming.

'Street cams are down,' says Simon on the line from GCHQ. My quartermaster is unflappable.

'Point of origin?'

'Unconfirmed. He is on the move. Signal interrupter.'

'So he's local, wherever he is.'

'Isosceles is down.'

The Western Europe super-satellite. Now *that* I don't believe.

'Are you serious?'

There are only a handful of hackers in the world who could take out Isosceles and none of them could do it from a laptop.

I lift the MP5 from the corner where I left it at the start of the evening. I check my boots with the eight throwing knives, I check the thigh holster ruining the line of my white satin evening dress. My reflection scowls in the glass panel of the door. A weaponised Grace Kelly.

My fingers drum the desk.

*Come on.*

Whoever the hacker is, he is going to have me hard on his heels.

All around me the security services are putting the hotel into lockdown. I couldn't care less. The hacker who could pull this off is a big fish, maybe even Halo, the biggest of them all – the hacker for the Prince of Darkness.

'Found him!' Simon's shout blurs the comm unit. 'He's moving fast.'

I am already slamming out of Security, taking the back stairs three at a time. I shove my way through the screaming crowds, cross the atrium, burst out into the chill night and slide behind the wheel of a Service Merc.

*

Smoking brake pads fill the air. I peer out through the windscreen at the bright lights ahead. Cuckoo-clock chalets cluster round an alpine church – Courchevel ski resort. My hands grip the wheel in the dark, trying to throttle the frustration. Two hours of chasing blind, with Simon in my ear. I thought I had the hacker trapped until I remembered the altiport, perched on the side of the mountain, a slice of concrete sticking out into nothing.

'You'll never close the gap in time,' Simon says. 'He's too fast.'

'Is Isosceles still down?'

'Yeah.'

*He is going to get away.*

Across the square, lights blaze from an outdoor piste bar I recognise. Ten years ago, I used to hang out there before a night run. Life before GCHQ... Is there anyone there who will even remember my name?

I ditch the car, swing the MP5 onto my shoulder and push through the crowd. Woolly hats bob to music twenty years out of date, a woman in plaits, a bikini and ski boots toasts the moon.

A red-and-white all-in-one dips and dives to the music – a ski instructor. Our shoulders collide. I palm his radio and make for the lighting gantries, pulling myself onto the lower rungs to improve reception. There are whoops from the crowd, a hundred arms punch the air, rocking the night. Above me, a searchlight swings and arcs in its cradle, lighting up the mountain with a bright circle on both sides of the valley. I'll never close the gap by road but there is another way. A much faster way.

I tune to the emergency frequency used by the piste workers. I'm amazed I can still remember it.

'Control Room, Control Room, Control Room. This is Winter, over.' This has to be the longest of long shots.

Silence.

'Control Room, Control Room, Control Room. This is Winter, over.'

Nothing.

The channel crackles.

'Winter? This is Control Room.' The voice is unsure, fearful. 'Winter? Is that *you*?'

*Jake.*

My night-boarding buddy. Ten years ago, he watched me jump off the Streif. No wonder he is unsure. He thinks I died a decade ago. He thinks I died the night GCHQ pulled me off a mountain.

*

It is heavy-going through the snow to the Three Valleys Command and Control station. White satin flaps against my legs.

I throw open the reinforced steel door. Jake sits in semi-darkness, his hands down his trousers, a black Kessler snowboard resting against the blinking control panel. Ten years and nothing has changed: he is still working the night shift, monitoring the safety of the piste workers. He is still stoned out of his skull.

'I have to get to the airstrip. I need your board. And your jacket.'

Jake stares. He was expecting a dreadlocked adrenaline junkie with a nose ring and a bad attitude, not satin and an MP5.

Cognitive dissonance.

I lean over and swing the board vertical. It is in great shape. 'Nice.'

'You're alive.' Tears hang in his lashes.

I close the gap between us and reach out, putting my hand behind his neck pulling his forehead to mine. The gun clanks against my side. Static from an open channel crackles.

'For now,' I say.

I cross the rubber matting of the waiting platform and swing myself into the nearest Apollo gondola. Jake's hands hover over the controls and the doors close, trapping me in the tiny metal compartment. His mouth opens and shuts like he has finally thought of something he wanted to say.

I pull Jake's jacket on and the comforting smell of weed envelops me. It must be minus fifteen up here in this tin can. I shrug the MP5 onto the bench seat opposite and swap my footwear, pushing my boots into the wide poacher's pockets, my fingers stiff in the cold.

The cable car lurches in the wind.

How long is it since I have been on a board? It is ten years since I flung myself off a mountain not caring if I lived or died. Ten years and Erik, my Head of Field, have taught me caution of a sort. I'm not sure what else they have taught me.

Not a lot, according to my last psych report:

*Overconfidence causes subject to underestimate all around her. Under pressure she falls back on behaviour that has served her well in the past: physical aggression or seduction.*

'Fight it or fuck it' in other words.

Now Erik is dead and I am on my own – no one has my back. He was father, brother and punchbag rolled into one. The constant in my life for the last ten years. The force that transformed me from teenage hacker to GCHQ field agent.

I stare into the black as the cable car starts to dock. Familiar muscles tighten and adrenaline floods me. No one else could make this run. I don't even know if I can make it. The door slides open in a screech of runners and I hurl myself across the rubber matting and curve down and round and straight off the mountain.

Less than a second later, I reach terminal velocity. I strain down into the darkness, closing my eyes to slits. The muscle memory kicks in. Thank God you don't forget. The grinding roar of the board is deafening on the icy piste. I haven't done this run in ten years, I have never done it in ten minutes.

The navigation lights of a helicopter starting its descent shine red and green above me, so close I could touch them. I am forced to slow for the off-piste route through the trees. The terrain changes from smooth piste to forest, the snow pooling in deceptive mounds around the tree roots. My dress whips my knees as I snake the turns. This is where it could go wrong. A stray branch smacks my bare leg, slicing the skin. I stagger, lose my balance and right myself. As I break out through the dark wall of pines to the slope above the runway, the helicopter is coming in to land.

I hurl myself down the vertical drop to the landing strip, crashing the final few feet onto the slick black tarmac. Ice grazes my cheek, hard as rock. The edge is beside me. Headlights slant across the empty space. A car door slams in the distance. The hacker.

My feet are trapped on the board. I kick frantically at the boots, my eyes on the helicopter. Someone is standing on the helicopter running board, riding the turbulence. He is floodlit by the landing lights, then slides into darkness. Then back into the light.

I stare.

His body flexes and bends as the tail swings sharply one way and then the other, his arm raised as he hangs from the strap. A white snake circles his right wrist and my heart thuds. A wide, white snake tattoo. A boa constrictor. A tattoo known to every intelligence service on the planet. There is an artist's impression of it on the wall in the GCHQ incident room and another beside my desk.

He jumps and lands with his back to me. When he straightens up I see he is broad with developed shoulder muscles, a shaved head and long legs in dark combat trousers.

*I don't believe it. The Prince of Darkness himself.*

The hacker walks forwards, his face a pale dot in the night, and his boss greets him with a forearm grip.

My bare feet slip and slide as I throw myself across the wet concrete. The MP5 smacks in the small of my back.

The hacker climbs onto the running board and the Prince of Darkness is right behind him, his arm on the open door. They are leaving. He has touched down to pick up the hacker and now he is leaving.

*Noooooooo.*

All I need is his face, just once, just a glimpse – my photographic memory and the GCHQ database will do the rest. Once we know who he is, we can find him. I don't need to bring down his websites if I can bring down the man himself. I see the Slashstorm homepage and a floppy-haired kid taking three hours to die. It is not happening again.

I accelerate across the gap, shouting out in the night but it is too far and my voice dies, a whisper, lost against the rotor blades. My chest heaves, my lungs burn with fumes and he stops, one long leg already on the board, as if he feels the sheer force of my will behind him.

He turns and dark eyes meet mine.

*Hot.*

I wasn't expecting that.

He steps down and I skid to a halt, etching his features straight into my memory, processing his face, top to bottom like a laser printer. Shaved head, olive skin.

*Bastard.*

'What do you want?' His voice cuts across the whirr of the slowing blades, the screech of metal, the sounds of a cooling helicopter. His accent hovers somewhere over Eastern Europe. Steam rises off the helicopter, mixing with the freezing fog.

*I want to know who you are.*

Behind him, three bodyguards jump from the helicopter, assault rifles in their hands.

*Not good.*

I crash sideways, drawing from my thigh holster, firing at the yellow underside of the helicopter. The blast carries the still rotating blades into the air, showering the site in shrapnel.

I am already running. The sprint across the open airstrip to my board stretches out, unravelling in front of me, miles and miles of black.

'Stop her!' shouts a bodyguard.

My feet find the boots still strapped to the board and I throw myself over the edge, out into nothing, his face safe in my head. I have got more than I came for.

Now I just need to stay alive.

# CHAPTER 3

I open my eyes.

I am curled in a ball. My whole body shakes. This is what they mean by teeth chattering. My head shrinks into the collar of Jake's jacket. I have no neck, I am a tortoise. A wall of grey touches my nose. There is a familiar feel about my ankles – restriction. One foot is attached to something. I try to move my feet and the pain rips through me. I close my eyes, wondering why there is snow all around me. A snow pocket. It is funny. As I lose consciousness I think how cold it is in this Winter-shaped snow pocket.

*I am dreaming. A man with a shaved head laughs at me. A boy with floppy hair pleads. I light match after match to keep his image alive, the sulphur as strong as the brightness of the flare of light and the pain of burnt fingers. Again and again I strike a match, and again and again the image fades.*

I open my eyes. The wall of snow glistens with texture. The grey has become brighter. Daylight. Water trickles and runs down my nose, down the back of my neck. It drips on my face. The grey-white hollow is alive with the sound of moving snow – the creak, slither and slide of it. The trickle of thawing water. It is so hot in this snow pocket, the heat has woken me. I burn with it.

Erik shouts in my head. *Get up NOW!* he screams.

'I'm fine,' I say. 'Fine. Just hot, really hot. I need to sleep.'

The trickle of water drowns him out. I close my eyes, drifting on a sea of molten lava. This must be the hottest place on earth. Erik is still shouting. I growl at him, but he doesn't stop.

*Hypothermia, Winter!* he shouts.

What is he talking about? His shouting is annoying when I am so hot and tired. The truth hits a second before the panic, and the panic kicks in hard. I need to move NOW. My arms and legs are pinned. Trapped. My comm link and locator are gone. I am buried alive. I try to remember the survival training for Siberia but my brain refuses. I close my eyes to focus. A laughing man with a snake tattoo blocks my way. Flames dance in his eyes.

A sound wakes me.

Chipping and jarring like a broken tooth. Digging. I curl tighter. I am going to hibernate until spring. Arms reach down into my hollow, into my cocoon, into my Winter-shaped snow hole. They haul at me, dragging. My legs scream at the movement. The pain pulls me into itself and there is nothing but black.


Jolting wakes me.

My head slams against a restraining bar. I am moving along the ground.

Sliding, a rescue sleigh. Arms lift me and the pain screams through me again.


The smell of diesel wakes me.

Diesel and rubber. I taste truck. I cannot see through the clumps in my lashes. I blink and blink. A rubber hose in my mouth. I focus on the dirty red pipe. The pipe hangs across a gap and disappears into a grill – I am breathing hot air straight from a truck's heating grill. The air burns my lungs. My head swims with fumes. My gag reflex cuts in and I choke on the hard rubber. Arms force a cup of hot liquid between my lips, it spills down my face.


Pain wakes me.

Arms are forcing me into water. My eyes open. I am in a bath, fully clothed. White satin floats to the surface. My body jackknifes. Arms hold me down in the burning heat. I scream and scream, thrashing like a martyr in the fire.


I open my eyes.

An orange pine ceiling slopes above me so close I could touch it. Cannabis and aftershave. Ten years slide away. Jake. A fetid duvet covers my mouth and nose, something hard and alien is pinned to my body under my arms, rammed up between my legs. Rubbery. Hot water bottles on the femoral artery. I can smell the rubber. Thank God for Jake's avalanche training. I push at the covers and a face appears beside me, looming above the mattress in a cloud of dirty brown hair and hash. He must have been lying on the floor.

'Oh, no you don't,' he says.

'I have to get up, Jake.' I am carrying the most wanted man on the planet in my head, his face as clear as a photograph. I thrust at the covers.

Jake clambers onto the bed and across the duvet, pinning me in place with his body weight. My arms can't shift him. I am made of jelly, a jelly woman.


It is night-time and the room is dark. Oinking is coming from somewhere and laughter. I turn my head and my brain crashes against my skull, bobbing around inside my head, smashing up against the hard surfaces. A small TV, the source of the weird flickering light, is propped up on a chest of drawers. The picture resolves. A Peppa Pig cartoon dubbed into French. I shift. Still wearing my underwear. And skiing thermals, a man's skiing thermals, the armpits smell of gravy. I try to move and the nausea hits me like a wall. Peppa oinks with a French accent.

'Do you want something to eat?' There is a hopeful note in Jake's voice.

He picks up a thin cardboard box balancing on a pile of clothes. There is stuff everywhere. The living area has shrunk smaller and smaller until it is a tiny space in the middle of the room. It probably happened so slowly he didn't notice the tide had pushed him off the sofa and onto the floor.

He holds up a slice of congealed pizza. My stomach spasms. I lie flat, dangling the slice above my face. My mouth aches as it drools with saliva. Salty and sweet, anchovy and pizza crust.

A black snowboard with a fork lightning motif lies across the end of the bed. I can just touch it with my toes.

'Were you looking for me or your board?'

Jake scowls. This has pissed him off for some reason. 'How did she run?'

I am exhausted by the effort of chewing.

'I made it.'


Peppa has gone and the news has come on. Jake nods at the TV. 'Can you believe someone shot John J. Traynor? The man was practically a saint. No one is safe these days.'

I think of the white hair and earnest face at the black-tie gala. When did someone shoot him? Was it while I was on the road chasing the hacker?

I stare up at the orange ceiling. 'I'm not sure about the beard.'

Jake removes his hand from his trousers and strokes his face defensively.

'You just need to rest.' He lights up a spliff, his hand drifting down the front of his trousers again. There is a rasping sound as he scratches.

How long since he had a girlfriend? Has he *ever* had a girlfriend? My eyes close and the waves of hash roll over me.

'Where have you been?' Jake asks. 'I thought…' he hesitates, his voice muffled, 'I thought you were dead.'

The varnish on the orange pine ceiling accentuates the knots and whirls in the wood. Tiny black holes into another life.

I shrug.

The mound of bedding muffles the movement. Barely a ripple disturbs the surface of the duvet. Jake turns away and flicks the ash off his spliff.

'Fine,' he says.

'How did you find me?'

'I thought it was an avalanche till I saw the smoke. When it got light, I found your tracks. Got out the Recco, got out the shovel – the rest is history.'

I stare at the ceiling. I have been lucky. Very lucky. Advanced avalanche training and a boarder's eye. Jake is one of the few people in the Three Valleys who could have found me.

'It's carnage at the strip. You should see it: sirens, fire engines, ambulances, every rescue service in the Three Valleys is there.'

'Anyone die?'

'Not that I've heard.'

I look up at the wooden whirls. They could almost be made of icing, they are so shiny and perfect.

'I'm hearing before the crash someone heard gunfire,' he says.

I turn on my side. 'Is that what the police are saying?'

Jake shrugs.

'People are asking questions.' He flicks his spliff. 'Russians. Serious Russians. They are knocking on every door in Courchevel looking for a blonde woman.'

Mercenaries. Hired muscle sent to clean up the mess. Does he know who I am? Are they looking for me? Or is he just being careful? Half dead or not, I need to get out of here.

I sit up, push back the duvet and swing my legs over the side. My head thuds worse than the time I was tasered. Dizziness sweeps me. I put my head between my knees. My feet are encased in thick red socks – the sort people used to ski in before they discovered engineered merino.

I stand up.

The bathroom is one short flight down, barely stairs, almost a ladder. There are other rooms off the corridor. Laughter. Gunfire coming from an Xbox. I open the door.

A snowboard stands on end, drip-drying in the small pink bath. I hunch in like an old woman, pull down the toilet lid and sit down. I can't move I am so exhausted.

I wake to the smell of male-shared bathroom. Whatever you are imagining, it is worse. I pull myself to my feet and yank at my thermals. Skintight on a man, they are baggy on me, hanging round my legs like wrinkled stockings. I look down at my bare body, sliding my fingers over the pink weals on my legs. Jake must have washed off the blood. The boarder boots saved my feet in the snow hollow. My fingers, protected by the long sleeves of Jake's jacket, are fine. Only the legs are showing damage.

I turf the board out of the bath, put the plug in and sit on the edge while the steam curls around me. I haven't got in a bath since my first week at boarding school. Childhood lessons are hard to shake. Hold someone's feet up in the bath and they cannot escape, no matter how much they squirm and buck, no matter how frantic their gasps for air. No one hears you underwater.

Boarding school – sink or swim. I mainly sank until I learnt to fight, no rules and no mercy.

The skin on my legs burns as I lower in. I duck my head, until only my face is above water and sit up again. Shampoo and soap?

I stand up, lean over and pick up a bottle of problem-skin face wash. Probably the same as liquid soap at ten times the price.

I step out of the bath and grab a towel – a hand towel but better than nothing.

There is a hesitant knock at the door.

'Are you OK?'

I ignore the thermals. No power on earth is getting me back into them. I knot the hand towel round my waist and slide the bolt. Jake's eyes widen.

'I'm going to need some clothes.'

Jake nods, his eyes huge.

'Jeans, T-shirt, some kind of coat. I've got my own underwear.'

He nods again.

I shut the door.


Back in his room, Jake stares. 'It looks good,' he says.

The previous owner of the T-shirt was a different body shape, it is tight across the chest. I glance down. '*Kiss Me Quick, Kiss Me Slow*' in pink sequins. I shrug on the jacket. The jeans are a perfect fit.

'Thanks Jake.'

I turn for the ladder hatch.

'You're not *going*?' His voice is high-pitched with disbelief. 'It's nearly midnight. Where will you go?'

He follows me down the stairs, scrabbling at my arm. At the front door, he tries to bar the way. 'Are you sure you're well enough?'

He has shaved off his beard. I wonder when he did that.

'I'll see you around,' I say.

I pull the hood up, zip the jacket to the chin and head out into the darkness.

# CHAPTER 4

The night is so cold it sucks the air. It hits your face and makes you gasp. Even right down here on the lower slopes, in the grey tail end of the season, the snow is deep, piled beside the road in great dirty slabs. I breathe in gulps of the dry air. It feels good after the closeness of Jake's room. The sky is covered in stars, like some kid has gone nuts with the glitter glue.

I need to get back to London and I need to do it without anyone seeing me. I can ID the Prince of Darkness, the man running Firestorm and Slashstorm, the man with a knife to the world's throat. He is going to be after me with every asset he has.

I pull the hood low over my forehead. Satellites work just as well in the dark. The days when only the intelligence services could watch you are long gone. Organised crime are now as good as we are.

The street is silent. Not that it is much of a street. The hamlet stretches out along the main road, an ugly ribbon development of ugly accommodation built to service the wealthy resort above, more concrete than cuckoo clock. Black spray from the road splatters the walls.

Fifty yards away, a group of men are standing beside a black four-by-four. Waiting. Their voices are clipped. I measure the distance.

*Serious Russians.*

A man peels off from the group and goes round the back. A sweep. They are flushing the building, working their way down the street.

His movements and hand gestures say military, his body language says mercenary. I feel down the side of my leg for the top of my boot. My knives are all there.

*Never turn your back. Never run.*

The free shuttle bus up the mountain swings round the bend towards us. Will it arrive before they notice me?

It pulls to a halt beside me in electric silence. The blue-and-chrome Courchevel livery gleams. The doors open and the driver looks me up and down.

'Out for a night on the town?'

'Something like that.'

I swing past the metal poles and sink onto a velour bus seat. The temperature inside is about a hundred degrees. Ski resorts – baking or freezing. No middle way. We lumber past the Russians at walking pace.

The shuttle bus stops in the central square. Alpine church to the right, cuckoo-clock chalets with expensive shops to the left. Opposite, the outdoor bar is still going full throttle.

I picture the message coming down to the team in the field:

*You have missed her. She has gone back up the mountain.*

The outdoor bar tables ring with the sound of ski boots. I scan the clientele. Not the right kind of punters. A red-and-white bobble hat lies forgotten on a bench, long red plaits hang down from the earmuffs. I slip it into my pocket and carry on up the street. Just below the Croisette, I see what I am looking for. A black-clad figure stands on the street, curly wire in the ear. Two-hundred pounds, six foot, and all muscle. I pull off my jacket and shake out my hair. The problem-skin face wash has turned it crazy. He looks me up and down, then back up again. His eyes stop just below my chin.

'"*Kiss Me Quick*"? Is that a request?' He leans in.

I duck under his arm, feeling his eyes on me all the way down the stairs.

The club is low and long and glitzy. It has changed its decor in the last decade but it is still high-end. It is still the place to go if you are loaded. White leather banquettes line the walls. Blue neon lights under the counters shed a weird glow. This is more like it. Beautiful women teeter on three-inch stilettos. I am spoilt for choice.

A tall blonde in skintight white Lycra slumps on a seat, dressed to match the club. Her pupils are wide. A party drug. I lift her bag as I pass, holding my coat as a shield against the bar cams and head straight for the corridor.

Some interior designer has had fun with the toilets. The ladies is straight out of a gothic horror flick. The gilt mirrors are hung with fake cobwebs, firelight flickers between the basins – cinnamon-scented candles, dry and choking. I can barely see my face in the gloom. A woman perches on a stool in the corner, nodding and smiling.

I close the cubicle door, sit down on the toilet seat and open the bag.

The great thing about ski resorts is that everyone carries their passport. I flip to the back cover. Ivana Litvinova. Good name. Our blonde is Russian. Two hundred and eighty euros in a little purse. A separate roll of dollars for the recreational habit. Eyeliner, a pearl pink lip gloss, Coco Mademoiselle in travel size. Factor 50 chapstick. Comb. A little bag of something. I hold it up to the light, twisting and turning the plastic sachet, not that there is any light in this gothic horror cubicle. If it is what I think it is, I need to get the bag back to her fast.

I lift 200 euros out of the purse and tip everything else back into the bag except the eyeliner, the roll of dollars and the passport. I slide the bolt. The woman jumps off the stool to turn the tap on. Algerian maybe. I put a twenty euro note in her bowl. She nods and bobs with delight.

I pencil on the eyeliner, watching her in the mirror. I wonder how much she has had to pay for this shift. The smile has gone, she is wary and weary, her eyes glitter in the candlelight.

'I have to get out of here.' My French is laced with a Russian accent. 'I'm sick of this place. D'you know what I mean?'

She nods sympathetically.

I tap the roll of dollars.

'My friend Omar can take you,' she says, catching on quick. 'His shift ends at 2 a.m. He's at Le Chabichou.'

I know the Chabichou hotel – high-end. I am halfway to the door before she speaks again.

'Men are looking for you.' She leans down under the counter. 'They were back again yesterday.' She straightens up, holding a postcard-sized picture. It is the photo from my GCHQ pass. The photo on file. Classified.

I stare.

*Overconfidence causes subject to underestimate all around her.*

The long fingers of organised crime grope for me, reaching into every corner, reaching into this dark toilet with its fake cobwebs.

A tap drips in the silence.

My knives hug my calves.

'It'll cost you,' she says. 'Everything you have.'

# CHAPTER 5

The path to the Chabichou is lined with twinkling little lights. Of course it is. There is no dirty concrete up here. The windows are golden with firelight and wealth. Through the door I can see the hint of a chandelier, a sheepskin rug thrown across a chair.

I stay out of the rectangles of light at the entrance and slide round the side and then round again to the back. The building is built into the hillside. The kitchen door opens onto a bank of snow. An open door, bright with strip lighting, shows rows and rows of stainless steel. Industrial fridges. The sound of clattering and running water and voices comes from inside. My boots crunch on the thick snow. No one clears a path back here.

I pull on the snowflake hat with the red plaits and stick my head round the door looking like a mad Gretel.

Three men load an industrial dishwasher.

'Omar?' I say.

They look up. Omar walks forward, drying his hands on a tea towel hanging from his waist. He is between forty and fifty. Tanned, compact, wiry.

'I need a ride.'

He looks at his watch.

'I know,' I say. 'You don't get off till 2 a.m. Can you take me then?'

'Where are you going?'

I hold up the roll of dollars. 'Wherever I like.'

He stares for a moment then nods and turns back to the huge conveyor belt. It is just like the conveyors at airport security but with water. Trays get loaded up, pass along the belt through the machine and out the other side. The steaming china is hauled off and stacked on trolleys ready to go back out.

I pull off my coat and stand at the clean end. The men look at me like I've dropped my pants.

'What are you doing?'

'Helping. I'm not going to wait out there in the cold for an hour.'

*I'm not going to wait outside while satellites hunt me like a dog.*

I feel my muscles ease. The slow, repetitive lifting is like being in the gym but with more steam. Memories of the cold are fading. They pale beside the longer, darker memories of cold. The dormitory under the eaves, one thin blanket per child. No help and no hope. Only the other faces and the endless silent endurance.

At 1.30 a.m. the flow of dirty dishes dries up. The end is in sight. Now the trays are coming in singles. At 1.50 a.m. I slide out into the darkness in case a supervisor is going to turn up for the end of the shift. No one comes except a waiter saying the tips are down because someone has broken something.

Omar appears in the lit doorway wearing a coat and pushing a cigarette between his lips. He leads the way down the path and into the darkness with a jerk of his head.

My monkey brain watches him. That instinctive part of me that watched in silent wakefulness all the long night hours in the dormitory. Has the woman in the toilet set me up? How much were they offering? *Serious Russians.* That could mean anything. Did she phone ahead? Tell him not to be too eager. Tell him to take me to them. Tell him to hand me over somewhere quiet, outside the resort?

Parking is at a premium here and he leads me through the darkness down the mountain. Finally, we hit a side road with one lonely streetlight and he stops at a green Renault as old as he is.

I smell him in the confined space. Nicotine and tiredness. He turns the heater on, opens the glove compartment and pulls out an ice scraper. He gets out and starts the slow business of clearing the car, the heavy soft *thwump* of powder hitting the deck, the scrape of ice against glass.

*He is waiting for someone to come*, my monkey brain says. *They are taking longer than he expected.*

He opens the driver's door and gets in, rubbing his hands. The wipers creak as they break out of their ice pockets. They scratch back and forth, back and forth. He wipes the inside of the windscreen with the back of his sleeve and releases the handbrake. The wheels spin on the powder until their chains grip. He eases his way out of the parking space slower than I can walk.

Omar's eyes meet mine in the mirror.

'Paris,' I say. I hold up the roll of dollars. '500 dollars. Everything I've got.'

His eyes go back to the road.

We pass the dirty concrete of the lower slopes, pass the building with Jake's attic bedroom. The black four-by-four has gone.

I breathe out.

We turn a corner and a police barrier blocks the road. A checkpoint. Neon flashes. Another black four-by-four waits in the shadows beyond the barrier.

Omar mutters. I can read his stress levels. He has something to hide. He yanks on the handbrake and a policeman walks over.

I pull the Gretel hat over my ears and wind down the window. My stream of angry Russian hits the gendarme in the chest. A verbal prod. French police don't take this kind of grief. Especially not from a woman. He hauls the car door open and jerks his head.

My fingers graze the tops of my boots as I step out.

'Passport.'

I hand over Ivana's passport with a mutter of Russian. He looks it up and down, he glares at me.

*Breathe in. Breathe out.*

A figure moves in the shadows by the four-by-four.

*They have my GCHQ photo. All they have to do is come over.*

The gendarme walks over to the four-by-four, holding my passport. There is no such thing as a straight copper these days. Organised crime and Firestorm have seen to that.

I count to twenty, leaning up against the car door. The gendarme walks back. Snow flurries in the headlights. He hands me the passport and jerks his head.

I snatch the passport and climb back in the car, leaving a torrent of annoyed Russian hanging in the air. The barrier lifts and they wave us through.

As we pass the four-by-four, curious faces turn my way. They are looking for an English woman. My Russian has saved me.

# CHAPTER 6

Three hours in, we pull up outside Lyon for petrol. The windscreen wipers are still working overtime. Omar peers through a porthole in the glass the size of his fist.

I fold myself out of the car door and stretch in the night air, pulling my arms across my body, pressing them against me. We have left the snow behind, but it is still cold. My breath curls away from me, the air twinkly with tiny snow crystals.

Four more hours to get to Paris. Plenty of time for a four-by-four to catch an antique Renault. When will the tall Russian notice her passport is gone? I picture her as I slid the bag under her legs, her head lolled, her legs splayed. Chances are she will be asleep for a while. Will she have noticed before I'm on the train and clear of Paris?

I pour myself a coffee from the service counter. A French motorway stop. The coffee is good. I consider the baguettes under the curved glass deli counter. Parma ham. It's almost a bacon sandwich. I pick up a canvas bag and a baseball cap from a rotating stand. I've got nothing to put in a bag but a woman without one is weird.

The toilet facilities are like service station toilets everywhere, worse than going in the bushes. Above the cracked sink, the mirror is dull. My face stares back at me. She is there again, the stranger behind my eyes. I drop the mad Gretel hat in the bin and apply more eyeliner.

*

I head back to the car, cradling the coffee cup between numb fingers. Two minutes later we are back on the road.

I open my eyes. A wall of glass stares down at me. The main entrance of the Gare du Nord. More cameras per square foot than an airport. The gothic stone arch of the old station is on our left, the sleek glass of the new extension on the right.

I pass the roll of dollars between the front seats, pull the baseball cap down over my eyes and step out onto the Paris pavement. Crowds mill around the main entrance. I turn a sharp right and hug the wall, skirting the cameras. It won't protect me from the central pillar cams and I turn my face to the wall, hunching my shoulders. I cross to the escalator that leads up to the Eurostar terminal. Ten steps in the open. There is a camera at the top of the escalator. I lean down to do up my boot buckle. 9.48 a.m.

A one-way ticket on the 10.13 a.m. to London St Pancras costs me 150 euros. I get my boarding pass at the same time, remembering not to say thank you as she hands me back my Russian passport.

I head for the turnstiles and feed in my boarding pass. I picture the call coming into the police department in Courchevel. Maybe the tall blonde goes in herself, maybe her hotel concierge calls. Either way, I have just put the passport in the system. A couple of checks and they can see it is currently in the departure lounge of the Paris Eurostar. I am out in the open.

Passport control. The line divides into two and then into two again in front of the glass booths. Four goldfish bowls, two men and two women. Policemen stand either side against the wall. These are not UK bobbies. They are French military police in body armour and carrying submachine guns. Rumour has it that, thanks to Firestorm, organised crime has the Paris police network sewn up. It is not a theory I want to test. I glance back the way I have come. It's a long dash to the turnstiles.

The queue is moving slowly as the UK defends her borders. I edge to the left and to the left again, trying to skew the male/ female probability. I don't want to risk a man looking in my eyes, checking me out.

A French kid stands in front of the goldfish bowl, hopping from foot to foot. She grips the ledge and pulls herself up, peering through the narrow gap. The passport woman smiles at her father. She hands back their passports with a comment I can't hear. The father laughs, reluctant to move away from the compliments.

Out of the corner of my eye, I see the male border officer coming free. I edge towards the father and daughter, hustling them along with my body language. They move off, stuffing passports in hand luggage, and I post my Russian passport and non-EU card through the slot. The passport lady is smiling, distracted.

'Cute,' I say, watching the little girl and working my Russian accent.

She is still smiling as she opens the passport and feeds it through her scanner.

She looks up at me.

Ivana Litvinova. Same colour hair, same sort of age. Otherwise we are not really alike.

'Have a good trip,' she says as she hands me my passport.

I am behind the father and daughter in the queue for the security check. The little girl stares at me over his shoulder. I wink. A pink rabbit slips from a gloved hand. She watches me pick it up. I hide it behind my back. She grins. It is a game.

Dad puts her down to focus on collapsing the buggy. It is the size of a shopping trolley. I pile my coat and my bag into a plastic tray. I haul up another tray and put bunny in it. I hold out my hand.

'I will take her through.'

Dad looks up in distraction. He smiles at the good Samaritan. 'Thank you,' he says, 'thank you so much.'

The little girl beams at me. Together we head through the arch. Security smile at the sight of us. No one asks a mother to put her boots through the scanner.

Beyond security, space is at a premium and passengers squash together under the arches of the original station. I head straight through the departure lounge and out the far end to the boarding gates, down the travellator and onto the platform. Stewardesses in blue and yellow stand ready.

I turn left down the platform looking for Coach 15. I find my seat and walk past it looking for another seat. Coach 15 is nearly full and the nearest spare empty seat is beside the aisle several rows away. The window seat is occupied by a guy in his fifties. He looks up, scowling in disappointment that he isn't getting a double seat to himself. Then he smiles. The '*Kiss Me Quick*' T-shirt has changed his mind. He grips his blazer to his side and shuffles his beige trouser leg over to make more room. I settle myself down, take the baseball cap off and lay out a little effort to be charming.


Half an hour later I know a lot more about the Channel Tunnel. My travelling companion is not a businessman, he is an enthusiast. It is his tenth trip this month. He waves his hands as he speaks, his tie flapping.

'The tunnel is 31.4 miles long, making it the eleventh longest tunnel in the world,' he says.

'Is that right?'

'Thirteen thousand people were employed building it and only eight died.' He laughs like this is a ludicrously small number for such an engineering miracle.

Time crawls by. Nobody checks tickets on the Eurostar. You need a boarding pass even to get on. There is a guard on the train, but you don't see him. You don't see him unless there is a problem.

We are nearly an hour in when the guard appears at the end of Coach 15. He stands the wrong side of the glass doors, scanning the row numbers on the overhead. His eyes stop at the row I booked. They drop down to find the seat empty. He turns away talking into a walkie-talkie. Reporting in.

*There's no one there.*

The doors open and he walks down the aisle, swaying with the 180 miles per hour speed. He has been told to go and check. To make sure. He pauses beside the empty seat then he carries on walking to the end of the carriage.

*Definitely not there.*

The windows black out as we start our descent. Twenty-two miles under the sea plus ten miles as the tunnel heads under the seabed. Cruising speed of a hundred miles per hour – twenty minutes under.

Worst-case scenario, they check every passport and ticket on the train. Dover to London: thirty minutes. The Eurostar takes 750 passengers. There is no way they have time for that. Most likely, the guard is told to do an eyes-on. A walk-through. They know they are looking for a solo woman traveller.

The train starts its ascent.

'If you hold your hand over the air vents next to the window just before Ashford, you can feel it cut out,' my fellow traveller says, his face shiny pink with the pleasure of sharing. 'This is where the train switches from the overhead cables to the "third rail" power.'

The grey wastelands of Dover come into view. The enthusiast is holding his hand over the heating grill. Nodding and smiling. We pull into Ashford, the last stop before London.

*Did the guard get a message through?* Uniforms walk up the platform. *Yes, he did.* British Transport Police. They disappear from view.

'That's unusual,' the enthusiast says. 'The Eurostar doesn't carry Transport Police.'

I nod but I am not listening.

The third option. The really worst-case scenario – they check every unreserved seat. They know their woman is on the train and they know she is not in the seat she booked. Ergo she has sat down somewhere else. Thirty minutes to check maybe fifty empty seats. Doable. Extremely doable. Coach 15 is towards the end. Will they start at the front and work backwards, or start at the back?

I pull the baseball cap hard over my eyes and watch the door.

'One of the four original pieces of boring equipment was buried in the tunnel,' the enthusiast says.

Faces appear in the gap between the carriages. Black uniforms. The Transport Police. They stand looking at a screen. They have Ivana's passport photo. The doors ping open. Can't be more than five empty seats in this carriage and I am in one of them. I check my knives down the side of my boots, sliding my fingertips into the soft leather, staring at the floor.

'The average depth below the seabed is 150 feet but it does get as deep as 250.'

They move up the aisle slowly, handing themselves along on the backs of the chairs, scanning the overhead numbers.

Ten rows away, six rows away, three rows away.

They are almost on me.

'I always book both seats,' the enthusiast says. 'But I'm glad you sat down.'

They walk past. The doors open to the next carriage and close behind them.

*What?*

I stare at my travelling companion.

'You always book two seats?'

'Yes.' He nods, embarrassed. 'I like the extra space.'

I close my eyes in disbelief. What were the chances? My whole body exhales. I grip his suit lapels and kiss him hard, plenty of tongue. Like the French. Only better. When I pull away, his eyes are closed and his mouth open.

# CHAPTER 7

At St Pancras, you walk straight off the train, up the platform and onto the station concourse. We file slowly off the train in the middle of the press of people fumbling with wheelie suitcases. I am back in the UK. Back in central London, only a couple of miles from safety.

At the entrance to the concourse, four armed police are standing like a pinch point – an eyes-on check.

*Not good. Not good at all.*

I think about the word going out. I think about Firestorm's infiltration of the police.

I zip up my jacket and pull the baseball cap low. A man is struggling out of a doorway backwards, dragging a giant buggy behind him. I look up into the face of pink Bunny.

'Let me help,' I smile.

He beams his gratitude. 'What a coincidence,' he says.

I hoist the kid into my arms. Little hands circle my face. Sticky little hands. Pink Bunny bounces on my head. He bounces all the way down the platform and out through the pinch point, the kid laughing and Dad pushing the buggy and pulling a suitcase and smiling at us both.

'You look like Elsa,' she says.

*Great. Drawn by Disney.*

'You can be Anna,' I say.

'I don't want to be Anna.'

*That's the spirit.*

The main concourse of St Pancras is wall-to-wall cameras. A woman stands staring at us like she can't believe her eyes. The missing piece in this family jigsaw.

'Maman!' the kid screams in my ear.

She comes towards us, her smile faltering.

I set the kid on her feet.

'Bye, Bunny,' I say.

The kid clings to my calf like a bobble-hatted barnacle.

I remember my last psych profiling. The part where they show you a picture and you say the first thing that comes into your head. I remember willing myself to say the right thing and the psych profiler turning up the picture of the woman in a pool of blood, where you are meant to say 'butterfly'.

'Butterfly,' I said.

'Are you sure?'

'Yep.' *I've so got this.*

Flip went the chart: little kid, big eyes.

'Liability.'

Silence.

'Liability' was not right. It was so far from not right that it earned me a tiny red flag at the bottom of the spreadsheet.

61% of respondents (I learnt afterwards) say 'Cute'.

36% (the less articulate) say 'Aw'.

And 3% say it how it is.

The station clocks read 12.05 p.m. Gray's Inn Road straight down to Holborn is the direct route, a thirty-minute walk in the spring sunshine. I picture my GCHQ photo under a counter in Courchevel, a French police barrier, British Transport Police searching a train. I won't be taking the direct route.

I duck along Platform 15, the final platform on the end before King's Cross, and out at the opposite end. There is no avoiding the Euston Road, a six-lane thoroughfare peppered with surveillance. I cross, head down, and dive into the mass of side streets below King's Cross.

An hour of zigzagging brings me within reach of the City. Now all bets are off. The Square Mile has almost as many cameras as workers. This is where I get to find out how good Simon really is.

Ages ago we made a plan. If I was compromised, if GCHQ was compromised, we would meet in a place only he and I know.

Will he have seen a stolen passport report come in? Will he have seen the passport was on the 10.13 a.m. train out of Paris and that border control could find no trace of it? Will he join the dots? A lot of maybes.

I skirt St Bart's, down Snow Hill and into Paternoster Square. A Starbucks is set into the old cathedral precinct. Glass and chrome meet a thousand years of religious history. I walk by. Not slowly, not quickly. Exactly long enough to see him sitting there with his messy hair and laptop, eyes lifting hopefully to the door.

I carry on walking. Surveillance is just as present here but the stripy awnings of the eateries that line the square were put up after the cameras. There are blind spots and multiple exits and multiple vantage points. I sit down on the steps of the fountain with the rest of the lunchtime crowd. Secretaries chatter, their sandals clattering on the stone steps. I watch the east exit of the square. The exit nearest to GCHQ. Traffic noise from New Change and Ludgate Hill fills the air: braking taxis, sirens, diesel engines.

I turn my attention to Starbucks. Customers come and go. Typical occupancy of a table: eight minutes. As many solo customers as there are couples. There are no groups. Team lunch and they hang out at the All Bar One on the corner.

Simon has a laptop out on the table in front of him. His hand moves rhythmically across the trackpad. Top to bottom, top to bottom. I study his face through the window. Dark-rimmed glasses, floppy fringe, messy hair. My calm, unflappable quartermaster. My man Friday. He looks tired. Actually, he looks awful.

I turn back to the east and watch the exit. An hour later I am sure. All the customers in Starbucks have changed. No one is with him. No one followed him. There are three entrances to Starbucks: the main entrance, the one on the side and the one at the back. I go in the back so he can't see me coming and plonk myself down, stretching my legs out sideways and twisting, trying to get sideways to the room.

He looks up and exhales like he has spent a week holding his breath. Close to, I can see his eyes are bloodshot. He has four days of stubble. I throw an open packet of sugar at him.

'God, you look awful. You'd better not be playing Solitaire.'

He twists the screen. CCTV stills of the Gare du Nord fill the page. Square pictures, five to a row, four rows on a screen. Thousands of images every minute. A tiny part of the tension inside me eases. Simon, he never lets me fall.

'How did I do?'

Sugar hangs off him like fake snow. He brushes at it.

'Good,' he says. 'The best shot is at the top of the escalator. I wasn't sure.'

'Yeah. You either crouch down or you turn like there is someone behind you. Either way you can't avoid it. They caught on quick. There were Transport Police on the train.'

He nods. 'They think it's the person they want in connection with the Courchevel terrorist attack.'

'What attack?'

'Apparently someone blew up a helicopter and half the airstrip.' His hand reaches across the table for me as if he can't help himself. He pulls it back to his coffee cup. 'Where have you been? Are you hurt?'

'Out for a day. Bed for a day. A day getting here.'

Pain flickers across his face, you'd think he would be pleased.

I lean forward. I can hardly bring myself to say the words out loud. As if giving them airtime will jinx it. 'You are not going to believe this.'

'What?'

'I met him. The man himself. The Prince of Darkness.'

Simon stares. Sugar slides off his shoulder.

'No way.' His whisper is hoarse. 'Who is he?'

I sit back shaking my head.

'Tall, shaved head. Eastern European. Maybe Russian. Hot as hell.'

Simon rolls his eyes.

'Between thirty and forty.'

'Young.'

I pick at the packets of sugar. 'We have a leak a mile wide.' *Can you have a leak a mile wide?* 'My GCHQ mugshot was all over Courchevel. Russians. The police. The Eurostar. I thought they would be watching you, once they were on to me.'

Simon looks around at the coffee drinkers anxiously. 'We have to get you to Control.'

I crane round. I hate having my back to the door.

'It's good to see you,' I say.

# CHAPTER 8

A flicker of relief crosses Control's wrinkled face. A shadow of a sigh but no more. I close the door quietly behind me. He was old when I was a teenager and that was a decade ago. He looks at me over his steepled fingers.

*No hug then.*

'Where the hell have you been? Correct me if I'm wrong, but you were on surveillance. Can you remember what that is? Geneva went dark on your watch. Half the Three Valleys have gone up in smoke.' He glares. 'At what point did your orders include causing an international incident? It is the same story all over again. You are too hasty, too rash, too overconfident. When will you think before you act?'

'I met him. The man himself. The Boss. The Prince of Darkness.'

I let it sink in.

Control stares.

I savour the moment. The first time in ten years I have got the drop on him.

'Who is he?'

Funny that Simon asked the exact same question. Somehow, they expect to know him.

I shake my head. 'I didn't recognise him. Youngish. Dark-haired. Ripped.'

The profilers have always struggled with age. The creation of Firestorm suggests youth, the iron control of the heads of organised crime says not. The Head of Yakuza is seventy-three, his Mexican opposite number, sixty-nine. Now I have met him, I have no trouble reconciling the two.

'We were right about one thing. Eastern European, or maybe Russian,' I say.

Moscow are less than helpful in the struggle against organised crime.

'So, search. Right now. Search until you have a name. We have to have him on file. He is the richest man in the world; by definition he must be a colossus.'

My bollocking is forgotten. Control is already picturing telling the NSA the news.

'And when we have him…'

'Yeah.'

Control doesn't need to say anymore. These days, with facial recognition software, you can kill someone from a mile away. He'll be dead by teatime.

'Go through the systems. Pull in everything we have. How long will it take you?'

I shrug. 'Twenty-four hours. Thirty-six with the debrief and medical bullshit.'

Control considers this.

'It makes you a target. Forget the debrief. Check in with medical.'

I picture the tall figure with the shaved head. He knows I saw his face and he knows who I am. Does he know about the photographic memory?

'I am a dead woman walking.'

'You'll just have to get there first,' Control says briskly.

Mutually assured destruction. Every Firestorm contractor on the planet will be after me, from the part-time hobbyists to the five-star goliaths like Solo, Aveline and the Guardsman.

He glares at me. 'Why are you still here?'

My hand is on the door handle before he speaks again.

'Winter?'

I turn.

'Erik is gone. It's time to grow up.'

# CHAPTER 9

Thirty minutes later, I am sitting on the couch in the medical suite pulling my clothes back on. The doctor has gone. The CAT scan has come back clear. I swear he was disappointed. Simon hands me a new locator. I clip it to the top of my ear. He is so relieved he won't shut up.

'I'll set you up next door. We will go through the profiles one by one.'

He is proposing to lock me in the detainment suite.

*Great.*

'You can't keep me a secret, Simon. Everyone will know I'm back.'

'This is the safest place in GCHQ. We will find the answer here. You don't need to go anywhere.'

The corridor stretches away with pairs of doors leading off it on either side. Not a lot has changed in ten years. The antiseptic TCP smell is just the same. Medical are at the far end – on hand, so to speak. They make me shudder. I can't even be in the same room as Everard, GCHQ's Chief Medical Officer. I meet a lot of people who make my skin crawl, but no one touches Everard.

I open the door to the observation room for Detainment Suite 5. It is just down from the one they brought me to when I was a teenage hacker.

The room is a dark box. Maybe ten foot by eight. Low polystyrene-tiled ceiling. One wall is a window onto the interview room. A thin strip of desk sits under it, workspace for the watchers.

Behind it, banks of terminals give access to the GCHQ mothership. The air is warm with the lingering smell of bodies.

I look around. 'Let's do this. I'll take a shower when I've found him.'

*I have the most valuable intel on the planet in my head.*

Simon loads the search:

*White, Caucasian, male 30–40, Eastern European/Russian.*

'I wonder if we'll still call him the Prince of Darkness when we know his real name,' I say.

'We won't call him anything,' Simon says. ''Cause he'll be dead.'

I pull up Slashstorm while I wait for the search to run. The twelve faces stare out at me.

Who are they? Where did they find them? The girl with wide brown eyes still looks into the camera. There is nothing behind her. Mirrors. Or a green screen. If it is mirrors behind her it would have to be the whole room.

*A mirrored room.*

The thought makes me shudder.

The counters scroll. More than a million votes already.

It is not happening again. Not if I can help it.


The GCHQ systems identify 12,582 possible matches. I think about the shaved head. Could be military, but not necessarily. I'm sure it's not a recent style decision. I take a gamble and screen for buzz cut or shorter. I have cut the matches by 80 per cent. I focus and start scrolling. A face a second. Three thousand six hundred an hour. Simon stands by my shoulder.

Two thousand faces in, I get up and stretch. It is counterproductive to push too hard. That's when mistakes get made. I sit back down.

'I'll get you something to eat. Lock the door behind me.' Simon goes out.

I get up and bring the bar down across the door. I go back to the screen. The buzz cuts are coming to an end. This proves nothing. I load the rest of the search and refocus.

*Where are you, Prince of Darkness?*

Now it is heavy going. A face every five seconds. Some of the shots are crystal clear, some lack focus, some grainy, some over-exposed, never two with the same problem. My eyes constantly have to readjust, refocus. They feel like parchment. A vein pulses beside my temple.

Simon is back with a loaded tray from the canteen. No bacon.

I feed my face with my left hand. My right hand scrolls. Pro-ductivity goes up. A face every two seconds. By midnight I have come to the end of the 12,582 possible matches.

Simon's hand is on my shoulder. 'How much sleep did you get last night?'

I think about the Renault. My face icy on one side and warm on the other. I shrug.

'Three, four hours?'

Simon nods like it was just what he suspected. 'Your work rate is way down. You need to sleep.'

I look down at the carpet tiles. Hairy. Grey horsehair. Identical to the Security Centre of the Hôtel Grand.

'I'll curl up here. You can lock me in after I lock the door on my side.'

Simon thinks about this. That might be OK. He nods.

'I'll get you a blanket.'

A few minutes later he is back, his arms crammed with bedding.

I push back from the desk, looking at the mound of blankets. I've had way worse – I spent two weeks sleeping upright, manacled to a wall once.

'Give me a couple of hours.'

Simon hovers. 'Lock the door behind me.'

I pull the bar down and hear the key turning in the lock from the outside. I am asleep before I hit the floor.

*Bang, bang, bang.*

Sleep crusts my eyes. I blink. My ribs ache. I have been lying on my left side.

'Rise and shine,' says the voice through the door.

I sit up shaking my head. My spine creaks at the neck. I get to my feet, raise the bar and pull the door open. Simon is standing there, a coffee in one hand, a white paper bag in the other and a change of clothes under his arm.

'What time is it?' I scrub at my eyes with the heel of my palm.

'Eight o'clock.' Simon puts the coffee down carefully.

'*What?* You let me sleep all night?' I sink down into the swivel chair and hold out my hand for the bacon sandwich.

Simon shakes his head. 'Shower, change, breakfast.'

Grumbling, I follow him out of the room and back down the corridor towards Medical. The place is deserted. The strip lighting flickers.

Simon shoves a pile of toiletries and clothes at me and pushes me into the shower room.

I stretch out my neck, putting my face in the scalding jet. I am going to widen the search – every white Caucasian male on our systems. He has to be there.

Back in the observation room I settle down for the long haul.

'Thirty to forty-five years old, white, Caucasian men. Global,' I tell Simon.

He says nothing but shakes his head at the momentary pause before the results come up. GCHQ has the fastest search capabilities on the planet, although the NSA might disagree. Any momentary pause is down to the scale of the search. Simon scrubs the data for files already checked. Ninety-four thousand eight hundred new names. I start scrolling.

My work rate is fast. Three hours in and I am averaging a face a second. Businessmen, sportsmen, politicians, criminals. The day stretches before me with an ever-shrinking pool of options. I am closing in, I can feel it. Determination drives me. Lunch comes and goes. There is no clue to time in the artificial light.

Six o'clock in the evening and my optimism is fading. My work rate has stayed steady all day. Two thousand names, break, get up, stretch and get the blood pumping. Get back to it.

Simon moves around behind me, coming and going. I refuse to believe that our kingpin has no footprint, no presence. He is the richest man in the world. If he exists at all, by definition, he must be a giant.

'Daniel called by the way,' Simon says. 'Someone is having a crack at the bank.'

Daniel: Front of House at the Colony Club in Mayfair, my second home. He has no idea what I do for a living, but he wouldn't phone unless he had a problem.

'What did you tell him?'

'I told him you were busy.'

Daniel was the Pit Boss when I broke the Colony's bank on my seventeenth birthday. He has never held it against me. A decade later, he is General Manager and the most highly paid front of house in London. He lets me come and go as I please. I can catch a card sharp faster than any pro.

I have never had much of a home, the Colony is as close as it gets.

I am down to the last hundred, then the last ten, then the last one. The final face fills the screen. A blond-haired, grey-eyed Russian with a scar along his jawline. I rest my forehead on the desk. The keyboard is warm beside my cheek.

I have got nothing. I jumped off a mountain for nothing. I blew up Courchevel for nothing.

# CHAPTER 10

Simon is leaning against the watcher's ledge, his legs stuck out in front of him, his hands in his pockets.

'Simon,' I say from my face plant on the desk. 'What happened in Geneva?'

'You mean apart from it going dark? Nothing. That's the weird thing.'

'Well, someone went to a lot of trouble. Who do we know that could take down Isosceles from a laptop?'

'No one.' Simon shrugs again. 'Max is convinced it's Halo.'

Max, the GCHQ Head of Research. Halo, the master hacker who works for the Prince of Darkness.

A memory is rattling around. *Dark, flickering light, cannabis.* I pin it down. Jake watching the news and telling me someone had been shot. A white-haired philanthropist, peacemaker and all-round good guy. The Traynor Trust: always first at the scene of any disaster, founding orphanages in war-torn hostile states, raising money from anyone who will listen. A one-man philanthropy powerhouse.

'What about John J. Traynor the Third?'

Simon's hands come out of his pockets. 'Oh, yeah. Makes you wonder who would do something like that.'

'We know who would do something like that. Traynor is exactly the kind of person Firestorm was designed to intimidate.'

'You don't take the whole of Geneva dark for a single hit. Isosceles was down. Overkill.' He grins. 'Like using a Sledgehammer to crack a nut.'

I roll my eyes.

I picture the scene on the mountain. Landing lights, rising steam, flames. 'The helicopter touched down to pick up Halo – or whoever it was – like he was the final man on a bank job. *Something* happened that night. Who do they figure for the Traynor hit?'

'Contractor, obviously.'

I search up the news reports. John J. Traynor III and his three bodyguards taken out in a Firestorm-style hit at the Hôtel Grand in Geneva. Bullets between the eyes. Definitely a pro. Eyewitness accounts mention a man in a baseball cap.

One of the news channels is carrying old footage of the Nobel presentation. Mr and Mrs John J. Traynor hold hands on the podium, pink with pleasure, the smiling faces of representatives of their children's charities around them.

'Check the feeds, every cam, the satellites, social media for Geneva that night. Halo – if the hacker was Halo – was in a hurry, he may have missed something.'

Simon fires up the spare terminal. 'What am I looking for?'

'A man in a baseball cap.'

It is Simon's turn to roll his eyes. 'Great,' he says.

'Around the Hôtel Grand. In the streets. Some tourist may have something.'

I go back to my terminal and after a few seconds the logo of the Geneva Metropolitan Police Department fills my screen. The systems administrator login gives me access to every file on the network. Pathology, blood work, forensics, personnel, IT. Who is running the John J. Traynor III case? Detective Andreas Godard.

*Hello, Andreas.*

I can see where he lives, where he works, what car he drives, its registration number, what his medical history is. I can see how long he has to retirement and I can see he is registered to the G: drive.

It is all here, phone records, bank account details. Pages and pages of interviews. The gun that fired the shots belonged to one of the bodyguards and was recovered at the scene. Andreas has been fast, efficient and methodical. A straight copper in a bent world. I feel kind of bad I'm hacking him. Not bad enough to trust him though.

'All the street cams were down,' Simon says in a defeated voice. 'All the Grand's own cameras, all the police cams, all the airport cams, even Isosceles. Basically, Geneva went pitch black the night you blew up Courchevel.'

*You blow up one tiny helicopter…*

'You sound like Control. It wasn't the *whole* of Courchevel.'

I have reached the autopsy files. My neck feels cold. The air con must be working overtime.

'This wasn't in the news reports.'

Simon comes to stand behind my shoulder.

Post-mortem photos. Three bodies with military buzz cuts and matching bullet holes in their foreheads. The white-haired fourth can barely be called a body. It looks like it jumped from the top of a building. It looks like it fell in front of a train.

I scan the John J. Traynor pathology report.

'Beaten to death with two heavy metal objects not recovered at the scene,' Simon reads over my shoulder.

Of course they haven't recovered the heavy objects. I feel like calling the pathologist – *that is what a body looks like when it has been beaten with knuckledusters.*

I think about a white-haired old guy, a man who inherited wealth and then did his best to give it away, living his life under the shadow of this threat.

Simon is back at his terminal, data trawling.

'Makes you wonder,' he says after a while, 'who would do something like this.'

'You already said that. We know exactly who would do this.'

'But even criminals have limits.' His voice is suddenly distracted. 'I think this might be something. On Facebook. I'll just pretty it up. A distance back shot. Outside the hotel.'

I stand by Simon's shoulder. The image pixelates at maximum resolution. My breathing stops. Simon scrubs the white cheek of the selfie taker from the frame. My hand grips the back of Simon's chair. I stare.

One shoulder and the back of a tanned neck.

*Hello, Handsome.*

'It's not a contractor,' I say.

'How can you tell?'

'Because it is the man himself.'

I have spent thirty-six hours looking for his picture and here he is on Facebook.

# CHAPTER 11

I stare and stare at the tanned neck.

'I bet it was Halo who took Geneva dark. He will be the support team, when the Prince of Darkness does wet work.'

Simon swallows. 'You mean he carried out the hit *himself*?'

'That's him, I'm sure of it. He was there, Simon. In person. He walked into the building. And no one knows this but us. You and me. We can't trust anyone with this. If we can get an electronic print off him…' I don't need to say anymore. An electronic signature can be traced to its source.

'Let's think about what we know,' I say. 'He comes across from where? Russia?'

Simon shrugs helplessly.

'OK, so let's just say he comes in from the East. Comes in to make a point, to teach John J. Traynor a lesson.'

Simon looks sceptical.

'Maybe he wasn't showing enough respect. Maybe he was refusing to bow to Firestorm. Whatever. He decides to administer a lesson, so he flies in.'

Simon shakes his head. 'No need to fly in. Comes in by road. Flies out when he's in a hurry.'

My mouth twists as I concede the logic. He is probably right. It just makes the inbound journey more or less impossible to trace.

'OK, so let's work it backwards.' I stare at the tanned neck. 'What did we get from the helicopter?'

Simon shakes his head. 'Swiftcopter Agusta 109S hired out of Geneva. Paid for in cash. Courchevel pickup. The pilot is still in hospital after what happened but he remembers nothing.' He looks at me a shade accusingly.

'What about an end destination? It must be on the flight plan. They were definitely on route somewhere.'

'Paris.'

Paris is a big city. They could have been going for any number of reasons or just passing through. I press my thumbs in my eyes and try to focus on what we actually have.

'At some point that evening he was here.' I jab the Facebook page on the screen. 'On his own outside the Hôtel Grand on the Avenue du Mail, probably with a burner phone. Isosceles was down, but the mobile networks were still up. I'm betting he had a burner with him, initialised that evening, and the same burner will have turned up in Courchevel a couple of hours later. Two locations, one phone. We need to find it.'

Millions and millions of electronic handshakes go on between devices and mobile towers every minute. To have any hope of pinning down one anonymous burner signal in all the noise we need a timestamp and a location.

I am accessing the surveillance feeds for Geneva before I remember that Halo took everything down. For a moment I am stumped. That is what ten years of government service does to you. I am so used to Isosceles and all the other GCHQ tools that I have forgotten how to do it like a normal person.

I go back to Facebook and check the upload time. 21.01 p.m. Monika uploaded her picture of 'Fun times in Geneva' the moment she took it.

That gives us a time.

Location discovery software is based on assessing signal strength between masts. It collects all the data and triangulates down to give a probable location. It is way more accurate in urban environments with the higher number of base stations. In central Geneva, we will be looking at picocells with a 650-foot range. With a bit of luck, we might even get a femtocell and narrow it down to thirty feet.

This kind of tool is used all the time by the intelligence services to find the location of an individual via his phone. I am proposing to use it to find a phone by locating the individual. A needle in an electronic haystack of needles. How many other electronic signatures were there in Geneva that night?

We are going to have to do the mother of all tower data dumps.

'We need to do this upstairs.'

The detainment suite doesn't have the range for this kind of data search.

'I'll do it,' Simon says, standing up fast. 'Not you. You don't need to go anywhere. Get some sleep. This will take all night to run.'

He is out of the room before I can argue.

I glare at the closing door.

*You don't need to go anywhere.*

As soon as we have a location for the man behind Slashstorm, I am going. There is no power on earth that could stop me.

I stare at the blank screen. How much exactly does the Prince of Darkness know about me? He has my leaked GCHQ picture, so he knows what I look like. Is the leak a person – a source at GCHQ? Or is he in our systems?

The thought holds me still and staring.

If he is in our systems, he will be able to see my GCHQ locator. See me coming. And I will be coming. A little blue dot bleeping my way towards him.

Can he see my locator? Can he see me now, holed up in the detainment suite, twenty-four floors below street level, cowering in a grey cell?

I open up Firestorm, searching for my own face.

Nothing.

Where is the contract on me? He must know by now that I have survived. But then, he might not take out a contract, he might send someone direct. They could already be on their way, tracking me by my locator, heading straight for me like a shark homing in on a drop of blood.

I stare at the grey wall. I know what is needed. Some kind of a controlled experiment. A test. Before I set out to track him down.

I need to put myself out there for a few hours as a trial to find out if they are tracking me. Out in the open, away from GCHQ but somewhere safe. If someone comes for me then I have my answer, neither my face nor the GCHQ systems are safe.

How long will it take Simon to run the software? Hours probably.

I pull up Slashstorm again. No change. Twelve faces. Twelve scrolling counters. Eleven days to go.

*But where is safe?* Just the very thought of me offering myself as bait would give Simon a cardiac.

I think about the Colony Club, my home from home. There is only one way into the Colony and that is through the front door. Past a doorman who has known me for a decade. The control room that runs their camera surveillance and stores the money has iron blast doors and was built as a panic room. If you had to storm it, you would need a battalion and armour-piercing rounds.

I think about the leak at GCHQ and the Prince of Darkness watching my locator approaching, and make a decision.


I slide cautiously out into the corridor. It is deserted. The strip lighting flickers. Silence from Medical, no one is in for interview. I creep down the passage until I hit the stairs, then I am tearing up them two at a time to the locker room. I peer in. Empty.

I haul out another white evening dress, yank off my clothes and scramble into it. I twist my hair on top of my head and pin it in place. The mirror on the back of the locker door shows red-rimmed eyes. Out comes the black eyeliner and the lip gloss.

Seven minutes after I left the detainment suite I am ready to go. I swap to heeled boots and check the knives. They are all there. I belt a holster to my right thigh. Check the chamber. I would like more firepower but the armoury is too much of a risk. There is no chance they won't tip off Simon. I head up the stairs to Reception. Everyone at GCHQ uses the lift. I used to think that Erik and I were the only ones that knew the stairs existed.

I stride through Reception, out onto the street and glare around at the night. The air is cold on my bare arms. The cameras of the Bank junction stare down at me.

I rotate a full 360 degrees, arms outstretched, hairs pricking on the back of my neck.

*Here I am. Come and get me.*

*Come and get me if you think you're hard enough.*

# CHAPTER 12

A taxi heads down the junction towards me. I climb into the back, watching the grizzled profile in the driver's seat. The interior is cold. *Is this it? This quick?* The taxi pulls off as I give the address.

Fifteen minutes later we stop outside a tall, thin Georgian townhouse. The garden square is dark behind its railings, the clamour of Regent Street far away. I pay the man and he drives off. I watch him until he is out of sight.

A carriage lamp above the door is bright in the dark. Harry's eyes crinkle at the sight of me. I climb the shallow steps towards him and kiss his cheek. Stubble grazes my face. He has stood outside the Colony Club, the oldest and most exclusive of London's gaming establishments, for more than twenty years. He was on duty the night of my seventeenth birthday. The night I broke the bank. It was Harry who intervened when the general manager discovered my age.

I turn and look out at the silent square, my locator a pulsing beacon in the night. There is only one way into the Colony Club and that is through the front door.

*Come and get me.*

'Harry?' I rest my hand on his arm. 'I need to know about everyone who comes in after me. Particularly anyone you don't recognise.'

His eyebrows cock and he looks down at me fondly. 'Are you in trouble, Winter?'

*You have no idea.*

I pat his arm. 'Nothing serious. Guy trouble.'

He nods, touching his earpiece, checking that it is fine.

'Daniel will be pleased to see you.' He jerks his head towards the interior. 'Someone's having a crack at the bank.'


The fire sparks in the grate, filling the hallway with wood smoke. I hang up my wrap and slip through the velvet drapes into the main salon. The room is full of punters, the sounds of dice, the clink of glasses, laughter.

I don't waste time getting a drink but head straight for the control room. A service door stands in the corner covered by wallpaper, a servants' door when this was a private house. The corridor beyond is dingy. Faded yellow lino on the floor, scuffed walls. The iron door with its armour plating opens before I have a chance to knock – they have seen me coming, tracking me through the building.

The control room is in darkness except for the glare from the screens. Everyone in the room is crowded around a single terminal.

'I can't see it,' one of the technicians is saying.

Daniel turns and relief blooms on his face at the sight of me. He pulls me into the centre and we watch the end of a hand. The stakes are massive. I take in the tension in the dark room. The fear.

'How much?'

Daniel tells me. The bank is going down hard. I lean forward. 'Who is it?'

The challenger has his back to me, but he doesn't look familiar.

'First timer. Kazakhstani billionaire. Arrived in London yesterday.'

'Name?'

'Konstantin.'

I shake my head. It doesn't ring a bell.

I study the side profile, dark floppy hair, high cheekbones. Cute. 'Young for a billionaire.'

'Kid brother of a billionaire,' Daniel amends. It is all the same to him.

The technician gets up and gives me the chair. I sit down and watch the six screens. Focusing in on the long fingers as they flick the cards. A dinner jacket – ideal wear for a card sharp.

'Why is he in the alcove?'

High rollers get the private room with double the camera surveillance.

Daniel is tense. 'We prepped the blue room after the call but then he just sat down in the alcove.'

'When did he call?'

'His major-domo called this afternoon.'

I zoom out on the audience. A neat, dapper little figure stands at the challenger's elbow. Personal servant in every line. 'Is that him?'

Daniel nods.

'Sounds like a sting.'

We watch the next six hands in silence. The bank is teetering on the edge. I push back from the screens and cross to the two-way mirror. I lean up against the window, watching the challenger's back, the set of his shoulders.

'He's cheating,' I say.

Daniel is beside me. 'How?'

I shake my head. 'I don't know.'

Daniel's face pleads. There is only one real answer to a card sharp. He knows it and I know it – a card counter running the table. What can I say to him? I can't go out there? Global organised crime are looking for me? There could be a price on my head?

'Daniel, I can't go out on the floor at the moment. Guy trouble.'

'Please, Winter. I'll close the doors. We won't let anyone in. No one is better than you.'

I think about my locator. I think about Simon noticing I am gone. I think about the might of global organised crime tracking me to the Colony's door.

'Has anyone come in since me?'

We listen to Harry on the radio saying I was the last person through the door.

*I must be mad.*


Daniel is out of the door and into the service corridor before I have time to reconsider. The salon is bright after the dark and it feels like everyone is turning our way. A Chinese woman in silver stares. Conversations pause as we pass. The thick red pile of the carpet pulls at my heels. It seems a vast distance to walk, the entire length of the room. We thread our way through the knots of people, Daniel in front.

The challenger looks up and smiles like I have just made his day. I try to picture what he is seeing. A woman in a white, full-length evening dress, blonde hair on top of her head – elegant. The croupier slides discreetly away and I step into her place.

'Hi,' says the billionaire kid brother.

I close my mouth to stop myself gaping. If he was good-looking from behind, he is a whole lot better from the front. I strip the cellophane from seven new packs of cards, empty the shoe and load it with the new packs.

'I heard they had an in-house card counter here.' He grins. 'I thought I might check him out.'

*Bring it on.*

'Not him, her. How about taking your jacket off?'

He stands up slowly and shrugs his jacket over one shoulder and then the other.

'I thought you'd never ask.'

*What?*

I watch the sleeves as he pulls his hands out. Nothing. He sits back down.

'Are we playing cards or are we talking?' someone asks.

The first round, the billionaire's brother goes down.

The second round same as the first. It is like he is playing an entirely different game.

I smile in satisfaction.

He looks at his new cards. 'How is the counting going?'

'I've barely got started.'

Around us the crowd mutter, disappointed. Rows of beautiful faces stare, murmuring in hushed voices, faces glistening in the heat from the chandeliers. Elnett and Chanel hang in the air. Sweat and lust and cocaine. Silver sequins glitter. I shake my head to clear it. Fluttering restlessness washes over the crowd, and disappointment. They thought the bank was going down.

I deal the third round. Two aces. The challenger looks up into my eyes and I feel the pull like the undertow on a rip tide. Attraction. He is messing with my concentration. The cards start to slip in my head. The golden room with its peacock colours flickers. A man with a shaved head laughs behind my eyes. Too many hours of looking at bad guys on screen has got me hot.

His chair screeches, he is getting up. He leans forward, cupping my chin. His other hand reaches behind my head and pulls something from the coils of hair. I feel it slide out of the knot on top of my head. The crowd gasps in shock. The Ace of Hearts. He adds it to his pair. The onlookers exhale, laughing, and break into spontaneous applause.

'Halt in play, gentlemen.' Daniel appears magically at my elbow. It is just the excuse he needs.

'Can I buy you a drink?' The challenger's dark eyes are laughing. *Absolutely.*

I lead the way across the main salon to the private room he was supposed to have. The Blue Room is lit by firelight. Teal velvet sofas with bolster cushions in turquoise satin line the walls, a small Carrera marble bar stands in the corner. The distinctive Colony smell of Pledge and lilac lingers. On the card table, new blue paisley packs sit neatly stacked. As he enters, I move smoothly behind him and lock the door. The key turns in the lock like a gunshot.

He laughs down at me. Dark hair frames his face. 'Now that you've got me here, what are you going to do with me?'

I consider him. Young and cute.

*I am going to eat you all up.*

Frankly, if this is a hitman, it will be worth it.

'How old are you?'

'Twenty-two.'

*Just think of the stamina.*

I back him up against the door. After a while, he picks me up and in one easy movement, reverses our positions, pushing me hard into the panelling. He has my dress up around my waist before he stops. I open my eyes, the skin around my mouth buzzes. He is looking down at my thigh holster.

I wonder what excuse to make.

A strange expression crosses his face and then his mouth covers mine again.

About the time I think the panelling may give way, the Blue Room camera winks and dies. Daniel has turned off the CCTV.

He is missing out.

You need to be pretty fit to pull off a standing orgasm.

*Check.*


'Roman,' the challenger says after a while.

'Winter.'

There is a discreet knock at the door. Harry's muffled voice comes through the battered panelling.

'Winter, there's someone outside asking for you.'

*Finally.*

'Says his name is Simon.'

Typical. Not a representative of global organised crime.

I look at Roman, his bow tie hanging loose, his shirt out. Just-fucked hair really suits him. I wonder how soon he could go again.

'Winter, did you hear me?' Harry asks louder.

I turn the key in the lock and pull the door open.

The hall is quiet after the main salon. I wait while Harry gets my wrap, resting my foot on the grate. The fire crackles and spits a hint of green. Simon's lanky frame appears in the doorway. He looks out of place with his dishevelled hair and crumpled clothing.

'Your timing sucks,' I say. Attack as the best form of defence.

The velvet drapes part behind me and Roman Konstantin stands on the threshold.

'I'm staying at The Ritz,' he says.

I head down the stone steps and up into the Service Range Rover. Simon puts his foot down before I've even got the door shut.

'What the *hell* are you doing?' His knuckles are white on the steering wheel.

*Baiting a trap. Testing a theory. Two hours out in the open and no show. Not long enough to be sure though.*

'Getting laid.'

'What? Who?'

'Some billionaire.'

Simon looks like he might be sick.

'How d'you know he's not a contractor come to take you out?'

I roll my eyes. 'How many billionaire contractors do you know? He was here before me anyway. He's been here for hours.'

Simon glares.

'What the hell are *you* doing?' I demand. 'You are supposed to be finding a trail.'

'I've got something,' he says. 'A prepaid. Initialised on Rue des Vieux-Grenadiers at 8.25 p.m. Enters the Marché de Plainpalais at 8.45 p.m. Disappears, reappears in the Three Valleys a couple of hours later. Goes dead minutes after you blow up the helicopter.'

*You blow up one tiny helicopter...*

'And?' On its own a prepaid tells us nothing.

'And I have a regular phone turned off 8.24 p.m. right beside it on Rue des Vieux-Grenadiers.'

I breathe out. I had been holding my breath.

# CHAPTER 13

The night streets of the City are deserted. We pass St Paul's on our right, its dome uplit. Paternoster Square is dark.

'I came to tell you,' he says. 'But you were gone.'

'I don't suppose the phone comes with a name and contract?' Simon shakes his head.

It doesn't matter. We can track its signature back up the line. He could change it every week and we would still get something. I stare out of the window.

Even with Max's algorithms we are looking at a vast amount of new data to sift through. Billions of signals criss-cross the globe. We need to track one unique signature mast to mast, finding the hand-offs one by one, like high-tech gingerbread crumbs. *Where will they lead? Where is home?* I'm sure it will be Moscow. Urban terrain. The picocell covering two or three streets.

A night cleaner is stacking stools on tables in the Pret on the corner.

Soon I will be on my way to Moscow and I need to know if he can see me coming. *Two hours out in the open. Not long enough to be sure.*

The Penthouse at The Ritz is another place with fortress security…

'Go back, find Max and trace it. Call me when you have an end location,' I say.

'Where are you going?'

'The Ritz.'

The Range Rover screeches to a halt in the middle of Cheapside.

'Are you mad? You can't be out here. Every contractor in Western Europe is probably heading our way.'

'There's nothing on Firestorm. No one turned up at the Colony. Get the programme running and call me when you have something.'

Simon is furious, I can tell just from the angle of his jaw as he squints in his mirror.

'If you have to go, I'll wait outside,' he says.

He wants to wait outside while I get laid.

*Classic.*

'Get back to the office and find me a location. It's time for you and Max to pull your fingers out.'

We have to go around the block to come at the road entrance to The Ritz, the right way up the one-way street. A doorman steps up to open my door.

'I am NOT happy about this,' Simon says.

'GO. You're blocking the traffic.'

Simon is looking in his side mirror as he pulls out. I slam the door on his reply.


The neat little major-domo answers the door to the Penthouse suite. I give him a winning smile.

'Hi.'

Nothing. Not a flicker.

'Is he back yet?'

He looks me up and down. 'Is this a social call?'

*As opposed to what?*

He blocks the door, one hand on the doorjamb, a weird mix of proprietary and protective. I make his mind up for him by ducking under his arm and walking in.

The sitting room of The Ritz Penthouse suite is black and gold and cluttered. What is it about penthouse suites and gold? I circle a couple of small tables and make for the sound of running water. The bedroom is empty, the sound is coming from the en suite.

Our eyes meet in the huge mirror.

Roman is standing with his back to the door, with nothing but a white towel wrapped round his waist.

He won't be needing that.


I stand naked, considering the room service menu. 'What shall I get you?'

Roman is face down on the carpet. He lifts his head, but no sound comes out.

I order steak for two and put the phone down.

'I tell you what,' I say, 'why don't you sit this next one out?'

I climb on the bed, spread my legs and use one finger so as not to block the view.

His head gets higher and higher and his eyes wider and wider until he is crawling up the end of the bed, across the sheet and on top of me.

'Christ,' he says as he sinks deep.

I hook his leg, flip him over onto his back and use his hands to move myself up and down.

'Don't mind me,' he says.

After I've come riding his perfect twenty-two-year-old body, I climb off and finish him in my mouth. Room service knock just as he grips the sheets, pumping down the back of my throat.

After that he doesn't seem to be getting up, so I eat the steak and chips myself, check the door and curl up beside his warm sleeping body, thinking about the twelve and their scrolling counters and John J. Traynor, a man who spent his whole life helping others, beaten to death by a pair of iron fists.

*

Early morning sun wakes me. 5 a.m. and still not a contractor in sight.

*Seven hours out in the open.*

I feel as fresh as a daisy. Roman is lying fast asleep on his side, the sheet hanging off his perfect washboard stomach. I lift the sheet. He seems to have recovered.

I push him back gently, straddle his hips and lower myself onto him. As I come down, his eyes open sleepily.

'Morning,' I say.


'When I was a boy,' Roman says afterwards, 'we had this tradition down on the plains. A race.' He rolls on his side to face me, the sheet hanging off him. 'The men would wait at the start line on their fastest horses and the women would gallop past them. If a man caught a woman before the mile marker, she was his for the night.'

'And what if they didn't catch them?'

'If they reached the mile marker without being caught, the women turned and the hunters became the hunted. The women carried long training whips. I was fourteen and there was this woman. Black eyed. Wicked. She lorded it over the others.'

I nod. I know the type.

'Anyway, I begged my brother to let me compete. I was already a good rider. Fast and fearless.'

I watch him, curious. 'And what happened?' I prompt when he doesn't continue.

He rolls onto his back, his arm over his eyes. 'He gave me the slowest donkey in the place. He said to me, "If you want something badly enough you will make it happen. Find a way."'

'And did you?'

'No. He won himself.'

I laugh. 'And what happened? He slept with her?'

'No.' Roman sits up. 'He just wanted to put me in my place. So, that night I crept into her house and made it happen. Women had trouble saying no even then.'

I push him over in disgust. He falls onto his back laughing.

Brothers. It makes me glad I am an only child.

'Why was it up to him?'

Roman's face twists. 'He is fifteen years older than me. I never knew my parents.'

I process this.

*Brought up by a domineering older brother.*

'He has no time for women. You should hear him.' His voice turns stern. '"Women are weak and they make you weak. They suck you in and drag you down, surround you with their soft pillowy limbs and suck the life out of you."' He rolls his eyes. 'He never stopped lecturing when I was growing up.'

'So… is he gay?'

Roman laughs. 'No. No. Definitely not. He's never met a woman yet who said no to him.'

'That tends to be the case for most billionaires, I find.'

Roman shakes his head, half jealous, half admiring. 'It's always been the same. You should see women with him. They just fall at his feet.'

'I'm sure.'

'I remember this one time, we were in a club and this woman went down on him.'

'That kind of club.'

'Yeah, that kind of club. And afterwards he went to tip her.'

'As you do.'

'And she said, "That's OK, I don't work here."'

'And what did he say?'

'I don't think he knew what to say. He never lets women get close. You know. Emotionally.'

My phone rings. I lean forward to get it from the tangle of white satin beside the bed. Simon.

'You had better not be checking up on me.'

'I have something,' he says. His voice is hopeful.

I smile. Quick work even for Max and Simon.

'Let's have it.'

'A live number.'

*I have the Prince of Darkness's phone number.*

'I'm on my way.'

I swing my leg over Roman's body and stand up.

'You can't go. Stay for breakfast.' He clings on, his cheek pressing into my bare back. 'Stay for supper.' I break his hold and push him backwards onto the bed by his face.

'I have to work. I'll see you later.'

What it is to be a billionaire playboy with nothing to do but fuck all day.

# CHAPTER 14

There is no grand, double height atrium at The Ritz, just one opulent lounge area leading into another, a series of antechambers. I make for the side exit on Arlington Street, reading the sight lines. The doorman raises his hat. He knows I came from the Penthouse suite, don't ask me how.

It is going to be a golden day. I head down the street, sucking in lungfuls of early-morning air, turn the corner and end up on St James's. The wide bow windows of gentlemen's clubs stare down at me.

I turn the corner into Pall Mall, past the flaming torches outside the RAC Club, past the broad wide stairs onto The Mall and out into Trafalgar Square. The steps are deserted. Come back in five hours and it will be packed: students – hair blowing in the wind, tourists with selfie sticks. I cross the road outside the grand art deco front of Charing Cross station and duck down a side alley.

It is the perfect morning to walk along the river to the City, but I am in a hurry and I force myself into the tube. The tired yellow tiles of Embankment look like a urinal. Smell like a urinal too. Even early rush hour is busy. Commuters crowd the platforms. The tunnels are warm and airless after the freshness of the day.

The train rumbles in the tunnel and comes into view. I keep my back to the curved wall. I saw a hit on a tube platform once. It stays with you. Never let anyone get between you and the wall. The train screeches to a halt, the doors beep and the crowd surge forward. I am the last on as the doors close. I throw myself at the gap, forcing it apart, squashing myself through. People tut until they see me. Then they smile. Evening dress in the morning rush hour will do that.

I lean up against the door, hanging from the rail. The proximity is comforting. It reminds me of my teenage years when I used to ride the tube just to feel close to someone. I close my eyes and the Prince of Darkness is standing there, smiling at me. I want to call out to him.

I get off at Monument station. The underground link to Bank station and GCHQ is deserted. This time of day everyone is in too much of a hurry to walk. I set off up the silent passageway.

Footsteps echo down the tunnel. Someone is approaching in a hurry. Running. I resist the urge to start running myself. Maybe they are late for something. I touch the GCHQ locator in my ear. Is this it? Have they tracked me to this deserted tunnel?

Closer and closer the footsteps come. They are running full tilt towards me. Leather shoes, not trainers, a man, light but tall, the strides are long. I stand still and wait. The runner turns a bend in the tunnel.

Simon.

Not a hitman. Someone allowed to track my locator. His messy hair is swept back with the speed. He screeches to a halt, rocking with the forward momentum and puts his hands on his knees, gasping. I breathe out, more tense than I realised and slap him on the back trying not to laugh.

'Firestorm, Winter,' he chokes.

Finally. There is a contract out on me and I actually feel relieved.

I pat his shoulder. 'It was to be expected.'

'No, you don't understand,' he gasps.

'Just breathe,' I say, amused. 'Christ, you're unfit.'

He stands upright and starts to drag me back down the tunnel the way he has come. He is surprisingly strong. I let him drag me, half laughing, half protesting.

'If it's less than fifty grand I'm going to complain.'

'One hundred million dollars,' he says. 'Flat fee. No auction.'

*WHAT?*

'It's a mistake,' I say.

He shakes his head and I see the panic in his eyes and the determination. Any minute now he will be trying a fireman's lift.

'Alright, alright.' I hold my hands up, conceding defeat, and we break into a run.

We pound down the tunnel and up the escalators. Now we are in Bank station, on the level below the ticket hall. We dive into the tunnel on the right and down a short flight of steps onto the westbound Central line platform. A train has just left and the platform is full of people hurrying up the platform for the exit. The air is thick with fumes. We thread our way along to the far end and duck through a scuffed service door beside a ladder to the track.

The spiral staircase is lit by emergency lighting. It ends in a tiny lobby. A fire door blocks the way. Simon heaves a huge sigh of relief as we enter the security capsule.

'Detainment suite,' he orders.


The GCHQ canteen is on the tenth floor below street level. Simon is still arguing as we hit the swing doors.

'You have to go to the detainment suite. It isn't safe here.'

I roll my eyes at him. 'What? You're worried in the GCHQ canteen? Now you are being ridiculous.'

I beam at the white-jacketed guy behind the counter. There are trays and trays in front of him. Bacon, hash browns, mushrooms, beans, sausages and eggs, scrambled, fried and poached.

'Everything, Winter?' He gestures with a spoon the size of his fist.

'Right you are.' I point at the food. 'Maybe it's poisoned, Simon.' I put my hands to my cheeks doing my impression of Munch's *The Scream*.

Simon scowls. 'Keep your voice down. It could be all the food in the place.'

'What? Just to get at me?' I grin. It is quite funny. One hundred million dollars is a hell of a lot of money to throw at a problem. Boy, does this guy value his anonymity.

Simon's mouth twists but he doesn't say anything.

The room is half full, well into the main sitting. GCHQ doesn't sleep. Technicians, data analysts, research analysts. The bug hunters sit together. The Doris and Dennis minders, support staff, cleaners – it is not a threatening line-up. The place rings with morning chatter, the clink of cutlery, the scrape of china, a hundred bodies in a confined space. There is everything and nothing to read.

A window stretches the full length of the room overlooking the Arena, a triple-height, football-pitch sized underground training area. I can see a couple of sessions in full swing. I breathe deeply. Bacon overpowers everything. I look at Simon's worried face.

'Relax,' I say, clapping him on the shoulder.

I plonk my tray on a table by the window and sit down. I have my back to the door and even here it gives me a prickle of unease. Curious eyes stare and look away. Everyone knows I was missing.

'What news of Slashstorm?' I say, thinking of twelve faces and the girl with wide brown eyes.

Simon sits down opposite me and pulls the bowl of sugar sachets towards him.

'No change.'

I look at Simon's tray in disgust.

'Is that all you're having? A coffee and a banana?' I have every one of the hot breakfast options.

Simon eyes my tray. 'Carb-loading?'

'Don't go there,' I warn, pointing my knife at him, my mouth full of bacon. I am not allowing him to dictate what I put in my face. That is what Viv did to Erik until he found himself eating egg-white omelette. The thought comes out of nowhere and blindsides me with sadness.

Simon is decimating packets of sugar. He is so wired.

'You really have to deal with your anger management issues,' I say.

His face flickers into a half smile but he doesn't say anything.

'So…' I prompt. 'What have we got?'

'It is a live number,' he says. 'Still triangulating down but looks like Italy. Rural.'

Someone is behind me. Too close.

Simon's face stills as he stares over my shoulder, then he is launching himself across the table at something above my head. I throw myself sideways off my chair and feel pain in my shoulder. A blade has made it through the satin. Right where my heart would have been a fraction of a second before.

I roll, bouncing up to face my attacker. It is a bug hunter, the evolutionary successor of a Bletchley Park codebreaker. He has a blade in one hand and a look of determination on his face. I see the knife coming and feel the adrenaline rise. I spin and plant a roundhouse kick to his jaw with all the strength I have. The bug hunter flies back against a white plastic table. The knife soars through the air, landing with a crash, and skitters across the floor.

A wall of noise rushes back. I am standing in an empty circle of space while people scream around me.

Simon is trying to press napkins to the hole in my shoulder. A couple of figures bend over the fallen bug hunter. Medics. I don't need them to tell me he is dead. I have killed him with a kick.

I slam through the canteen double doors. They smash against the wall.

*In my own bloody office. Son of a bitch.*

Simon follows in the wake of my anger, jogging to keep up. His shirt is splattered with fried egg. He lunges at my back, trauma pad in hand. I shake him off. A corner of me wonders where Simon has found a trauma pad so quickly. Maybe he carries them around with him. I hold my right hand to my shoulder. Blood wells through the fingers.

'It is nothing, nothing. Surface,' I tell him.


The GCHQ incident room is the size of a boardroom and the best place in the UK to run a live op. The room is dark, the air cold on my face. I flick the switch and the lights burst into life down the long room. The light bounces off rows and rows of equipment ready and waiting for action. Banks of blank screens. It smells of cold.

This is the ultimate. A hacker's wet dream. There is nowhere this room can't go. The Bunker can handle most things, but I am taking no chances.

Simon stands by the door. Indecision pours off him.

'Get Max here.'

'Winter, this is the last resort. Let's not waste it.'

'Do it.'

Simon shakes his head but sits down at a terminal, pulling on a headset. Two minutes later Max walks into the room. His beard has crumbs of Crunchie in it. He has been running and is trying not to let it show. It is ten years since I hacked the service on his watch. He still hasn't forgiven me.

'Get a trace started.' I pick up a headset and wait, tapping my nails on the desk.

Max is already firing up the kit. He personally modified the location software. He needs no persuasion to use it.

'Dial the number,' I order.

'Once we light up the line that will be it.' They both nod their heads in agreement. Synchronised bobbing.

'Do it.'

Simon looks across, waiting for Max's OK. When it comes, he sighs as he presses the number he has just traced into the dealer board.

This is it.

I wipe my fingers on my white satin and press the headphones to my ears.

The Prince of Darkness answers on the first ring.

'You missed,' I spit.

There is laughter. I close my eyes as I picture him, laughing at me. He is so close I could almost touch him.

'Come and do your own dirty work. Coward.'

There is an intake of breath and silence. The laughter has stopped.

*That has shut him up.*

Then he is laughing again, laughing so hard he holds the phone away from his face and now there is real amusement in his voice. I can see him on the Courchevel airstrip, backlit by flames, laughing and laughing. *You're so funny little girl.*

'Get out of my head,' I whisper.

He stops laughing.

*'What?'* he says, his voice quiet.

Silence swirls around us, cocooning us in a bubble of intimacy. I can feel him on the end of the phone. I can hear his breathing. I can see the strong line of his jaw, the curve of his lips as he holds the phone to his face, considering. The satin feels hot.

Max holds up his finger. He is close to a full trace, but I don't care. I stare down the long empty room.

'I am coming,' I promise, my voice full of venom.

'I'm looking forward to it.' I can hear the smile.

He pauses, then cuts the call.

On the other side of the desk Max gives a double thumbs up. Relief mingles with surprise on Simon's face. He can't believe it. I throw down the headset and rush round to look at the findings.

'Tell me it's Moscow,' I beg. It's all slotting into place.

'Umbria.'

'Umbria?' My mind goes blank. 'Umbria... in Italy?'

It has to be a mistake.

'It's the same mast again. A microcell.'

It is not a mistake. He set out from there to go to Geneva five days ago and he is back there now.

Simon is coming to the same conclusion. 'Umbria is home? I can't believe it.'

# CHAPTER 15

Control looks up as I burst through his office door. He keeps looking at the door as if trying to make a point.

'Self-defence,' he says. 'I'll write it up as a training accident.'

*What?*

Ah yes, a broken body lying on a white plastic table.

'In the canteen?'

'I can't understand why you were out of the detainment area in the first place. Don't leave it again until you have a name.'

I have a better plan.

'Viv,' I say. 'I need her help.'

Viv was Erik's quartermaster and the only person bar Simon I trust with my life.

'Anyone else, Winter. She is on psychiatric leave. She is never going to get cleared for duty.'

Viv went postal after Erik was killed.

I fold my arms across my chest. We stare at each other. I can see him weighing it all up. Me vs. Medical.

Silence.

Across the room, tiny silky moths flutter against a piece of sticky cardboard. A pheromone trap. They throw themselves at it again and again. It makes me want to help them. I turn away so I can't see their struggles. The silence stretches out.

Apparently the balance tips in my favour because eventually he nods once quickly.

'Go via Erik's office,' he says.

I don't bother to thank him as I head to the door.

'Winter?'

I turn.

'Don't leave the detainment suite again. That's an order.'


I stand in the doorway of Erik's dark office for the first time since he died.

Why has Control sent me in here? What is he expecting me to find?

I walk in without turning the lights on and sit down in the swivel chair. The monitors are black. The air is still, like it hasn't been disturbed for years. Erik is there in the air – even though he spent all his time in the Bunker. The scent of him. It knocks the wind out of me, blindsides me again.

I stare at his blank screens. Tiny particles of dust are stuck to the static. I pull open a desk drawer at random and my heart lurches.

A padded A5 envelope with my name on it. A farewell letter.

I pull out the single sheet of folded paper.

> *Dear Winter,*
>
> *It is down to you now. You must find the way. You are the best field agent GCHQ has ever had. I knew you would be from about ten minutes after I met you. A Dalmatian onesie is a hell of a disguise. The enclosed box is for my quartermaster. Please make sure she gets it. Don't be sad. That's an order.*

Erik's heavy signature scrawls across the bottom.

I open the black velvet box. A single teardrop diamond ring, dull in the half light. A world of 'if onlys' in a box. A litany of things he never got around to saying to her.

*Too late.*

The saddest words in the English language.

Tears well up through my sinuses, my nose tingles. I drop my head in my hands.

*Don't leave me.*

Something blocks the light. A figure in the doorway. Simon.

'Are you OK?' he says.

I rub the desk with my sleeve.

'Fine.' I stand up. 'Fine. Where is Viv?'

Whatever Simon was expecting me to say, it wasn't this.

He shakes his head as if to clear it. 'No one can reach her. She is in pieces. Good for nothing.'

*I know the feeling.*

'Take me to her.'

He blanches. 'Winter, you cannot leave the building. One hundred million dollars. Who knows what the hell is out there?'

'It has to be me.'

He swallows. 'But, Winter, there are probably snipers on every rooftop. We will be lucky to avoid someone ram-raiding the building.'

We take a squad car in the end. I don't trust any of the tube exits and Simon refuses to let me out on the street. As the car skirts Old Street and heads down Bethnal Green Road, my heart sinks. I have a bad feeling about where we are going. We pull up outside a terrace in Mile End in East London, a GCHQ safe house. Viv has gone back to the last place she saw Erik.

Pain twists in my gut. I wasn't there for him. Neither of us were. He will be forever lying on the floor in a dirty hotel bedroom with a 9 mm hole in his forehead.

I undo my seat belt slowly.

Simon shakes his head. 'It's not good,' he says. He doesn't meet my eyes. 'I can't reach her. I've been trying. She would have given her life for Erik and she wasn't even there.'

I am surprised by the sensitivity of the comment.

'At least she wasn't drinking coffee and playing Solitaire on the job like someone I know,' I say, prodding his shoulder. Not that I have ever actually caught him at it.

Simon looks away. He starts to unbuckle his seat belt, but I stop him. 'I'll go on my own.'

'What are you going to say?' he asks.

'I have no idea.'


I open the front door and close it softly behind me. The house is silent. I can guess where she will be and I make my way wearily up the threadbare stairs. The boards show through the red patterned carpet. The smell of old house fills the air. It is in the very bones of the place. You could take out every stick of furniture, every rug, every piece of carpet and it would still be there. I reach the top of the stairs. The door to the bedroom is open.

Viv is sitting on a chair with her back to the door. How long has she been like that? Today, there's no draught from the windows. It is a warm day.

I touch the black velvet box in my pocket, turning it over and over with my fingertips. Erik's slate-grey eyes beg me to do it right.

She stares out at the garden. There is nothing from her back, not a flicker of movement, nothing to acknowledge my arrival. I walk round until I am standing between her and the window.

I don't know what I was expecting to see in her eyes, maybe tears, maybe pain. Something. There is nothing. Empty black pools of nothing, enough to drown us both.

And suddenly I know what to do. I shove the ring box back in my pocket.

*Some day, but not today.*

*

I turn away, then spin back, my left hand extending and the full force of a knife-hand strike smacks into the side of her face. I feel it connect and wonder how many bones I am going to have to break. It is my last moment of detachment.

It is a very long time since anyone landed a blow on Viv and even longer since she took a hit to the face. She falls to the floor but the eyes that look up at me through a tangle of dark, lanky hair are angry and focused. I leap out of the way of the round kick that would have broken my ankle and boot her straight in the guts as hard as I can. There is a crunch of rib. She rolls away and now she is rising on the other side of the chair, her face murderous.

I lunge across the gap, capitalising on my superior reach but she dances and blocks and lands a kick to the chest that knocks me backwards. Her fists are up and she weighs in with a classic attack pattern. As a fifth *dan*, she technically outranks me but the advantages of being combat-ready are all with me. I block and land a second knife-hand strike on her neck that takes her down. I stand, my fists clenched, breathing hard, but she is not getting up.

I crouch down beside her and lift her head by her lank hair.

'I need you,' I say.

I explain to her what I want. It is terrifying. Her eyes close and she nods.

As I sweep out, she whispers something that might be 'thank you'.


Simon is waiting for me in the car.

'That was quicker than I expected. How is she?' He takes in my heavy breathing and leans forward. 'Is someone there?' he demands. 'Another hit?'

I shake my head and sink into the seat. Tears prick the corners of my eyes. I rub at them with my wrist.

\*

The squad car drives us back through the titanium blast doors and into the holding bay. The underground car park is quiet, lit by the usual flickering strip light. I hesitate outside the security capsule. Simon's hair stands up in small peaks he is so tense. I don't trust GCHQ. I don't trust the squad car. I pull Simon into the shadow of a concrete pillar and whisper in his ear. Not very high tech.

'I'm going off-grid. Viv is going to wear my locator and pretend to be me.'

Simon stares.

'No one can know. Lock her up in the detainment suite and say I am looking at faces 24/7.'

'Where are you going?'

'Umbria.'

'No way, Winter. Are you mad?'

'Full appearance transfer. I need you to book me in. The works. Facial implants. Hair, everything.'

The thoughts scud across his face, one after the other. There are so many things about this plan that he doesn't like. He homes in on the biggest one. 'No locator?'

I shake my head. 'Think about it. We're full of leaks. That is bad enough at the best of times. Now there is 100 million dollars' worth of incentive.'

Simon's face grapples with the problem. 'But then how can I support?'

I grip his arms. 'We are dealing with someone with live assets in the GCHQ building, someone with government grade surveillance capabilities. If you can see me, he can see me. I need to slip under his radar and I have nine days left to do it.'

His mouth twists as he concedes the logic.

'So, we give him something to watch. He probably knows by now I have a photographic memory. He knows I know about the contract. He will expect me to sit tight and find him in the systems.'

'What does Control say?'

I shake my head. 'I'm not going to tell him.'

'Shit,' he says.

'But you will help me?'

He stares at me for a long moment then he looks away. 'You don't need to ask.'

# CHAPTER 16

Smooth olive skin and dark hair fill my thoughts. I call The Ritz. The major-domo answers.

'I can't come round later,' I say. 'Something has come up.'

There is a muffled conversation off-line and then the major-domo is back.

'He's wondering if you can meet him for a quick drink?'

*Why? Does he think I want to date him?*

He names a bar within five streets of GCHQ, almost like he knows where I am.

It must be fate.

Maybe for fifteen minutes. Twenty max. I pull off my locator and leave it on the desk for Simon to take to Viv.

I climb the stairs, two at a time, and arrive in Reception via the stairwell lobby. Reception is busy. It always is. I stroll out through the main doors like I haven't a care in the world. I figure with four subterranean – plus a road – exits to GCHQ, no one will be expecting me to walk out the front door. I don't pause to scan the rooftops but cross Cheapside briskly, weaving through the lines of cars like a bike courier and ducking down a narrow alleyway that leads to Gresham Street.

A minute later I am in King's Arms Yard, an alley stretching between Coleman Street and Moorgate. A hangover from medieval London's street layout.

The bar sign creaks. The Highwayman. It would be a perfect place for a hit. Good lines of sight. I glance up at the roof as I duck under the threshold.

Roman stands at the bar with his back to me. A fine wool suit stretches a perfect fit across his shoulders and hangs from his hips. The barman smiles up at him. The halo effect. Roman was probably born thinking the whole world smiles. He turns away with a word of thanks, carrying a bottle of beer and a long, tall drink. His hair flops down across his face. I remember it plastered across his forehead as he begged me not to stop.

He catches sight of me and smiles and the room lights up. I hunch my shoulder away from the bar cams and walk over. He is close enough to touch when his trouser pocket starts to vibrate. I lean forward.

'Is that a phone in your pocket or are you just pleased to see me?' I grin as I palm the phone. 'Retro,' I comment, looking down at it. Not what you would expect from a billionaire playboy.

He scowls when he sees it in my hand, thrusts the drinks down on the table and tries to snatch it back. I hold it out of his reach, looking at the caller ID. The Cyrillic characters catch me out for a moment and I squint down at them.

'It's your brother,' I say.

Roman swears some more and grabs it from me. I drop the phone and back off, holding my arms out, palms up in surrender. I get a picture of the stern older brother lecturing about women. Roman cuts the call without answering and throws the phone down on the table.

'You can answer,' I say, puzzled. 'I don't mind.'

Roman shakes his head. He stares down at the phone.

'What is it?' I ask, reaching across the gap, half amused, half concerned. 'Don't say he is cutting your allowance.'

The joke is in poor taste, I see the anger in his face. His eyes rake the bar, scanning, as if he is looking for trouble. He glances behind him. He shakes his head irritably.

'Forget my brother.'

He leans forward and takes my hand. I notice my split knuckles and pull it away quickly. He stares into my face.

'What happened to you?'

I drag hair over my sore cheek.

'I walked into a door.'

'With your fists?'

It is a fair point. The phone on the table between us shrieks in the silence. It does a little jig on the polished wooden surface.

I sit back and gesture to it. 'You'd better speak to him.'

Roman stares at the phone for a moment then snatches it off the table, rising and turning away. He is annoyed – and something else.

I rein in my libido. *Time to go.* The bright lights of the operating theatre and facial alteration surgery await. I should never have come in the first place. I slide out of the booth, drink untouched, and head for the exit. At the door I pause for a moment to watch him. He is speaking rapidly and urgently in Kazakh.

By the time he turns, I am gone.

# CHAPTER 17

It is night by the time Simon drops me at Gatwick Airport. I am more than eight hours early for my morning flight to Perugia, Italy, but he would brook no arguments and after the facial alteration people had gone to work on me for hours, I was in no mood for a fight.

Airside at Gatwick is one of the safest places in the UK and, as far as Simon is concerned, it has the added bonus of there being no possibility of me skipping off. If he had his way I would spend my life airside. There is more military hardware held there than there is at the Barracks in Hyde Park. They are on red alert. They are expecting a terrorist attack, they are expecting hidden weapons, they have trained for a ground assault on the terminal.

I wait patiently in line at check-in. Around me the airport is still full. Tired drawn faces, mothers with little kids up hours past their bedtime, business travellers heading home.

I am next in line. I walk up to the desk and smile at the woman behind it. She is young and groomed and glossy with a wide smile and a neat little red scarf around her neck. There is something about air hostesses… like you could ask them for a happy ending.

I put my passport on the desk.

*Who am I today?* I squint down at the passport photo.

'Did you pack the bag yourself?'

*No, it was packed for me by my quartermaster. I don't even know what's in it.*

'Yes.'

'And has it been out of your sight since you packed it?'

*This is the first time I've seen it.*

'No.'

'Do you have any of these?' She pushes a card of prohibited items towards me.

*Apart from the eight ceramic throwing knives?*

'No.'

'Have a nice flight.' She hands my flight documents over the counter.

*Nice?* I revise my views on the happy ending.

I stare at myself in the vast, grey airside bathroom and someone else stares back. The smell of commercial toilets catches in the back of my throat. Stale urine mingles with industrial bleach. The brilliant white light hurts my eyes.

My hair has been cut and new hair woven onto it. It hangs in black waves to my shoulders. Pale skin, black hair, red lips – I look like Snow White. My dark eyes sparkle. Brown contacts. I trace the silicon beneath my cheekbones and along my jaw. The surgeons have done an unbelievable job. Snow White's face is heart-shaped after the inserts. Winter is gone.

Snow White sounds like a Firestorm contractor handle.

*Snow White, my hitman alter ego.*

'Hi,' says the woman in the mirror. 'Snow White. Nice to meet you.'

I down a couple of ibuprofen for the swelling and Snow White winks at me. She is hot.

Midnight and the main concourse is brightly lit and bustling. There is no such thing as night here. The place is open 24/7. The shiny glass shopfronts never close.

I drift past confectioners, coffee shops, doughnut sellers, miles and miles of duty free. Every shop counter has tiny pieces of product to taste. You could survive here on freebies. Warm offerings line up on the counter of Hotel Chocolat: Tequila Sunrise specials, caramel puddles. You could survive… until the diabetes or the scurvy or the boredom got you.

I stare up at the nearest camera, wondering if Simon is watching. There are more cameras here per square foot than the Bank interchange, but facial recognition software works on nine contour points on the human face. You only have to alter four of them to baffle the software.

I walk all the way around until I find myself back at Hotel Chocolat. The place is a huge hexagon, there is no escaping. A weird microcosm of a world, an ecosystem of scarves and bags and chocolate and bright, smiling shop girls, their heavy foundation almost orange in the harsh lighting.

I sit down on one of the plastic chairs in the very centre of the shopping mecca and stretch my legs out in front of me. The chairs are linked together in a continuous piece of moulded plastic. It is seriously uncomfortable. The curved shoulders of sleeping bodies stretch out on the narrow chairs, heads pillowed on hand luggage rucksacks.

There is nowhere you can get your back to the wall. I am never going to sleep here. What am I going to do for the next eight hours?

I get up and go back to wandering the shopfronts. Everywhere I look, someone is trying to sell me something.

A bored late teen sits in front of racks of earrings, hair bobbles, bikinis. She is doing the merchandise justice – she has at least eight piercings that I can see. Golden eyes look up and meet mine and I find myself wondering what else she has pierced.

I wander over.

'Late shift?' I ask.

She nods, sizing me up. 'I've just come on.'

A silver ball on the end of her tongue flashes as she speaks. I think about what you can do with a tongue stud. Several things you can do.

'I'm worth 100 million dollars,' I say.

*Snow White is crazy.*

She laughs. 'Bullshit. Who has that kind of money?'

She is right. Very, very few people. He should be easy to spot in a five-mile radius. I smile. I pull a polka dot bikini off a nearby rail and hold it up against me.

'Do you think this is my size?'

She considers, eyeing up my figure.

'You need a bigger top,' she concludes.

I close the gap between us and hold the polka dot bikini up against her chest.

'You try it,' I suggest. I put my head on one side. 'So I can see what it looks like.'

'Are you fucking with me?' she demands, her hands on her hips. Apparently this is an unusual request.

I picture her on her knees. 'If you like,' I say.


The changing room cubicle is small. Two polka dot bikinis stand side by side, looking in the mirror. The girl with the tongue stud's golden eyes are wide. Snow White pushes her to the wall. I cup her jaw in both hands, her hair feels silky beneath my fingertips. My thumbs trace her lower lip. I bend my head and whisper, feather-light against her mouth. Her lips open. The stud is warm on my tongue.

When I look back in the mirror, Snow White is pushing the shop girl to her knees and leaning back against the door. I close my eyes and grip the silky hair, controlling the movement. After a while, my hands brace against the walls.

I sweep the clothes off the chair, sit down and slide her bikini bottoms off. I pull her backwards onto me and my eyes hold hers in the mirror. Her mouth forms a perfect 'O', with a tongue stud in the middle, as my right hand moves downwards.

I speed up and slow down until her head thrashes from side to side and her skin is sheened in sweat. It is not long before her back arches and she screams against my neck as her body jackknifes over and over.

I yawn and stretch. There is a speckled laminate wall two inches from my nose. I jerk fully awake. *Where am I?* A laminate cell about four foot by four foot. No wonder I was dreaming about stretching. The changing room is completely enclosed, there is no gap at the top or bottom and I realise I have slept soundly for hours.

I sit up and the strange woman with the brown eyes and the long dark hair stares at me an infinite number of times. I grin back at Snow White as memory fills in the blanks. Why have I never thought of a changing room before?

My watch is flashing 6.30 a.m. My flight is probably on final call. I unlock the cubicle and step out. The girl with the tongue stud is standing at the till ringing up a basket of scarves. She must have let me sleep. She waves at me.

'They are just so beautiful I had to have them,' the customer is saying.

'Yeah,' the girl with the tongue stud says. 'Yeah. I know what you mean.'

# CHAPTER 18

It is 10 a.m. in the UK, 11 a.m. in Italy by the time the plane taxis to a halt. I step onto the flimsy metal gantry and the wall of hot air hits me. There is no sign of the fortress security of Gatwick. Here they see two flights a day. One flight in the morning and the same flight back in the afternoon. The man at border control looks into my eyes, not at my passport.

'*Ciao, bellissima,*' he says. 'Welcome to Italy.'

As I cross the main concourse heading for the taxis, I can't even see a camera. The place is deserted. I buy a guidebook from the only kiosk and watch the taxi queue. The fourth driver along is stuffing pizza into his face, balancing a cup of something on his dashboard. As he moves forward, I head out from the shadows and slide into place in the queue. He is still stuffing pizza in his face as we drive off.

'Welcome to Italy,' he says.


Umbria rolls past, walled hilltop towns and golden vistas. Across the opposite valley I can see a field of olive trees, silvery bushes in neat lines. A pale road snakes its way between the fields, disappearing out of sight behind the borders of dark green. The haze dulls the middle distance and beyond like a movie shot through Vaseline.

I see our destination from miles away. The sandstone walls of an ancient fortress town rise out of the treeline. Medieval slit windows in the castle tower watch the plain. It is the home of our microcell and the centre of the search area. Somewhere in its small radius is the most wanted man in the world and he has no idea I am here.

Anticipation flares. I am closer to bringing him down than anyone has ever been, closer to ending Firestorm's reign. I picture the twelve faces and the twelve vote counters on the Slashstorm home page and my heart starts to race.

*Breathe.*

The road disappears behind scrubby trees as it starts to climb, hiding the town from view. We pass little brown houses, their windows blind in the heat, and squares of golden flowers, fields of maize. Suddenly, we round a bend above the treeline and the stone walls come into view.

I climb out of the taxi and thank the driver in my broken Italian. He is still eating as he drives off. The squat clock tower in the main square sounds a single echoing note, an iron bell ringing the half hour from rusty chains. The white painted clock face is unreadable.

A cobbled street too narrow for cars leads to the stone castle with its high tower. The place is deserted. Even the birds are silent in the midday sun. There is no sign of the mast but I know it is there. The local government preserves the integrity of the ancient monuments like a mother guards a child. It will be there.

As I climb higher, the houses are built into the stone castle walls. Once they were probably little better than hovels, now they are painted and tiled and gentrified. A small plaque on a corner reads 'Jewish Quarter 14th–19th Century'. I round the bend and I am at the top, at the foot of the tower. It is a ruin, a facade with nothing behind.

A spreading cedar grows on the corner of the parapet, buckling the stone wall with its mighty roots. It stands on the very brink. Below it, the sheer wall of the keep fortifications and below them, the city walls themselves. I can see tens of miles across the plain. I can almost see the sea.

*Where are you?*

He was here six days ago, and he was here yesterday. This has to be home. Where does the most powerful man in the world call home?

Tiny little houses dot the valley floor, churches. Monasteries. I try to picture the Prince of Darkness in a monastery. It makes me want to laugh.

Where to start?

I peer over the railings on the town side. A roof terrace. Neat clipped box hedges, bougainvillea, rosemary, lavender. A scent tsunami. Coiled green hoses curl through the flower beds. It is as good a place as any.

I vault over the handrail and drop the fifteen feet or so to the terrace below, rolling as I hit the deck. The roof terrace of a private house, double doors with slatted wooden blinds stand open onto a room beyond. I step through. An old man and his tiny wife sit in armchairs looking out at their roof terrace. Octogenarians. I take in the faded grandeur of the decor. I smile winningly.

'Just passing through,' I say, heading for the stairs.

They watch me go without interest. At their age nothing surprises them. I fight my way past pot plants on stands and armchairs on the curve of the stairs until I am in the hall. Spider plants die against the wall. The Prince of Darkness doesn't live here. I open the front door and I am out on the main street.

I cross the road. The houses on this side have the plain at the back. I duck into the dark doorway of the house opposite. A bead curtain slaps my bare shoulder as I push through. A small square room leads directly to the back of the house. My mouth drops open. A plate glass window overlooks the plain, hundreds of feet above ground level.

A woman enters carrying a basket of sheets. She looks at me in surprise.

'I am so sorry, Signora,' I say, smiling. 'I wanted to see the view.' She stares after me as I turn to go.

*

Two hours later I am footsore and weary with nothing to show for it. I have checked every possible option in this walled town and drawn a blank. I head to the café in the main square and order a coffee. The wooden tables are sticky, but the café owner smiles. Snow White gets a lot of smiles. Lime trees hang heavy over the tables, dripping sap.

Beside me an English couple speak slowly and clearly, their vowels precise as they try to order lunch. The café owner stands patiently, tea towel in hand, making no attempt to help them out. The English man's linen jacket hangs limp over the back of his chair. I lift his phone while he frowns with the effort of communication.

'Should it be this hot at the beginning of May?' he says, like it is a personal affront.

Simon answers on the first ring.

'Nothing in the town,' I say. 'I'm going to check the outliers.'

'I've got fifty revenue returns in the higher tax bracket and one super tax,' he says. Population data mining.

I can't see the Prince of Darkness filing a tax return.

'And one Ferrari owner.'

'That sounds more promising.'

He reads out the location.

'Check for square footage,' I say. 'There's no way he lives in a bungalow.'

Simon grunts.

'How's Viv?'

'Fine. Waiting to kick some butt.' I can hear the smile in his voice.

'Anyone suspect it's not me in there?'

'No,' he says. The smile has gone.

*

I cut the call. No one had long enough to get a trace and if the GCHQ systems are compromised, Simon is in the detainment suite and not on his own workstation.

I peel a note from the wad Simon has given me and leave it on the table, weighted by the coffee cup. The Englishman has noticed the absence of his phone.

'I definitely had it,' he is saying. 'Just now. I was checking the cricket scores.'

*And we wonder why Europe was happy to let us go.*

'Maybe it's fallen out?' the wife suggests.

He growls irritably. 'How can it have fallen out?'

I lean down and pretend to pick something up out of the dust.

'Is this it?' I say. 'Lucky it's not smashed.'

It is bloody hot. The Englishman was right. He should try wearing Kevlar mesh in this heat. I head back to the viewing terrace at the very top of the citadel for a better look at my surroundings. On the other side of the castle, the southern side, the land slopes away sharply – dry, dusty terraces punctuated with clustered forests of dark green.

A line of tall thin cypresses curves up the opposite hillside out of the valley, their long, pointed horizontal shadows a ladder against the green. They curve from the valley floor to the brow of the hill and disappear over the top carrying the eye up and over, beyond the middle distance and into the far away. My eyes give up trying to distinguish colour and form, the hills are silhouettes against the pale blue sky.

Crowning the summit of the far valley, almost hidden from view by the tower, is another castle. It makes up the pair. These two castles guarded the plain a thousand years ago, looking down from their opposite sides. I squint into the distance. Is it a ruin like this one?

I stare at the forbidding walls. My neck feels suddenly cold. The stone shimmers in the haze, moving in and out of my vision.

It is just out of our five-mile square but I like it. I like it a lot. For the first time since I arrived I can see somewhere the Prince of Darkness might call home.

It is 4 p.m. and still hot by the time I reach the settlement on the opposite side of the valley. I walk into the main square, the tarmac soft beneath my feet. My bare arms prickle, my hot skin scenting the air. Little stone houses with pots of red geraniums at their windows line the square on three sides.

The place is deserted, the stone houses shuttered against the heat. Not deserted. Sleeping. The only movement is from the fountain in the centre. A bronze swan reaches up to the sky. I watch the water fall, the play of light through the curtain of silver. Hundreds of wasps dance a mad dance of aerial suicide.

A ramp the width of a car leads up to the castle. It disappears out of sight round a bend. No cameras that I can see. A tourism plaque is nailed on the wall at the bottom. That throws me. I take a few hesitant steps up the ramp, to the corner.

An old fig tree grows on the bend. I hang in its shadows reading the space. The green musk of fig, sweating through sandpaper leaves, is everywhere.

I walk on into the castle courtyard. There are brackets for torches all around the walls. Medieval. A low brick wall in the centre could be a well. Dark green moss circles the rim, bleeding down the wall and out across the dusty gravel. One side of the courtyard is a tower, the other three sides look like barracks, squat and unfinished. Monstrous stone hounds with collars of iron stand guard. It is completely deserted. Not a car, not even a cat. No sign of life.

There are iron bars on the windows that look out onto the courtyard. I peer through chicken wire. The gloomy little cell is derelict. A pigeon shuffles across the dirty floor. I turn to face the castle. In the corner on the far right, a tiny doll-sized door is propped open.

I skirt the edge of the courtyard and stand undecided, peering into the gloom through the tiny door. The stillness is absolute. I take a step inside and then another. The room is cool, several degrees cooler than the afternoon sun, and high, with windows above eye level. It leads into a huge hall with a domed ceiling. The space is completely empty. No furniture. No signs of life.

A magnificent Renaissance staircase rises, gracious, to the first floor in three even stages. I creep slowly up the stairs, an intruder in the Beast's castle, my tourist guidebook in front of me like a shield.

I pause on the landing, listening. Nothing. The door in front of me is ajar, I nudge it open. Inside, faces stare down at me from the ceiling. It looks like the Sistine Chapel. The room is empty. Tall windows flank the fireplace. It is a spectacular view, all of Umbria is laid out before me. At the other end of the room the window stares out across Tuscany. The sister castle crowns the opposite hillside. I am staring right back at myself from this morning.

And I am wasting my time. This is a scheduled ancient monument, not a home.

# CHAPTER 19

I stand in the main square, in the shade of a carved loggia, leaning my head against the stone columns, letting the disappointment wash over me. The dark green smell of fig fills the air. Fig and asphalt.

Fig, asphalt and something else…

My eyes narrow and my head wheels round as I try to locate the sudden smell. In the corner of the square, beside the ramp, are the castle bins – big green commercial dumpsters, taller than a man.

I cross to the shelter of the ramp and squeeze my way into the narrow gap between the bins and the stone. A gecko darts up the vertical stone wall, making me jump. I lift one lid after the other. The third in the line holds what I am looking for. I raise the lid quickly and with one hand on the edge, vault swiftly over the side and drop in.

The dumpster is more than half full and I land on piles of soft, squishy refuse sacks. It is about a thousand degrees. My body won't take this heat for long. My brain reports this and then goes off to shut down all nasal function. Fresh rotting food on top of old rotting food on top of stains that are years old. I crawl forward on my stomach, my face close to the bin bags, searching, my tongue tasting the air.

I rip open bag after bag and get nothing but fish bones and cat shit and deodorised kitty litter. Someone has a lot of cats. On the fifth attempt, I hit the jackpot.

My fingers investigate in the dark, sliding over the hard features. The stubble a few millimetres, a strong chin, a big aquiline nose, soft hair. Advanced rigor mortis. The body is hard but warm from the dumpster. Things are probably hatching in it, a whole microcosm being born. I feel in the dark, crusted hole between the eyes. Nine millimetre, dry and sealed. An execution, muzzle to the forehead.

I lay my cheek down on the face and there it is, the distinctive cologne. It doesn't need the daylight from the open crack to confirm what I have already guessed. Dominique St Vire, the Parrain, head of the Paris Milieu, France's de facto head of organised crime. The last time I saw him, a couple of years ago, he tried to put a bullet in me. What is he doing hundreds of miles from home in an Umbrian dumpster?

You know that well-worn phrase, 'he had cold eyes'? And you think, *what does that even mean?* No one has cold eyes, eyes are the warm vivid living part of the face, someone without their eyes looks like a shell. Well, Dominique St Vire had cold eyes, as cold as an iron-hard January day when tears burn your pink cheeks.

I remember looking into his smiling face with the pale skin and the smell of spice like Christmas. I remember his white teeth and his French charm and I remember looking deep into his eyes and seeing what was really going on. And shivering. Because by then I was too close and had lingered too long.

*Who does a man like Dominique call 'Boss'?*

And I know the answer to that. The Prince of Darkness was on his way to Paris to see Dominique St Vire when I blew up his helicopter.

Head of the biggest crime network in France chucked in a dumpster like he couldn't even be arsed. Like the Prince of Darkness doesn't need to bother. It tells me a lot about the scale of his reach and I don't like it.

I crawl out of the dumpster, cross to the fountain and stick my head under the cascading beads. Icy water hits my hot skin, soaking through my T-shirt, running down the stained trousers. I hold my hands up to the water. My gag reflex calms in the icy shock.

I clamber out of the fountain and make for the middle house in the terrace opposite the castle, my footprints glossy black in the dust. There is no front door, just a brightly coloured curtain keeping the flies away. Beads slap against my wet arm.

I inch silently down the stone corridor and peer round the first doorway, a laundry-cum-junk room, the walls rough. The corridor ends in the twist of a stair. I look back through the bead curtain to the bright square beyond. Still siesta time. Maybe they are all asleep. My hair drips down my back, pooling in little puddles on the stone floor.

'Hello?' My voice is shocking in the silence.

Above, a chair scrapes against a tiled floor. A woman's voice. Footsteps. A man ducks around the bend in the stairs, tucking in a shirt with rough, dirty fingers. Blue collar. His eyes widen at the sight of me. I can just imagine what I look like dripping water everywhere. His eyes stop at a point about six inches below my chin and stay there. Italian men. You have to love them.

'Who lives in the castle?'

His eyes snap back to mine at the speed of fear.

'I'm sorry I can't help you,' he says, stepping off the bottom stair. He comes down the passageway, hustling me backwards.

I consider my options. I am hot and tired and have just spent ten minutes too long in a baking dumpster with a dead body.

'Sorry, *Bello*. This is nothing personal.' I step to meet him and a moment later he is kneeling, his back against my legs, my left arm circling his windpipe. He chokes out a spluttered word.

'Signora?' I shout to the floor above. 'Can you come down?'

A moment later a face peers round the corner of the stairs. The wife. A tea towel hangs limp from one hand. She stares at her husband.

'The castle,' I say. 'Who lives there?'

The woman looks at me with worried eyes. She is making up her mind. 'There is no one there.' She looks at her husband again. 'They were all here two days ago.'

Two days ago. So close.

'They?' I prompt.

The woman shrugs. 'Men, politicians, leaders. A conference. I don't know. They left in a hurry.'

'I see, and when will they be back?'

The woman shrugs again. 'Next year?'

She turns to go back up the stairs. 'Don't let me stop you,' she says, glancing back at her red-faced husband.


I back out into the square. The fountain is still the only thing moving, the water sparkling in the sunlight. I fight the temptation to put my head under again. At the far end of the street, the last in the run of houses, a tiny café has opened its doors.

The café is bright and white. An ice cream counter leans against the far wall. A woman stands behind the high Formica counter beside racks of Tic Tacs, Haribo, Mentos. What has she seen here in this tiny café? Does she know the most wanted man on the planet? Does he come in here for a beer and an espresso?

I order a Limoncello for the sake of it. To break the ice. It stays frozen. Not a flicker of interest. Not a flicker of curiosity about this woman dripping water all over her café.

'Can I use your phone?' I ask, trying direct.

She stares.

I peel off a note from my wad, slap it on the counter and she puts her hand in her pocket and pulls out a smartphone without a word. I nod my thanks and take my drink and the phone to the far corner. No reception. I gesture outside and the woman nods.

Simon picks up on the first ring.

I tell him about the settlement on the other side of the valley. About the second castle. 'He was here but he's left.' I shut my disappointment down. 'Just find out who owns it.'

'On it.' Simon cuts the call.

The street is starting to wake up. The little stone houses are opening their doors, unshuttering their windows.

Three minutes later Simon calls back. 'I've traced the owner.'

I close my eyes in relief. 'Thank God.' All we need is a name.

'It is owned by a company.'

'Go on.' I get a sinking feeling I know where this is going. 'Cayman Islands?'

'You guessed it.'

*Great. A paper trail of subsidiaries leading nowhere.*

In my head, the Prince of Darkness laughs and laughs.

An untraceable company. What else have I got?

A body.

A body that will open doors. A body people will be grateful to get back.

'I need to get a body out of here. Send me a cab and a suitcase.'

'What? Who?' Simon's voice is annoyed. 'You are on recon.'

'Not me. Book the cab for a journey.'

'Where to?'

I cut the call on his questions.

I go back into the café and give the woman her phone.

'Who lives at the castle?' I ask as I turn away.

She shrugs. 'It is empty. Sometimes there are people there. Conferences and stuff.'

*Conferences.* Does he gather all his senior leadership together? Like he is running some kind of multi-national?

Her heart rate is calm. She is bored. She knows nothing. I take my Limoncello and sit down in the far corner to wait for my taxi.

A man appears on the terrace and looks through the open doorway. He sees me and ducks out of sight. Another face peers in. I shift slightly, resting my hand on the top of the boot I have propped on a chair. Blue-collar guy has some friends. How long will it take Simon to get a cab out to me? Twenty minutes maybe. A cab with a suitcase? Call it forty. Two new faces look round the door.

I just need to get out of here with the minimum of trouble. I wish my Italian was up to being charming.

Chairs scrape on the terrace. They are sitting outside. The woman comes out from behind the bar. A moment later she is back pulling bottles of beer off the shelf. If they are content to stay outside that suits me fine.

To kill time, I try the wooden salon door with a crude stick man drawing on it. The unisex toilet is all I was expecting. A china upright and a small sink. I lock the door. I squint at myself in the tiny piece of broken mirror. Snow White is not looking her best. I smooth her dark hair and reapply her black eyeliner. I pull out my folding toothbrush. The sink's single tap is operated by a foot pump. Judging by the smell it is more urinal than sink. I fight off the stomach clench and brush my teeth.

I slide the door back and come face to face with a roomful of people. They weren't content to wait outside. I sit back down at my table and put my boots up on the chair. One guy by the bar, two by the door, three sitting down. I have four blades in each boot making eight blades in total, leaving room for error. On the other hand, Simon will get annoyed if I make a mess. I am steel toecaps in a butterfly house.

Someone is coming over. I raise the Limoncello to my lips.

'Who are you?' he says. He is swarthy and dark and has absolutely no interest in the answer. A hint of cigarette hangs in the air when he speaks.

I put the Limoncello down on the table and raise the guidebook.

'Just passing through,' I say, waving it. *'No comprendo Italiano.'*

He leans forward placing his hands squarely on the table. I look down at them, assessing their position. I raise the glass to my lips while my other hand rams a blade between his outstretched fingers. The handle vibrates upright in the table. He screams and shoots backwards, tripping over a chair.

*I didn't even touch you.*

Blue-collar guy leaps into his place, swinging for my head. I bend sideways and give his arm a jerk as it sails past my face. The momentum carries him on and I give his ear a clip to help him on his way. He crashes headlong into the curved ice cream display. The woman behind the counter shrieks.

I sit back down again and pull the blade out of the wood and grimace at the woman in apology. I spin the blade on the palm of my hand. I throw it in the air. It somersaults twice before I catch it. I roll it over the back of my hand. Suddenly, blue-collar guy seems to have fewer friends.

A man stands in the doorway. Stubble, check shirt, jeans. He is carrying a huge pink suitcase. Nineteen minutes.

*Good work, Simon.*

'Taxi?' he says, looking round, bewildered.

I get up and take the case from the taxi driver, handing him a fifty euro note.

'Buy everyone a drink,' I say, clapping him on the back. 'I won't be long.'

Amateurs, civilians. A million miles from the men with the Prince of Darkness. The door closes on the hubbub behind me and I head back up the street.

I wheel the suitcase out of sight beside the green bins.

*How to do this?*

I wriggle into the gap between the castle ramp and the dumpster, brace my shoulders against the wall and push. The dumpster is on wheels but is hard to shift. I drop to the floor. I have pushed it about three feet from the wall. The opened suitcase fills the gap.

I take a deep breath. It is almost too much for my gag reflex, as if I have become sensitised by my time in the dumpster.

The Parrain was a big man and is now a dead weight. It takes me several long, hard minutes to haul, heave, push and roll the bin bag out into the suitcase. I sit down heavily on the lid to get the case shut, my heart thundering, my breathing heavy. I wheel it over to the fountain and stare at the water for a minute then I climb in.

When blue-collar guy and his friends and the taxi driver come out of the bar I am standing in the fountain, my face in the cascading water.

# CHAPTER 20

The Merc's back seat is worn, the leather satin-smooth in places. It was probably quite high-end when it was new. About twenty years ago. Now the red has faded to a stained brown. If the driver was surprised the case was now so heavy – it took two of us to heave it into the boot – he didn't mention it.

At some point in the preceding twenty years, the air con has packed up. I wind the window down with a plastic lever, surprised it doesn't come off in my hand. My wet hair blows in the breeze. My soaking T-shirt sticks to the seat. I hope the car will make it. The last thing you need if you break down is a dead body in the boot.

I review what I know about Parisian organised crime. Violent, chaotic and cruel. Somewhere along the way I am going to need to pick up some firepower.

Darkness falls. The motorway rises above the countryside on stilts. Wooded hills slide away on either side, invisible save for the odd settlement picking out their contours. We are travelling nose to tail at a steady sixty. Every now and then, headlights fall on parking areas beside the road. Sometimes they are proper parking bays with a bank of trees screening the road, sometimes they are just indents, the cars huddled together against the roar of passing traffic.

I think about the route we have taken, we must be near Bologna. At the next parking warning sign I touch the driver's shoulder.

'Can you pull over?'

He grunts but a few moments later he slows and turns off into a proper parking area. Red taillights from the passing traffic flicker through the low scrub between the parking and the road. Two canvas chairs sit at the corner of the lay-by swaying, buffeted by the passing traffic. They are empty. A container lorry stands with its running lights on.

I open the car door and the wall of warm air hits me. Exhaust fumes fill the night, almost blocking the smell of hillside. I stretch my shoulders, walking round to let the driver know I will only be a moment. The tarmac is still soft under my feet.

The lorry cabin curtains are closed. I resist the temptation to climb up, knock on the window and tell him to hurry up. I lean against the metal side and fold my arms.

I don't have long to wait. The cab door opens and a pixie boot emerges followed by two skinny legs, a neon pink miniskirt, a black string vest over black underwear and finally a mop of spikey brown hair. She clutches the rail through a handful of baby wipes. I lever myself upright with my shoulder blades and stand in her way. I'm betting hand job.

'What did he have?' I ask conversationally.

She stares at me with stoned eyes, a sweet wrapper stuck to one knee.

*Blow job.*

'I need to score,' I say, appealing to her compassion.

'I've got nothing.'

I sigh and pull out my stack of bills. Her eyes widen. I hold a fifty just out of reach.

'Tell me where to go and who to ask for.'

She gets less than that for blowing a lorry driver. She gives me a name, snatching at the note. Track marks crawl up her arm. I raise it higher.

'And who does he work for?'

She looks at me, her thin face sullen in the headlights. I produce a second fifty euro note.

'Giovanni. Café Stefano. Piazza Maggiore.'

*Giovanni. Just like a proper Godfather.*

I give her the notes. Her thin fingers tuck them away somewhere in her waistband with the rest of her stash.

'Where's the other girl?'

She shrugs.

'Shouldn't there be two of you?'

She turns away.

I wonder as I walk back to the car whether there is a lay-by hierarchy. Whether the secluded option gets better trade. The taxi driver is sitting with his engine still running.

'Bologna,' I say. 'Piazza Maggiore.'

His eyes hold mine in the mirror but he says nothing.

The outskirts of Bologna teem with bad-tempered drivers. Horns blare and insults fly in the hot Italian air. The further we get into the walled medieval city the narrower the roads, until they are less road and more alley. Tables and chairs, the awnings of cafés, fruit and veg stalls block the street. We have gone as far as we can.

I leave the giant Merc and its driver in a dead-end alley and continue on foot. Everyone is heading in the same direction and noise levels ratchet up several decibels as I follow the crowds. Is there a festival on, or is Bologna always like this?

The alleyway opens into a medieval square as wide as a football pitch, with elegant arched porticoes. The reddish brick reminds me of the cities in the south. Tourists, entertainers, pickpockets. A fire-eater plies his trade. Next to him, a man unwraps a hoop as long as his arm. He dips it in a blow-up paddling pool. When he stands a huge bubble corridor flows behind him.

Cafés line the square, their awnings red or white. On one awning, in curly, flowing golden script are the words *Café Stefano*. I head over. It is grander than I was expecting, linen table clothes and proper menus and small candles in glass dishes.

'Giovanni,' I say as soon as I am within hailing distance.

The waiter waves me through to the inside. I walk between the outdoor tables on the old flagstones, under the colonnades and through a glass door into the restaurant.

The air conditioning stops me dead. It is like stepping into a freezer. I look around. An upmarket restaurant about half full. A couple of men sit at a table in the middle, talking. The table is empty except for the linen cloth. They are both wearing shoulder holsters. They look up when I come in, and away. I am no threat.

Stretched across the back of the restaurant is a long family table. Kids, elderly grandmas, young men. It *is* like something out of *The Godfather*. My eyes flick back to the guards at the table in the middle. Fat lot of use they would be against automatic weaponry. They must be for show. Giovanni is not expecting trouble. I walk over to the guards.

'I want to see Giovanni,' I say. They look at me incredulously. I know what they are thinking. I am thinking the same myself. I look over at the family table. A man catches sight of me, his slicked back hair shiny in the light and he pauses in his meatball shovelling to say something to the Adonis beside him. The young man looks up. He rises slowly and comes towards me. He should be punting down a canal in Venice.

I rein in my libido. *Now is really not the time.*

'*Ciao, bellissima,*' he says. His eyelashes are as long as mine. 'How can I help you?'

*How to put this?* He is in the middle of a family dinner.

'I need a weapon,' I say. 'I don't mind what it costs.' I pull out my wad of notes.

Giovanni junior raises his eyebrows at me.

'You have a problem?' he says, lowering his voice, full of concern.

*Yes. Damn right I have a problem. There is a 100 million dollar price on my head and I am losing my mind.*

I nod, trying to look sad and battered.

'Where is your problem?'

He doesn't want trouble here.

'Paris,' I say quickly. 'Paris.'

He looks at me thoughtfully for a moment then turns on his heel and heads back to the table. I am not sure he is buying it. I try to look nonchalant, wondering what plan B is going to be and wishing my clothes were a little less garbage stained. He leans down to speak to the older guy, his body angled away from me. The meatball shoveller nods as he listens. His eyes rake me once. He says something into his meatballs. The verdict is in. Tall, dark and handsome stands up and heads back my way. He is smiling but that means nothing.

'Come.' He touches my arm to follow him.

We step out through the restaurant doors into air twenty degrees warmer. He sends me a sidelong glance, flashing a white smile that hits me in the pit of my stomach.

He crosses the Piazza at a brisk walk and dives down a narrow alleyway. Three streets later we are away from the tourist hustle and bustle in a deserted alleyway. He slows and the adrenaline kicks in hard. He points out a flight of stairs down between two houses. I hang back at the top and he motions me to go down ahead of him.

*You have to be kidding.*

I shake my head and he laughs, runs down the stairs and bangs on a door halfway down.

It opens.

'Jamel!' he shouts into the darkness, his eyes on me.

He heads back up the stairs. 'Jamel will help you,' he says as he passes me. Then he is gone without a backward glance.

I look after him uncertainly. Is he leaving me here?

I head down to the open doorway. The room below is lower. A crude stone bar. Cold air, red wine and damp, red leather bar stools, a couple of upturned barrels acting as tables. Parma hams hang from the rafters.

A man is coming towards me, traces of beer in his draggling moustache. Moroccan maybe. He shoots me a cursory look and pushes past, leaving me to follow.


He opens a locker below the table and pulls out a handgun. I don't even recognise it, it is so ancient. Nothing worth having would be in an unlocked cupboard.

'Two thousand,' he says.

I smile. 'What else?'

He leans down to the cupboard and comes back with a Beretta. He puts it on the table between us. It is missing the slide.

'It is a good gun,' he says. 'Keep you safe.'

*I don't have time for this shit.*

'The only use I would have for this lump of metal is to club you to death with it.'

His eyes widen in surprise. I can see him re-evaluating.

'Show me something you would use,' I say.

He meets my eyes for a moment then puts his arm in his clothes and takes out a Glock 17 Gen4. I hold out my hand. He hesitates for a moment then releases the double stack magazine. Fair enough. Doesn't want to hand a customer a loaded weapon. He passes it to me.

The fourth generation, full-sized Glock 17 has thirty-four parts. But for easy maintenance it strips down to five main components:

the barrel, the slide, the frame, the magazine and the recoil spring assembly.

It takes me less than six seconds to field strip his gun into the five pieces. His eyes narrow as they watch me. Now he is interested. I look down at the pieces on the table.

'Watch my face,' I say to him.

I close my eyes and put the gun back together blind. It doesn't take me any longer this time round. I open my eyes. The moustache twitches. It might be a smile, who knows? I lay my money on the table.

'I want the best you have.'

Locked doors lead to a small, metal-lined storeroom with wire shelves. This is more like it.

Twenty minutes later I have found a friend. He waxes lyrical about the merits of the Springfield XDS. We argue the toss over the Glock. We agree on the Steyr.

'My boss thinks they're antique... thought,' I correct myself and his eyes watch me in understanding. I remember the first time I fired a handgun. The recoil dropped me like a hammer blow and Erik laughed so hard he nearly joined me on the floor.

He touches my arm. 'This is the one for you,' he says. He holds out a pale grey gun. The suppressor-ready version of the CZ P-09. The P-07's big brother.

'I've never tried one.'

'Light,' he says. 'Glass fibre. Very accurate for distance work. No recoil.'

'No recoil?'

He shrugs. 'Less recoil.'

I weigh the gun in my hand. He is right, it is light. Its thin, flush-fit magazine is great for a woman's hand and has the highest capacity on the market. Twenty-one plus one bullets. If you need more than twenty-two bullets at close quarters you are in deep shit.

'Omega trigger system. Tritium night sights.'

'Previous owner?'

He shrugs again, noncommittal. 'It is clean.'

*Well, that's a comfort.*

'Can I try it?'

'Sure.' He hands me a single bullet.

We go out into the alleyway. The night is quiet, the sounds of the bustling centre a few streets away. There are no streetlights, everywhere is in shadow.

'Good up to fifty yards,' he says.

I look up and down the street, screwing the suppressor on to the threaded barrel. At the far end a clock face glimmers, a hint of white on an ornate church front. He lounges away from me against the wall. I level my arm, it must be 100 yards or more. From his place in the shadows he follows my gaze and laughs.

'No way,' he says.

'Six,' I say.

I take aim. Even with the silencer, the noise is seriously loud in the night street. A clipped pop. Like the sound big clippers might make trimming bushes.

There is no smell. These days you don't get a lot of smell off a gun. No gunpowder, cordite or sulphur. Maybe a bit of hot oil from the gun itself, maybe a tiny hint of firework. Depends on the ammo obviously.

'Did you hit it?'

'I hit it.'

'You are very confident.' He looks me up and down.

I shrug. 'Knives are more my thing.'

He glances sideways at me but doesn't comment. We head up the street.

There is a bullet hole through the number six. Jamel laughs in disbelief.

'How much?' I say.

'A grand for the pair and I will throw in some straps.'

A pair? I am elated.

As he buckles the worn leather round my shoulders I feel unstoppable.

'Thank you,' I say. I hold my hand out.

He hesitates for a moment then he takes it. His hand is slick with oil. 'No problem.'

As I retrace my steps to the taxi I am filled with gratitude to Italian organised crime.

# CHAPTER 21

I round the stone corner. The taxi driver hasn't moved. He sits, head down, in a pool of soft light, cocooned from the street noise of night-time Bologna. When I open the car door a flood of classical music spills out. Bach maybe. He is reading by the weak light of the overhead bulb.

'Sorry,' I say. 'It took longer than I expected.' This seems inadequate. I hold up two long baguettes filled with Parma ham.

The taxi driver closes his book deliberately.

'And now?' he says.

Ah yes. I haven't told him where to go.

'Paris,' I say, settling down on the back seat. 'Wake me up when we get there.'

As we pull off my eyes are already closing.

The change in tone wakes me. I yawn and stretch. My neck and shoulders ache. The cab has left the smooth tarmac run of the motorway and slowed down. Potholes and horns and French sirens. The outskirts of Paris. The streetlights in the suburbs cast an orange glow over the concrete wasteland, an experiment in urban planning gone spectacularly wrong. Graffiti-ridden suburbs fly by, deserted except for the foxes and the shanty towns that have grown up there. Refuse lorries crawl along, their orange lights rotating.

And then suddenly we are travelling down wide, gracious boulevards and tree-lined avenues. After the concrete nihilism of the suburbs nothing prepares you for the beauty of the centre. I gaze out of the window at the Haussmann architecture, tall pale buildings with twirly, spindly iron balconies and ornate balustrades.

I have a sudden flashbulb image of Simon searching for me, picking his way through thousands of street cams, no facial recognition software to help him, doing it longhand, face by face. He will be in the detainment suite. Keeping Viv and my locator company, waiting for someone to turn up to collect on the 100 million dollars. He is always there on my shoulder. Viv is not the only one I have put in the firing line. *Here in Paris*, I tell myself, *I will find the answer.*

'George V,' I say.

The cabbie doesn't turn, but there is something about the way his shoulders flex that tells me he has heard. It is not a shrug but it might as well be. It says, *if she is crazy enough to turn up at the chicest hotel in a city of chic hotels in the middle of the night smelling of garbage, that is her problem.*

We pass the lit scaffolding on the front of Notre-Dame, pass the Île de la Cité, pass the Louvre and the Place de la Concorde and up the Champs-Élysées. I pull a thousand euros and a pair of sunglasses out of my bag. Then we are turning into the Avenue George V and the Merc is slowing. The black-jacketed bellhop opens the car door and I climb slowly out, heading for the main entrance. Behind me the cabbie is opening the boot. I hear the muffled conversation then the grunting as together they heft the suitcase out, the scrape of suitcase wheels on pavement.


The George V lobby is wide and white and high and minimalist, and quite unlike the rest of the hotel where Louis XIV gold filigree rules. My case appears silently beside me courtesy of the invisible bellhop. I drag it over to the Reception desk. The smiling night manager sits in front of a vast old master landscape. He wears black and white like the lobby.

4.43 a.m.

I love the George V. Old school glamour. You can't fake it.

'Checking in. No reservation,' I say.

'*Mais bien sûr*, Madame.'

And there you have it. That is the George V for you. Any other five-star would raise an eyebrow.

He types rapidly into his system and I turn sideways so I can watch the lobby. A giant flower arrangement dominates the centre. Hundreds of vases hold a single peony. Their perfume hangs in the air. The bellhop stands just inside the door with his hands behind his back, looking out into the night. Otherwise it is quiet.

Something is wrong.

I listen: traffic from the street, a distant siren, faint tapping on keyboard. Nothing is moving. It takes a while, but I get there. *Rotting meat*. I glance down at the suitcase. If I can smell it, how long before everyone else can too?

I turn back to the night manager and lean up against the polished counter. He has finished typing and is folding a key card into an envelope.

'Can I have my case vacuum wrapped before my flight?'

'*Pas de problème*, Madame.'

He hands me the key card. I look down. He has given me a Superior.

'I need a laptop delivered to my room.'

'*Pas de problème*, Madame.'

'And a pair of jeans, size 8, long, and a T-shirt.'

*Yes, that's right, I have nothing but the filthy clothes I am standing in.*

He writes down the measurements.

'*Aucun problème*, Madame.'

I leave the white-marbled minimalism of the hotel lobby and make my way through deserted salons. It is all gilt and chandeliers and little tables. Stand still long enough and someone will paint you gold.

I let myself into the room and walk to the window. Third floor, garden courtyard, wide windowsills. I feed the key card into the slot and every light in the room comes on. I strip my clothes off: hoodie, T-shirt, holster, Kevlar, bra, jeans, pants, and leave them in a heap by the door.

There is a knock. I stand to the side of the door. Never look through a spyhole.

'*Oui?*'

'Laptop, Madame.'

I pull the CZ P-09 from the heap of clothes and wrap a towel around me.

I open the door. He is young. His eyes widen at the sight of the towel. He's not to know there is a gun behind the door pointing at his heart. At this range it would blast a hole all the way through him.

I take the laptop in my free hand and kick the door shut with my foot. I sweep all the bedclothes off the giant bed. Take the phone, hotel directory and box of tissues off the desk and lift it high onto the centre of the mattress. I throw the top sheet over it, making a tent, plug the laptop in and crawl inside, dragging the sheet down behind me. The smell of cotton-fresh hotel linen surrounds me. I don't have the time or kit to deal with any surveillance and now I don't need to.

Now to deal with the online eyes. I sit cross-legged and open the laptop. There is no way the George V will not monitor activity on their own laptop on their own network.

It takes me maybe twenty minutes to drill down through the operating system and down to the kernel to see if the hardware is carrying any surveillance. Nothing. This doesn't reassure me. It just means I haven't found it. I close it up and turn the slim case over. I feel every inch of the silky-smooth surface with my fingertips. Nothing. I turn it on its end and look into the USB ports. Nothing. I shrug. Maybe the George V are confident they have their own network locked down. I open the laptop up again. It logs in automatically to the hotel Wi-Fi.

I override the command settings.

*Looking for other networks…*

It takes a moment to think about this. Then a list of nearby routers pops up. They are all locked. I choose the one that looks the most like a domestic address and try a brute-force attack.

Step one.

I back out of the tent leaving the attack to do its thing.

The shower is scalding bliss across my shoulders. It hammers away the queasy, sweet smell of decay, pummelling my muscles into submission.

Twenty minutes later and my mini programme still hasn't cracked the domestic password. I watch the little circle go round and round as the laptop bombards the neighbouring router with millions of passwords a second. I am just wondering whether to give up and try another when I am through.

I login to the GCHQ remote server and pull up Slashstorm. No change. Counters still scrolling. Millions of votes already cast. Eight days to go. I have already had nearly a week.

I close it down, open the file on the Milieu – Paris organised crime – and start to read.

It is seven o'clock and the hotel is waking up before I close the file.

It is not the first time I have been on mission in Paris. I knew a lot about their organised crime before but now I am up to date.

And I don't like it. There is no requirement to be creative about death. Dominique St Vire has turned murder into an art form:

genital mutilation, hot wax down the oesophagus, corpses skinned, dismembered, decapitated. Young women with their bodies cut. My rock-hard stomach feels queasy.

His wife is the safest option. The Marquise de Mazan, an aristocrat, old money. She has kept her own name. A patron of the arts. The picture on her file looks like Coco Chanel. Charity and good works. How does someone like that end up married to Dominique St Vire? Maybe I will get to find out when I take her his body. Either way, she is going to help me. Revenge is a powerful motivator.

I crawl out of my tent and pick up the phone, considering the breakfast menu. My underwear and Kevlar are dry. I put Snow White's brown contacts back in. She stares at me, standing in my underwear, in the opulent white marble bathroom.

'Get on with it,' she says. 'Chicken shit.'

This morning the stranger in the mirror looks like she means business.


The bellhop is back with my breakfast and a bag of clothes. I stand aside and let him wheel it in. He stares at the tent bed and at me in my underwear.

He is out of the door before I have a chance to tip him. I can't say I blame him.

I dress like I am going into battle. Kevlar, T-shirt, holster. I have checked both magazines three times. I strap the spare bullets round my waist, though if it comes to that kind of a firefight I am in trouble. My knives are all in place. I feel down the tops of my boots, smoothing down the soft leather. They never find my knives.

I lift the silver domes on the hostess trolley. Bacon and eggs. Porridge. Eggs Benedict.

I can picture Simon's face. *Carb-loading?* he'd say.

How many people have tried to get into the detainment suite since I've been gone? How long before someone twigs it's not me in there?

The George V has carpets that deaden sound. I can just hear the muffled clink of crockery, the odd low voice. The corridors are running with black and white clad staff. Four people say good morning to me before I make it to Reception.

I pause by the newspaper stand, just outside the lobby, checking the sight lines. The flower arrangement has changed. There must have been a whole team of florists in the early morning, setting up their step ladders, black buckets of new flowers at their feet.

I pull up my hood, cross the lobby quickly and go out through the main exit. The Avenue George V is bathed in early morning sunshine. It is going to be a beautiful day. I put my shades on. Sun shines bright through the gaps in the buildings, the pavements are dappled with the shadows of moving plane leaves. I can identify a dozen cities by sound alone. In Paris, the ambulances wail and the horns are high-pitched.

# CHAPTER 22

I pass the Hôtel de Condé, home of the Marquise de Mazan, on my left, and keep walking.

The street is tall and narrow. Perfect Haussmann. An architectural gem. The whole street should be a scheduled ancient monument. High black double doors lead through to inner courtyards and the thing about inner courtyards is there are not a lot of escape routes. I check out the roof line. Circular windows, ornate parapets, all silvery spires, turrets and mini towers.

I know how these streets work. They are built on a grid system. If you see them from the air they look like neat rectangles. I turn right at the end of the street, walk a block and turn right again. The road is broader with the cheery awnings of pavement cafés every few yards. They back the buildings opposite the Hôtel de Condé. I need to find a way through.

The first couple of cafés I try are self-contained units, a front of house, a kitchen, a storeroom, toilets, no access to the rest of the building. I work my way along the street, prodding and prying, testing, pushing my luck.

Between the cafés, residential front doors glossy with varnish and well-maintained brass work lead to apartments above. They are nailed down tight, video entry phones and suspicious residents.

At the third café I come to, breakfast is in full swing, the air thick with coffee, hot chocolate and croissants. Round tables with plastic wicker chairs spill out onto the pavement. I stand under the awning watching the street. A man is fumbling with his keys, bags of shopping at his feet. Two long baguettes wrapped in triangles of white paper are jammed under his arm. I scoop a discarded cigarette packet off a table and smile my best smile.

The baguette carrier looks up and blinks when he sees Snow White. I hold the heavy door to the apartments wide, he backs in, profuse in his thanks. I close the door behind him and slide the cigarette packet into the gap.

I start to count.

Do they have a lift? These old apartment lifts can be slow. I wait and I wait. When I can't bear it, I make myself wait some more. Then I push the door open and close it swiftly behind me.

A narrow hallway, as expected, a high ceiling, a red carpet, a small chandelier, lavender, a plug-in air freshener for the communal hallway, no sign of the baguette carrier. Individual post boxes hang on the wall. The stairs stretch away in front of me. No lift. I jog up the first flight, pausing on the turn in the stairs to check out the floor above. Two apartments on each floor, one on either side. So far all as expected. I carry on with the jog, pause, look routine until I have reached the top floor.

The top floor apartments are in the roof, servants quarters originally. This is the floor with the circular windows and the parapets. A push-bar fire escape. I look more closely. Hooked up to the fire alarm. I trace the wires back from the contact point. I don't normally have to deal with this. A word to Simon on the comms link and he disables it. I run my nails behind the cables as they feed along the skirting board. Heads: the alarms go off as the circuit breaks, tails: they don't.

*Fifty/fifty.*

I yank the wires.

Silence.

I push down the bar and duck out onto the roof.

I edge along the slick squares of rooftop, slippery as an ice rink, leaning over the parapet to get my bearings. It is a sea of small grey mountains glossy with rain, not a flat surface anywhere – a parkour course of parapets and sloping roofs and aerials. So many aerials.

I pick my way, inching along gullies, peering into triangle windows, staring over the edge of internal courtyards where pigeons flutter and mutter, their jerky little heads bobbing.

A valley steep and slippery enough to trap a child marks where one street backs onto another. Now I have to be more careful. I jump and scramble and keep moving in a crouch until I am looking over the parapet down onto the Marquise's street. A low wall of columns, Grecian style, stands between me and death by pavement.

The Hôtel de Condé is directly opposite me. I watch the rooftops for any sign of movement. I am expecting a guard at the least. Snipers, worse case. Nothing but aerials. Lots of aerials.

I peer in the triangle window beside me. Inside it is empty, deserted, dilapidated. Not just empty. It looks like it has never been lived in. The street that is so well maintained from the front is derelict. It reminds me of that square in London, removed to make way for a railway, with only the facades left.

Something moves in the corner of the empty room. I jump away from the window, cursing myself for presenting a silhouette against the bright sky, and freeze on the slate slope in an awkward crouch, heart thumping, gun in hand. I tilt my head a fraction, listening. Far away, a siren. Close to, the sound of a fire escape door opening.

Footsteps.

I have both hands on the CZ P-09, my arms at full extension. A man shuffles into view behind a chimney pot. Crazy beard, crazy staring eyes. Smell. Christ, there is no faking that smell. Urine cut with meths. A tramp. He ducks out of sight, leaving me with my gun pointing at nothing. I peer round the chimney pot. The fire escape door stands wide. There is nothing but blackness beyond.

My gun makes it into the building before I do. I creep over the threshold and stand listening. Two rooms, one on the right, one on the left. I opt for the one on the right – the room I have just been peering into – and swing round, gun first. He is squatting there in the corner, his eyes bright in the gloom. He nods at me.

'They are watching,' he says, pointing upwards. 'Now the sun is out.'

His voice has a forty-Gauloise-a-day habit. It is too loud in the still air. I stare around quickly in case I have missed cameras – unlikely. The place is as dilapidated as I thought. Cold, the chill of old damp houses that are not lived in. He points at the ceiling again. He means the sky. That's why he wanted me to come in.

'Who are watching?'

'They are. In the sky.'

You're right, I want to say. They *ARE* watching. Paris is watched by Misty. It can see the individual hairs on your head. And it doesn't need sun – satellites see through cloud. Clouds are only water droplets after all. Shift the spectrum just slightly to the left and the image clears.

'Are they?' I say.

He nods emphatically.

*Nutter.*

I lower the gun. 'I'm just going to have a look around if that's OK?' I can feel myself mouthing the words.

I move slowly down the stairs, gun still drawn. A townhouse – the building has never been an apartment block. Bare walls, bare floors. Empty. I move onto the first floor, the grand reception rooms. A pile of newspapers in the corner. The windows look out at the house opposite from behind a film of dust.

I check out the Marquise's front door. No cameras that I can see. No video entry. Just a bell. I head back up the stairs. The crazy guy hasn't moved.

'How long has this place been empty?'

He looks at me blankly.

'All empty,' he says. 'All the houses. She owns the whole street.'

I feel my spine prickle. Actually, it is more like my whole body.

'The Marquise?'

He nods. 'One day she will come out.'

'Who? The Marquise?'

'My little one.'

*Right.*

A whole street of prime real estate stands empty opposite her house. I don't know what to make of that.

I go back down the stairs. A glass-paned door on the left leads to an inner courtyard. Wooden doors big enough for a coach and horses lead to the street. A small pedestrian door is set into the left-hand side.

I twist the double mortise and it creaks open. I jam a tiny piece of newspaper in the corner of the door, opposite the hinge and slip through. The door looks closed, but it isn't. I stride away down the street, the Hôtel de Condé on my right, my steps too loud in the silence.

Ten minutes later I am leaning against Reception waiting for my suitcase. A different bellhop wheels it across the white marble. The pink fabric is swathed in cellophane. It looks organic, like a chrysalis. I breathe in. Nothing.

I know the layout of the Hôtel de Condé now. There are two main ways in and out and I know there are no external guards. I am done pussy-footing around. How much trouble can the widow be?

# CHAPTER 23

It is a proper front door, the varnish old and thick, many layers deep, the brass knocker glossy with regular polishing. Hôtel de Condé is written in swirling copperplate on a small gold plaque.

The silence draws out, leaving me to wonder if the bell has actually rung somewhere inside or whether I should use the knocker.

Footsteps in the courtyard. Young, light footsteps. A woman? A girl? A maid. I breathe slow and steady to calm my heart rate, my hand curling round the gun in my pocket. The door swings open. A maid stands on the threshold – I know she is a maid because she is wearing a tight, short blue dress and a frilly apron and a little white cap. Dark lashes frame eyes so blue they are almost purple. I peer past her. Where are the bodyguards? The men with semi-automatics?

'Is the Marquise home?' My French has a Russian accent.

I push her backwards, yanking the suitcase over the lip behind me.

'*Oui,* Madame,' she says, flustered, inexperienced. Her hands grip together in front of her apron.

I roll the case into the courtyard. No one. No security. Nothing. The maid eyes the suitcase uncertainly. It teeters on the cobbles. I stand it upright.

'I'll leave it here.'

The glass-paned door on the left leads through to a grand entrance hall. Wide stone steps with a red carpet sweep straight up to a half landing. It is like arriving at the opera.

My head slews from side to side. I grip the gun in my pocket. Too many pillars. Too many blinds. The maid turns after a few steps to see if I am following. She is young and fresh and beautiful. Someone has an eye for the ladies.

Ancestral portraits look down from the broad landing. There is a room directly opposite the top of the stairs. The maid nods encouragingly when I stop on the threshold. The room is empty. Four floor-to-ceiling French windows look out over the Seine. At the far end, double doors are open, leading to another room, its blond parquet flooring streaked with brilliant sunshine. I whistle as I take in the view.

The maid heads off down the corridor leaving me to rehearse what I am going to say.

*I am sorry for your loss.*
*Your husband, Madame.*
*I am sorry for your loss.*
*I am sorry for your loss.*

Sunlight pours through the long windows, covering the panelled room in gold. It hits the mirror above the fireplace, it reflects through the crystal drops of the chandeliers to spatter the room in dancing dots of light.

A woman stands in the doorway, more Coco Chanel than Coco Chanel. I could snap her between my thumbs. In my pocket, my hand relaxes.

'*Magnifique n'est-ce pas?*' She gestures to the window. 'Juliette de Mazan.' She holds out her hand. Her dark hair sways thickly as she moves. The soft scent of jasmine reaches me as if she has sprayed it in her hair. Pale grey eyes stare into mine. The colour of a winter's day. Her creamy fifty-five-year-old skin is unlined, taut over a firm jawline.

We shake hands.

'*Je suis desolée, Madame—*' I drop into my rehearsed patter about her husband, nodding towards the door as I mention the case in the hall.

The Marquise's eyes follow my gesture before they return to my face.

'Are you a fan of the Impressionists?' she says.

'What?'

There is a painting on the wall behind her, a Georges Seurat study, the strange mauve figures motionless as if they have been cut out of felt and stuck on. I hadn't noticed it when I came in – this room is all about the view.

I shrug. 'I prefer the early Impressionists. There is something artificial about Seurat.'

*Are we having this conversation?*

She inclines her head. I have been caught showing off like a schoolgirl. 'You prefer nature's ephemerality,' she says.

There is silence. The pale eyes rove all over me, the pincers of a hundred tiny crabs.

I think of the entourages people surround themselves with. The richest man in London – a prisoner behind his own CCTV screens, Giovanni in Bologna with his armed guards and this woman with nothing.

'I am so sorry for your loss, Madame.'

The maid comes in with a rustle of starched cotton, bending over the low coffee table and the Marquise's eyes lift, distracted, to watch her. She indicates a sofa with a graceful gesture.

'Will you join me for some English tea?'

I sit down on one of the spindly sofas. It could have come from the George V. Doesn't she want to know what has happened to her husband? I had been picturing a load of mobsters, leaning on her for answers. I am ready for a fight. Now I feel unsure, wrong-footed, a gap where a step should be.

She smiles at the maid as she passes. A lip twitch of acknowledgement, nothing more. A heavy silver teapot stands on a silver tray. Two cups wait ready. Fine porcelain with gold tracery. They are probably priceless. She leans over, pouring a steaming amber arc into each cup.

'Milk or lemon?'

I add milk, stirring slowly. She spears a slice of lemon from a saucer and retreats to a chair.

She sits down in a graceful sweep, crosses one leg over the other and considers me. Her chestnut hair curls into the curve of her jawline, cupping it perfectly. There is something about her… the Seurat picture fits her. Elegant Parisian fashions, a little too precise, a little too cut-out and static. A mask. A grieving widow is unpredictable. Not that it feels as if she is grieving. I get the sensation of an outer shell, as if her face is painted onto a wooden cover while the real face lies behind.

'What is it I can do for you?' she asks finally.

Somewhere nearby a bluebottle buzzes, whirring round the room with random urgency.

What to say? What to say to this French aristocrat with no interest in her husband's fate?

*You can help me catch his boss. You can help me track down the most powerful man in the world.*

I need something to work with – grief, anger, something I can twist and mould and hone into a thirst for revenge.

'I am looking for someone.'

The pale grey eyes stare.

'An *amour*?' Her voice is soft.

I shake my head. 'No. An enemy.'

A ghost of a smile lights up the parchment face. 'So often it is one and the same,' she says.

'Not this time.'

'Are you sure?' She raises the china cup to her lips and takes a delicate sip. Her nails are short and blunt and unpainted. Incongruous.

*Yes, I'm bloody sure.*

'He's not my type.'

The tea is warm and sweet. Aromatic. I swill it round my mouth. The warmth is soothing against the implants in my face.

She watches me. The drone of the bluebottle circling lazily suddenly stops. I resist the temptation to turn and see where it has landed. The air is charged with awkwardness and something else. The Marquise taps her index finger with its blunt nail slowly against her painted lips.

'And what is your type?' she asks softly, her accent thickening. *You cannot be serious?*

I shrug and jerk my head to indicate the recently departed maid. 'That is my type,' I say.

The Marquise looks at me for a long moment.

'*Moi aussi*,' she says.

Behind her, the felt figures on the Georges Seurat painting start to twirl. Droplets of light from the chandelier whirl and sparkle in a kaleidoscope of colour, dancing away from me across the ceiling, and the floor comes up to meet me as I tumble forward, knees first.

# CHAPTER 24

Blood thuds round my body, throbbing in the soles of my feet. My muscles ache. My face tingles, the soft skin round my mouth buzzes. Fingers slide across my skin, exploring. My brain fizzes with colour. Sunlight streams through the windows, bright white squares on the blond floor. Long shadows from the windowpanes cut across the squares, dark and defined as bars. They burn the floor.

Somewhere different, brighter, the light cold and hard. A figure bends in cream silk. Her lips taste mine. Teeth tug. Fingers swarm over my body, their blunt ends pushing into every crack and crevice. They crawl into my mouth, my nose, my ears, down my body, between my thighs. My legs are gently spread. The fingers linger, touching, stroking, assessing, then they are inside me. I am paralysed, only my eyes can move.

I open my eyes. Twilight. The sun has gone. The room is cold. Parisian chic. An antique sofa, silky against my skin. I am naked. Oil glistens on my body in the track marks left by blunt fingernails.

On the table where the tea tray sat, someone has lined up two guns, eight white knives and a number of bullets. They are the same distance apart. There is a pile of clothes beside them, neatly folded, a Kevlar vest on top. My gaze moves around. The Marquise is watching me from a chair by the window. She has changed her clothes.

I sit up and swing my legs to the floor.

*Drugged. Goddammit.*

My head aches worse than when I was tasered. Again.

'So, you've established I'm not wearing a wire. I hope you had a good time.' My voice sounds sour. 'Can I put my clothes back on?'

She shrugs. Gallic.

'And you have established you can trust me with the truth.'

And I realise she is right. If I couldn't completely trust her, I would be dead.

*My enemy's enemy is my friend.*

My hand shakes as I reach for my pants. No wonder she keeps her nails blunt.

'Tell me where you found him,' she says.

'In a dumpster. Single bullet in the brain. I was tracking someone else.'

She nods.

'When I arrived, the man I was looking for had gone. I just missed him. And then I smelt this smell.'

*It was so bad it made me heave. It was so bad I had to get in a fountain.*

'I got the body out. Got in a cab here.'

'Where was this?'

'Umbria. Near the Tuscan border.'

The Marquise's eyes bore into mine.

'A Tuscan hill town outside a castle.' I step into my jeans, drag them over my hips and zip them up. I turn for my bra.

'How did you know who he was?'

'I recognised him.'

'Who are you?'

'Ex-FSB.' I step up the Russian accent. 'This is personal.'

She yanks me, bra in hand, to the window and out onto the balcony. My skin warms at her touch. The breeze whips against my naked top half, making me shiver. Below us in the greying light, pleasure boats still circle the Île de la Cité.

'I know who you are looking for.' Her voice is hard.

My throat dries so fast it is almost painful as my face asks the question.

She shakes her head in response. 'I don't have a name. He commands from a distance. Anyone who threatens him is removed. My husband was a proud man. He hated that he was not the Boss. He hated criticism.' She looks out across the river, leaving me wondering about the criticism.

'But he knew him? They met face to face?' I can feel my excitement rising.

'Yes.'

'And what is he like? What did he say about him?'

'He is what you would expect. He is the most powerful man in the world. He has charisma.'

'Charisma?' I remember how his voice cut across the helicopter noise. I remember how he stood laughing. 'I don't know what I expect.' The man in Courchevel was all black-ops squad. All muscle. Not an intellectual. 'But is he a fighter? A thug? A planner? A thinker?'

'Let me tell you a story about him. Some men took something from him once. When he caught up with them, he beat them to death with his fists. One by one in a castle courtyard. There were twelve of them. It took him more than three hours. Does that answer your question?'

I think about this. It tells me he is a thug, a bare-knuckle fighter, someone who protects his own. He has come up from the streets – he wasn't born wealthy, he knows how to inspire fear, he knows he has to do it himself. And yet he knows the story will be told and told and will do the work for him. Does that make him a thinker? I ponder the point.

If nothing else, it means he is fit. Extremely fit to be able to punch that hard for that long. And I told him to do his own dirty work. I am standing half naked on a balcony, my skin covered in goosebumps. Above me, the sky threatens rain.

'What about a personal life? Does he have a family? What is he into? Women? Men? Both?'

'Women,' she says shortly. 'An ever-changing line-up. The moment anyone gets close they are gone.'

Kinda lonely. But then what emotional needs does a psychopath have? He must inspire loyalty. He must have a whole group of people he relies on.

'Anyone he is close to?'

She looks at me thoughtfully, her eyes roving over my naked top half, lingering on my stomach where the muscle disappears under the waistband of my jeans. She hasn't laid a finger on me and my skin is heating under her gaze.

'I wonder…' she says to herself. She stares out at the river. 'How good are you?'

'Good enough.'

'And I think you are determined, yes?'

I nod.

'There is a way.'

*There is always a way if you want something badly enough.*

'But the price may be higher than you want to pay.'

'Tell me.'

'There is an event every year that he attends. An event he never misses.' Her lips sneer. 'A tournament, if you will.'

'What type of tournament? Who goes?'

'I think it is a fight to the death, although I may be mistaken.'

'*What?* Between who? Does he take part?' I can hear my incredulity.

She shakes her head. 'It is an exercise in machismo. A statement of power. Every area, city or state sends representatives. They fight for supremacy. For status. For money. This year Marseille will go. Paris is finished.'

*Marseille, the number two city, steps up.*

'So, when is it?'

'Very soon. My husband was waiting for the call.'

'Where?'

She shakes her head. 'He is collected.'

'Where is it held? France?'

'I think not. One year, the journey was seventeen hours.'

*Japan? Australia? Singapore?*

'Another year it was only four.'

*Morocco? Algeria? Kazakhstan?*

I can feel the little bubbles of excitement fizzling out. The sky has darkened while we've been standing on the balcony and a great fat wet drop lands on my bare skin. How can I crash a meeting that could be anywhere at any time? I look into her pale eyes and see she already has the answer.

'You will go with Marseille,' she says.

# CHAPTER 25

I walk slowly down the curving staircase, pausing on the half landing. She is standing outside the salon, looking at me over the iron balcony. She waves her hand gracefully and turns on her heel. I walk down the rest of the flight alone. There is no sign of the maid. The pink case is gone. When no one stops me, I grip the top and bottom locks on the street door and pull.

I step over the lip into a downpour. It suits my mood. I pull my hood up and huddle my hands into the sleeves. The wrists are already grimy, the oil on my skin bleeding through the cotton. What did she do to me? My overconfidence makes me sick. How could I, of all people, so grossly underestimate a woman?

The sky is lower than it should be at four in the afternoon, the cloud cover impenetrable. The clear blue skies and bright sunshine of this morning are gone. Everywhere lights are coming on. Traffic sounds far away. Muffled.

I let myself into the building opposite through the door I wedged this morning. The air is warm and the decay stronger, as if the damp has brought it oozing out of the plasterwork. The empty house is as deserted as it was earlier, but now I am fearful. We are descended from people who knew going into dark, creepy places alone is not a good idea. The best modern training in the world struggles to overcome instinctive fear. It is in the bone.

I creep slowly up the main staircase, my head twitching at nothing. A broken gutter gushes somewhere. Lights move across the ceiling. Headlights from the street.

The crazy guy is there in the gloom, standing just inside the attic room.

'You came out,' he whispers. 'You went in and you came out again. I saw you.'

'You were watching?'

He nods and I picture the pile of newspaper in the first-floor reception room. 'They never come out.'

I shiver. The rain must be working its way under the Kevlar. I picture a maid fumbling in her inexperience, smell the oil on my naked skin and feel fingers with blunt fingernails working their way over my body, intimately, lovingly.

'Who are you looking for?... A friend?... A daughter?'

The crazy, watery eyes fill with tears.

*A daughter.*

I hunker down beside him, crouching back on my heels. She really isn't coming out.

I don't know how long I stay in the room. The rain hammers down in the darkness beyond the high window. Sometimes he speaks, most of the time he is quiet. He rocks backwards and forwards, the newspapers rustling under his weight. After a while I go back out through the fire escape door.


Up here on the roof, the rain thuds down, pouring in torrents along the gullies, pouring into the gutters, drumming on the slate and stonework. Water hangs off my nose, soaking through my cotton hoodie. Now I am cold. Without the Kevlar I would be shivering. I turn my face to the sky and let the rain beat down on it. Far, far above me Misty is spinning in its orbit.


*'I will make a deal with you,' the Marquise said to me. 'I will send you to Marcel in Marseille. If you do well, he will take you with him*

*when Marseille go to the tournament. And in return, you will deal with the Boss.'*

*Marcel Furet. Ferret by name and Ferret by nature, a street-hood made good. A Chicago-style gangster. The head of Marseille's organised crime.*

*'Marcel is expecting a shipment tomorrow night,' she said. 'An unusual shipment. I will send you to oversee it.' She looked me up and down. 'You must make him accept you. He will not take you with him to the tournament unless he trusts you.'*

*'What is unusual about the shipment?' I asked.*

*She stared out at the river. Revenge versus discretion. Revenge turned to face me. 'It will be the first shipment of partially refined heroin to be landed on mainland Europe in a decade,' she said. 'Six months ago, it had a street value of five million euros. Do you know what it is today?'*

*I shook my head, a queasy feeling in my stomach.*

*'Five hundred million euros.'*

*The unseen consequences. All because the methadone substitute coming out of the UK has dried up. And whose fault was that?*

From up here, the rain looks like grey vertical lines, a child's drawing. It is settling in for the night. Great rivulets drag dirt off the road, cigarette butts, food packaging. Pedestrians jump from doorway to doorway. Young women office workers in silk blouses and short skirts are caught unawares. Raindrops flash in car headlights. Puddles two feet wide form on pavements. People edge single file around them. The bare-legged girls, soaked and sad, battle their way, flimsy handbags held two-handed above their heads, hair running wet down the sides of their faces.

The anger that propelled me across Italy, through France to Paris, is fading. I don't have to do this. Walk into the enemy camp all alone. Agents have tried infiltrating the crime networks before to get to the man at the top, Americans mainly. They never come back.

No one knows Snow White. I could just vanish. Disappear without trace. I have been trained to be invisible.

Sounds are muffled up here: the trickling in gutters, the thunder on pavement, the swish of car tyres, the screech of brakes, the shriek of the unlucky pedestrian caught beside the pooling black water.

*I could just disappear. Vanish like the rain. Slide down the gutter and disappear into the dark.*

I think of Simon and Viv barricaded into the detainment suite to give me this chance, and I think of Erik.

I think of Daniel in the dark of the Colony's control room. 'No one is better than you,' he says.

I think of a man with matted hair waiting for a daughter who is never coming home and a floppy-haired kid taking three hours to die.

And I think of twelve new faces and their scrolling counters.

*No one is waiting for me to come home.*

The Marquise can get me in. But no one can get me out. This has long since stopped being about identifying him. My life for his. It is down to me and I will succeed or I will die trying.

I go back through the dark empty house that smells of damp plaster and out onto the wet street. It is the work of five minutes, maybe less, to lift a phone from one of the shrieking office girls.

What can I say to Simon? Oil trickles down my back, down between my buttocks, down the back of my thighs. I don't think I can face telling him I spent most of the afternoon unconscious with my legs spread. I can picture what he would say if he knew I was planning to go to Marseille to hang out with the Ferret.

'Thank God,' Simon says. He looks exhausted. Behind him I can see Viv in the shadows. They are in the detainment suite. 'Why are you FaceTiming? Are you crazy?'

'Any luck with the Cayman Island listing?'

Simon shakes his head. 'It's not looking promising.'

*Of course it isn't. They aren't amateurs.*

'What about Slashstorm?'

'No change.'

'Anyone else try anything?'

'Just now.'

'One of ours?'

He nods.

'I just wanted to say goodbye.'

'WHAT?' He scrambles to his feet.

'I'm going in Simon.'

*The lion's den.*

'I won't contact you again until I am done. It is the only way. I am going in deep. If they are in our systems, anything you know they will know. Every time you watch me, they will see too.' I hold my hand up in a gesture of farewell. I feel choked. 'Good luck, guys. Give me as long as you can. Thank you.'

'No, Winter! Tell us where you are going, at least—'

My sinuses prick as I cut the call. I pull the phone apart as I walk, snap its SIM card, chuck its battery into the torrent in the gutter. A few streets later, I grind what is left of it beneath my heel on the wet pavement. I pull my hoodie tighter round me and set my face for the Gare de Lyon.

At least Marseille will be warm.

# CHAPTER 26

I walk slowly across Marseille's main square towards the street café. The rain of Paris is forgotten. The midnight air is soft and balmy and my oily skin warm in my jeans. The air is full: roasting meat, Gauloises, bins, coffee. Streets just need a bit of heat to release their scent. The breath of the streets. The orange and neon lights dance in front of my eyes. There are ghosts everywhere. When I looked in the mirror on the train, Snow White's eyes were ringed in dark shadows and the hand applying eyeliner shook.

The key to good cover is not having to think about it. Snow White is Russian and I will have no problem maintaining that. My Russian is perfect. Impenetrable. I dream in Russian. Ex-FSB gone rogue. *Close enough.* Grew up in a Moscow orphanage. I think of my bleak Surrey boarding school – *close enough.* She is a fighter and I've got no problem with that. Weapons competent. *Likewise.* The key to good cover is not having to think about it.

*I am Snow White. I am Russian. I am a hitman.*

Café tables spill across the pavement with the standard red-and-white check cloths and plastic wicker chairs. Most of the café's customers are outside smoking, eating, chatting, drinking. It is not clear where outside begins and inside ends.

I duck under the awning. More of the same tables and chairs, a proper wooden bar with a proper barman behind it stacking glasses.

And there he is. Marcel Furet. The Ferret. The biggest mobster in a city of mobsters. The Chicago of the south. I would recognise him anywhere. He is sitting at a table with his back to the wall, surrounded by henchmen. The table is covered with whiskey glasses, ashtrays and piles of silver foil. My heart sinks. Users. A tableful of people and they are all high. Dangerous. Unpredictable.

Ferret starts when he sees me and half rises off the red padded bench. The Marquise has already spoken to him. His eyes flick up and down, up to my face, down to my jeans. Checking. Matching me to what he has been told. Not a flicker of interest. Snow White does not do it for him. *What has the Marquise said?* Whatever it is, he doesn't like it. There is anger and irritation in his face and something else. Resentment? Does he resent Paris issuing orders?

Two men sit either side of Ferret, flanking him like great man-shaped bookends. He says something to them and nods towards the back of the café. This is it. Time to find out what the Marquise has said. Maybe she has sent me here for the Ferret to deal with.

He jerks his head at me. I can see the back of the restaurant. A corridor. Darkness beyond. I hesitate. Forget the vest, at this range it would be in the head. He jerks his hand as well as his head, like a pantomime of a hitchhiker.

I curl my lip.

*Don't jerk your thumb if you want to keep it.*

I walk past him without a backward glance.

The corridor is filthy, the lino stained and scuffed, piles of crates, old brooms, broken tables squashed up against the walls. I walk forward. It goes nowhere. I can feel the shape of a trap in the air. Two rooms, one on the left, one on the right. It will be the one on the right. That is the one that backs the restaurant.

The room is in darkness. Behind me someone reaches out and throws a switch. I flinch. There is a desk, a sofa, a safe, a picture of a football team, no windows. The air reeks of acetone. The whole place is rank with it. The feeling of a trap intensifies. The door closes. There are four of us: me, Ferret and two meatheads.

*I am Snow White. I am Russian. I need you to accept me.*

Ferret pushes past me, rounds his desk and drops down into his green leather chair. Close up, I get sweat, aftershave and rotting meat. The skin below his eyes is strangely droopy, I can see a ring of pink socket under the eyeball. His face is a mass of creases. He is more Bassett hound than Ferret. His weird sunken eyes stare meaningfully over my shoulder. One of the meatheads steps forward.

I move sideways and catch his hand. I have judged it perfectly. He has no training. I look up at him – and up and up. One of the man mountains. *Crusher.* His massive forehead lowers straight onto his cheeks with barely a space for eyes.

*Note to self – do not headbutt this man.*

The Ferret laughs. 'Apologies, Madame. A wire check, nothing more.'

I look down at the hand I am holding, then up into the big face. He has a handheld signal locator clenched in his meaty fist. Slowly and deliberately, I squeeze, bringing pressure to bear in just the right place. His face whitens and his eyes widen in surprise as his legs buckle, forcing him to his knees.

*Don't mess with me.*

I keep eye contact as I release him.

'No sudden moves.' My French is coated with guttural Russian.

Crusher wobbles. Then he puts one foot forward and presses down on his knee trying to lever himself up. I resist the temptation to give him a hand. He is breathing heavily. Unfit. He's got nothing but size.

The Ferret watches us in silence, but now there is a tiny crease between his brows as if he is trying to work something out. He toys with a glass paperweight the size of a tennis ball, spinning it and catching it and spinning it again.

I stretch out my arms for the wire test. Crusher runs it up my arms and down my legs. It is a cheap model but effective. Not good enough for the Marquise though, apparently. Crusher stands back, shaking his massive head.

'Phone?' demands the Ferret.

I shake my head. Ferret stares. He finds this more unbelievable than me bringing Crusher to his knees.

'Gun,' he says. 'Slowly.'

I unzip my hoodie really, really slowly, staring him down, pull out one of the CZ P-09s and place it on the desk. If he has any idea what he is doing, he will have seen the brown leather of the shoulder straps and know there must be another one.

'And the rest,' he says, annoyed.

I pull out the other one and lay it beside its brother. This seems to satisfy him. He can't imagine someone preferring knives to guns.

Silence.

'So, the Marquise sent you?' The question hovers in the air.

'Yes.'

'She thinks you might be useful,' he sneers.

I shrug. 'I returned her husband's body.'

More silence.

'You were in Italy?'

This is way over his pay grade. The disbelief rings in his voice. And something else. Now he is wondering what I know. He is wondering if I work for the Boss. He is afraid.

'*Da.*' I answer in Russian. I stare him down. There it is on the air, clear and pure as vodka, overpowering even the chemical haze. Fear.

*He must accept you.*

I sit down in the chair opposite Ferret and lounge back, resting one booted ankle on my knee.

'What do you know of Italy?' I steeple my hands in front of my face like Control.

'Nothing,' says Ferret hurriedly. 'I know nothing. Dominique used to go.'

He falls silent. He is thinking about Dominique. He is thinking he caused trouble and now he is dead and this Russian bitch delivered his body. He is thinking there has to be more to her than meets the eye.

I stay silent, my face cold, keeping him guessing, forcing him to speak. Power play. Something else I learned from Control.

'In what way can you be useful?' His sneer is back.

'Are you a Marseille fan?'

I know he is, I can see the signed photograph above his head, Ferret surrounded by the Marseille football team. He doesn't look any better smiling.

'Why?' He turns to look, and as he moves I put a blade though his tiny photograph forehead. There is a hiss of indrawn breath and a flurry of movement from behind me. I hold up my hand to stall them. *Too slow.*

It takes Ferret a moment to realise. He stares at me. My ankle is still resting on my knee, I haven't moved.

'I'm a useful person to have around.'

He leans back in his swivel chair and clamps a phone to his ear. He rotates as it is answered, so he has his back to us.

'She is here.'

The Marquise – it has to be. He listens, throwing the glass paperweight in the air and catching it again. He nods.

'This will not be a problem.' He waves his free arm airily. 'We are more than capable at this end.'

*Expansive.*

The call ends abruptly. She has hung up. The news is good. He rubs his hands. He looks past me at the meatheads.

'We are going on a little trip,' he says. 'The day after tomorrow, if all goes well.'

His eyes come back to rest on me and he scowls. Did she order him to take me with him to the tournament? I'm guessing not. It is up to me.

*He must accept you.*

I stand up, circle Ferret and yank my blade out of the wall. It has gone in a long way. I return it to its sheath.

'I'm going to need somewhere to stay.'

Ferret's face smiles, his cheeks a mass of creases. His brown teeth are pointed like his little carnivorous namesake's.

'You can stay with Henri.'

The henchmen laugh. The boss has made a joke.

*What joke?*


We drive through the night streets of Marseille, through the medieval alleyways of the Vieux Port. The colours are soft, muted reds, oranges, cream. Side streets wind away from us, narrow and twisting. Every window has painted shutters. To our left, the old fort rises above the harbour.

*Henri's.* I can just picture it, a bar downstairs, the clink of glasses, Gallic laughter, paint peeling, the name on the outside barely legible – Hôtel Tanger – rickety wooden stairs, half landings, peeling wallpaper. A creepy old lady.

We leave the old port and head out into the suburbs. The buildings have changed from old and painted to modern and bleak. Apartment blocks. We pull up on a busy street. Downtown Marseille. It is not picturesque.

I get slowly out of the car, looking around me. A sixties block. Concrete. Colourless. A line of shops below, with six floors above, an all-night kebab house, a pawnbroker, a 7-Eleven, its windows covered in posters.

Crusher walks over to a door between two shopfronts – an ordinary door behind a metal grill. *Keeping people in or keeping them out?* He talks to the intercom. The voice on the other end blurs with electronic distortion. The grill buzzes. It swings outwards. He opens the front door. I peer round him at the corridor beyond – another corridor, another potential trap, it stretches way back, as far as the shops are deep. This time Crusher goes ahead. His swagger increases, he is on home turf. He is amongst friends.

The corridor opens out into a reception area. A counter faces the door, a wooden staircase rises up to the floor above. You have to go past the counter to get to the stairs. There is a slightly thinner version of Crusher sitting behind it. I catch the words '*Russian*' and '*bitch*'.

'Hello, Henri,' I say with my best smile.

He ignores me. I lean up against the counter and look over the edge. A thick blue diary is open. An A3 appointments diary. Names down the sides, times running across. Times? *Not a guesthouse then.*

Henri rummages around and brings out a key with an enormous fob. He hands it to Crusher. Crusher heads up the stairs, breathing with effort.

'Thank you,' I say to Henri as I pass.

Nothing. Not so much as a grunt of acknowledgement.

I follow Crusher up the stairs, round the corner and onto a long corridor. It is exactly what I was expecting, plyboard doors with numbers on. There are five on each side and a room at the end. That will be the bathroom.

Crusher stops at a door halfway down on the left. He puts the key in the cheap Yale lock and it opens inwards. It wouldn't stand up to a good kick. It wouldn't stand up to a shoulder barge. I bet the girls know this. I bet Henri counts on them knowing it. Room after room, huddling behind their weak locks, one eye on the door.

'Thank you,' I say to Crusher.

He holds the door for me to enter then he throws the key at me.

Behind him, the door opposite opens and a man in a suit comes out. He stops abruptly at the sight of us. Forced social interaction he wasn't expecting. His eyes check me out. He winks at Crusher as he passes.

*Give her one from me.*

# CHAPTER 27

The door closes and Crusher's massive frame thuds away down the
corridor. I look around at my new home: unmade bed, pink sheets
soft with use – the brushed cotton worn smooth – greying net
curtains, toilet and basin cornered off by a partition that doesn't go
all the way to the ceiling. No one is ashamed of bodily functions
here. I lie down on the dirty sheets, my arm across my face.

In the corridor, doors bang.

*Changeover.*

I count door slams – fewer than half of the rooms change. Henri
was relaxed about giving up a room. Maybe it is a quiet night.

I open my eyes and sit up – I need to take my contacts out.
I screw down the little round pots and put them on the bedside
cabinet. The drawer is half open. It must have been white once,
now it is yellow, the plastic peeling, the round china knob sticky
with handling. Condoms. Unopened boxes. Shiny foil packets,
purple, red, silver. A tube of lubricant, jumbo-size. I shut the
drawer and roll across the bed and open the drawer on the other
side. A Bible.

*Figures.*

I peer down between the cabinet and the bed. There is a ledge
where the bed base protrudes beyond the mattress. The cabinet has
been wiped clean by use, the constant touch of clothing or body
parts, but this ledge is protected. Halfway along I can see a piece
of chewing gum like a miniature brain. The dandruff detritus of
decades is down here, layers and layers of human dust, each with

its own story. Yeast and eucalyptus. The smell is familiar. I can't quite place it. The colours – orange and green.

It comes to me in a rush of olfactory memory.

*Olbas oil.*

A working girl with a cold, trying to clear her blocked nose. Still working.

I roll over on my back and watch the play of light across the ceiling. The neon from the kebab shop sign fills the room, bathing it in a pink glow. Every now and then, police blue slides across the ceiling, killing the pink. Left to right and back again.

The corridor is empty. I can tell because every arrival and departure echoes in the room, shaking the doorjamb. I can hear the low rumble of voices. The sirens are nonstop, a constant Doppler blur. What are the police doing? Driving around all night with their sirens going? What can they do? Take out Ferret and someone else is put in his place. There is only one way to clean up a whole town.

*The Prince of Darkness laughs and flames dance in his eyes. 'I thought you were never coming,' he says.*

*There is a blade in my hand. It curves into my palm. He laughs and laughs. My face burns, the tears rush, stinging my eyes, ready to pour out. I back away before he can see I am crying.*

A door slams in the corridor. I open my eyes. The sound of sobbing throbs through the cardboard walls, through the thin door with its ineffectual lock. It gets as far as Henri sitting behind his big counter and he probably smiles with satisfaction because it means capitulation. It rips at me, a nail peeling back from the cuticle. I wish it would stop. I am there in that attic school dormitory again, watching the play of light and listening to someone sobbing.

Footsteps on the stairs. A heavy tread. A big man. Henri? Come to sample the product at the end of the night shift? He stops. I raise my head, listening. A key in the lock, the door opposite clicks open. The sobbing is louder now. I swing my legs off the bed, stand up and open my door. The room is so small I don't need to take a step.

Henri has his back to me. He looms over the woman in the doorway. I can see her under his arm – dyed hair, bare feet, huge pupils, high as a kite. She shrinks against the doorjamb. He looks up in surprise as my door opens. For a split second he can't remember who I am.

I hold his gaze and feel the anger rise in him. Eye contact is a challenge. I see it in his reddening face, in his twitching fist, in the vein on the side of his neck. I hear it in his quickening breathing and in the stillness from the girl behind him. I smell it in the air.

I know the type, a puncher. He shoves the girl into the bedroom and slams the door on her. The frame shakes.

For a moment he stands undecided in the corridor. Should he make something of it? Then he stomps off towards the stairs, trailing his fist along the wall.

I open my eyes. I am holding a knife in each hand. It is daylight. The hum from the street has changed. I lie listening for the unique signature sound that is Marseille. Nothing. I could be anywhere. The room is pale grey, monochrome in the morning light. The neon pink has gone, the orange street lights have gone. Daylight filters through the grubby net curtains. The corridor is silent, no footsteps, no opening and closing doors, no sobbing. I get off the bed and go to the window. It is disappointing by day. The pink and orange gave it atmosphere, now it is just dreary. The *Pharmacie* opposite has a lit green cross. It is the only point of colour on the whole row.

I slept in my jeans. If I'm here for a couple of days I'm going to need to get some clothes. I clean my teeth, put in my contacts and head for the stairs, bracing myself for Henri. Reception is deserted, the counter neat. The passageway to the front door is long and dark. I am still wondering how I will release the grill when I get there and find it is standing wide open.

The sky is overcast, the glare coming off the clouds hurts my eyes. It is going to be a hot day. Breakfast, clothes, then I am going to investigate the room at the end of the corridor. Somewhere there has to be a shower.

*He must accept you.*

I have no idea how I am going to make that happen.

I search the street for that authentic French café experience. It is not promising, but the French can't do food badly. They just don't know how. On the corner I find a Tabac selling newspapers and cigarettes, magazines and sweets. It has a few stools at its counter. The coffee when it comes in a big bowl is rich and milky. The baguette is still warm from the bakers. I eat it with cold, hard, unsalted butter and strawberry conserve. On impulse, I buy a packet of Gauloises and a silver lighter.

Don't get me wrong, I am not a smoker. And nor is anyone who has to rely on their body's performance. But there are times when a prop is good. A prop helps you to fit in. A prop can make the difference between life and death.

Outside the Tabac, I scan for cameras. Nothing. That would be unheard of in the UK. Further down the street, a dark gap leads to a rundown mall. Mall may be overstating it. A quarter of the shops are boarded up, their windows covered in fly stickers, leftover stock gathering dust bunnies in the corners.

I find jeans, T-shirts, socks and a baseball cap in one of those huge cheap emporiums that sell everything from camping stoves to slippers to mobile phones. They even have jackets – knackered black leather. I shrug one on over the hoodie. Snow White raises her eyebrows at me in the long mirror. Her black hair curls around the collar.

*You have to look the part*, I tell her. *Black leather really suits you.*

I ask the guy for underwear. He stares as if I am stark raving mad. *You sell hardcore porn*, I want to say. *What is wrong with pants?*

'Madame Jo Jo's,' he says.

They have burner phones behind the tills. I buy three just in case.


Out on the street I look around and there it is in among the rundown takeaways and launderettes – a lingerie shop. It wouldn't be out of place in Knightsbridge. I cross the road. An old-fashioned bell above the door jingles as I walk in.

What is it with French women and underwear? It is actually impossible to buy pants without the matching bra. The idea that you might need one but not the other is inconceivable. I buy three white cotton sets of underwear and go back out onto the street feeling like I have disappointed Madame Jo Jo.

The grill door is still open as I walk up the street, which is a relief, because I had been wondering what I was going to say to the intercom.

*Henri, it's me.*

*Henri, it's me... Yes. Dumb, Russian bitch.*

*Hi, Honey, I'm home.*

*Let me in, you bastard.*

I am nearly at the door when a figure blocks my way. It is one of the meatheads from last night.

'Marcel says you are to come.'

His greasy dark face is blank but there is something about him. Something that makes the monkey brain part of me sit up and take notice. Something has got him hard.

'I'll just drop off my shopping.' I raise the bags.

He would like to argue, but I am already striding away from him.

*

No one has been in my room. Kevlar check, knives check. My hand shakes as I put the cigarettes in the jacket pocket with one of the burners. I put my sunglasses on and head back down. Still no Henri. The meathead is waiting beside a black sedan, the tension pouring off him. He was worried I might do a runner. He watches me in the mirror, looking away every time our eyes meet. His sweat fills the air.

I have a bad feeling about this. A really bad feeling. I slide my fingers down my boot. I am starting to recognise parts of Marseille. We are heading for the Vieux Port, the old part, the expensive centre.

We reach the harbour's edge and turn right running along the port road. Past the Marina, the high-end yachts, the gin palaces, past the old fort on the hill behind us and round to the commercial heart of Marseille. A huge red-hulled container ship sits at anchor, boat cranes loading and unloading. Warehouses and boxes and sea containers. The clinking of chains. The surface changes under the wheels – we have left tarmac and are driving along the ridged concrete of the dock edge. We round the corner, another run of warehouses. Corrugated steel, bolts on the doors. The car stops.

He jerks his head. *In there.*

A huge metal door stands slightly open. I get slowly out of the car, taking stock, assessing the scene; the wind soft against my cheek, the traffic far away, the screech of a seagull, the smell of docks and diesel. There is a weird sound. Like a whine. Behind me, someone releases the safety clip on a gun. I don't bother to look round.

I feel it in my veins. The adrenaline. I know the physiology. It is charging round my body, going to where it is needed. My skull thuds with it. When people say they were so frightened their bowels went to water they are talking about adrenaline. A big shot. Cold pins and needles run down my arms. My body is telling me what is coming. My blood is pumping, my heart rate is up, my skin cold. I slide the door further and look into the big empty space. My body told me what was coming. It still didn't prepare me.

The weird whine is the sound of someone screaming without a tongue. A man is chained to the wall, naked from the waist down. One glance tells me he is missing his eyes and his genitals. He is bleeding out.

A second glance shows me Crusher and the other meatheads – one, two, three of them – and Henri holding a machete. And in the corner, his creased, droopy face watching me, is Ferret.

This show is for me. The stage is set and now I have entered, the principal actor, the star of the show. Applause.

*What are you going to do?*

I'm not good with suffering. Other people's suffering. I have to finish it. I don't even like watching moths in a trap. My own suffering? I'm OK. I go into my head and it takes quite a lot to get me out of it. It took Everard five hours in the GCHQ medical centre to break me during training.

The guy in chains is as good as dead.

Snow White walks forward. Her cold eyes rake the scene. She stops in the middle of the warehouse. She pulls a cigarette packet out of her jacket, shakes one out, puts it between her lips, flicks the lighter. The flame dances and flickers, the only movement in the big, empty space. She takes a huge drag and blows it at the ceiling. She shakes the flame out. She is the star of the show. Her eyes find Ferret.

'What is this?' The cigarette arcs through the air. Her voice is as hard as her eyes.

Ferret takes the machete and holds it out. 'Time to make yourself *useful*.'

Snow White stands smoking.

'What's the matter, *Mademoiselle*? No balls?'

*Make it stop.*

Snow White swaps the cigarette into her left hand and pulls a blade from her boot. It whistles through the air towards the man in chains. It goes straight through his jugular and into his windpipe. His head lolls. She takes a deep drag of her cigarette.

'What are you?' She waves the cigarette at the corpse. 'Amateurs?' She turns on her heel and walks slowly out.

My heart is pumping so fast I would be hyperventilating if it wasn't for the smoking controlling my breathing.

The concrete is warm in the sun. Huge boat cranes line the harbour. I stand in the sun smoking and waiting. The door grinds behind me. I don't turn. Ferret and Crusher. They have left the others to deal with the mess. Ferret holds out my knife. The blade drips crimson. I take a final drag pointing at the floor and grind the stub into the wet concrete.

'Get it cleaned,' I say.

The car is still there, the black Merc. I slam the door behind me, leaving Ferret and Crusher looking at each other. Ferret goes round to the other door and gets in beside me. Crusher is left with the driver's seat, a demotion. I watch the docks slide by, the container ships, their huge hulls high above us, coils of rope, broken boxes. Now we are skirting the Marina, rigging slaps against aluminium masts, seagulls wheel and shriek. The big car moves slowly in the daytime traffic, stopping and starting, stopping and starting, through the old town and out into the suburbs.

*He must accept you.*

We pull up outside Henri's without a word being spoken. I leave the knife lying on the seat between us and climb out.

# CHAPTER 28

I sit on the edge of the bed. My bags of shopping have been tipped out, a T-shirt lies crumpled on the floor with a heavy brown footprint across it. I collect up a clean set of everything and go out into the corridor. The sobbing is back. The strip lighting flickers. There is a smell I can't trace. I scan the empty corridor with the cheap white doors and the scuffed paint. It is the lino – endless people marching up and down in outdoor shoes.

The room at the end is a small bathroom, white enamel and functional. Snow White stares at me in the mirror. Her eyes are wide and dark-rimmed. When she puts her hand up to straighten her hair it shakes. I lean forward and peer at her face. Her eyes are shiny like she might cry. She scowls at me. I turn to the bathtub. Dangling from the thin metal shower rail are row upon row of stockings. I lift them down gently and loop them over the lip of the basin, careful to keep their order.

I unbutton my jeans, pull off my socks and boots, pull off my jeans and T-shirt. I unbuckle the Kevlar, take off my bra and drop them all in a heap beside the bath. A rusty rail holds a hand shower just above face height. The water drums on my head, scalding my scalp. It runs down into my shiny eyes, down my face. I put my hands out in front of me against the tiles and let my head hang down. The water hammers on my shoulders.

I can still hear the sobbing.

I look around through rain-drenched lashes. Razors, Veet, bottles and bottles of shampoo and conditioner. Shampoo that says 'hair is not the most important thing in life but it is a good place to start'.

I pour some into the palm of my hand and rub until my head is covered in bubbles. The shower pounds against my back. I turn the shower off, listening. There is something else besides sobbing. I glance at the flimsy bolt and lean out of the shower to find a knife.

Heavy footsteps climb the stairs. A man. Henri? His breathing is laboured. Overalls rustle. The footsteps stop in the corridor, he is listening to the sobbing.

Tap, tap, tap.

The knock is cautious. Apologetic.

*Not Henri. A punter.*

The sobbing starts up louder than ever. I drop the knife and stick my head back under the hot water. I hang my head down, bracing my hands against the tiles. The corner of the plastic curtain is dark and mottled with mould.

Tap, tap, tap.

*A man sways in his chains, his mouth open in a silent scream. Moths flutter against a trap, caught by their own pheromones.*

I turn off the shower and climb slowly out of the bath, soapsuds and water streaming off me. I slide the bolt and open the door.

A man stands in the corridor in the blue overalls of a dock worker. His face is smeared with engine grease. He holds workman's gloves in one hand while the other knocks. His sweat fills the space between us.

His handlebar moustache droops. He has just been paid and here he is in his lunch hour. He turns to look at me, his hand half raised as if he had meant to knock again and thought better of it. The sobbing has thrown him, it doesn't fit with what he is expecting, what he is hoping. He stares at me, soaking and naked with my hair full of bubbles.

The sobbing hangs in the air between us.

*Make it stop.*

'I'm free,' I say.

# CHAPTER 29

I put my clothes on after the punter has gone and let myself out of the room. The corridor is still. The sobbing has stopped. I go down the main stairs. Reception is empty. The street is quiet in the afternoon sun. A cat dozes on the pavement. When I head off up the road a shadow detaches itself from a doorway and follows me.

I walk through the suburbs of Marseille until the shops become smart and the apartment blocks have concierges. I keep walking until I am in the old town, with its sandy-coloured brick and its Moorish whitewashing. Here the streets are narrower, cobbled in places with flights of broad, shallow stairs.

I turn a corner, duck into an alleyway and wait for my tail. The knife fits snugly in my palm, an extension of my arm. He hurries past, he has lost me. He is young, with the dark curls and tanned skin of a Marseille native. He gets to the end of the street and looks each way. Then he looks back the way he has come. He was waiting tables in the café last night. I slide the knife back into my boot. He is muscled and keen, but just a kid. That means it is not serious, Ferret is just keeping an eye on me.

I can read his frustration. *Damn it.* His hands pump the air in annoyance. I sidle up behind him in a parody of that kid's game, Grandmother's Footsteps. I get all the way up to him before he realises.

'Hi.'

He is relieved and then horrified I have busted him.

'Show me the way,' I say, smiling at his dismay, my grim mood lifting. 'I'm lost.'

He stares at me. Unsure. Hesitant. Then his shoulders do that French Gallic thing like the Marquise. *Pouff.* And he gestures down the hill.

I think about the crowd in the warehouse. It takes a particular type to go through with that kind of scene. This kid doesn't feel like that. What is he doing with Ferret? Then I get an image of Everard, GCHQ's chief medic and interrogation expert, with his floppy dark hair and great smile and remember that appearances mean nothing.

The restaurant is quiet, the lunchtime crowd gone. A few sit over coffee looking out at the square, checking their phones. I walk straight through into the back, ignoring the meatheads. They sit with their backs to the wall, watching the room. The door is closed. I walk in without knocking. Ferret is alone. I sit down in the seat opposite him. He has changed his clothes.

*He must accept you.*

Fuck that. I am taking over.


'Paris is a spent force,' I say. 'There is no control.'

'We have control here,' Ferret says quicker than the speed of thought. I look at him until his gaze slides away.

'Paris is finished,' I say. 'It is time for Marseille to step up.'

'What about the Marquise?'

I wave my hand dismissively. 'The Marquise knows. She knows it is time for Paris to take a back seat. This is why she has sent me. Soon we will be getting a call from the Boss. An invitation.' I pause significantly.

His eyes are eager with ambition. 'We are more than ready to step up. Tonight will be the biggest shipment Europe has ever handled.'

'And it goes without saying, it must run smoothly.'

Ferret fiddles with his fingers. 'About this morning…' he says. His voice trails off.

I stare him down. 'Control,' I say. 'That is what is expected. Efficiency.'

'We have control,' he repeats, as if saying it is going to make it true.

I lean back and put my feet up on the edge of his desk. 'Show me the books.'

Ferret's eyes pop. *Why does she want to see the books?*

I open the leather-bound volume. I can't believe it. It was a figure of speech. The book is red and as big as a bank ledger. Doesn't everyone use a laptop these days? There are rows and rows of figures. I glance down them. I have not the slightest idea what I am looking at. GCHQ narcotics training. That's about it. What do I know about Marseille?

It has the biggest port in the western Med. It used to be the heroin capital of the world before the opium trade was trashed by the Taliban. Nowadays it is cannabis from Morocco and cocaine from South America coming up through West Africa.

I look back down at the columns of figures. The numbers are either weight or monetary amount. I have no clue. I don't even know if it's heroin, coke, or something else. Ferret smiles complacently. He thinks I am pleased.

'We are averaging fourteen at the moment.'

*Whatever that means.*

I nod. Any minute now I am going to say something ridiculous. 'And everything is ready for later?'

His irritation is back.

'Yes,' he says, 'we have it all under control. I don't know why she thinks…' His voice peters out. *I don't know why she thinks we need you.*

Ferret opens a desk drawer and leans down. I brace myself but when he comes back up he is holding out a twist of paper.

*Coke.*

'See what you think,' he says.

I shake my head.

He looks surprised. 'How can you tell the quality of the merchandise?'

I shrug. 'I am not a chemist.'

I close the book and push it towards him.

'My guns,' I say.

He leans back down to the same desk drawer. One, two. They hit his desk. I stand up and put them back in their holsters.

'And my knife.'

He hands me a plastic bag that has been sitting on the corner of his desk. Whatever is inside is long and thin and heavy. My knife falls out onto my palm. It is shiny clean.

Ferret's bloodshot eyes watch me. 'What is it made of?'

'Ceramic.'

I don't feel the need to tell him I have another seven. I slide it carefully into its gap on the inside of my left leg. My go-to blade. There is no point in having throwing knives if you can't get hold of them quickly.

Now I get to sit beside Ferret. Crusher sits on his other side. The meatheads from the warehouse surround us. The junior muscle stand. My tail from earlier hovers, waiting on the table. No one meets my eyes. My status is confused. They know where they stand in relation to Ferret but what about me? Snow White is keeping them guessing.

The table is covered in bottles, glasses, half-smoked cigarettes, packets of foil. We have had steak and frites with Dijon mustard and green salad. Now we are playing cards and drinking. I glance at my cards. *Vingt et un.* Everyone is cheating. Counting is pointless.

The Ferret snarls in a fug of cigarette smoke, bad teeth and bad temper. My presence is making him edgy. Grit in his shell. He doesn't know where he stands either.

My tail from this afternoon catches my eye. He winks at me. *Boy, is he an optimist.* The thought makes me smile. He catches the smile and thinks it is for him. He picks my burner up off the table and taps a number into it. I glance at the phone when he puts it down. *Léon.* Cute.

He leans down, 'What say after this we go back to my place?'

He is braver than he looks.

'To your Mum's?'

The English puzzles him.

'Get lost,' I clarify in French.

He grins.


8 p.m. and we are moving out. I pull my baseball cap on and tuck my hair up inside it. I am in the back seat with Ferret, pride of place. Crusher is still not happy about it. He sits in the front passenger seat. At least he doesn't have to drive. We go through the old town and out into the suburbs and then out onto the ring road. No one speaks. We leave the dual carriageway at a maintenance slip road.

An underpass. I could look out of the window in a dozen cities in the world and see the same thing, the huge bare expanse of concrete, graffiti, gang tags, supermarket trolleys. I can hear the thud of traffic passing overhead. Water drips down a column, staining the pale grey.

I catch sight of a stranger in the driver's mirror, her eyes are scarlet under the eyeliner.

*What the hell are you doing?* she says. Her face is chiselled, not heart-shaped, and her eyes are green.

I laugh.

The man beside me shifts in his seat. He steals a look at me. For a moment I can't remember who he is. Lights behind him spiral away across the concrete, twirling and dancing. I lean my head against the window, pain throbs in my right eye, my head buzzes.

Powerful headlights sweep the underpass, lighting up the cardboard boxes and supermarket trolleys in the dark corners. The movement is slow, a lumbering beast with giant wheels. I peer past Ferret at two enormous headlights moving towards us. It has to be a lorry, a huge container lorry. Crusher gets out of the car and walks over to the headlights. The driver's cab is above his head. He stands talking to the driver then he sets off back our way, head down, job done.

*All set?* Ferret's face asks the question. Crusher nods. The lorry moves slowly forward past our windscreen and comes to a halt beside us. Our headlights light up the red words and the blue, yellow and red flags and the little red bird. Auchan. The supermarket chain.

The Merc starts up, out through the underpass, up the slip road and back towards the city.

We pull up short of the water's edge in the shadow of a rusting container, our bonnet to the metal, our boot pointing at the sea. The scene hasn't changed much since this morning: shipping containers, port lights, pools of stagnant water shiny with oil, coiled rope as thick as a man's arm, mooring bollards. I scan the rest of the dock, through the back window, back and round, up and back and round.

Another red-hulled container ship is being unloaded, crate upon crate swinging on the loading platform of the huge dock crane. The leading line on the crane tightens as it swings up and off the deck, the loading platform now piled with crates. They are wedged up under the pyramid of chains. Men guide it to the ground, release the chains. Back the crane goes, leaving the workers loading a forklift.

I try to calculate what 500 million euros of heroin looks like. How heavy is it? Surely not heavy or bulky enough to need a dock crane?

A man is walking down the gangplank. Dark-skinned, tall, competent, the Captain. Crusher opens his door. A muscle twitches on Ferret's face. The Captain reaches the end of the gangplank and raises his hand in a half salute. They walk to meet each other, stopping in the bright white pool of light. Crate after crate is piled up on the quayside, being organised, marshalled, forklifted off. Crusher and the Captain look back towards the ship where the latest load is pulling off, the chains tightening. Is this it – the golden crate?

The dark faces of the crew mill around. Algerians. In the centre, Crusher and the Captain stand in their pool of light watching the dangling cargo.

*Get out of the light.*

I open the car door. Ferret turns to me, his face twitching. He lays a hand on my arm. I shake him off, climbing out of the car, scanning the shipping containers and the shadows that surround them.

The tableau playing out under the dock lights pauses as it spots me. For a moment I am the only thing moving quayside as they watch me skirt the pools of light, walking in the shadows. Crusher says something and the scene starts up again. Little clockwork people. The forklift backs away from the crane, a single crate in its jaws. It beeps as it reverses up to the Merc.

I walk right up to the crates, up to the workers. There is a rhythm to their movements, to their activity – *bend and stack and lift*. A harmony of movement with a discordant note. I stand watching the worker dripping with sweat, his eyes scanning the dock like mine. Just like mine. Watching the boxes being wedged into the Merc's boot. His shirt sticks to his sides oddly. It flexes wrong. You would never notice unless you know what it means to workout in Kevlar mesh.

I walk right up to him, scanning him from head to toe. His dark eyes roll, the eyeballs discoloured like the blueish tint on a hard-boiled egg. The fear pours off him, sharp in the heat. He has several hoops and studs in his ears and one of them, not a lot bigger than a pinhead, is a short-range receiver. A wire.

Before he can move or think or scream, I have my gun rammed in his face.

'On your knees if you want to live.' I pray he is quick on the uptake. It is one thing to risk my own life but another to risk his.

'The police are here!' I shout.

The workers freeze. Across the dock, Ferret's door opens. I spin the gun, bring it high across my body and down against the wire-wearer's temple. He keels over sideways, safely unconscious.

A bullet wedges between my shoulder blades. My vest takes the damage but not the force. The impact picks me up and tosses me across the dock floor. I can hear shouts, running, gunfire.

There are men on the shipping containers at the far end of the dock. Police. I knew it. They must have been there all along, waiting. The gunshot has thrown me onto my face between two crates. I taste blood in my mouth.

# CHAPTER 30

*'GET UP!' Erik shouts. 'Are you going to lie there and drown?'*

*My muscles scream as I dip again. Hands in water, Erik's foot on my back. How far will he let it go? I collapse, a tangle of splayed arms, my face hitting the water…*

I open my eyes. I am lying face down in a puddle. Instinct takes over, panicking, flailing, I am a fish on a hook twisting and writhing and gasping. I lift my arms, put my hands beside my shoulders and push. There is nothing. My arms burn, my lungs burn.

I twist my head.

The dock is on fire, golden fireworks of flame, dancing on the concrete. Half the crates smoke black and oily. The smell is chemical, choking. Heat scorches the side of my face. I lever myself up on my elbows. It feels like I've got a hundred-pound rucksack on my back. I swing my head from side to side.

*Nothing broken.*

A kill shot – centre of the body mass. Lucky it wasn't the head.

I commando crawl to the end of the crate alley, peer round and look straight into the unconscious face of the guy wearing the wire. He is still alive. Thank God. A perfect single teardrop of blood hangs from one nostril. He probably has a wife and child somewhere. Beyond him I can see the police behind a red-and-white shipping container. Answering fire comes from my end. An old-school police bust. And I thought Firestorm had killed police independence stone dead.

Bodies lie, awkward, splayed in no man's land: workers, the driver, the Captain, Crusher. There is no sign of Ferret. On the top of the container, a police marksman lies flat to the metal, his legs splayed, the thin barrel of his sniper's rifle protruding over the lip. My eyes narrow. I am a better shot, even with a handgun. *Lucky for him.* I take careful aim. My bullet hits his arm. He screams and I offer up a silent prayer of gratitude to my friend in Bologna.

*Where the hell is Ferret?*

I search the dock in short sharp bursts – duck, look, duck, look. He is crouched low beside his car, spraying the shipping containers with bullets. The arrival of law enforcement is a personal affront. The containers look like giant metal colanders.

I duck my head back in. The crates smell of wet pine, damp and rough beneath my fingers. How strong are they? Something is trickling through the gap – my knees are covered. Water? Oil? Blood? It is distinctive, the way it pools. I peer through the crack. A worker lies where he has fallen, an assault rifle beside him. I need Ferret and I need the drugs or Marseille isn't going anywhere.

I put the CZ P-09 back in its holster and count.

*One, two, three.*

I burst round the end of the crates scooping up the assault rifle, praying it didn't lock down when it fell. I fire a covering arc and sprint into the vacuum. The dock stretches out ahead of me, miles and miles for me to run, target practice for police marksmen.

The assault rifle clunks in my arms, eleven pounds of scrap metal, I cannot fire and run. I pound closer and closer to Ferret, listening to my gasping breathing, counting the paces out, one by one, measuring the distance. I throw myself into a full-body slide beside the car, my heart hammering in my ears, my breathing coming in great rasping gulps.

'We are leaving. NOW!' I scream.

Crouched low, I open the far passenger door and drag him by the scruff of the neck towards it. He chokes as he writhes in my hold and for a moment it looks like he is going to turn his gun on me. He is not strong, just reluctant. Beyond us, the police have seen the door open and their bullets thud into the car panels. A window shatters, crazy-paving the glass, the pieces still hanging in the frame.

I slither and slide and squirm between the front seats and belly flop down. Shrapnel pings around me. My hand gropes blind, scrabbling for the ignition. I could cry with relief at the jangle – the keys are still in. As soon as I turn them, the Merc's main beams flood the police position with light. The handbrake digs into my stomach. Head nearly on the floor, I ease off the handbrake, put the car in drive and slam my hand down onto the accelerator. The car roars forward.

The last thing the police expect is a car accelerating towards them without a driver. I scramble upright into the seat as the police scatter in a sudden storm of panic. The wall of the shipping container hurtles towards me and I brace for impact. We hit the container at about forty miles per hour and still accelerating. Enough to ram the steering wheel into my ribs. My neck snaps forward and back, my shoulder blades scream and Ferret slams into the driver's headrest behind me. A figure falls off the shipping container, hits the roof of the Merc and lands behind us. The sniper.

In the driver's wing mirror, the body on the concrete tries to roll. I've gone to all the effort of disabling him safely and now I am going to have to run him over.

What is the clearance under a Merc? I hope he has the sense to stay still. In front of me, police are recovering. I slam into reverse. The car surges back with a screech of tyre spin. The sniper's eyes are wide with horror. We shoot straight back without a bump. I crane forward, peering down the length of the bonnet.

*Legs, torso, head.*

*Is he still alive?*

Police vehicles pile forward in the gap between the two shipping containers, sirens shrieking. They are trapped, the body of their colleague is blocking them in. They can't run him over. The Medea defence. They will have to find a way around.

I back a wide arc, slew the wheel and slam my foot down. I can see nothing in the mirror except the Merc's raised boot lid. I picture 500 million euros of heroin sliding around in the open boot.

I tear down the dock. The port road exit is closed off by a barrier of police cars, lights flashing. The sirens behind me are working themselves into a frenzy of rage. High-pitched shrieking panic. I pull hard right onto the pedestrian walkway beside the Marina. There is a loading ramp up to the port road ahead. It is steep and narrow but my only bet.

The Merc's wheels spin on the steep incline, the engine chokes and stutters, maybe the tank is hit, both hands fight the wheel. At the end of the dock, the sudden roar of acceleration tells me the police have made it past the marksman on the concrete. Ferret is out cold. The burner is still in my pocket. As the Merc levels up, I pull it out. I need help. Now is not the time for overconfidence. I have to face the fact that I cannot do it alone.

The wheel spins again at the top of the ramp and I slam my hand back onto the steering wheel to hold it. I punch the buttons before I change my mind.

I can see him sitting sadly in the café. Left behind. Too junior to be involved. Left with the whisper of something big going down.

Léon answers on the first ring, his cute Marseille accent full of enthusiasm.

'Hello, lover,' I say.

# CHAPTER 31

Sirens shriek – every police car in Marseille is heading our way. I throw the car sideways and take one of the alleys that leads away from the docks. A one-way street. The road is empty. I take the next right, running parallel to the port road. There is barely room for a single car up the middle. A great place to get trapped. No street cams.

*No street cams?*

A great place to hide.

A lot of these apartment blocks have underground parking. Black double doors stand open all the way along. I stare at a dark opening – the ramp leading downwards beside me – trying to make a decision.

Rule 1 of car chases with the police. Don't get into a car chase with the police – there is one of you and many of them. They plot your movements on street cams, set up roadblocks and hunt you from the air.

Rule 2. If you *are* in a car chase with the police, stay where you are. They expect you to run. Drive around the corner and park.

Behind me sirens turn off the port road. I spin the wheel, pitch forward down the steep ramp and cut the lights. Residents' parking. The place is half empty, more spaces than residents' cars. I pull into an empty bay and turn off the engine, watching the car park in my mirrors, listening for the sirens, my heart thumping.

I open the car door. It is cooler down here, several degrees below the night street.

*So, that is what 500 million euros of heroin looks like.*

The cardboard is in good shape considering it has just been in a gunfight. I slam the lid shut and head back to the ramp, my footsteps echoing in the empty space. The concrete is streaked with green algae. Somewhere water is running. I pull out the burner as I walk, trying to get a hand to the throbbing pain between my shoulder blades. I am halfway up the ramp before the phone has reception.

'Where are you?' His voice is breathless, the roar of traffic loud.

I stick my head out of the shadows at the top to see if I can spot a street name.

'I am nearly there,' he says.

'Halfway along. Residents' parking.' I cut the call.

Fast work. I retreat back into the shadows to wait for the cavalry, watching the police sirens dash past the end of the road. A police car turns down into my street and speeds past. They are not suspicious yet – they are still chasing. I watch it disappear around the end of the road. A red moped drives slowly up the street, the rider looking up and down, scanning.

*A moped?*

No wonder he was quick.

As he draws level with me I step out of the shadows. 'How exactly is that suitable transport?'

'Place is gridlocked, every copper in town is here.' Léon is hurt. 'How else could I have got here so fast?' His eyes widen as he gets a better look at me. 'What happened to you?'

'I was shot.'

He gapes.

*Adjust and adapt.*

I scan the street. 'We need an old car. A really old car.'

He catches on quick. He points at an ancient brown Renault 4.

'Seems a shame,' I say as we draw level. 'It's a classic.'

I put my elbow through the driver's window. The splintering echoes in the quiet street. Léon is already leaning past and pulling the wires from under the steering console. The Renault 4 splutters into life.

Carjacking – it's a lost art.

I step back and jerk my head towards the entrance to the ramp. Léon climbs into the driver's seat and backs up the road until he is level with the opening.

'At the bottom on the right.'

I wheel the Vespa down the ramp into the dark, flexing my shoulder blades. I am going to have one hell of a bruise tomorrow.

Léon is out of the Renault, staring at the Merc.

'Back it up.' I clap him on the shoulder. 'I want them boot to boot.'

It is a sweaty, swearing business unloading the Merc. We shuffle awkwardly sideways, up a bit, left a bit, up a bit. Overhead, the sirens play.

How long before someone comes? How much more collateral damage am I going to accept? *The ends justify the means.* What an easy, pat saying.

The final box is out. I slip the burner inside and shove it down until it hits the cardboard bottom. It's not much but it's better than nothing.

Every square inch of the Renault is stuffed with brown boxes. The front passenger seat is piled high. On the dashboard, a yellow straw hat bears witness to the Renault's owner.

*One careful lady driver.*

Which is more important, Ferret or the merchandise? I can't protect both. Without Ferret I have nothing. Without the drugs he has nothing.

*Get through today, live to fight again.*

He needs an alibi and fast.

I open the Merc. Ferret is still slumped in the footwell.

Léon stares. 'Is he dead?' he asks in a small, horrified voice.

'Knocked out. We need to get him back to the restaurant. It has to look as if he never left. It has to look like he's been there all evening.'

Léon can't believe this. He thinks he should be running for his life.

I pat him on the shoulder. 'Never run,' I say. 'It is what they expect. Sit tight. Wait for them to prove it.'

He leans past me and gets hold of Ferret under the armpits. I grab his legs and we half carry, half shuffle him to the Renault. There is no way in God's earth we are going to get him in as well as the 500 million euros of heroin. We reach the same conclusion simultaneously and half lower, half drop him to the concrete.

*Adjust and adapt.*

'He will have to ride pillion. We've got to wake him up.'

Léon looks at me, helpless but willing.

I jerk my head at the Merc. 'Wipe it down, everywhere, d'you understand? Back of headrests, steering wheel, handbrake – everywhere.'

'No problem, boss.'

It won't be good enough. Forensics can find out what you had for lunch if they really put their mind to it, but it should be good enough for now. I don't need perfect. I just need good enough.

I look down at Ferret. Concussed. Smelling salts would be the best bet. It's what they use in the ring. It's not what they teach you in the field. I look around for the source of the running water. A tap on the wall dribbles a thin thread, the washer blown. I grab an empty bottle from between the front seats of the Renault and hold it under the tap. Icy water runs over the back of my hand. Half a bottle. I carry it back to Ferret.

'Help me get his trousers down.'

Léon's curly head emerges from the back seat of the Merc. '*What?*' His expression says it all.

I yank at the suit trousers. Léon watches me for a split second then he backs up to help.

Forget all that slapping around the face business. Ice water to the testicles is where it's at. Ferret springs to life, folding at the waist. His legs come up, his head and shoulders come up. Zero to sentient in a split second.

I slap him around the face anyway. Because I want to. Because it is all his fault and it has been a long night and it is not over yet. The slap echoes like a gunshot. My palm smarts. I scowl.

*Now you have hurt my hand.*

He stares at me, at the dripping concrete ceiling and slowly sinks down onto his back.

*Oh no you don't.*

I roll him onto his side.

'We need to get you home.'

Self-preservation kicks in and he pushes at the concrete, trying to get himself onto his knees, his head hanging down. Groggy. Léon backs the Vespa until it is right beside us. Ferret levers himself up the bodywork, hand over hand, clambering like an ugly toddler. Between us we push and pull him over the seat. Léon yanks Ferret's thigh, pulling his leg over. Ferret flops forward onto the handlebars. Léon climbs on the back, his arms circling. I eye the pair of them.

'Should we tie him on?'

Léon shakes his head. 'I'll be fine. It's just like he's drunk.'

I lift the helmet off the back of the Vespa and ram it on Ferret's head. I rap on the visor.

'Is there a back way into your office?'

He nods.

Sirens are heading down the street. We freeze. I pull the CZ P-09. Lights slide past the top of the ramp. They are moving slow now. They have stopped chasing. Now they are looking. Time's up.

I lean in, my whisper urgent. 'I'll need you to pick me up. You know the underpass on the outskirts beside the flyover?' Léon nods. 'I'll see you there. Drop him in his office via the back way, then meet me.'

He looks round at the Renault. 'Is that where you are taking it?'

I nod. 'Trust me, the police are the least of our worries.'

Léon and Ferret set off at a crawl, Léon's legs stuck out like he is on a fairground ride.

I climb into the Renault, take off the baseball cap and squash the straw hat on my head. Now I feel the part. The door has a thin tinny sound when it shuts. Not the clunk of the Merc. Flimsy. I hope it is up to the weight it is carrying. I pull the wires out from under the steering wheel, wishing I had got Léon to start it for me. I know the theory. I have just never done it.

*Step one: release handbrake.*

My hand gropes. I look down. There is no handbrake. Where the hell is the handbrake?

It is sticking out of the dashboard.

*Step two: release wires from steering console – already done.*

*Step three: blue wire against brown, metal to metal.*

Nothing. I try again. Nothing.

At the end of the car park, a light comes on. A lift.

Someone is using the lift. Someone is coming.

*Breeeeeeathe.*

Metal to metal. Nothing. I think back to Léon doing it. Almost casually like there was no possibility it wouldn't work. Rage pricks at my sinuses. I slam the dashboard and the engine kicks into life. I hold my breath as I put it in gear. God knows how I will get it started again if I stall. The ramp looms ahead of me, 1:2. The ultimate hill start.

*Please don't stall, please don't stall, please don't stall.*

Behind me, I hear the lift doors grind open. I nose, painfully slow, up the ramp and out onto the street. I retrace my steps, turning the wrong way up the one-way street and then out onto the port road. The Renault 4 creaks along, heading towards the sirens, very, very slowly. The port barricade has gone. The road ahead is closed. Traffic police direct the line up a side road. I glance across at the cardboard boxes. We crawl along.

I draw level with the traffic cop. Her whistle sprays saliva. I sit tight, eyes front. We are right by the docks. Eventually they will circle back. When that fails, they will come for Ferret.

It takes me fifteen minutes to reach the ring road and my nerves are in shreds. Holding the car on the bite has my calf muscle aching and my heart lurching every time the engine stutters. The motorway is busy but moving, thank goodness. I keep the needle on a steady fifty miles per hour and pray.

I squint into the kerbside darkness. Where was the underpass? I spot the maintenance slip road ahead and the worry that I have been keeping locked down hits me.

*What if the Auchan lorry has gone?*

I kill my lights, ease down the slip road, riding the clutch, trying to quieten the Renault's engine. The underpass is in front of me, empty.

I sob with disbelief. Fliers, dust, empty. And then I come round a pillar and see it, parked hard up against the slope lengthways.

*Oh thank God.*

I can feel tears of relief. I drive a wide circle, back up to their loading doors and get out. The air is still warm. No one moves. My back throbs. Eyes glitter in the giant wing mirror. They are not expecting a woman in a Renault 4 with a floppy straw hat. They are expecting a Merc and armed men. The cabin door opens and a man climbs down. Six foot, military. He looks past me at the Renault. He pans back round the way I have come.

'Is it all there?' There is an Eastern European lilt to his French.

*Adjust and adapt.*

This is a professional.

'Yes.'

Overhead I can make out the sound of a Vespa coming down the slip road. Léon has got Ferret to the restaurant and back here in the time it took me to drive the Renault one way. The Eastern European has a gun in his hand before I register he has moved.

'It's my ride,' I clarify. I jerk my thumb at the Renault. 'It will need wiping down. You don't have a lot of time.' I fling the hat into the back.

He nods. 'Bonfire.'

I climb on the Vespa behind Léon. As we turn up the slip road, I look back. They are already unloading the boxes, fast and efficient.

# CHAPTER 32

Central Marseille is still gridlocked, horns blare and sirens screech. We weave through the stationary cars, past the fountain, past the restaurant, left down a side alley, left again into a residential street and pull up outside an apartment block. We are somewhere behind the restaurant.

Léon yanks his helmet off and turns round. Whatever he sees makes his eyes widen and he seizes me in his arms, shielding the bullet hole. Pain splinters across my back. He puts his face against mine and kisses me.

It is OK. Not as good as I would have been at his age, but not bad.

A squad car draws level.

*Nothing to see, officers.*

It drives past.

He is still going for it. I bring my hands up between us and push. Not hard, not like I would if I was breaking a hold, but enough to give him the idea. He pulls back. His eyes are closed.

In the communal hall, Léon disappears down a flight of stairs into the darkness. The stairs go right down. A sub cellar. Cold comes up to meet us. Léon flicks the torch on his phone and starts to run.

The key to being a good field agent is to know when not to ask, to know when to take charge and when to follow. I follow.

Any minute now, armed police will be in the restaurant, filing in, deploying. I am working out how far we have come when Léon stops and I cannon into his back. He starts climbing. Far above us, a square of light says trapdoor. I accelerate, snapping at his heels. Léon flies up the ladder. As we get close, I can see the corner of a rug rolled back and a hanging ceramic pendant: Ferret's office. Are the police already here? Am I too late?

I heave myself over the lip, slam the trapdoor down and pull the rug back over. Ferret is lying, out cold again, on the sofa. Léon peers through the spyhole into the restaurant.

'The police are here.'

I push him aside. Police in riot gear deploying exactly as I had feared. Assault rifles. Expecting a firefight. They cannot possibly have a warrant, but they don't need one. They are in pursuit. They just need probable cause. Their leader signals them to left and right. Customers stare, halfway through their supper.

*What about the civilians?*

They start to shuffle the tables of people out, almost as if they have heard me. Customers are slow to react, picking up their bags, arguing. It is just the delay we need. I pull Léon to the spyhole.

'See that guy by the bar? That is the boss. This is what I want you to say to him.'

Léon's eyes widen as he listens. 'Seriously?'

I nod. I am already pulling my jacket off. The door closes on him. I yank my T-shirt off, the Kevlar vest.

My back throbs like it has its own pulse.

I pull off my boots, unbutton my jeans. I ram it all under the sofa. I can smell the scorched Kevlar. Hopefully I will be the only one. I put my boots back on. Bra or not? Not. Nothing says don't shoot like a pair of naked breasts. I crane to get a look between my shoulders. I wish my hair was longer.

Over by the bar, Léon is putting in an Oscar-winning per-formance. He grins, he shakes his head. *He won't thank you for spoiling his fun.* The hands in pockets are a nice touch. Casual. Not worried. You can't shoot someone with their hands in their pockets. If they are any good, they will know Ferret isn't into chicks. But they might not know what he is into.

I slap Ferret round the face. 'Time to play.'

He opens his eyes. If I needed any confirmation that I am not his thing it is there in his face. The horror. A pair of breasts at point-blank range.

'What is happening?'

'I am saving your ass,' I say. 'Get your trousers down. The police are outside that door.'

I have to hand it to Ferret, he is not slow on the uptake, he pulls at his trousers while I search the desk drawers. It doesn't take long to find exactly what I am looking for.

'Just to the knee is fine. Turn over and leave the talking to me.'

Ferret's bemused eyes watch me. *Turn over?*

'And try and look as if you are enjoying yourself.'

I can hear them in the corridor now. Booted footsteps shuffling along, the leader mouthing orders, signing them to left and right.

*Drums in the deep. They are coming.*

The door flies open.

*Showtime.*

If there's one thing I know, it is how to work a room naked.

*I've got this,* I tell Snow White.


I hold the pose a moment longer than necessary. A lithograph of Victorian porn, boots, pants, metal ruler. The ruler lashes down across Ferret's naked buttocks, leaving a bright pink weal edged with blood. He screams. I go a second time, just for maximum effect. I smile a slow smile at the officer in the doorway.

'Hel-lo, Off-i-cer.'

I take my boot off Ferret's backside and stroll towards him. He stares. This is really not what he was expecting.

*Adjust and adapt.*

Over his shoulder, Léon laughs. 'Sorry, boss. I told him you were busy.'

Behind him, the corridor jostles with halted momentum, the cops at the back craning to see what the problem is, the ones at the front just craning.

'What can I do for you, Officer?' I purr.

His eyes stare, they travel down to the boots and back up to the breasts. It is all there in his face – *I could consider a life of crime myself if this is where it gets you.* He is dark, a Marseille native, and earnest. A copper untouched by Firestorm. A copper trying to do the right thing.

'I love a man in uniform.' I circle the tip of the ruler with my tongue.

He gapes.

I slap the ruler across my palm.

'Is there something I can do for you?' I say.

*Suck you until you scream?*

He pulls himself together. You can see the mental process. Scrambling back from the extremities. Gathering his wits. He looks past me to Ferret, face down on the sofa. He can see the weals on his bare buttocks.

'Where were you at nine o'clock this evening?'

I walk backwards – *don't turn your back, don't turn your back* – until I am level with the sofa. I put my heel on Ferret's head and flex like I am doing aerobics.

'He was here. With me.' I bite the ruler suggestively.

The police officer's eyes widen.

'What, *all* evening?'

'Yes.' The metal ruler slaps against my palm. 'I like to take my time.'

He can feel the bodies behind him pressing forward. He is flustered. He thought he had probable cause. He wasn't expecting to have to create it.

'My name is Fresson,' he says. 'There was a firefight tonight at the docks, a number of officers were wounded. We need you to come to the station.'

'And have you got a warrant, officer?'

It is a rhetorical question and we both know it.

'In that case, I am working.' I turn away. 'Come back later.'

His mouth opens but I don't give him a chance.

'You can find me at Henri's if you need me.'

That has done it, the convincing little detail. He knows Henri's. The Commissioner is probably a regular. I shift gear, walking back towards him. More sashay, more catwalk.

'Unless…' my voice is a breathy whisper, 'you'd like to stay?'

The question hangs in the air.

*RUN* says his monkey brain.

*STAY* begs his libido.

# CHAPTER 33

His eyes search the room, looking for some kind of angle, any probable cause. Time to give him more of an incentive. I go back to Ferret, put my foot on his neck and lash down again. The scream runs through the room, out into the corridor. Fresson has to stand firm to hold back the press of people pushing for a better look. I hook my fingers in my pants like I am about to remove them.

'Staying for the show?'

This is too much for him. He shoves his colleagues back into the corridor.

'We will verify your claim that you have been here all evening,' he says.

Fine. The restaurant is full of people who will swear blind that Ferret has been here. The door closes. Ferret raises his head, listening. I lash down again, just to keep up the good impression. The scream makes me smile.

He rolls over at the same time as trying to yank his trousers up. He lies back, closing his eyes, his hand on the side of his head. He fingers the matted area, feeling for a break, feeling it crusty with dried blood. We listen to the sound of retreating footsteps in the corridor.

'What the hell is going on?'

'An ambush. You haven't been paying the right people.'

Ferret's eyes open at this. He probably pays out almost as much money as he makes. The port authorities, the police, the deputy police commissioner, half the magistrates. Those who can't be bribed can be threatened.

I watch them file out into the empty restaurant.

'What are they doing now?'

'Unlike us, they have to play it by the book. If they have no CCTV records, no street cam shots, no fingerprints, no DNA, they've got nothing to tie you to the shipment. They need a magistrate for an arrest. We have to wait it out.'

I scrabble around under the sofa and pull out my bra. Ferret watches me trying to get it on. I give it up. The pain is coming in waves, throbbing up across the shoulder blades, throbbing down my arms. I try to get a hand to it but bending hurts too much. Ferret shudders.

'Where is the shipment?' he says.

'I'm glad you asked. Given that it was in the middle of a fire-fight' – Ferret's eyes close in pain – 'it was surprisingly undamaged. Delivered intact and on schedule.'

*More or less on schedule...*

'But I think that is worth checking, don't you?'

He grunts. 'What about the car?'

'Dumped it not far from the dock. Compromised.'

*What with all the bullet holes.*

Ferret shifts uneasily on the sofa. 'Are you going to put your clothes on?'

I peer through the spyhole. The police are still milling around, it will be time for statements soon.

'No.'

Léon is handing round bottles of beers. No one is taking them.

'What if they come back?' I say. 'How can I be rocking your world with my clothes on?'

I put my leg up and sit astride him in pants and boots. Drum my fingers on his chest. The white cotton gusset stares him in the face. A full body shudder runs through him.

I grin. 'What's your thing? Tell me. What are you into?'

He stares at me, terrified and repelled.

'Boys? Beards?'

Nothing.

I swing off him. I haven't got the time to get to the bottom of it now. His red-rimmed eyes slide to the metal filing cabinet in the corner of the room.

'Oh no. You need to focus.'

He nods miserably. He is wondering when I became the boss. I go back to staring out of the spyhole. Léon is leaving the main restaurant heading for the back. There is a knock.

'Boss? Are you decent?' His voice is muffled.

Ferret looks at me. I nod.

'Come!' shouts Ferret.

Léon shuts the door carefully behind him.

'That was unbelievable,' he whispers. 'Un-fucking-believable.' He looks at Ferret. 'They want to talk to you.' He grins. 'If it is convenient.'

I nod to the trapdoor. 'Who else knows about that?'

'No one,' Ferret says.

I try to stay patient. 'When you say no one do you really mean no one? Henri? Who?'

'No one who is left alive.'

So that means plenty of people knew. It isn't going to take the cops two minutes to find it once they come back with a search warrant. Which will be tomorrow. I will need to hold them up a bit.

'Come find me tomorrow with a laptop,' I say to Léon. 'Early. I'll be at Henri's.'

'Right you are, boss.'

Ferret glares. He may not know where he stands when it comes to me, but he is in no doubt about Léon.

'Get out.'

Léon backs out, still grinning.

'Make the call,' I say.

Ferret gets slowly, awkwardly, to his feet, leans over his desk and picks up his phone. His landline.

I catch his wrist. 'Not your phone. Everything, everywhere is bugged. You have no idea.' I scrabble around under the sofa. I shake Snow White's jacket till a burner falls out. I hand it to him.

Ferret sneers. *Not very high tech.*

I roll my eyes. 'Beware the person carrying a burner. Really beware the person carrying nothing – they work for the government.'

He dials the number. 'It is done.' He nods. 'Yes, on its way.'

The call cuts and he throws the burner down on the desk. *Now you need to destroy it*, I want to tell him. *Now you need to dismantle it, take the separate pieces and grind them into the dust.* I don't say that. I put the burner back in my jacket.

That's it now, the die is cast. Has it been enough? Will the Boss be pleased? Will Marseille still get the call up for the tournament?

I give him the burner's number.

'We are going on a trip, remember? It will be very soon now. I need to know when you get the call.'

Ferret nods reluctantly.


Léon drops me off on the Vespa at Henri's. I am too tired to argue and it is by far the quickest way to cross Marseille. He pulls his helmet off. It rotates in his hands.

I clap him on the shoulder. He has had a field op masterclass tonight. If it was a training exercise, I would say he had done well. Really well.

'Thank you for your help tonight.'

*I couldn't have done it without you.*

He nods. There is something about him that reminds me of Jake, my boarding buddy. Like he wants to say something. I can feel his eyes on my back as I cross to the grill door.

I press the buzzer.

'Let me in, Henri.' I haven't got the energy to be charming.

Henri is waiting behind the counter. He gets up and bars the way.

*Here it comes.*

'Henri, I like you. I really do, but you are just not my type.'

Henri lets out a snort of laughter. He moves with one quick practised swerve and pins me against the wall.

*He's done that before.*

'You are a cheeky bitch,' he says. 'I don't like that.' Spittle flies. I look back at him. Eye contact. His expression darkens.

'Henri,' I say, 'it has been a long night, a very long night, and I cannot be arsed to deal with your body. For that reason and that reason alone I am going to let you live. And also, and here I want you to listen carefully, I am leaving you in possession of your manhood.'

I glance down. He follows the glance. A white blade jabs his groin.

*Bitch.*

It is my depressing experience through many long boarding school years that, contrary to popular belief, bullies do not back down when they are challenged. There is a reason why they rule the school. His arm pulls back. It is going to be in the face. Nose-smashing. A proper injury. The blade rams in. A centimetre. Enough. Not all the way. I pull it out. He sinks to his knees at my feet, cupping his groin with both hands. I wipe the blade on my jeans and pat his shoulder.

'Next time, Henri.' I promise us both. 'Next time.'

I climb the stairs wearily. The pain across my shoulders hits like a hammer, rising and falling in waves of spasm. The girl opposite is standing in her open doorway, smoking. End of the shift. The room beyond has yellow walls. There is a teddy bear on a wardrobe. It looks like someone's bedroom.

I turn to my door.

'Are you new?' she asks.

'Just passing through.'

She nods. She drops her cigarette on the lino and stubs it out with one turn of her velvet mule. The fur is peeling away from the plastic.

I put my key in the lock and shut the door behind me. The room is bathed in pink light. I lie down on the bed and the banging doors, the footsteps on the stairs and the sirens lull me to sleep.

# CHAPTER 34

Tap, tap, tap.

The knock is cautious, hesitant, either unsure of its room or unsure of its welcome. Not Henri, not Henri in a million years of knocking.

'Come in!' I shout.

The door handle rattles. I swing off the bed and open the Yale.

Léon is standing on the threshold looking bright-eyed and perky. His eyes peer past me at the room, checking it out. With the morning light it has returned to its habitual grey. I hold the door so he can get past.

'Did Henri tell you where I was?'

'He's not there. I looked in the book.'

God knows how I feature in Henri's blue book.

'Did you bring the laptop?'

'Yep.' He pats the satchel over his arm.

'Make yourself at home. I'm going to shower.'

I head down the corridor. My neck and shoulder muscles scream as I try to undress. The tendons on either side of my neck are hard as ropes – whiplash. I take another couple of ibuprofen and put my head under the tap. The skin between my shoulders stretches. Everything aches. I squint at it in the mirror. My back is a mess. I turn the shower on before I get in and ratchet it down until it is only a weak, warm trickle. Even so, it hurts so much I am dizzy with nausea. I lather up the soap and wash all over.

Léon is sitting on the bed playing on his phone when I come in. He looks away quickly when I drop the towel. I smile at the rising tide of red across the back of his tanned neck – teenagers, half flash and half foolish. I crawl into a clean set of everything. Getting a bra on is a serious trial. Teeth, contacts, eyeliner, towel dry hair. Ready. The Kevlar reeks. I kick it under the bed.

Reception is empty, as promised. We head out, scanning the street – no one is there. The morning is fresher, clearer than it was yesterday. The end is in sight.

'Where are we going?' he asks.

'Breakfast. Two birds with one stone.'

I prop the laptop on the counter between us while we wait for our coffee to arrive. The Slashstorm home page hasn't changed. Twelve faces, five days to go.

'What's that?' says Léon.

'Nothing.'

I close Slashstorm and pull up the search engine.

'The thing about government systems,' I say, like I am teaching a class, 'is they are Leviathans. They grew up organically, piecemeal, patch by patch, upgrade by upgrade. There is always a way in.'

Léon nods seriously. The logo of the Marseille police force fills the screen. I search the sitemap. Employee technical support. The help desk. It even has a contact address for IT. As an extra bonus they are in a different building to the main police force. I jab the address.

'Where is this? Is it Marseille proper?'

Léon considers. 'Suburbs,' he offers.

I pull out a spare burner and initialise it. 'What Trojans do you know? Rowhammer?'

Léon shakes his head.

'It was massive about ten years ago until a hacker invented an even worse version of it: the Sledgehammer.'

Léon is still looking blank.

I sigh.

'*Anyway.* Everyone in IT from the help desk upwards knows the signs of a RAT attack.'

'RAT?' He is still looking blank.

'Remote Access Trojan. Do they teach you nothing at school these days? We'll go with one of the really early ones.' I hand him the burner. 'You are going to phone the help desk and tell them about your problem.'

Léon looks worried.

'I will type your answers. You can just read them off the screen with a bit of your acting flare.'

He cheers up at this.

I dial the number and put it on loudspeaker.

'Support desk, this is Clementine, how can I help you?' The woman's voice is young and bored. Her job is fifty per cent resetting passwords and fifty per cent asking if you have tried logging off and logging back on again.

'Hi, this is Detective Fresson, I am having problems with my remote login.'

'Can I take your username?'

'Wow, that is fast, how did you take control like that? That is amazing. Is that you typing? What does kilerat stand for? Isn't technology amazing?'

'I'm sorry, sir, did you say kilerat?'

'Yep. It's OK; it's gone now.'

'Can I put you on hold, sir?'

'Sure, sure no problem.'

Léon grins at me and I give him the thumbs up.

Clementine has gone, now someone called Felipe is on the line.

'Hi, is that Detective Fresson? I want you tell me exactly what was on your screen.'

'It's fine now – it has gone away. Something about a kilerat.'

'Sir, are you in the office?'

'No, I'm on my laptop.'

'I need you to turn your device off now and disconnect it.'

'I can't do that. Did you not hear about last night's operation? I need my PC. I have urgent shit to deal with.'

'Sir, you may be the victim of a remote access attack. You need to turn your PC off, you could infect the whole network.'

Time to go for broke.

'OK, I'll just send a couple of emails first.'

I cut the call on Felipe's anguish.

Léon looks at me taking the burner to pieces. 'What was that? Did we do it? Did we hack the police network?'

I snap the SIM card, shaking my head. 'No need. They'll try and call you back.' I hold up the bits of phone. 'Then they will use their system administrator access to shut Fresson down. With a bit of luck, they might take the whole network out as a precaution. Safety first. Because you were on your laptop, using the remote access tool, it becomes plausible. Just. Once they think about it, they will know kilerat couldn't have got through their virus net.'

Léon shakes his head. 'You know some amazing shit.'

We have a second bowl of coffee and a second baguette while I give Léon a potted history of Remote Access Trojans. I wish Control was here to see me playing mentor.

Léon sits back, lighting up.

'You shouldn't smoke,' I say.

'You don't like it?'

What a cute question. I am about to tell him it doesn't matter what I think, when I remember my new-found mentor role. I have a once in a lifetime chance to do his lungs a favour.

'Smokers are no good in bed,' I tell him. 'No stamina – it messes with lung capacity.'

Léon drops his half-smoked cigarette like it has burnt him.

'*Really?* I never heard that.' He stubs it out in the saucer and inhales and exhales a few times checking his breathing is OK.

I turn my face away.

'So, what would you look for in your ideal man?' he says, fiddling with the bits of phone.

I check the other burner. Still no word from Ferret.

'Sexual prowess.'

'No, seriously.' His puppy dog eyes are earnest.

'Strength, I guess, mental and physical. I don't want to be able to push him over.'

He nods. 'He has to be able to beat you in combat. Like Artemis, goddess of the hunt.'

I stare. 'You don't know what a RAT is and you are quoting Greek myths at me? Why is it always about defeat and submission with men? It is not about being defeated. It is about being equalled. A mental and physical equal.'

'So in your case, you are basically looking for a God?' He sounds disgruntled.

'I am not looking for anyone.'

'Have you ever been in love?'

'No,' I say, reaching for the bill.

# CHAPTER 35

The text on the burner makes me jump. All this time I have been waiting, listening for it, desperate as a girl who has been on a date and yet when it comes, it catches me unawares. I look at it confused. What is this? Where did it come from?

*Looking forward to your kiss Hershey X*

I look at it for a long moment. It is what I have been waiting for, but what does it mean? I put it back in my pocket. Then I get it out again.

'What would you say that meant?'

First, I'm mentoring, now I'm asking for a second opinion. Control would fall off his chair.

Léon considers, his forehead furrowed.

'It means Ferret needs you to come over now but can't say that, so is making it sound casual.'

He sits back, pleased with his decoding.

I need to get the Kevlar. The call to go and see the Boss has come. I picture the tall figure with the shaved head and adrenaline floods me.

*Finally.*

'Where can you buy Hershey's Kisses in Marseille?'

Léon is baffled. 'Are they peanut butter?'

'No. Not the peanut butter cups. The kisses. You know? Little, disgusting silver-and-gold chocolates?'

He gets it now.

'Nowhere,' he says.

Of course not. Like I said, the French don't do food badly.

'Intermarché, maybe? Has to be the only place. Big. Out of town. We used to hang out there as kids. Furniture and stuff.'

I get the picture. A retail park.

'We'll have to get a car. I'm not going on the Vespa again.'

We head back up the street. The gate is still wide.

'Wait here,' I tell Léon.

The corridor is dark. No Henri. I charge up the stairs, my heart hammering. There is nothing much to collect from the room. Toothbrush, contacts pots, Kevlar. The jacket reeks of gunfire. I can't risk going where I am going without body armour. I put it in one of the plastic bags that held underwear and hurtle out of the room. Total time in room, less than a minute, and in that time Henri has come back.

*Damn.*

Judging by the voices, he is not alone. I peer through the wooden slats at the top of the stairs. I have a great view of the top of Henri's head. He perches awkwardly on his stool behind the counter, shifting uneasily like he can't get comfortable. A fly buzzes round his head and Henri swots at it ineffectually. His tone is jovial.

'Back so soon, Jean Luc?' he says.

Jean Luc must be a regular.

'Is it your birthday?' Henri laughs.

The punter steps forward under the single bulb. His sombre black suit has a strange creased look to it, as if it has just come out of deep storage.

Henri stops laughing. 'Has someone died?'

The punter's cap rotates in his hand. 'I want to see the new girl,' he says.

Oil glistens on the top of his head.

'What new girl?' Henri says irritably. 'You see Natalia once a week.' *As regular as clockwork with your pay cheque.*

'No, last time I was here, I saw someone else. The new girl,' says the punter patiently.

'There is no new girl.' Henri is mystified.

'Black hair, long legs, big brown eyes.'

*Ah…*

Henri stares, but before he can answer there is the sound of a new arrival. Henri stands up quickly, his body in hard lines.

'No special rates for coppers,' he says before the newcomer can open his mouth.

There is a pause, like the new arrival would like to say something but is thinking better of it. He steps under the light.

'I am here on business,' Detective Fresson says. 'I am looking for a woman who works for you.'

'I have permits for all of them,' Henri says quickly.

'I am sure you do,' Fresson says. 'Nothing like that. I am not immigration.' His voice is warm. *I'm not those bastards in immigration.*

Henri laughs heartily. 'That is a relief. You never know, no matter how much you pay, when immigration will come making difficulties.'

'I would just like a few extra words with her on a routine matter.' He pulls out his Blackberry. He fiddles with it. In goes the password once, twice, three times. No luck – his account is locked down.

He gives up in a flurry of frustration and reaches into his jacket pocket. He lays a grainy black-and-white picture taken from a CCTV camera on the counter.

'I have a better one on my phone,' he says.

They all lean over the counter.

'That's her!' says Jean Luc in triumph.

*

I am already sliding backwards. The corridor is a dead-end. No windows in the bathroom. Nowhere to run. Ten rooms. Five on the front, five on the back.

The last door on the right beside the bathroom gives way to a kick. Thank goodness it is empty. I close the door quietly behind me, hoping the doorframe splintering isn't too obvious. The same net curtains cover the windows, beyond them is a narrow alley and the back of a building. One floor up. About ten feet.

Footsteps on the stairs. Heavy, booted footsteps. Jesus, they are all coming: Henri, Jean Luc and Detective Fresson. They stop outside my old door.

I try the metal casement – the handle is stiff, it hasn't been opened in years. It gives suddenly, jerking out of my hand. The window opens horizontally, the latch hanging down. Not the easiest of escape routes. I hang one leg out, lean my stomach on the edge and roll my body over. The latch catches against my clothes. My shoulders burn as my arms take the weight. The plastic bag with the Kevlar hangs from my wrist. I look down and see bins – the back of the 7-Eleven.

The thud is plastic not metal. I land heavily, rolling my shoulders.

The back door to the 7-Eleven is propped open, cardboard boxes line the floor, piles and piles of stock. I push past and into the main shop. The street window is so covered with posters and flyers I can't see what is going on. How many police are there? Has he brought a police van? I dial Léon.

'Start up the Vespa.'

'The police are here,' he says.

*No shit, Sherlock.*

He has the Vespa outside the door in under two minutes. As we turn the corner at the end of the road I look back. Detective Fresson is coming out of Henri's, his shoulders slumped. No Blackberry and no witness.

# CHAPTER 36

We pull up outside the retail park. Léon has sold it short – five out of town retailers and an Intermarché. Massive. I scan the space. Hundreds of cars, plenty of people. If the police are here, I can't see them. Léon pulls up onto the pedestrianised forecourt, right up to the Intermarché's glass doors. Concrete bollards keep the traffic out, but they are too widely spaced to bother the Vespa. He takes his helmet off.

'Get me a Fanta while you are in there,' he says.

I nod and smile and pat him on the shoulder because I know I will not be coming out.

*I am never going to see you again.*

At the doorway I do a quick scan. Léon is fiddling with the strap on his helmet, still astride the Vespa. A mother with a buggy and a walking toddler, an old man with a stick, a car full of watchers, a man on his phone, another car full of watchers. OK, so the police *are* here. Did they follow Ferret inside or are they waiting for him to come out?

The store opens with the flower section. Black buckets up to the ceiling, a downmarket version of the George V atrium. It widens out into fruit and vegetables. Homewares and clothing to the right, bakery to the left. I turn left, confectionary has to be after bakery surely? Magazines are after bakery, then toiletries, then snacks. I scan the ceiling signs and back up.

The confectionary aisle is empty. I check behind me. They've got every chocolate bar known to man. The Hersey Kisses are down at the bottom beside the Peanut Butter Cups. You have to be keen to find them. I pick up a packet and shake it. The little gold chocolates dance. Almond. I turn it over. I look back at the empty space on the shelf. I shuffle all the Hershey's bags to be sure.

I carry the packet to a till and wait. The line crawls forward. The woman in front of me has a trolley overflowing with pet food. She must have a dozen dogs. Finally, the dog woman is shuffling off.

The till girl is harried and hassled and generic. If there was some terrible crime and I had to describe her I would be falling back on words like grey, nondescript. But efficient. She is being timed. Any till girl slower than the pack risks having her basic wage job taken away. She looks up at me as I hand her the money.

'Are they a gift?'

Curious question.

'Yes,' I say, 'they are a gift.'

'Have you tried our in-store café?'

'No, I haven't. Perhaps I will.'

She nods as she hands me my change, already lifting the next customer divider bar, not wanting to slow her run rate.

I put the change in my jacket pocket, pick up the Hershey's and look around for the café. I follow the sign – a bowl with steam rising off it. It is pointing towards the back. I round the final aisle and a woman is standing there.

She is dressed like an air hostess, but she carries herself like special forces. Neat little blue suit, skirt a shade too short, silk blouse, stripy scarf, great legs, shiny French plait. Air hostess with a hint of extra services thrown in. Set against this are the double bulge under each arm (holsters are a bitch under slim tailoring), the coil of wire behind the ear and the way she scans the corridor up and back and round, up and back and round. Just like me.

She focuses on the Hershey's Kisses and then on my face and steps into my path. We are in the far corner of the store. The archway to the café is down at the end. No cameras. A blind spot.

She turns to a fire escape door behind her, pushes the horizontal bar, pulls me through and shuts the door quickly. I imagine a tail, rounding the corner of the aisle and carrying straight on, entrance to the café ahead.

'Nice,' I say to her back. 'Neat.'

A service corridor stretches the whole length of the store – rough breeze blocks, the bare bones of the shopping mecca. Customers never see back here. I watch her walk in front of me. Slight awkwardness in left stride, too slight to be a gun – thigh knife.

She walks fast and I am expecting her to stop at the loading bay, but she carries straight on, all the way to the end, through another fire escape door and behind the scenes in the next unit along. What did it sell? Beds.

The loading area is the same as the Intermarché's but much less busy. How many beds come and go in a day after all? Rows of Grand Litier lorries line up, their loading ends pointing to the store. She climbs onto the running board of the nearest lorry. I brace as she throws up the tailgate, my hand clenched inside my jacket.

It is not what I was expecting. I had been expecting a lorry full of plastic-wrapped mattresses and bedsteads stacked on end. And then I realised that this is a transfer vehicle to take us to the Boss, so I was expecting empty.

The huge trailer interior is filled with sleek chrome. A double-decker Airstream. The sort that might transport a pop star. A vehicle within a vehicle. I pull myself up. The air hostess is beside me talking into her wire and the tailgate closes.

I edge along the Airstream's silver side. It is so massive there is barely any room to squeeze through between it and the truck wall. Metal steps lead up to the open door at the front. Laughter, muffled voices, the sounds of guys having a good time. I put one foot on the bottom step, stretching up like an ostrich and see a narrow lounge area, banquettes, a built-in table, Ferret and the three meatheads making themselves at home. My eyes narrow.

They are already high. The Boss is putting on a party and they have gone large on the free handouts.

*Idiots.*

I glance towards the driver's seat. Empty, no keys. If we wanted to get out, how easy would it be? A steel container locked from the outside, with a limited air supply, an air supply that could be altered? There are so many ways this could go wrong. What if the Boss is angry about the screw up of the first major heroin shipment to be landed in years? What if they have got us here to punish us? What if the Marquise has found out who I am and is delivering me straight to him? What if she has double-crossed me?

'Make yourself comfortable,' the air hostess says, a hand on my arm. The hostess act is deliberate, she is here to escort us.

'How far have we got to go?'

'It is a fair way,' she says, smiling.

*A fair way?*

'So how long? Give it to me in hours.'

'It is best that you prepare yourself for a long journey.' Her voice is soothing.

It closes me down. I feel myself relax. My eyes droop and then I get it, something is making me dopey. I am on her in a second, my adrenaline pumping, my knife at her throat.

'Why is the oxygen down?'

She stares up at me. Calm. She hasn't moved. 'It is nothing to worry about. It is a really long trip – overnight, trapped in a steel box. We are just trying to make it pleasant.'

My head swims. I stand back, scowling. I have spent over a week trying to get into this position, to get into his orbit, since Slashstorm began counting down. Trying to get into his inner circle. And now I am actually on my way to see him, I don't like it. What is this? Last-minute nerves?

She is walking away from me now, adjusting overhead lockers. I follow her long legs up the turning stairs. A double-decker. There are no seats on the top floor. More like low couches, cushions – a party bus.

'Where are the hookers?' I ask sourly.

'They will be joining us later.'

*What?*

'What about me?'

Her eyes consider me thoughtfully.

'What would you like?'

'Gymslip and pigtails?' My voice is laced with sarcasm. There is nothing about this situation I find erotic. And really, that is saying something. 'I'll be fine,' I say in case she takes me seriously. 'I could do with a good sleep.'

I remember a line from that psych report: *subject is a sexual predator with a moral compass that points due self.* And Control and Erik laughing and laughing.

'That's psychoanalysis for you,' Erik told Control. 'A day of in-depth interviews to find out she's selfish.'

I still don't know why they found it so funny.

I peer out of the windows into the dark of the container. The lorry is moving but the feeling is subtle, like high-speed train travel, the coach's suspension cushioning us. I imagine Léon, his face starting to worry, looking up and down the forecourt. He will go inside. He will do what I did and track down the Hershey's Kisses. He will ask the management if anyone has seen me. How long will he wait?

I go back down the stairs, my balance all over the place. Ferret and the meatheads are out for the count. I turn back to her, suspicion making me fast again.

She holds out a tiny clear pot with a blue pill inside.

*What, no red pill?*

'You know I am never going to take that.'

It could be anything. I give her the full eyeball treatment.

'It is to put you to sleep.'

I roll my eyes.

*Obviously.*

'So you can do what?' I say, thinking of the Marquise.

'It is a precaution to disguise the location of our destination. A weapons and wire check.'

'And if I refuse?'

'We will let you all out and you can go home. We are still in France.'

So, we are heading north. That's not what I expected. I take the pill in its tiny clear pot and stare down at it. I smell it. Cellulose. The whole situation reminds me of something.

'How long have I got to decide?'

She shrugs. 'I can give you a few more minutes.' She heads back towards the stairs.

I stare around at Ferret and the meatheads, out for the count without needing any persuasion. Easy. Embarrassingly easy. I kneel beside them, checking their vitals. Heart rate normal, breathing deep. I pull back an eyelid. The pupil has rolled all the way to the top of the head. Drugged.

When she comes back, I am still staring at the pill in my cupped hands. I breathe her in. She is calm. Nothing is riding on this. Could I fake it? Probably not.

*Breathe in, breathe out.*

I tilt the pill pot and jerk the pill to the back of my throat. It is down in one big gulp of bottled water. Her wide eyes watch me as I sink back onto the bench. I can see another pair of eyes, dark and glittering in a cobwebbed toilet in Courchevel. *It'll cost you*, the eyes said, *everything you've got.*

As I lose consciousness, I remember what all this reminds me of: an old movie. A man took a pill to find out what had happened to his missing girlfriend and woke up in a coffin. Buried alive.

# CHAPTER 37

*I stride along a desert floor. Powder slides beneath my feet. Mountain ranges hide the horizon. My strides pound forward. The wind blows my hair back, it blows like a hurricane until all my hair is gone. Flames douse my body, cocooning me in a pyramid of flickering gold. My clothes shrivel and curl, my skin crisps and burns, the flesh falls from my arms, from my face, from my body. My arms are gone, my legs are gone but still I limp onwards on my twisted stumps.*

*I am standing in the courtyard of a castle, the golden stone warm under my palm. The doors open and he is there in the shadows.*

*'Welcome, Winter,' he says. He is huge and scaled and when he tilts his face the shafts of sun from the window sparkle on his cheek. I am a tiny doll, a matchstick girl. His huge scaly hand strokes my cheek. 'Welcome,' he says.*

*I am lying on my back, naked. A mirrored ceiling is above me. Hands travel up my body, long fingers feather-light stroke my skin. They glide over my breasts, circle my nipples, slide across the cotton-soft skin of my stomach...*

I open my eyes. We have arrived. I am lying fully dressed on the bench. My feet are bare, my knives are gone, my holsters with their guns have gone, my phone has gone, the Kevlar has gone. I tilt my head to look out of the window. The lorry has gone. The coach is on a huge dusty plain, a mountain range on the horizon. The sun is low over the mountains but pale. Is it going up or coming down? I am alive. That is all that matters.

Murmured voices come from upstairs. Everyone is awake. I sit up. Out of the window, I can see lines and lines of coaches, silver in the sun. Someone is hurrying down the stairs. Ferret rounds the corner. He looks just like he did when my gusset was in his face and I know exactly what is going on upstairs. The hookers have arrived. He slows at the sight of me. Awkward.

'So, we're here.' My gesture encompasses the coach park, the desert, the mountain range.

He peers out of the window like he hasn't even noticed.

'Have you got any of your weapons left?'

He shakes his head.

'What about your phone?'

He shakes his head again.

I let myself into the tiny toilet. I dig out my toothbrush. I smooth Snow White's hair. Her big brown eyes are red-rimmed from sleeping in contacts. Something feels uncomfortable and I twist my arms behind me. The movement is not as painful as it has been. My back is greasy to the touch. My bra is loose. I pull off the T-shirt and squint at my back in the mirror. The bruise feels easier. I scrape my nails across the skin, smelling the thick ridges under my nails. Arnica. Someone has put Arnica on my bruise while I was sleeping. In the mirror, Snow White shrugs. She doesn't know what to make of it either.

I need to eat. The mini kitchen has a pile of baguettes in plastic on the side by the tiny sink. I rummage around, taking out every item in the cupboards to see what else there is. Salt, sugar, Nescafé. Yellow Lipton. Yellow bloody Lipton. Powdered hot chocolate. It feels Eastern European. If we were in the West, the coffee would be better.

Fresh products, that's what I need, items that might have been bought here. I open the fridge door. It is inserted ingeniously under the countertop. Bottle of fresh milk. Well, that narrows it down. You don't get milk like this in India, China or Japan. I pick the bottle up.

*Lait écrémé.*

French. It was bought in Marseille.

I slam the fridge door.

What weapon opportunities does the kitchen offer? I throw open all the drawers, peer into every cubby hole, examine every tiny space. A corkscrew is the best I can come up with. It is one of those simple ones – a handle with a corkscrew spike in the middle. I slip it into my back pocket.

*Better than nothing, way better than nothing.*

Ferret is still sitting awkwardly at the little table. His hand shakes, a vein below his eye twitches, his fingers feel for the scar in his hair. He is coming down. I sling him a baguette sandwich.

'You need to eat.'

He stares at it.

I sit down at the tiny table opposite him and unwrap my sandwich. Processed ham, tomato, cucumber, lettuce. The bread is western. You wouldn't get this kind of bread in China. But then again it could have just come in, like us, on a lorry. So basically, a processed baguette can tell you everything or absolutely nothing. I bite down.


'Let's look around.' I make it sound upbeat and cheery, like we've just arrived in a holiday camp. I need to work out where the hell we are.

He glances back up towards the turn in the stairs. 'Do you think we're allowed to?'

'Sure.' I gesture at the door, hanging wide.

'Maybe we should wait,' he says, looking back up the stairs.

'Why?'

I stand up. The metal floor is cold under my bare feet – we have been stationary for a while. It is a drop to the ground. The air is warm. The grass underfoot has bare patches of soil. I fall to my knees, running my fingers through the dirt – almost sand. Behind me, Ferret jumps down. The caravan beside us is a hundred feet away. I circle the Airstream. The ones in front and behind are the same, close enough to block our view but far enough away that they are not on top of us. It would have to be an active decision to visit the neighbours. You couldn't sneak up on them.

Quite a logistical operation, setting all this up. I wonder what it looks like from the air. Something ought to be showing up on a satellite somewhere. How many coaches like this are there? How many party buses?

High ground, that's what is needed. I stare up at the outside of the coach. It is two storeys of sleek chrome and glass not designed with footholds in mind. Then I remember the skylights on the upper levels. I pick up a broom from the kitchenette on the way through.

The girlie show is in full swing on the top deck.

'Don't mind me,' I say, skirting nipples, 'just passing through.'

I stand on a couch and lever the skylight open. It stops at the typical two-inch mark. I ram the broom handle into the gap and lean against it with all my weight. The hinges will give or the handle will snap – could go either way.

The naked gyrations slow and the nearest girl stops to watch. Gymslip and blonde pigtails. I pass her the broom handle, punch out the skylight, put my hands either side of the opening and hoist myself up. A full-body pull-up. My biceps burn, my stomach flumps down on the metal edge, my legs dangle. I wriggle and push. It is not elegant, but it gets the job done. I clamber to my feet.

This is more like it. I can see the full scale of the coach park. About eighty coaches. Each vehicle is parked very precisely, an exact distance apart with a line of floodlights between it and its neighbour. I squint in the brightness. Millimetre precision. I turn a slow 360 and my mouth drops open. Khaki as far as the eye can see, supply tents, a jeep park, a landing strip, a structure as big as a warehouse. An army.

I am here to kill a man with his own army.

A green canvas watchtower winks in the sun. Field glasses. Someone is watching me. I wave and grin, giving a thumbs up.

When I drop back down onto the top deck, the action has moved on. I step over the bodies and head for the stairs. Gymslip and pigtails stands forlorn on the side.

Ferret is sitting at the table looking out of the window.

'You really don't want to go up there,' I tell him.

The air hostess appears, minus her shoulder holsters. Unarmed. I guess there is no point in disarming us and then walking in with more weapons. Time to get some answers.

'How much did you get for this run?'

For a moment I think she's not going to answer.

'Fifty,' she says.

That seems a bit tight. Especially if she is expected to put out.

'Fifty thousand dollars,' she clarifies.

Some lost respect slides back to the man at the top. Fifty thousand dollars. For that she is not just going to put out, she is going to do what it takes. Whatever it takes. One woman and a bunch of thugs? She must be good.

'Have you ever met the man at the top?'

'He interviewed me. I am on the staff.'

On the staff. Like he is running a bloody multi-national.

'So, what kind of interview was it?' I ask with a hint of suggestion in my voice. 'Do you think I could get a gig like this?'

'He doesn't fuck the staff,' she says flatly. Then she laughs. 'More's the pity.'

'So, what are you? Ex-special forces?'

She shrugs, noncommittal.

'Where are we?'

'You need to relax,' she says. 'It is several hours to wait. You seem very tense.'

I am going to get nothing out of her without breaking something. I need a softer target.

Pigtails is coming down the stairs, wide-eyed and needy as an Athena kitten poster. Stripy black-and-white tie, short games skirt, freckles painted on, school satchel over her shoulder. A pleading look in her eye.

She was booked for me.

*The things I do in my job.*

'Come on,' I say.

I haul her towards the back of the coach. She shrieks girlishly. Probably part of the service. I push the door open on the bedroom, throw her down on the bed and kick the door closed behind me. Cue more girlish shrieking.

The contents of the satchel make me smile, not very schoolgirl.

I unbutton my jeans and drag them down. Step out of my pants. I leave my bra and vest on. No point in overdoing it. I crawl up the bed and kneel either side of her face. She looks up the length of my body, a little unsure, so I sit on the fake freckles until she gets the idea.

A camera winks in the corner of the room. I blow it a kiss. I hope I am making some bored guard's day.

When I am done, I swing a leg over her and go back to the satchel. She watches me from the bed, her face glossy.

The harness buckles over each hip. I choose a double-ended, slot it into place and slide one half inside me. I kneel back on the bed, flip her over and push up the gym skirt. No pants. Nice.

By the time I have come three times, I am feeling a lot less tense.

'Where are we?'

Her face has left smears across the sheets where she has been thrashing.

'Who knows?' she says, barely opening her eyes. The girly shrieking is gone. 'I took a pill and woke up here.'

*Like the rest of us.*

I pull out, unbuckle the straps, step out of the harness. I got her off. No one could call me selfish.

I slide into my jeans and turn for the door. 'Thanks,' I say.

She waves a boneless arm from her face plant, her skirt still up around her waist.

'No problem.'


The air hostess is making a really big show of stacking kitchen cupboards.

'Everything OK?' she says.

'Fabulous.'

I move into her personal space and keep going. She smells good. I back her right up against a teak cupboard, pressing my body against hers. She is wondering if I am going to stick my tongue down her throat. I get the impression that would be OK. Her hands are wide, not resisting, evaluating. *Adjust and adapt.* I spin her against my body, my arm round her throat. A classic chokehold. I squeeze.

'Where are we?'

She doesn't answer. All in a day's work. She knows I have no reason to kill her. She needs incentive. The corkscrew is out of my back pocket and in her face. She drops straight to the floor rotating. She moves to scythe my leg but I am ahead of her. She's good but I am better. I stamp down and then my knee is against her neck. A guillotine choke.

She croaks into her wire.

I can see her counting as she stares into my eyes.

'1, 2, 3, 4, 5, 6—'

The corner of the work surface comes up to meet me as I topple forwards.

# CHAPTER 38

I open my eyes. Bars on the ceiling. Narrow truckle bed. Earth on the floor. Some kind of prison. Khaki canvas – military prison. I am in the camp. I sit up and swing my legs over the edge of the cot, tracing my right eyebrow with my fingers. Dried blood. Something hit me hard. The teak countertop swinging up to meet me. Knockout gas. Whatever they used was really fast. I guess it has to be.

*You underestimate everyone around you.*

The canvas flaps and a soldier comes in. Coincidence, or was he watching? Buzz cut, six foot, thirty, no weapons that I can see. He crosses to my cage, pulling keys. The door opens outwards.

He jerks his head.

*On your bike.*

I stay where I am.

*Come and get me, big boy.*

He is not falling for that.

'I can stand here all day,' he says in bad English.

'Where am I?' I try in Russian.

'Taking up space in my holding bay.' His Russian is fluent, way better than his English. 'Come on,' he says, 'you'll miss the show.'

'Is that it? No slap on the wrist?'

The tent jerks up and down as I stand. *Sheesh.* The headache is punishment enough. I put my hand to my eye.

'Caught yourself a right shiner.' He grins.

Even scowling hurts. I roll my shoulders, flex my neck. He holds the flap open for me to pass.

Night-time. How long was I out? The huge sky is filled with stars. We are right in the middle of the military base. I can see the warehouse structure, the landing strip, the watchtower. A military Chinook is coming in to land. We watch its tail end swing, twin dots of red against the starry sky. Cold edges up the backs of my arms.

I shiver in my T-shirt. It must be ten degrees cooler than it was – cold, clean desert air for miles and miles. We walk between lines of tents until we are on a wider stretch, a main avenue full of soldiers dressed like my guard, not a weapon in sight. I feel the glances on the back of my neck, the sidelong stares. Everywhere, everyone is heading our way. The crowd hums with anticipation.

We slow up at the entrance to the warehouse and the press of bodies mills, throngs, bottlenecks pushing to get in. I have spent over a week trying to get into the same room as this man and now finally I am going to do it. The entrance is dark before me and then we break through into the dazzling light of a huge arena.

The place is massive – an aircraft hangar-sized space. The warmth and smell hit me before my eyes have had time to adjust: testosterone, men – the cream of global organised crime – and then above them on the higher seats, rows of khaki. I scan the faces. They are all here. Yakuza, the Bratva, the Mafia, the Triads, the 'Ndrangheta, the Cartels. Organised crime. I am right at its heart.

*Breathe in, breathe out.*

Two soldiers stand in the aisle controlling the crowds, sending people to the back. When they see my guard they wave us through. I am a VIP, not a soldier – I get to take my place on the lower tier. A ringside seat.

*A ringside seat at what?*

Metal barricades circle bare earth and in the centre is a raised podium and a cage. Mesh stairs lead up to the cage door. Thumping, pumping rock music hammers its way along the plank seating, vibrating the metal uprights of the scaffolding. We have had the girlie shows and now it is time for a bit of no-holds-barred violence.

Cold trickles down my back and I shiver in the warm air. How many times have we drilled the dark web looking for kill cages? Looking for millionaires paying to watch a fight to the death. Gladiator conquests.

I search the rows for Ferret. He is near the front, sweating hard, his droopy face sallow. His eyes flick back and forth along the rows. He is with the big boys now. He is terrified. The meatheads sit beside him, relaxed, they are looking forward to the show. They don't have the imagination to be as afraid as they should be. I point them out to my guard. He watches me edge along the metal gantry seating.

Ferret looks up at the disturbance, the shuffling of feet, the sideways swing of knees. He sees Snow White edging her way along and anger joins fear.

'What the hell were you thinking?' He mouths the words over the pumping rock music. 'You are going to get us all killed.'

*He is right.*

'Eye of the Tiger' pierces my skull, drilling like a woodpecker on my eardrums.

'What are they fighting for?' I shout in Ferret's ear.

'A billion dollars.'

*Blimey.*

'And a promotion.'

A billion dollars, a promotion and as much sex and drugs and rock 'n' roll as you can manage. The Prince of Darkness sure knows how to throw a party.

The lights go down and spotlights cut through the darkness, beams of white brilliance rolling around the audience, lighting up faces and then moving on. 'Eye of the Tiger' plays on repeat. The border of earth around the podium, inside the barricades, fills with smoke. Dry ice. The cloying, choking white fumes crawl over the lower tiers filling our lungs. Sirens sound and police lights on the corners of the cage start to rotate, pulsing on and off, flooding the cage with blue neon.

The compère climbs the podium stairs, a microphone in one hand and a bunch of keys in the other. He jams the mic in his armpit, wrestling the padlock. Behind him, two giants stand guard. His words are lost on the rising tide of sound, the thunder of hundreds of heels drumming on wood as the first contender makes his way down the main aisle, bare chest gleaming with oil as the spotlight locks onto him. Huge and tattooed, South American.

Now the spotlight is picking out his opponent on the other side of the arena, another tattooed meathead. Columbia vs. Mexico. They are climbing into the ring, the compère is trying to tell us something about the rules but his words are lost in the wall of sound. He backs out of the ring, slams the gate and locks the padlock.

A klaxon sounds.

The fighters throw themselves at each other with a thud that vibrates through the seating. No circling.

The difference between every MMA bout I have ever watched and this one is the end. The first submission hold is the last. The audience groan.

The padlock is opened and the giants guarding the stairs are in the ring dragging the body out. A smear of blood sweeps down the centre of the grey cage floor.

A new contender is making his way down the aisle accompanied by his own theme tune of pumping rock.

The second bout follows the first – short and to the point. The klaxon screams.

The third starts and then the fourth and I begin to understand. Battles are being fought, arguments are being resolved, grievances are being aired – cage-fighting as a way to settle turf wars. It will go on until there is one man standing and then the Boss will come, to see and be seen, in the ring to congratulate the winner. The only time in the year he is out in the open. The one chance. I scan the crowd. He is here somewhere, watching and waiting, getting ready to come down and slap the victor on the back.

As the seventh bout starts, the Mexican Goliath in the ring is looking unbeatable. The sweat rolls down his blue-green back, his fists shine with blood. He raises his hands in the air and the crowd scream their delight. He holds his hands above his head in a slow hand clap.

*Is it all over?*

Any minute now the Boss will be in the ring congratulating the Mexican. Then he will be gone for another year.

I blink my contacts out onto the palm of my hand and drop them on the floor.

I slide the sole of my heel aside and take out the small plastic sachet. The Go pills. Round red pill: Dex IR, green and white: next generation stanazolol, white caplet: codeine and keratin. The ultimate performance boosters relied on by soldiers facing enemy fire and insuperable odds, the last resort of the desperate. I have only taken them once before in my entire GCHQ career and that was outside a nuclear facility in Siberia.

Even instant-release they will take thirty minutes to work. I don't have thirty minutes. I crush the pills in their plastic with my heel until there is nothing but a mess of powder. I tilt my head back and tip it into my mouth before I can change my mind. I made my decision on a rooftop in Paris.

How good am I hand-to-hand? Pretty good. I was a black belt when I was a teenager and that was before ten years of government training. But, and it pains me to admit it, I am breakable – every rib, an arm, my left wrist twice. Some fingers. Never a leg, thank God. So, I have to be fast and accurate and lucky. One good hit, maybe two in the right place, by someone who knows what they are doing, and it is game over.

I dry retch as the Dex hits my system. I hang my head between my knees, the blood thudding in my ears, my hair grazing the concrete. The air is rank with bodies. I raise my head and the room spins. The neon lights on the corner of the cage flash a dazzling kaleidoscope of colours, the silver bars sparkling in the rotating rays. It is beautiful. The roar of the crowd is drowned out by the pounding in my ears. My heart rate is accelerating. My skin feels too tight for my body. I get to my feet, my eyes raking the crowd. Anger floods me. I hate them all. The victor stands in the cage roaring with blood lust and self-satisfaction. I want to punch his face. I want to knock his teeth through the back of his head.

I run down the makeshift planks and onto the dirt floor of the arena.

*It is not over. It has only just begun.*

# CHAPTER 39

I vault the metal barricades and leap for the gangplank. Behind me Ferret shouts. He is nothing beside the rage building in me. The padlocked gateway hangs open. The giants back down the steps, dragging the previous challenger. His face hangs down, dripping. I push past them into the ring.

The compère looks at me, in jeans and a T-shirt, pulling my hair back into an elastic band. He doesn't get it. I ball my fists trying to contain the surging power. Now he gets it. He shakes his head emphatically. *No way.* The cage sparkles with light, glitter hanging in the air, gilding the victor, crowning his head with silver.

My kick catches the compère at chest height. The bars clang as his head snaps back against them. The crowd screams its disapproval. He slides down the metal, crawls to the gateway on his stomach and pitches through. As he padlocks the door, his face is vicious.

The victor stares. He cannot believe it. He turns to the audience looking for sympathy at this insult to his manhood.

*His mistake.*

He has a hide like an old bull elephant. I could pummel him all day long even with my Dex-fists and I wouldn't knock him out. I know what he needs. I leap for the overhead bars and bring my heel down on the back of his neck. He crumbles in slow motion from the knees and the crowd roars.

The fury spits through me. I turn a 360, my canines bared. The arena looks different from down here. Light surrounded by darkness. I can hardly see the crowd, but I can hear them baying for blood. Anger at this collective insult to the natural order of things. The spotlights shaft pools of brilliance in the darkness. The lights dance against my eyes, messing with my vision. I shake my head against the buzzing in my blood.

The compère is undoing the padlock and then he is back, skirting the edge of the metal, his eyes on me, his face wary. A spotlight shaft picks out a tattooed figure hurling himself down the main aisle towards the arena. A challenger. I hang in the corner, my arms stretched wide behind me, holding back the power. I try to control it, to choke it down, to focus.

*Concentrate.*

Blood hammers round my body.

The challenger is climbing into the cage, huge and muscled, shaven headed and tattooed. He could be the bull elephant's brother. He is not going to get caught the same way. He charges straight for me before the compère is out of the gate. I slide sideways but he grabs at me, fast for such a big man. It will be game over if he gets his arms around me and for the first time since the Dex, I feel the fear.

He takes an elbow to the face, snatching at my arm. His fingers tear at my T-shirt and he is forcing me to my knees. I dip and heave and he goes over my shoulder, landing hard on his back. Triumph burns through me. The blackness descends. I open myself up to it, drawing it around me like a mantle. I kick him hard to the head. Once, twice, three times. His nose streams with blood. I watch Snow White from above, kicking a corpse. Sound returns. I face the crowd screaming my defiance. I throw myself at the cage wall, spitting with anger.

The next challenger is in – fit, athletic, a bare-knuckle boxer. I feel the shock as the blow connects with the side of my face. I spin away but he clips me again and I can taste blood in my mouth.

*Close it out.*

I punch and spin and kick, a sweeper kick to the head. He goes down. I am taking no chances and I punch him once, twice on the canvas.

As the next opponent climbs into the cage, the crowd quieten as if they recognise him and everything goes slow motion. He is Yakuza, wiry and fresh and vaguely familiar. He pulls off his jacket. He is wearing a T-shirt and trousers. He didn't come dressed for cage fighting either. His eyes hold mine. I wipe my face on the shoulder of my T-shirt. The white comes away scarlet, the blow from the bare-knuckle boxer has opened the cut above my eyebrow.

He steps forward. We bow. He steps back.

The cage fight has just turned into a martial arts exhibition match. He stands in *manji gamae*, the preparatory position, ready to strike – one arm raised above and behind the head, the other blocking low in front of the body. I raise my arms in the corresponding block position and we begin.

*Shuto yoko ganmen uchi* – knife-hand strike to head, *shuto jodan uchi uchi* – inside knife-hand to neck.

*Knife-hand meet keri waza*

I launch into the kick strikes: front knee kick, front jump kick, circular knee kick, crescent kick. He is backed up against the bars. I round off the sequence with *nidan tobi geri* – double front kick – and he is down, bouncing off the bars and hitting the deck and I am on him and there is nothing technical about my hand in his hair, my fist in his face.

His sweeper kick saves him, but not before I have broken his nose. The bones are sharp under my fist. Gashes have opened between my knuckles from the force of my punches. I spin away and he is after me. I meet *ura zuki* – the uppercut punch – with a dropping forearm block and feel my weak left wrist crack.

I run for the corner, spin, grab the ceiling bars and kick out. Both feet connect with his face. He flies backwards and is back on his feet with an arcing curve of his lithe body. Blood streams from his nose, his pupils narrow to tiny black dots in his dark eyes, and I read the murder in them. *Close it out.* My swinging head kick has my full weight behind it. There is a snap like gunfire. His body keels over, neck broken.

I drop down from the bars, spitting blood. My hair hangs in my eyes, out of its band.

A man is walking slowly down the wide concrete stairs of the main aisle. He is tall and broad with long legs and a face that haunts my dreams. Silence follows in his wake, it funnels out from the aisle, spreading through the arena like ripples in a pond. The crowd at the front turn and watch.

Shaved head, olive skin, hot. He wears a white T-shirt and black combat trousers, his hands in his pockets. My eyes lock onto his as he stares down at me.

I hang from the walls plotting his movements, holding back the power. I swing my head to clear it and my brain jolts against my skull. I taste the Dex.

He is at the stairs. He says something to the giants and the padlock pops and they are in the ring dragging the body away. He is on the top stair. He is climbing into the cage. He comes towards me. He is as big as I remembered. I am going to plaster him across the bars. I am going to smash my fist through the back of his skull.

*My life for his.*

I hurl myself across the cage.

He grabs my cracked wrist and then he is behind me. Fast. Faster than Erik. Faster than anyone I have ever fought. His arms wrap around me from behind. My wrist stretches across my throat. Even through the Dex, the pain burns like a brand. My good arm is pinned to my body.

*NO.*

I buck and strain in his grip. I stamp and twist and bend.

His chin rests on my hair. I smack my head back, but his face is down by my ear. Stubble scratches my neck.

I bend at the waist, crashing him back against the bars, shifting, trying to gain some purchase against his weight, lowering my shoulder. My arms burn in their sockets, my wrist screams on a frequency just below agony. My legs buckle. Black bubbles pop in my line of sight, a band wraps itself around my chest, squeezing, crushing my ribs. They are cracking one by one as the band crushes them. Blood thunders in my ears. The wooden planks ring with the sound of drumming heels, the thudding keeping time with my heart.

*I can't breathe. I can't see.*

# CHAPTER 40

Cold air hits my face. He hauls me between the tents, fighting and flailing. My wrist is hard across my mouth, my good arm pinned in a half nelson. Nausea hits me with the cold. Hot and cold. My Dex-blood burns. Amphetamine overload. Black bubbles still pop in front of my eyes.

We reach a tent entrance. Two soldiers stand outside like Praetorian Guards. He says something to them and then he is pushing me forward through the tent flap. A commander's tent: military khaki, desk, seating, a central tent post.

The flap lifts and a guard is back with a pair of handcuffs and chains. The Boss snaps a handcuff on my good wrist. He drags me to the central tent post and throws the chain round it and closes the other handcuff. He has left my broken wrist free. He goes over to a drinks cabinet in the corner and pours a drink. An inch of amber. Veins stand out on his forearms as he raises the glass. The white snake on his wrist comes into focus. It's not a tattoo – it's a scar, a wide scar, pale against his tanned skin.

He walks slowly towards me, filling the space. The light is dim, his face in shadow. He looks down at me, a frown on his face. Chest muscles like slabs, six foot five, 220 pounds, slim hips, lean, strong jaw, olive skin, dark eyes, stubble, sharp cheekbones. *Warrior.*

When he finally speaks his voice is appraising, the English tinged with Eastern Europe.

'What have you taken?'

'Dex.'

He nods like he had guessed as much and holds the glass to my lips.

Whiskey fills my mouth. I spray it in his face. He stands stock still while whiskey drips down his forehead, off his chin, down the front of his T-shirt. He walks to a basin in the corner and turns the taps on, reaching over his shoulder and dragging his T-shirt off. Muscles play across his tanned back. Plenty of scars, no tattoos. He balls up the T-shirt, throws it in the corner, drops his head to the sink and splashes his face. He picks up a towel and turns back to me. The light flickers across his chest.

There is a voice from outside.

He goes to the doorway, talks to someone, drying his face.

The voice has gone.

He pours another drink and walks back to me, bare-chested. There is nothing spare about him, not an inch of extra flesh. A line of dark hair trails down his stomach to below the waistband. He takes a swig of whiskey and grips my jaw with one hand. The long fingers are as hard as the arms were. This is what the Marquise meant by charisma. His physical presence is intimidating. Sculpted lips close over mine. Whiskey pours down my throat.

'Swallow,' he says against my mouth.

His bare chest is hot.

Choke or swallow? I swallow.

The whiskey burns my throat.

I swing my good arm around his neck and throw myself backwards with all my weight. Whiskey flies as he crashes over, the chain looping around his neck. I get my knees and then my feet up to his chest and haul on the chain with all the Dex-strength I have left.

*This is it. Shit or bust.*

It is awful, ugly, desperate. Twisting and turning in a puddle of whiskey. My face cowers from his punching, flailing fists. His fingers scrabble at the chain but he can't get purchase. He is so strong. My arms burn. It goes on and on.

There is an almighty crack and all the tension goes. The tent post has cracked. The chain flies free. He is on his hands and knees, choking and heaving great dry retches, pulling the chain off his neck.

He has me at the door, bringing me down with a bone-busting tackle and yanking my arms behind me. Something hits me on the back of the head and it all goes dark.


*Burning feathers.*

I choke and gag, jerking my head away from the fingers under my nose. My body jackknifes. Restraints hold me down. Ankles and wrists. Bands across the body.

The bright lights of an operating theatre.

Hard fingers on my chin, a needle torch above my face. The fingers take the pulse in my neck. They grip my chin, urgent.

'Can you understand?' he asks in French.

Why is he speaking French? For a moment I can't remember. And then I realise. He has found Ferret. He knows I came with Marseille.

*You are going to get us all killed.*

'Who sent you, Snow White? Who do you really work for?'

'I'm sorry,' I whisper in Russian. Tears prick the corner of my eyes. 'It was the Dex. It made me crazy.' I scrabble for his hand. 'Please believe me.' Tears track down my cheeks. He touches them with a fingertip.

'You are a lying bitch.'

'Fuck you.'

'Amo.' His voice snaps the order, his hand, palm up, impatient. His fingers are long. He pulls my right arm straight, a needle rams into the vein.

Amobarbital. The only thing I have no defence against. The thing that Everard used to crack me during training.

ALEX CALLISTER

He smiles as he sees the fear in my eyes.

'You will tell me everything,' he whispers beside my cheek, gentle as a lover. 'Everything. Until there is nothing left but your bare soul.'

Above me the operating lights burn white. The whole room burns with brilliant flame. I see Simon and Everard and Erik. I see the Marquise. I see twelve faces and their scrolling counters.

His face swims above me, a black silhouette against the brilliance. The needle is out but something is left behind. An IV. I tilt my head. Flashes of white dance on the syringe emptying fire into my arm, the liquid floods through my body, burns through my veins.

A defibrillator hovers above my chest, waiting. No one is going to let me have a heart attack. I shove Winter down as far as I can. I shove her below the operating level, below the kernel.

*Run,* I tell her. *Hide.*

*I am Snow White. I am Russian. I am a hitman.*

# CHAPTER 41

Muffled voices, the beep of medical machinery, pain in my wrist. *Still alive.*

I can remember nothing. Nothing about the amobarbital. What have I said? My eyelids flutter and squint. Canvas roof, medical supply boxes – a field hospital, not the operating theatre. I have been moved. There is a new IV in the back of my hand like they have given me a general anaesthetic. I follow the clear tube to the swinging bag above me.

My arms are lying on the bed beside me, pinned to my sides, as if I have been laid out for burial. I flex my left wrist. In a plaster splint. The tap is still in my right elbow. Bands hold me down on the bed. There are murmuring figures in the shadowy space, outside the pool of light. Doctors. Two of them.

I close my eyes and take a deep breath as they approach. I can hear them muttering, checking monitors. One leans down to pull up an eyelid and I snap my head up and smack him full in the face. Something cracks. I haul my good arm free, skinning the back of my forearm, and pull him down on me, circling his throat.

'Untie me,' I hiss.

The other medic stands horrified. Paralysed. I tighten my grip and he hurries to comply. I strain towards the door as he fumbles with the buckles.

I am free.

There is a needle and tube stuck in the back of my hand. I rip at it with my teeth and the tube comes away leaving the metal still embedded. Thick, red blood wells up around it. The pain is so bad I want to close my eyes. Cold shivers of nausea grip me.

The medic is limp against me. I thrust him away from me and he falls to the floor. I swing off the trolley and face the other. I have to take him down. My legs are like jelly. He opens his mouth to shout. My knife-hand strike gets him in the throat and he keels over backwards.

The one with the broken nose is the smaller of the two. I strip off his khaki. My fingers work his buttons in a frenzy, my splint making me clumsy. Why have they put a splint on? My limbs stagger, like waking from deep sleep. Adrenaline is keeping me up. I pull the top and trousers over my hospital gown. His boots are massive.

*I need to go NOW.*

*Never run. It is what they expect.*

I grab a scalpel from the tray and throw myself down behind the medical supply boxes lining the shadowy edge of the tent, forming a long low wall.

I am barely there when there is a flurry of movement outside and the sound of a canvas flap being pushed aside, and the Boss is striding into the tent.

'Son of a bitch.' He swears long and low as he sees the empty bed, the unbuckled straps. His anger and disbelief fill the room. He swirls around and I think for a moment he sees me but then he is looking at the guy in his underwear and realising I am dressed in khaki in a camp full of soldiers, and now he is really mad.

He raps out orders in rapid Russian closing the main gates. Then he is gone and I can hear him issuing orders outside, marshalling an army to find me. Anger rings in every syllable.

Medics pour in through the flap, kneeling by the bodies, bringing round their fallen colleagues.

I wait a long time in the dark. Ten, twenty minutes, maybe more. The longer I can leave it, the better chance I have. Panic fights training. My body shakes with the adrenaline comedown. I am cold, the fear making me clammy. I can hear searching. Pursuers. I bite my hand on the panic.

*Wait. Breathe. Wait.*

I cut a tiny hole in the canvas beside me. Supply tents. Medical. Back-to-back. I cut a long, low slit six inches off the ground and tuck the scalpel down inside my splint. This is it. My head swims as I try to move. I crawl through the gap and flatten out, my heart pumping. The night is cold and dry. Desert dry. I can see an aisle between the tents. It is busy. Soldiers marching back and forth. When they can't find me, they will search the trailer park then they will widen out, open the gates. Either way they will be using their vehicles. I stand up and walk confidently out between the tents to the aisle. Not quick. Not slow. People searching are trained to look for quick furtive movement. Move slowly right beside them and they don't see you.

I hit the main aisle, my legs shaking, and try to get my bearings. The cage is behind me, the main gate in front. I turn right and walk towards the jeep park – not quickly, not slowly. A hundred yards in the open. The watchtower stands over to my right, full beams circling like a lighthouse.

I remember the jeep park from my 360 on top of the trailer. There were more than fifty. I walk down the line. Ten, fifteen, twenty, nothing. The panic is rising in my throat when I see a glint of silver keys in an ignition and I almost sob with relief. I pull open the driver's door and slide behind the wheel.

In the darkness behind me there is the click of someone taking the safety off a handgun.

I put my hands up.

'Turn around.'

He is still, fading into the shadows.

Silence.

'Are you on your own?' I say.

'Yes. Because I know how you think, Snow White,' he says, answering my question before I ask. 'FSB-trained. *Never run.* I knew you were there behind the boxes.'

'If you are going to shoot me, do it.' I spit the words. 'Spare me the monologue.'

'Oh no,' he says, 'you don't get off that lightly.'

'What d'you want? Didn't you get it all from the amobarbital?'

He waves his hand dismissively. 'I don't want information. I want capitulation. I want submission. I want to break you. You think you can turn up here and crash this party?' He puts the safety back on and puts the gun in its holster. 'Do you know what happens when two predators meet?'

'One of them loses?'

'I want your surrender.'

*My surrender.*

My fingers find the tip of the scalpel in the end of my splint. 'And which one of us,' I say, 'is still holding a weapon?'

I hurl it in his face.

It is not one of my throwing blades, but I am an expert.

He is fast. So fast. He throws himself sideways and the blade slices across his forehead, leaving a red line. I have the truck door open and a leg out, but he is lunging across the seats grabbing me and I know it is game over. I couldn't take him when I was juiced up with Dex, I am not doing it now.

'Jesus,' he says, wrapping his arms around me and dragging me into the back. 'You are starting to be a real pain in the neck.'

Iron bands circle me again. I squirm and buck, slamming my head back.

'Give it up,' he says into my hair.

I don't. I fight like my life depends on it.

'Jesus,' he says again.

He throws open the door and drags me out. I hit the ground heavily. It knocks the breath out of me. I lie bruised and panting, nothing left. His legs are beside me. I can feel his boots under my shoulder. He is pulling his belt off. He pushes me onto my front and holds me down with his full body weight then he is belting my wrists behind my back and hauling me to my feet.

'Are you going to walk?' he says.

I stamp back against his shin.

'Fine,' he says, picking me up and throwing me over his shoulder.

'I think I might enjoy this,' he says.

# CHAPTER 42

Darkness and deafening, throbbing, vibrating noise. A helicopter. A helicopter at night. Green lights from the flight deck. The floor throbs under my cheek. The metal vibrates. I am on the floor, my wrists handcuffed behind me and chained to my ankle cuffs.

There are boots behind my neck. I lift my head. I am lying at his feet like a slave girl. Hatred burns white hot inside me. A scowling man sits opposite watching.

The whine of braking metal. We are coming in to land. I roll my head, there is nothing but darkness below and then legs are stepping over me and he is climbing out onto the running board. He leaps and a moment later we are down, the runners grinding on concrete, the blades slowing to a stop.

Arms haul me out and then the tension goes between hands and feet as the chain is released. He holds me against his chest like a baby, my hands still cuffed in the small of my back.

Wind buffets my face. There is another sound in the background, a crash and fall. Waves. Lights bob through the night, flickering and moving in the wind. He strides towards them carrying me.

A stone staircase disappears up a cliff into the night. The bobbing, moving lights are flaming torches in iron holders. I can just make out his face above me.

The last thing I see before the darkness covers me is his head bending over my body.

\*

There is a cool breeze on my face from an open window and a distant crash and swell. It fills the room, an invisible constant. I have been lying listening to it for hours, the crash and swell of water pouring from a great height.

I am in a large white bedroom, flimsy gauzy drapes at the windows. Everything is white – white walls, white ceiling, white-painted wooden floorboards. I can see miles and miles of flickering sea dappled with dark movement. My arms and legs are chained to the four corners of a bed. There is a tap in my elbow connected to an IV. A bag swings above my head. I am dizzy. Morphine. I shift, my wrist throbs. I am wearing a T-shirt, a huge, white, man-sized T-shirt and nothing else. Someone has stripped off my clothes. My ribs are taped. My hands are bandaged from the wrist to the first joint of the fingers. White spatula hands.

Panic sends me upright, but the chains hold me back. Pinning me down. I cannot sit up. Claustrophobia chokes me.

*Adjust and adapt.*

If adrenaline is blood charging round the body, fear is an absence of movement. The fearful dart of the eye when a board creaks, the single solitary thump in your chest, the body rigid, stock still, listening.

*He is sweating you*, I tell Snow White. *Calm the fuck down. Nothing is worse than your own imagination. If he plays it by the book no one will come for hours. Maybe even days.*

*I want to break you.*

My mind throws up all the ways you can break a soldier. A woman soldier. And I swallow the rising panic over and over. My heart races, my skin is damp with sweat. Just because I know what he's doing doesn't mean it isn't working.

I brace myself against the fear. It breaks against me, throwing me onto the rocks. It will smash me to pieces if I let it. My head goes under again and again, drowning in panic.

I practise the techniques I learnt from Everard during inter-rogation training. Mind control. The decompression they teach to submariners facing nine months below the weight of the ocean. I plan half a dozen ways to escape. But when the footsteps come I am still chained to the bed.

Footsteps in the corridor. A long quick stride. Adrenaline thuds. *Showtime.*

The door opens. He is dressed the same as before. The T-shirt sticks to his six-pack. Either he has been working out or he has been punching someone. He leans against the wall and folds his arms. His biceps bulge. A vein beats in his neck.

Tension spirals away from us, circling and winding round the room. I shift as vertical as I can in chains, the sound deafening in the silence. The room is suddenly too small.

'How are you feeling?' he says finally in Russian.

'If you think this is going to break me' – I lift the cuffs – 'we are going to be here a long time.'

He watches me, his mouth curving in a slight smile and I wonder whether he can hear my heart beating, whether he knows how much the brave face is costing me.

'Tell me about the Marquise,' he says.

*What have I said?*

'She hired me to kill you,' I say. It is more or less true. 'You know this.'

'Did she tell you why?'

'You killed her husband.'

He crosses his ankles and looks down at them. 'I put a bullet through his forehead. Do you know what he did to the last person he killed?'

I shrug. 'I can imagine.' I've read the file.

'I let it go on far too long. Men are monsters, but that doesn't mean they have to be monstrous.'

'Says the man who runs a torture website.'

The room fills with his anger. It pushes me back against the pillows. He puts his hands in his pockets and when they come out they are encased in metal. He walks over to the bed.

'Be careful,' he says, stroking an iron-clad knuckle down my cheek.

My heart stops at the look on his face. Then he is gone.


The door opens and the scowling man from the helicopter backs in with a tray. He puts a drink down beside me. I watch him under my lashes. Small, squat, not Russian. Somewhere else. Ex-Soviet Bloc. His personal chemistry gives nothing away.

*Not starving me then.*

'What am I doing here?'

He shrugs.

'Is he going to kill me?'

Nothing.

*Make him talk.*

'How long have you been with him?'

'A long time.'

'And you would do anything for him?'

'I would die for him.'

'I felt like that about my old boss.'

He grunts and his eyes meet mine, but now there is a flicker of a connection.

'What should I call you?' I say.

'Kristophe.'

'What is he like to work for, Kristophe?'

'Demanding.' His face creases. 'No one could do what he does. The power over people, the control. No one else could have calmed the arena.' I can see him in my mind's eye standing in the Cage.

'What was the problem?'

He stares at me.

'*You* were the problem.'

'What did I do?'

Kristophe looks at me as if I am crazy. 'You are an insult. The Cage is sacrosanct. Scores are settled, dominance established. And you wrecked it. He stopped the Cage, he didn't let it run its course. He has *never* stopped the Cage before.' Kristophe shakes his head. 'Kobe are furious.'

*Yakuza.*

'If we had stayed in the camp, you would be dead.'

I sip the drink when he has gone. It is thick and delicious, some kind of protein shake. My mouth burns. My face feels puffy. I put my hands up to my cheeks, but I can't feel anything with my spatula hands. I consider the wrist splint and the bag of morphine, the bed pan beside me, the padded cuffs, the padlocked chains loose enough for me to get comfortable, and it makes me more scared than I have ever been in my life.

# CHAPTER 43

It is morning. Still alive. Gulls scream overhead. The sea is calm with dancing white flecks, mesmerising. Something catches my eye in the bay, a discordant note, something driving through the water, purposeful against the randomness of the waves. I sit up in bed as far as I can, trying to see. Broad shoulders angle out of the water, carving round and down in a powerful front crawl. The swimmer disappears out the left of my limited view and a few minutes later he crosses my line of sight again. Right to left. He is back where he started. I am on an island.

I watch the speed and strength. Strong swimmer. Twenty minutes. About a mile around. A really small island.

The door opens and Kristophe enters carrying a tray and puts it on the bed. Its little feet tent my legs.

'Is that him out in the bay?'

Kristophe goes to the window and peers out. He stills as he catches sight of the swimmer and his body relaxes. He puts his hands on the windowsill.

'Yes,' he says.

'He's a very strong swimmer.'

'Yes.'

'Has he swum all the way around?'

'Probably. He doesn't like doing nothing.'

I clank my chains. 'I know the feeling.'

Kristophe's eyes meet mine and his lips twitch. It is not a laugh, it is not even a smile really, but it is something.

The door slams behind him. He stomps off down the corridor.

I lift the lid. I cannot believe it. Eggs and bacon. I am so grateful my eyes burn. My mouth aches as I chew.

Footsteps in the corridor. I recognise the tread. The long quick stride. The door opens. Long trunks dripping wet, bare chest, towel round the neck.

'I know what you are doing,' I say.

'And what is that?'

'Softening me up. I spent two weeks in the hold of a pirate ship once. Can't say it softened me.'

'Were you chained?'

'Yes. And not like this Fifty-Shades set up.' I pull at the padded cuffs, wave at the billowing drapes.

'Fifty Shades? As in total power exchange? Sex games?' His eyebrows raise. He rubs a hand over his stubble. He hasn't shaved.

My eyes find his.

'Relax,' he says. 'If I wanted to fuck you I would have done it by now. You look like a squashed peach.'

'Thanks.'

'And you're not my type. I prefer my women compliant.'

'Me too.'

'Yeah, I saw the footage from the trailer park.'

*Great.*

'Did you escape from the pirate ship?' he asks when I don't reply.

I shake my head. 'My boss rescued me.'

'And then you went rogue. Tell me about the life of a professional hitwoman.'

'No.'

He looks at me from under his black brows. 'Play nice.'

'Why?'

His eyebrows raise again.

'Didn't you get enough of my backstory when I was under?' Now I just sound sulky.

'Tell me what you were like as a child then.'

He sits down on the end of the bed, folds his arms and waits. Water beads on his tanned skin. There is not an inch of fat on him. And there is something in his voice. I don't know if it is the note of command, or the barely contained threat, but I know not to push it.

So I tell him about my childhood. The coldness in the dormitory. The bitter night chill, no heating and one thin blanket per child. The desperate jockey and trade for a thick wool one. The dirty daily fights, the miserable physical endurance of the hungry body, tired and worn from nights of fearful wakefulness. The cold the body never shook off. The core staying solid as a block of ice. Stiff and unbending, like a child trying to dress without uncovering.

'I remember the cold,' he says. 'The cold of a tired skinny body. So cold you would do literally anything to get warm.'

I tell him about the windows, mansards set into the steep pitch, too high to see out of. I tell him about the small hole rimmed with grey mould, wet like an open mouth. Lying on ice-cold sheets, night after night, watching the play of wet and light, the hole seemed to speak. The wind, as it hit the side of that window, made a buffeting, slithering sound. I close my eyes, crawling back into myself, my mind fleeing the memories.

He listens to me in silence, leaning up against the bed post, and when I falter his face tells me to carry on, that he is listening, that he understands, that he wants to know more.

I tell him about waiting all day, choking with excitement at being taken out of school by a distant uncle and aunt. Relatives of my own. The twenty minutes of brittle, bright chatter then their sidelong glances at their watches, the polite excuses, the relieved jollity to be heading back, a chore nearly done.

I tell him about Lord of the Flies who ruled. Sink or swim.

I tell him about the endless sobbing. I tell him about the night someone lost the daily, dirty survival game. The desperate buck and kick. The pleading. The humiliation. The noise she made as she fell, scrabbling and scrabbling against the tiles, still begging. *She was always talking about climbing on the roof*, they said afterwards. And I never said anything.

I tell him about adolescence, about the adrenaline junkie on a self-destructive path. I tell him about the service and Erik: father, brother, punchbag. In my version he is FSB, but the essentials are the same. The training, the skill set. I tell him more than I have ever told anyone, until the sun is shining straight in the windows and it is afternoon and I am in the open, running across virgin territory, spilling my guts.

'I remember the fear too,' he says. 'The fear and the hunger and the cold.' He is still sitting on the end of the bed, leaning against the bed post in a shaft of sun. His face is dark with his back to the window.

'Why am I still alive?'

'I have my reasons.'

I watch his shadowed face. It is utterly unreadable. A vein pulses in his neck. A tell.

'Can I get up?' I hold up my cuffs.

He stares.

'Come on. We both know you can take me. What am I going to do high as a kite? Let me use the bathroom.'

He leans over as he unbuckles me. Skin and sea and sweat. This close I can see his eyes are flecked with gold. Tiger's eyes. My head swims.

'What?' he says beside my cheek.

I shake my head. 'You have the most amazing eyes.'

'That is the morphine talking,' he says as he hauls me up. 'Mess with me now and you are in trouble,' and I know he means it.

I hang my legs over the bed onto the white painted floorboards. My knees buckle as I try to stand. The T-shirt skims the top of my thighs. He watches for a moment then he scoops me up like a baby, his arm under my bare legs, crosses to the door in the corner and opens it with his shoulder.

A bathroom. He plonks me down on a chair in the corner.

He leaves the door ajar.

Basin, toilet, simple stone shower in the corner. Elegant but not luxurious. No mirror.

I finger the scar above my eyebrow. How bad is my face?

*You look like a squashed peach.*

I try to stand but my legs buckle again. I settle for crawling around the room exploring. A cupboard in the corner holds soap and toilet paper. No potential weapons.

'You have a lot of women back here?'

His reply is far away and then he is standing right outside the door.

'I don't bring women here,' he says. 'If you care, your enemies have all the leverage they need.'

I nod on my side of the door. It is why GCHQ recruits orphans like me. 'D'you have a lot of enemies?'

'You have no idea.'

*Good.*

'I'm surprised you didn't try that first,' he says.

'What?'

'The soft approach.'

'I expected to take you in the Cage.'

'Really?' He sounds more surprised than annoyed. 'But in my tent. The chain. It didn't exactly play to your strengths. It is hard to throttle someone.'

Great, I am being given pointers by my victim.

'You're wondering why I didn't try seduction.'

'Yes.'

'Never crossed my mind.'

The door opens. He looks down at me on the floor. 'Really?'

'No amount of money would be worth it.'

He slams the door.

I crawl to the basin, climb up onto my knees and turn the tap. My knuckles burn. A brand new toothbrush and toothpaste stand in a holder. I am so grateful I don't stop to wonder if it is a good idea. My spatula hands are clumsy, the bandages on my right hand get soaked, toothpaste burns my mouth.

I spit out into the basin. The foam is streaked with blood. Nausea rises, it sweeps up my face bringing the cold with it. Saliva rushes into my mouth. I rest my forehead against the white china edge of the basin and he is back, lifting me under the arms.



Late afternoon he comes again. This time we talk about world politics and regime change. About the passage of money and global trade. He moves around the room as he talks, his hands expressive and I catch a glimpse of the orator that calmed the Cage.

'Technology changes everything,' he says. 'The world is tiny now. Satellites can see what you are having for breakfast. You can kill someone from a mile away. And man has yet to develop the emotional maturity to handle this new sophistication. The internet forced a thousand years of development into ten years. It develops, magnifies, enhances all the worst parts of human nature. And what do you do about that? You control it. Man is a pack animal, he responds to strength and order, there is a natural hierarchy. In many parts of the globe it still takes a dictator to bring peace. Did Iraq function better once Saddam Hussein fell? Did Libya? Law and order are an illusion.'

'Surely democracy is the ultimate goal?'

He looks at me as if I am mad, indulging in some kind of existential debate. 'What is democracy? Electorates are easily manipulated. Justice is easily bought.' He sounds weary and disillusioned, as if his role is not one he has sought. 'Every genera- tion makes mistakes. Is *allowed* to make mistakes. Not this one.

Technology changed that. If we make a mistake, we could wipe out the whole planet. And then where is democracy?'

I am silent.

'I don't know,' I say finally.

I have said the right thing.

'How old are you?' I wonder aloud.

He is surprised and suddenly the question seems strange, too personal, too intimate, and I wish I hadn't spoken. He is sitting on the end of the bed again leaning up against the bedpost beside the padlock.

'I don't know,' he says. 'Thirty-seven maybe. Why do you ask?'

I shrug because I don't want to say I spent hours and hours trying to guess his age.

'Tell me about the twelve men you beat to death with your fists,' I say.

He stares at me then he scowls.

'I think you are forgetting who the captive is here, Snow White.'

The rejection is whip sharp. He walks out and the room rings with the sudden silence. I want to tell him I am sorry. I want to beg him to come back. I want to grovel.

I watch the waves until the light fades to twilight and then to dark and I can only hear the sound of the sea breaking against the jetty.

*He is sweating you,* my training says. *Capture bonding. Trust and then rejection. Textbook.*

It doesn't help.

# CHAPTER 44

The next day, he comes and I am so grateful it chokes me. His long fingers hold my hair back from my forehead while he considers the scar above my eye. He has a matching line from the scalpel. A deep, dark cut.

He takes down the IV drip, leaving the tap in my arm. He unwinds the bandages on my spatula hands. There are butterfly plasters over the battered knuckles. I flex my fingers. I am dependent and vulnerable and obscenely grateful.

'Where did you learn your medicine?' I ask.

He shrugs. 'Here and there. All over. Gunshots, trauma, broken bones in the field. I go a lot of places where there is no decent medicine. Half the time it is just pain control.' He sighs. 'The world is full of people dying with no relief thanks to the crack down on opium. We develop it all the time in our labs. Next-generation morphine derivative.'

He tells me about the opium trade, how it was decimated by the war in Afghanistan and how, when a new world order emerged, it became international and organised, the Triads, the Tongs, the Russian mafia all coordinating in the free passage of narcotics around the globe. Opium flowing one way along the Golden Crescent, and refined product the other.

His mood is reflective, almost melancholy.

'Haven't you got more important things you should be doing?'

'Like what?'

*Running the world.*

'I don't know.' I shrug. 'Prince of Darkness shit.'

'Prince of Darkness?' He shakes his head.

'I guess even you probably have enough money by now.'

'You think it is about the money?'

I look at him standing by the window in his habitual T-shirt and dark trousers, his hands in his pockets now the first aid is done.

'Before I met you, I would have said it was all about the money,' I reply.

'And now?'

'Now I would say it was all about control.' My shoulders shrug again and my chains rattle, making my point for me. 'Tell me about Firestorm.'

'What about it? Any improvements you would like to suggest?'

*Jesus.*

'Did you create it?'

'I killed the man who created it.'

'Tell me about Slashstorm.'

His face is in shadow. 'Slashstorm is over.'

'Over?'

*I don't believe it.*

'Slashstorm is finished,' he says. 'You have my word.' He scowls when I say nothing. 'Do you think I am behind Slashstorm?'

'Isn't it an offshoot of Firestorm? It must be very lucrative.' I try to get into his mindset. 'Like those old TV contests. Money from every vote then a second round from the viewing figures.'

'Let me ask you a question.' His poker face is on but his voice is hard. 'How many child contracts are there on Firestorm?'

'I don't do under 21s. Not many, I guess.'

'Try again.'

'None?'

'Yeah. None.'

He looks at me like *I'm* the monster, then he walks out.

# CHAPTER 45

I stare out at the sea, turning his words over and over. There was no mistaking his reaction. The mention of Slashstorm made the Prince of Darkness angry. And then there was Dominique St Vire.

*I let it go far too long. Men are monsters but that doesn't mean they have to be monstrous.*

It makes me wonder. Was he administering rough justice? The Prince of Darkness as dark policeman? I turn the idea over. And what about John J. Traynor? How could that have been rough justice?

*You have my word. Slashstorm is finished.*

I cannot explain it even to myself, but hearing the words from this man makes the huge knot in my gut dissolve. The surge of panic that comes every time I think of Slashstorm is gone. If he says it is finished, then it is finished. The relief is like a tidal wave.

That afternoon when Kristophe comes, he brings two plates. My heart rate accelerates waiting for him to arrive and I can't decide if it is Stockholm syndrome at work or Lima, its reverse.

What does the world's richest man eat? Steak. Like all men. It is really good. Salad, chips.

'Who does the cooking?' I ask when he arrives.

'Kristophe.'

'No chef?'

He shakes his head. 'Not here.'

And I wonder, not for the first time, who else is on this island and what I am doing here.

'Do you always eat this much?' He is smiling. He approves.

'Yeah. Especially when I don't know where my next meal is coming from.' I am about to tell him Simon calls it carb-loading but I stop myself. The corners of his eyes crinkle, I notice, when he is amused. His sculpted mouth doesn't move but his eyes crinkle. I can't believe I ever thought him hard to read. He has a thousand poker tells.

'In my experience, women pick at their plates and then eat less than budgies.'

'You are probably dating supermodels.'

'I guess.'

'There you go. You don't eat with normal women.'

Now he is laughing and his whole face lights up.

'I wouldn't call you normal,' he says.

He gets up and stacks our plates on the tray and the action is so domestic my head reels.


He tells me about the four main Yakuza families, the biggest based in Kobe. He tells me about the many different branches of the Mafia and the Camorra and the inter-relationships and the cooperation. He tells me about Los Zetas and about MS-13 – Mara Salvatrucha, violent and tattooed, disorganised and cruel. The regional heads focused on their subjugation and integration. The trouble they cause.

I watch him speak, watch the play of emotions across the hard lines of his face.

'And what happens if they can't be integrated?'

He shakes his head in a gesture which means 'game over'.

'Tell me about the twelve men you beat to death.'

He scowls. I am crossing the line. He looks at me under his brows. His tiger eyes are dark. He puts his hands in the pockets of his black trousers and when they come out they are encased in metal again. My throat dries at the expression on his face. He crosses to the bed. I want to cringe, to grovel, to flatten myself on the mattress. Instead I sit up, staring him down.

'They took something from me.'

'What?'

'A child.'

'You have kids?'

He shakes his head.

'A kidnapping? Did you get them back?'

He nods, but the look is wary.

I stretch out a cuffed hand. 'Can I see?'

He stares at me. He wasn't expecting this. No one has ever asked this before.

He slips the rings off the knuckles of his right hand and holds them out. His fingers brush mine. My chains are loose enough that I can bring my hands together. The rings slip through my grasp onto the bed.

'So heavy.' I turn the warm metal over and over in my hands. I slip them on my knuckles and consider. They are ludicrously massive. Like a child wearing grown up shoes. I hand them back. 'I would like to try a pair,' I say simply.

He turns them over in his hands and I know I have crossed some kind of Rubicon.

I reach out and touch the white skin around his wrist with the tip of one finger. 'Did you do that to yourself?'

Close up, I can see it is an uneven, jagged scar, years old.

He turns away. 'Yes.'

'When you were a child?'

'Yes.'

I know what caused it now, a manacle that dug too far into the skin. He must have cut it out himself.

'I killed for the first time that night,' he says, staring out of the window.

My throat is dry as I swallow. 'How old were you?'

He shrugs, shaking his head, still turned away from me, and I understand that it's not that he won't tell me, he just doesn't know.


When I wake, he is standing by the bed looking down at me.

'Were you watching me sleep?'

He smiles.

'Look, I appreciate this whole Bluebeard show you have going – island, castle, billowing drapes, maiden chained to bed – but what am I really doing here?'

'Maiden?'

'Maiden.' I am firm.

'I'm the bad guy here?' He shakes his head. 'I'd feel pretty sorry for Bluebeard with you in his castle.'

'Damn right. I would grind his bones to dust. And spit on them.'

'And then scatter them to the ends of the earth?'

'Probably.'

'*You*, a maiden? I saw the trailer park footage, remember? Your face relaxes when you are about to come – did you know that?'

*Marvellous.*

'That is what a woman looks like when she is about to orgasm,' I say patiently. 'It may be a new look for you.'

He chokes and his tiger eyes burn. 'Don't push your luck,' he says. 'Your ribs aren't up to it.'

I would like to fold my arms but there isn't enough give in the chains. I narrow my eyes at him. 'How many times have you watched it?'

'I don't know. A couple. Maybe five.'

I raise my eyebrows.

'Call it ten.'

*Jesus.*

'It's kind of quick,' he says. As if that is an explanation.

'Well, you know…'

'Yes?' He looks amused.

'This is beside the point.'

'There was a point?'

'What the hell am I doing here?'

'Wait,' he says, going to the door.

'Yeah. Chains. Padlocks. Kinda hard not to!' I shout at the closing door.


He is back with a folder.

I look down at it.

'What's this?'

'A monster. You need reminding what real monsters look like.'

I open the folder. My heart skips. A face stares up at me. Winter's face. It is my GCHQ file.

'Who is this?'

'A job. This is what you are doing here.'

I glance down at the file. 'A job? Why do you need me? Who is she? I would have thought you have thousands of people who could deal with this.'

'So would I.' He turns to watch the sea. 'A couple of weeks ago she caught up with me. I thought she meant to take me down, but I was wrong. She has a photographic memory. A very special skill set. It makes her uniquely dangerous. She is locked up in a titanium fortress five-hundred feet below ground level looking at faces trying to identify me. I'm sure you appreciate the implications if she finds me.'

Silence.

'So, what have you tried so far?' My heart is beating so hard and so fast I can't believe he can't hear it.

'I have sent every asset I have in GCHQ. None of them have come back.'

'Really? She doesn't look very dangerous.'

'I even sent my brother. He couldn't get near her. She was too well guarded. Locked up in the GCHQ fortress.'

*Brother? There are two of you?*

'The contract out on her is 100 million dollars. Deal with her and you can name your price.'

I stare.

'Set a woman to catch a woman. You will succeed where everyone else has failed. I know you will find a way.'

*Oh the irony.*

I swallow. 'Can I think about it?'

He looks at me under his black brows. The vein throbs in his throat. His poker tell. 'Don't think too long. Or I might go back to my original plan.'

'Which was?'

'Breaking you.'

I put my hands up to my head. My hair is hard and matted, stiff like dreadlocks. 'Dreadlocks,' he says, reading my mind.

He disappears out of the room and a moment later he is back with an electric shaver in his hand.

I stare. 'You aren't going to use that on *me*?'

He rubs his hand over the back of his head. 'Not like this.'

I study the line of his stubble. There is a clear clean line where the hair meets the olive skin of his neck. He hasn't shaved for a couple of days. The sideburns are more pronounced, the line across his upper lip makes him look like a pirate.

I eye the shaver. 'Kinda disappointing.'

He raises his eyebrows.

'I thought you would use a cutlass for shaving.'

He rolls his eyes. 'You have some very strange ideas.'

He gets a towel from the bathroom and sits me between his legs on the floor with the towel round my shoulders, then his long fingers are in my scalp. The shaver buzzes and I can feel matted clumps of Snow White's hair falling onto my shoulders. I lean back against his warm legs and close my eyes. It is actually relaxing. A weird lassitude creeps over me.

He has stopped, his warm fingers rest each side of my neck. I shiver, the skin feels sensitive. I put my hand up. My hair curls in wisps round my ears, my fingers brush his. He scoops the corners of the towel together and straightens up. He disappears into the bathroom. Then he is back, standing in the doorway considering his handiwork.

'It suits you,' he says. 'It makes you look elfin.' He uses the English word and it surprises me that he knows it.

I must have pulled a face because he laughs.

I am on the floor, the perfect place for a supplicant.

'Can I get up?' I ask him. 'This is an island, right?' I smile up at him. 'I've got nowhere to go if you are worried about me skipping off.'

He looks at me thoughtfully and I can feel the conflict in him. 'I guess the Dex is out of your system.'

'Please.' Even I know how to plead when I have to.

'OK.'

'YES!' I pump the air.

'You can go anywhere except the locked room in the hall.'

'You have a locked room? I knew it. Bluebeard.'

He laughs. 'You have no idea what horrors lurk in there.'

I look around. 'Can I have my clothes?'

'No.'

'No?'

'You can walk around in my T-shirt, like installation art.'

'What about underwear?'

'No.'

*Bastard.*

'Actually, I have no problem with nudity.'

'Why would you?' he says.

# CHAPTER 46

After he has gone, I wait a bit then I try the door. I didn't expect it to be locked and yet it is still a surprise when it opens. The corridor is pale white with views onto a courtyard on one side and bedroom doors on the other. It is deserted. Wooden floorboards. I have been listening to footsteps on these boards for what feels like days. It is weird to see them in reality.

The room next door is just like mine. The bedding is thrown back. I pick the pillow up and hold it to my face. My head swims with the hit of him. This is his room. I search the bathroom first. No mirror, no razor. I turn my attention to the drawers: T-shirts, trousers. No underwear. Weird. All the money in the world and this is what he spends it on? And it occurs to me, I am wearing his T-shirt because he had nothing else. All that time I spent reading something sinister into it. It is as simple as that. The other thing that occurs to me is I am no longer afraid. The monster eats steak and likes swimming, his eyes crinkle when he is amused. He listens. More than anyone has ever listened. Getting to know the man, I have forgotten the monster.

The rest of the bedrooms are unoccupied. I drift down the corridor, listening. Silence. The screech of gulls, the crash of the sea and nothing else. Stone stairs curve round in an elegant arc of iron filigree bannisters. It reminds me of the Hôtel de Condé and the Marquise. On the half landing, I peer at the hallway below. A black-and-white tiled floor. A closed door.

*The locked room.*

From here I can see all the way out through the wide, wooden front door, through the semi-circle of window above it, to a jetty and a speedboat and the sea beyond. I have a memory of stone steps and flaming torches and a long climb. Is it a memory or was it a dream?

I creep down the stairs, silent on my bare feet, breathing and listening. Where is he? He is somewhere watching me. Cat and mouse. I stand in the shadow of the front door looking down at the stone steps carved into the cliff face, at the small concrete harbour, just big enough to land a helicopter.

I turn back to the house. Two grand doors lead from the hallway, their brass handles golden. The first door opens onto a drawing room with French doors and a balcony overlooking the sea. An old-fashioned chandelier hangs from a *trompe l'oeil* ceiling rose.

A door stands ajar at the end of the room. It swings open under my fingers – a music room with a frieze of mandolins and an upright piano against one wall. The room is on the corner, its windows stand wide. I touch a piano key. The sound is violent in the silence, discordant. Sea breezes are no good for piano strings.

I retrace my steps to the hallway, close the door softly behind me and stand listening. It feels like something. Not a trap. Nothing sinister, something from childhood, a narrative that I have heard play out a thousand times before.

I open the second door. A bright yellow room, part breakfast room, part kitchen. French doors lead to the courtyard at the back. An entire wall is taken up by a stone fireplace, the grate at waist height. A huge black metal kettle sits on a wooden table with a marble top. In the corner, weird and incongruous, a Wega industrial coffee machine. Copper pans hang on the walls. I take one down and weigh it in my hands. Heavy and unsubtle. A sideboard topped with the same white marble is laden with glass bowls of fruit: nectarines, grapes, apples and pears. I bite into a yellow pear and the juice spills, syrup sweet, down my chin. I haul open the drawers. No knives.

The sunny courtyard is as deserted as the house. I breathe, slowly tasting the air: coffee, ash from the fireplace, roast meat, pear, sea.

A flight of rough stone stairs leads down to the basement. There is a green twilight in the depths and the warm cotton smell of laundry. The walls are whitewashed. It is the least threatening basement I have ever been in. I peer in the first door on the right of the stairs. A laundry: three great industrial machines and four blue cylinders. A wide tunnel stretches the whole length of the house and ends in a huge open door to the outside. It is the source of the soft twilight of the basement level. The sweet smell of over-ripe fruit hangs in the cool, still air. Through the open door I see an old mangle on its side, wild geraniums spilling over it. This is the domestic side of the house: washing lines, piles of logs, two wheelbarrows upside down and stacked against the wall.

Stone stairs lead up to the courtyard. I climb slowly, my palms flat to the warm stone. At the top I lay my head against the sharp corner of the building and tilt my head to feel the breeze on my face. I know what it reminds me of, that narrative I've heard play out a thousand times before – it reminds me of a fairy story.

*Where are all the mirrors?*

The gravel crunches under my feet. I go back into the house, through the kitchen French doors and into the drawing room, suspicion making me fast. Above the mantelpiece the paint is darker, with a pattern around the edge from an elaborate frame. Where is the mirror?

He stands in the open door, black against the brilliant light.

'What do you think?' he says.

I am tempted to give him a smart answer but whether it is the traces of morphine in my system or the gracious old house, I don't. 'It is beautiful,' I say. 'Unexpected.'

His hard, aquiline face lights up, softens. His tiger eyes are black with his back to the light.

'I'm going to show you my favourite place.'

He takes me down the stone stairs. Through the soft twilight of the basement.

*Where are you taking me, Bluebeard?*

We come out by the old mangle with the geraniums, beside the wood pile. There is an axe sticking out of the stump, I didn't notice it before. The sea is framed like a perfect picture between the trees. It is beautiful and quiet.

He sits down and pats the bench beside him. 'This is my favourite place,' he says. 'And of all my homes, this is my favourite. I never let anyone come here.'

'So, this is your favourite place in all the world?' I say, but I am not listening because I am measuring the distance to the axe. Fifteen feet.

'Sit down and talk to me.' He stretches his long legs out.

I wander to the right, picking at my splint.

'I want to make you an offer.'

'Yeah? I'm not that kind of girl.' I laugh because I know that's not what he means.

'Get rid of my problem in London and come and work for me.'

'And do what?' The shock has me still and staring.

'Whatever you like. I know how you handled the Marseille shipment. I saw you in the cage. Ex-FSB, you are probably weapons competent.'

*That is one way of putting it.*

'How many Dominique St Vires are there in the world? You could troubleshoot. Clean the place up, raise standards. Like I said, men are monsters but that doesn't mean they have to be monstrous.'

*Leave that to the women.*

I close the final few feet, the handle of the axe slides out easily and I turn and throw it in his face. Point-blank range.

Mid-air, it comes apart into two clean pieces. The head falls short but the shaft hits the wall beside his ear. A perfect shot. It would have been a perfect shot.

He hasn't moved a muscle.

My guts curdle at the look on his face. For a split second I am frozen. I can see every golden fleck in his dark eyes.

*Fight or flight?*

Sometimes you have to run. I turn and run for my life. Into the house, back up the stairs and out through the front door, my breath coming in great gulps. I hurtle down the cliff stairs, the gravel slipping under my bare feet, expecting at any moment to hear the heavy footsteps and feel the iron bands closing around me.

I throw myself into the twin-engine powerboat. My knuckles burn as I turn the key in the ignition – the cuts have opened up again. And I am gone.

I look back at the island to see where the pursuit is. Nothing. I turn back to the wheel and max the speed. Sea air blows in my face. I turn again and catch the glint of glass. Binoculars. It reminds me of standing on the Airstream. Someone on the first floor is watching me through field glasses.

Five minutes later, the engine dies.

The dials are all reading normal but there's nothing normal about this. It has been set up to fail. Enough petrol to get me away and then die. The axe had been set up to fail. There is a reason I didn't notice it the first time. It wasn't there.

I look around me at waves as far as the eye can see. I am not good with water. Will he make me walk the plank? I lie down in the bottom of the boat.

It is not long before I hear the sound of another speedboat. It pulls up alongside. He doesn't say a word as I climb across the boats. As soon as I am in, he opens the throttle and we roar back. At the quay he jerks his head for me to get out, his expression black. I step out awkwardly onto the hot stone and he roars off. He has gone to get the other boat.

I walk back up the stone stairs and into the house and up to my room to wait.

A few minutes later a long stride sounds in the corridor and he comes in. I brace myself, heart pounding, back to the wall. He gestures to the bed. His face is grim. I stand in my T-shirt with my bare legs and bare feet set to refuse.

'Get on the bed.' His voice is full of menace.

Hairs stand up on the nape of my neck. There is no way this can end well. I will lose. Painfully. I climb back on the bed and he buckles me down. Hot tears of humiliation prick the corners of my eyes. He yanks the straps on the cuffs. They bite into my wrists.

'That was really stupid,' he says at the door, contempt on his face.

He is right. Fucking stupid.

The door slams behind him.

# CHAPTER 47

Hours go by. I lie in the bed watching the curtains billow, the breeze chill on my wet cheeks, wondering if it is my last hour on earth. Wondering what I can say to excuse myself. Wondering why he doesn't come.

Maybe no one will ever come again. Maybe he will leave me chained here to die.

*You are too hasty, too reckless, too self-confident. Arrogance makes you underestimate everyone around you.*

A motorboat roars across the bay. It slows approaching the jetty. I strain to catch sight of it but it has disappeared from view. Footsteps climb the cliff stairs. The murmur of voices. Many sets of footsteps and now I am afraid. Someone else is coming to deal with me.

When the door opens, I cringe, but it is Kristophe with a tray. He puts it down by the bed and starts to unload it.

'You're not starving me to death then?'

Kristophe is awkward, uncomfortable in my presence.

'What will happen to me, Kristophe?'

He shakes his head. 'He is mad.'

*Yeah.*

'Who's here?'

'Yakuza.'

*This cannot be good.*

'I thought he didn't bring people here?'

'He doesn't normally. They are here for you.'

*The final cage fight.*

'To kill me?'

'Maybe.' He shrugs. 'It is not as simple as that. Here, you are under his protection. They are on his ground. They owe him allegiance. But they want revenge.' He picks up the tray. 'This is politics. He has to give them a good reason to spare you. He can bargain for your life.'

'Or not.'

He inclines his head. 'There is a blood price. Someone must pay it.'

The fear trickles down my spine. Cold between my breasts. What possible reason can I give him to bargain for my life?

'Kristophe,' I say quickly, the words tumbling out in my haste. 'Tell him I will do what he wants. I will deal with this woman in London he seems to think is such a threat.'

'She is a threat,' Kristophe says. 'The worst threat he has ever faced.'

'Go,' I say. 'Go and tell him.'

The door closes behind him and I hear him move off down the corridor. I start to count seconds and then minutes. My nerves are stretched taut. Finally, I hear footsteps in the corridor. I stare towards the door.

Kristophe.

His scowl is back.

'They want to see you.'

I shrink against the bed.

'Why?'

'He has asked them to spare you. He has said he has you under control, that you are no threat, that he has a use for you.'

My body sags in relief.

'You need to prove it.'

I understand. I hold up my cuffs. 'Unlock me. I will come down and do exactly what is needed to convince them.' I put the full

force of Snow White's stare into play. 'I don't know why he would
do this after I threw an axe in his face, but I give you my word. I
will do nothing to harm him. I will do what is needed to convince
them, then I will come back up here and put the cuffs on myself.'

He stares at me.

'Kristophe,' I say. 'Please. Help me to help him.'

He unbuckles me.

'You have my word,' I say.


I run lightly down the stairs in my T-shirt. The front door is still open,
the breeze blows cool on my bare legs. I stop in the doorway to the
drawing room and a roomful of Japanese faces turn my way. Three
seated, four standing. The three seated are older. The man facing the
door must be in his seventies. My heart thumps as I realise who it is.

Cigarette smoke fills the air. Everyone is scowling. A long blade
rests on the table. A long Japanese knife. The kind you might use
for sushi or taking someone's skin off.

The Prince of Darkness stands listening. Even silent, he dominates the room. He turns and I read the message in his dark eyes.
*Now is not the time to be stupid.*

Whatever else he is going to do with me, he is not handing
me over to Yakuza. Relief washes over me. I step forward but
the force of his will stops me and I stand unsure, my bare legs
strangely vulnerable.

He laughs, saying something in Japanese, waving his hand in
my direction.

Movement ripples round the room. Some smiles. Some nods.
*What has he said?* The mood has changed. His hands are in his
pockets as he walks over, relaxed. He puts his arm around my waist.

Now I get it.

They think he is screwing me. They think I just got out of
his bed.

*She's no threat, she's joined my harem.*

The room laughs as it breathes out, a collective exhale as the tension abates. It chokes me that I have to pretend to be his plaything and that they would believe it. I glance around the room, measuring the distance to the knife. Could I take them all?

He laces his fingers through mine, crushing my hand. *Put up with it or die. Right here, right now.*

The atmosphere has changed. Smiles and nods. This is a story everyone can buy. This is acceptable. Even plausible. *Why kill her when I can screw her?* Humiliation and shame, Japanese erotic staples. Only the old man is still scowling. His narrowed eyes watch me, roving over the pair of us, reading the body language.

*He doesn't believe it.*

He says two words and I feel the challenge in the air, in the stiffening in the body against mine. The mood has turned ugly with two words. Has he called him a liar?

The room falls silent. Waiting.

*Waiting for what?*

The Prince of Darkness looks down at me, anger on his face. He hadn't bargained on this. He reaches a decision. He pulls my arms behind my back, holding my wrists in one hand. Then he bends his head and his lips touch mine.

*Now is not the time to be stupid.*

He is hot through the thin T-shirt. I stand rigid in his hold, trying to let him know I understand. Then he is kissing me and I taste him against my tongue and a surge of heat sweeps up my body swamping my senses, buckling my knees. I press against him and he drops my wrists. My good hand circles his neck as the kiss deepens. The iron bands curve round me, hands move in my hair. My fingers slide up his back, under his T-shirt feeling the hot silky skin, tracing his spine, pulling him to me. Blood pounds in my ears. The roaring blocks everything but his hard body and his tongue and his mouth kissing mine like both our lives depend on it.

Suddenly he pushes back and I open my eyes. He is angry. The room spins. All around us laughing faces whistle and catcall, drumming their heels with delight and the old man is smiling and nodding and smiling and nodding like we have just told him we are going to make him a grandparent.

Now he believes.

# CHAPTER 48

The room is chill and grey. I lie down and Kristophe helps me with the buckles.

'Please find out what is happening,' I beg.

Kristophe shakes his head. *You deserve nothing.*

I wait and wait in my room, padlocked down, but nobody comes.

I wake to the clink of china, the rattle of crockery on a tray. The sounds of a conversation outside my door. I lift myself up on my elbows straining to hear. Voices murmur. I catch the word 'Slashstorm' and then footsteps are striding away down the corridor. The door opens and Kristophe backs in carrying a tray.

'Where has he gone?'

'I told him to go to the mainland and get laid. He couldn't leave with Yakuza here.'

I can see him lounging back at his ease while pole dancers circle him. *Compliant.* Eager. On their knees.

'What happened to the blood debt?'

'It was paid.'

'How?'

Kristophe says nothing.

'He didn't pay it *himself*?' I can hardly get the words out.

Kristophe scowls as he decants the tray onto the bedside cabinet.

'Tell me. *Did* he pay it himself?'

He glares at me. 'I am not supposed to tell you.'

'In blood?'

'Yes.'

'How much blood?'

'A pint.' The words are clipped.

*Jesus.*

'Why so much?'

'It is not a lot for a life. It is normally a finger.'

The door slams behind him.

Why would he do it? Why would he save me at all? Why was I not dead before Yakuza came? I can understand him not conceding to demands on home turf but why not just deal with me before? I wouldn't put it past him to have staged the whole thing to collapse my resolve. But to what end? Does he really want Snow White's services that much? Is she really the only person who can deal with Winter? There are plenty of other hitwomen out there.

If he wants someone dead, they are dead. If he says Slashstorm is finished, it is finished. There is no grandstanding. I would bet my life on it and I've been betting my life on a lot less recently.

He just saved me. For some inscrutable and subtle reason of his own, but none the less, he just saved me. He gave a pint of his blood for me. There is something powerful, primitive about the idea. It is inspiring. I am grateful. Eye-prickingly grateful.

The day is long and lonely. I watch the door, but he doesn't come. He is out having a good time.

*In the shower, I wash every inch of my body carefully. Then I shout. His voice sounds in the bedroom. He is getting up. Now he is on the other side of the door.*

*'Are you OK?' he says.*

*I lather up the soap until bubbles run down my chest. 'No.'*

*He opens the door and his eyes widen. He stands staring. It is the first time I have seen him surprised. His mouth opens and closes. Snow White is hot, I can see it in his face. He comes over, his eyes wary and his expression rueful as if he has just lost a battle with himself.*

*'I hope you're not going to get me wet,' he says.*

*His fingers reach out, tracing the line of bubbles down my stomach and I pull him against me. The water drums on our heads as his mouth finds mine.*

I open my eyes. Daylight. It was a dream. The disappointment is sharp. A wet dream. Jesus. Like I'm fifteen. Sun shines across the water. Gulls scream.

The door opens and it is Kristophe.

'Where is he?' Impatience is making me irritable.

'Down on the jetty.' He looks worried. 'He doesn't really have time for this.' The wave of his hand encompasses the bed, the room, me. 'He has a lot of things that need dealing with. I told him about you giving your word before and he says I can let you out to use the bathroom.'

I nod.

'And he said' – Kristophe twists his hands – 'that I was to tell you that if you hurt me he will hunt you to the ends of the earth.'

'Kristophe. I wouldn't touch you. You know that.'

'Then why—' He stops.

'Why what?'

'Nothing,' he says.

He unbuckles me and I fly to the bathroom window. The air is warm. A man is climbing out of a speedboat. I squint in the bright sunlight. I can hear the shouts of greeting. Laughter, warmth, they are close. Voices float up the cliff face.

'Even you won't be able to sort this out. What are you doing here anyway? I can't believe you stopped the Cage for some woman.

World War III is breaking out and you are here messing around with some chick? What's she like? Does she throw you to the ground and squeeze you between her massive thighs?' The newcomer laughs.

'It is not like that.'

'Is she really here?' The new arrival is confused. 'I didn't think it was actually true. I can't believe this, Alek.'

*Alek?*

'I've never known you to bring a woman here. What do you always say? "Emotion is for fools. Women are weak and they make you weak. They suck you in and drag you down, surround you with their soft pillowy limbs and suck the life out of you". Boy, you must have it bad.'

'Don't be ridiculous.' I can hear the scowl in his voice.

A terrible premonition hits me. I peer through the slats. They round the final flight of stairs. The stranger has long dark hair. Even in aviator shades he is unmistakable.

*Roman.*

Brothers. The same olive skin and chiselled features. The laughter. The recognition. They even look alike.

*I am the world's biggest fool.*

It was no coincidence Roman was at the Colony Club. He had already been sent to find me. It was no coincidence he turned up in a bar beside GCHQ. He was there to kill me.

They stand facing each other shoulder to shoulder and I am back on the Courchevel airstrip watching two men greet each other. And I realise it is even worse.

No wonder he uses Halo as his ops team. Halo is his brother.

They turn and disappear into the house.

Alek and Roman Konstantin. What a talented pair.

For an hour, maybe more, there is nothing, then I hear footsteps on the stone outside. Murmured voices. Serious. Thoughtful.

Voices that have spent an hour in discussion and are now going their separate ways. Someone is going down the cliff steps. A speedboat leaves the jetty.

Have they both gone?

Footsteps in the corridor. A long quick stride. They haven't both gone. My heart beats a single painful beat. The door opens.

He is wearing holsters round each thigh. My eyes widen at the hardware and I realise I have never seen him with a single weapon. It is serious.

'I have some things to sort out on the mainland.'

I look at his forearm. I want to say thank you for the blood debt, but I don't know how.

'I am going to take your IV out before I go.'

He opens the drawer and removes a dressing pad, a bag of cotton wool, surgical tape and a pair of gloves. He disappears for a moment and there is the sound of running water from the bathroom. Then he is back, snapping the gloves on his wrist and straightening my arm.

He lifts the tape gently. I look away from the surge of blood that comes out with the needle. The tiny piece of rubber hose wiggles out through the hole. He presses the cotton wool down hard.

I watch his face, willing him to talk to me.

'Keep the pressure on for ten minutes.'

'Yeah.' I say. 'It's not my first time.' The voice doesn't sound like mine.

He sticks the dressing over the puncture wound and holds it down with the surgical tape. He turns his back, stripping off his gloves, looking out of the window.

'You are free to go.'

*What?*

He releases my ankle cuffs. He bends over my body, unlocking one wrist then the other, not meeting my eyes.

'Where?'

'Wherever you want.'

'I don't understand.'

'I wanted your loyalty, Snow White, but I am not going to force it. You are free to go if you want.'

Seagulls screech outside the window.

'How long will you be?' I whisper.

'I don't know. We'll talk when I get back.' He is looking out of the window. 'If you are still here.'

Then he is gone.

# CHAPTER 49

I let myself out of the room and stand in the corridor listening to the silent house. Alone. I pad down the corridor, down the stairs and stand in the hall looking out through the open front door at the sea and the jetty and the speedboat ready to take me anywhere I want to go.

The floor by the door is gritty with sand.

The memories are flooding back. I can see him climbing the steep cliff stairs in the night, his head bent to shield me from the cold.

I go down through the twilight green of the basement and out into the bright light. Is this really his favourite place? The ground is baked hard, strewn with rusty pine needles. They lie in slippery pools, the earth beneath cracked into hexagons. Pine and washing powder. The smell is comforting, domestic.

I go back to the hall. The black-and-white tiles are cool under my bare feet.

*You can go anywhere, but not into the locked room.*

Is it a cupboard under the stairs or is it an actual room? I trace the crack around the door with my finger. The lock is small and flimsy and new. Like the locks at Henri's. It wouldn't keep a child out. He must know that.

*What have you got in there, Bluebeard? Is it a server room? The Firestorm hub?*

I go back out through the open front door. The stone on the terrace is so hot I can barely stand. The locked door watches me from the hall.

*

The lock gives way with one good kick from my bare heel like I knew it would. The frame splinters, the door flies back. An internal room, not a cupboard. Crammed full. Its contents glitter. I walk in slowly right to the end.

Mirrors. Elaborate gold frames, full-length dressing mirrors, wooden frames from a bathroom. They glimmer in the dim light, stacked against the walls. My fingers reach out to touch a huge embossed frame.

Winter stares back at me, her face thin and chiselled after Snow White's. Her short blonde hair stands out from her head like a halo. Her green eyes sparkle. There is a thin slash above her right eye. I touch her face, her yellow cheekbones. She looks ethereal, a wild creature.

I turn and a thousand Winters turn with me.

'He has always known,' she says. 'Your implants came out in the camp.'

# CHAPTER 50

Daylight. A new day. Still alone. I flex my shoulders, turn my neck from side to side. My ribs feel comfortable, my knuckles are healed and the bruises on the back of my hands are turning yellow. My mind is hiding something from me, I circle round and round, not facing it. I think about all the men I have known and all the women and how they measure up. They don't measure up. I cannot hide from this.

I wash every inch of my body carefully. I wrap a towel around myself and clean my teeth. My jaw still feels sore and now I know why. My implants were taken out on the operating table in the camp. That's why it felt like I had had a general anaesthetic. Surgeons carefully deconstructed Snow White's face and reconstructed Winter's.

*Why?*

I stand at the windowsill. A single speedboat is moored up on the jetty ready to take me anywhere I like. If I want to go.

In his bedroom, I press my cheek against his pillow.

What did I find in the locked room?

A mystery.

He patched up a government agent, set her broken arm, nursed her back to health. He protected her. He paid her blood debt.

*Why?*

I wait on the stairs, looking out of the high window across the waves. My heart thumps in my chest. A speedboat is crossing the bay with a single occupant, racing the early morning wind. The throttle chokes as it slows.

I am on my feet, swinging off the handrail, clattering down the stairs and out through the front door. The day is already warm. I fly down the cliff steps and he looks up, a question in his eyes. I stop on the jetty suddenly shy and he leaps out of the boat not waiting to tie it up.

'You are still here,' he says. 'You didn't try to run off.'

I shake my head, grinning like an idiot. Then I am throwing myself into his arms. His body armour is hard. He lifts me off my feet, swinging me round, burying his face in my hair. I can feel his stubble and happiness bubbles through me.

I pull the gun out of his right holster with my good hand and shove him away from me. His arms drop to his sides, his face set. The vein in his neck pulses. I level the gun. Time stretches out.

Snow White watches us, facing off on the jetty.

'You know you said I wasn't your type?' I say.

He nods.

I lower the gun to my side and then offer it back to him, magazine first in surrender.

'I want to be compliant.'

His face blazes with triumph. He puts the gun in its holster and pulls me roughly back into his arms, his expression full of conquest.

'There's something I need to tell you,' he says.

'Later.'

I turn my face up to his and he kisses me. The heat sweeps up my body. The jetty fades, the baking sun, the grit beneath my bare feet and there is nothing but his mouth on mine, his arms around me, his hands in my hair. I skate my hands up the body armour tugging at the straps. He gives a low laugh as he pulls away and a moment later, he is dragging the breastplate over his head.

I slam him hard on his bare chest, a mighty blow with the heel of both hands, and he crashes over onto the concrete, back and head. For a moment, he lies stunned and still and I wonder if I have knocked him out.

Then he is struggling with his body armour and getting to his feet and I am in his speedboat turning the key in the ignition.

'What are you doing?' he says.

Even now he doesn't get it.

'It's been a pleasure, Alek Konstantin.' My voice is as hard as my expression.

Now he gets it.

He is up and hurtling to the jetty edge. I am just out of reach. His eyes narrow as he measures the distance.

'Get back here,' he says. He pulls the Glock.

'You know it's not loaded.'

*I know how you think – it's a test just like the axe.*

He turns to the other speedboat moored on the jetty.

'You aren't going to catch me in that either. It was set up to fail.'

'Winter,' he whispers. His final card.

'Goodbye, Alek.'

'What do you think will happen if you take me down? The world is a safer place with me in it, Winter.'

'Tell that to John J. Traynor.'

As I open the throttle, the last thing I see is him standing on the jetty, his face full of anger and frustration and sadness.

Finally, finally I have learnt.

What did I find in the locked room?

Myself.

# CHAPTER 51

The welcome committee on the flight deck of HMS *Albion* salute as I leave the Chinook like I am a national hero. God knows what Simon has said to them. I am a strange kind of passenger in a T-shirt and bare feet. They marshal me straight down to medical.

They have diverted HMS *Albion*. They have pulled it from its patrol of the Mediterranean, its search for asylum seekers braving the waves. They are so worried about reprisals that they hijacked a battleship to bring me home. It will turn up in Portsmouth months before it was supposed to. How do you hide a woman? Dress her like a chicken and put her on a boat with a load of other chickens.

The on-board sickbay is just like every other berth on a battle-ship and nothing like the white sterile GCHQ detention floor. The Chief Medical Officer is a commander with three gold bands around his cuff and the two crimson stripes of his profession. He is bluff and cheerful with fat sausage fingers. He gives me the once over. Checks my splint, checks the implant scars inside my mouth and takes my blood. Trace morphine, nothing else. I tell him about the knockout gas and the Dex and the amobarbital and he purses his lips.

The young SBA comes in carrying a pile of uniform. She looks at me from under her long lashes. 'Is there anything else I can do for you? Anything at all?'

I consider this carefully. 'No, thank you,' I say.

'You are to report to the incident room,' she says. 'For debriefing.'

I stare down at myself in uniform. The boots are awful. I have never wanted to be in the military. There is a cadet outside my door, like I am a prisoner. He escorts me down the metal corridor, up ladder stairs, along another corridor and holds a door open for me.

'After you, ma'am,' he says.

The ops room is about a quarter of the size of the GCHQ incident room. A man with Captain stripes is standing by a monitor. He shakes my hand.

'Captain,' I say.

'It is an honour.' He sounds like he means it.

He sits me down at the terminal and logs me in and a moment later Control is on screen tapping the microphone.

'Is it on?' He is talking to someone off camera.

'I will leave you to it,' the Captain says.

Control is smiling.

'From the beginning, Winter,' he orders.


'So, he killed John J. Traynor?' he says when I'm finished.

'No doubt about it. I have seen the murder weapons.'

'So, when did he blow your cover?'

I shrug. 'I must have cracked under the amobarbital.'

He looks down at his notes. 'If you had amobarbital, it would be in your blood work. You never had it. You had a general anaesthetic to take your implants out and set your arm. Which means he knew before that. You didn't crack under questioning because you were never questioned.'

He is smiling so much I can actually see teeth. Unnerving.

'He was waiting for you. The Cage was the obvious place to come at him. He was expecting you to come in on your knees, services for sale. I'm betting they ran DNA on every woman in the place and there you were – not a hooker, a hood. A perfect DNA match.'

*The blue pill.*

'There was arnica on my back when I woke up in the trailer park…'

'He probably went to put a bullet in you. There you were, unconscious and naked from the wire search and he reached for the first aid, not the Glock.'

'Dumb decision.'

'Maybe he wanted to see what you would do. He could have pulled you in any time, after all. I'm sure he didn't expect you in the Cage.'

'That is why I walked out of the holding-cell scot free.'

'I leaked your full file after Courchevel – DNA, everything,' Control says. 'I knew he would be intrigued. A man like that? How many times does he meet an equal? Especially an equal that looks like you. It is lonely at the top.'

*I don't believe it. I have been set up by my own boss.*

'I knew it was working when the 100 million dollar contract on you got cancelled,' he says.

'*What?* When was that?'

'A week ago.' He is still smiling. 'Alek Konstantin, the world's most powerful man, fell for a honey trap, the oldest trick in the book.'

'You knew I would go rogue?'

'It's why I hired you. Only a woman who walks on both sides of the moral divide could have pulled this off. You have always been… conflicted.'

I'm speechless.

'You will succeed Erik as Head of Field and my number two.' He smiles. 'It is good to see you all grown up, Winter.'


'So, what happened to Slashstorm in the end?' I say.

'Nothing.' Control waves his hands dismissively. 'We'll get a lot more data later obviously.'

'Later?'

'During the live transmission.'

The room rocks. I grip the desk. For the first time I actually feel like I am on a ship.

What does he mean 'the live transmission'?

I pull up the Slashstorm home page, my heart hammering. Twelve faces, twelve counters spinning so fast the numbers are unreadable. Business as usual. Millions and millions and millions of people voting.

*You have my word. Slashstorm is finished.*

The betrayal feels like a body blow. Slashstorm is in perfect working order with six hours to go.

I swallow hard to stem the rising panic. 'So, what have we got?'

Control waves his hands again. 'It is irrelevant.'

'You mean we've got nothing?'

Control shakes his head. 'We'll get a lot more from the actual event.'

'What? So that's the plan?' I am struggling to keep my voice level. 'We wait for someone to be tortured to death to collect the live data?' My sinuses burn.

Control's voice is hard. 'One life. You of all people, should be able to see the bigger picture. Once we have Alek Konstantin, we will dismantle his sites one by one.'

'He's not behind it. He pretty much told me it wasn't him.'

'It's not the first thing you admit to the woman you are trying to seduce.'

I scowl, leaning into the screen. 'It wasn't like that. I was chained to a bed. He could have had me any time he liked.'

Control looks at me like I am missing the point. 'I'm not talking about sex, Winter. He cancelled the contract out on you. What do you think that means?'

'I'm not his type. He said so. It's beside the point anyway.' I pinch the bridge of my nose. *Men are monsters but that doesn't mean they have to be monstrous.* 'If anything, he was trying to fight it. He told me it was finished.'

'Irrelevant.'

'I am coming back to London *now*. I will run the incident room on this.'

'Fine.' Control sits back. 'The war is won, Winter. This is just one life. Collateral damage—'

I switch him off mid-sentence.

It takes a while to get me airborne and frustration pulls and claws at me until I am a bundle of bad-tempered nerves.

*You have my word. Slashstorm is finished.*

Why did I think I could believe anything the Prince of Darkness said?

The blue of the Med shimmers below us. The countdown clock is showing four hours.

Twelve faces stare out at me from my laptop.

*You have my word.*

I can't explain the feeling of betrayal. I shiver in my combats. The Osprey is empty except for me and the pilots. An unscheduled run to London. The buffeting, grinding roar drills into my skull. Throbbing behind my eyes. My sinuses still burn.

I study the faces again, one by one. I can feel myself ranking them in preference order. The girl with large brown eyes stares out of the screen at me. I picture the knife getting to work on her, slowly, lovingly sliding under her skin. A scream crawls up my throat. *Please not her.* If I had a phone, I would be dialling the vote counter right now. My gut twists in self-disgust. It is exactly this sentimental human trait of choosing and empathising that has made Slashstorm the success it is. We just can't stop ourselves having favourites.

I go back to assessing like a policeman. I blow the images up, analyse them frame by frame. The same room. The same chair each time. One after the other. Definitely a mirrored room. Perfect for this kind of camera show. I worry at them like pieces of a jigsaw, turn them round and round, pick them up and put them down again.

We are hugging the Spanish coast. A strip of blue meets urban sprawl. My shoulder straps bite as we accelerate. A military aircraft hurrying me back to the incident room to watch a murder live and do nothing to stop it.

I *know* Alek is not behind Slashstorm. He may control the world's hitmen, but he has a moral code that stops well short of torturing for entertainment. But what made me tell Control he was fighting it? Nothing but my gut and wishful thinking. It turns on its head everything we have assumed.

I remember our conversations on the island. The Prince of Darkness as dark policeman. He killed Dominique St Vire for crossing the line. So why did he kill John J. Traynor III? What had *he* ever done? And why did he do it himself in such a brutal way, as if he were sending a message? Men are monsters but that doesn't mean they have to be monstrous.

*Leave that to the women.*

I turn the idea round and round.

The grey of the English Channel, foam-flecked, flies past, bringing me closer to London and the cold incident room. There is rain up ahead.

The countdown is moving towards the final hour. The digital clock fills the screen. I will be lucky to make it to GCHQ in time. Already the tracers will be in place, the analysts at their monitors, Max scowling over the data feed, a problem to solve. All around the world, people are getting ready to watch the show. Maybe they are watching to see if their favourite is safe, maybe to see who got the fewest votes, to see who was the least popular, but they are watching all the same.

I stare at the screen again. Willing it to show me something no one else has seen. I can smell jasmine in the cold closeness of the helicopter, a phantom nasal hallucination. I hate mirrors, they show your real self. As if your face is a mask and the mirror you is the real you.

Something clicks.

I sit frozen, staring, not even moving my eyes, trying not to lose the feeling. It is there at the back of my mind. Adrenaline floods me. *I know something*. My brain flails, searching. I can't pin it down. I can't grasp it.

Elegant fashions, a little too precise, a little too cut-out and static. A mask. The sensation of an outer shell, a wooden cover while the real face lies behind.

A forest of silver aerials, high-tech transmitting equipment on the slippery grey of the wet roof opposite.

The Marquise bends over me, engulfing me in jasmine. Her hair curves down either side of the back of her neck. Blunt fingernails run over my naked body. In a corner, a camera on a tripod films the scene. A fist slippery with oil pushes inside me. Her exposed spine is knobbled like some prehistoric creature as she leans over me, spread-eagled beneath her. I am watching from above, looking down on my unconscious self.

I am staring up at a mirrored ceiling.

A mirrored room.

I have been in the Slashstorm room.

# CHAPTER 52

The Osprey curves a wide arc as we burn the turn, the grey of the Channel flying by as we swoop low, streaking back the way we have come, back towards Paris, my heart pumping louder than the thudding rotor blades.

Fifteen minutes to go.

The thin line of motorway leads straight into the heart of Paris. Even with the auxiliary tanks we were running low on fuel. Now, with an unscheduled fifty miles added to our journey, we are flying on fumes. I shrug off my shoulder straps and buckle on the harness. The pilot is navigating blind following the Seine. The Eiffel Tower glints in the sun. I clip on and throw open the door. The wall of air hits me hard as a fist. Ice cold. Two thousand feet up. It is like toy town down there. I move my wrist in a circle, ordering him lower, the buffeting wind drowning my words. The Haussmann grid system is identical across the city.

On my laptop, Slashstorm starts its sixty-second count down. I get ready, check my buckles, check the line. There is no one to control the winch, no one to slow my descent. It is going to burn like hell.

Air traffic control scream in the cockpit. The radio blurs with urgency. An unscheduled flight path right over the heart of government, they will be scrambling fighters. The pilot catches my eye as I hang over the edge, then I am gone. I fly down towards the fairy-tale rooftops, the wire skinning my palms.

It is worse than I feared. I land heavily, the line dragging me towards the edge. I brace against the parapet. My hands are raw and bleeding, my fingers numb and useless as I fumble the release. The line flies free and I throw myself across the rooftop to the fire door, slipping and sliding on the slick surface. The heavy door is cold against my burning palms. The door is locked. I press my forehead to the cold metal, frustration stinging my eyes.

Behind the door, a girl screams. The metal vibrates with it. Desperate, panicky screaming.

*Think.*

I stare round at the forest of aerials.

Disrupt the signal. Kill the transmitter.

I half slide, half scrabble my way down into the gully. The evil bit of metal vibrates under my sore fingers. My palms sting. The aerial hits the roof with a clang.

I scramble back to the door. The screaming has stopped. Sobbing. Someone is climbing stairs in a hurry. I pull myself round and up onto the ledge above the door.

A shape on the roof opposite catches my eye. Alek is silhouetted against the skyline. My heart thumps once in recognition and the feeling of betrayal evaporates. He has an assault rifle slung over his shoulder and he watches me impassively.

The fire door crashes open and a hooded figure comes out wearing the dusty black robes of the Slashstorm contractor. How did we not notice the size before? How delicate the gloved hands are? The door stands open below me. The sobbing is clear now. The figure picks its way carefully across the fairy-tale terrain. Bare feet. She throws back her hood. The Marquise is scowling. Her perfect swinging hair hugs her jawline. The heavy hood frames her face. She could be arriving at the opera.

A woman, not a man. I will never listen to psych profilers ever again. She slips and slides across the rooftop just like I did.

Her feet are bare. She pulls the transmitter upright, resets it and turns back. Now excitement gleams in her eyes. Her face is alive with brilliant, vivid vitality. The mask is gone. Anticipation hums through her like Christmas morning.

I jump down from the ledge, barring her way.

Rage flashes across her face, forked-tongued and malevolent, and finally I understand this woman and I am glad I don't have a weapon. I want to use my fists. The strange grey eyes slide over me, lingering on my mouth. My skin crawls. She comes a step closer.

'I know you,' she says. Her head tilts and her tongue comes out as if tasting the air. 'You are different.' Her hand reaches out towards my lips. 'I never forget a mouth I have had. Why did you leave him alive? That wasn't part of our deal.'

'New deal.' I say, and punch her in the face hard enough to break her jaw. My skinned palm screams but I don't care, the need to take her down burns through me.

She stumbles backwards, scrambling across the slippery terrain, terror and realisation lending her speed. The scrabbling reminds me of someone else on a rooftop long ago. She slips and slides, trapped by the steep slope of the gully, the folds of material caught in the forest of aerials. The robe comes free in my hands. She backs away. I stalk across the roof like a hunter with a wounded doe.

'Who are you?' she says.

'A monster.'

I hit her again and again. Her face is broken. This is why Alek uses knuckledusters, fists don't do enough damage. I drag her to the parapet, her bare feet kicking and sliding. I pull her to the edge, to the row of low columns and up onto the stone. Now I understand what it was in Ferret's eyes when he thought of the Marquise. It was fear.

Her blunt fingernails claw at the ledge, a frantic, desperate fight for her life. Terror gives her strength.

I hold Alek's eyes as I shove her over. He hasn't moved. There is a sound like a gunshot as she hits the cobbles. The sound of a skull hitting stone. I put my palms on the ledge, breathing hard. And the knowledge hits me.

I killed her deliberately. Because it needed doing.


The fire escape stands wide. Somewhere in the house a girl is sobbing in heart-clutching fear. I lunge down the stairs following the sound. I am on the floor with the ancestral portraits and the thick carpet.

A door stands open.

Mirrors. A room panelled in mirrors.

A girl tied to a chair.

I fall to my knees at her feet.

'Who are you?' I say. 'Where do you come from?'

The wide brown eyes stare, unblinking.

I take in the ill-fitting clothes and suddenly I know where she comes from.

'I am Traynor Trust,' she says in broken English.

Of course she is. I get an image of a white-haired body beaten to death with knuckledusters. John J. Traynor. The missing piece in the Slashstorm jigsaw. An endless supply of teenagers we couldn't trace. The Prince of Darkness as dark policeman. That was his way of dealing with it. Sending a message. That was why he used knuckledusters. It was to make a point. And I remember Dominique St Vire dead in a dumpster and Alek telling me 'Slashstorm is over'. He thought he had dealt with it then.

I get to my feet and turn to face the camera. The red light of live transmission winks. I stare down the lens at the millions watching and for a moment it feels like they are so close I could touch them.

Blood from my palm drips on the parquet.

The girl's brown eyes are wide.

I lift the camera off its stand and hurl it at the wall and the mirror shatters into a thousand tiny fragments.


My skinned palms burn as I tear at the cords binding her to the chair, my raw fingers clumsy. She tries to stand but her knees buckle out from under her. I lean down. Her arms go around my neck and her legs hook my waist. She is surprisingly light. I edge out onto the landing, the house is silent. Dust motes dance in the shafts of sunlight. The smell of jasmine is everywhere. The need to get out chokes me and I throw myself down the stairs, taking the opera red carpet at a run. I try to put her down to open the street door but she clings to my neck, hanging on my hip as I wrench the lock and then we are out in the fresh air and the world is full of approaching sirens, a street away at most.

The door of the house opposite creaks under my hand. I slide through and shut it quickly behind me. Just in time. Cars screech to a halt outside. Shouts. Running footsteps. The other side of the door, the emergency services are arriving but in here we are protected, isolated, cocooned in soft, dusty silence.

The stairs flex and shift under our combined weight but somehow the creepiness has gone. Maybe it is the warmth of the day. Sun pours through the dirty windows.

I call as I climb. 'ALEK!'

I should have known Alek would come himself to clear up this mess. He is running for his life and he still came. He said Slashstorm was finished and he meant it. I should have trusted my instincts. I should have had more faith.


My lungs heave. My thighs burn with the effort of running up six flights with the girl in my arms.

The bearded man stands in the doorway as I hit the top landing. Adrenaline spikes.

'Where is he?'

His eyes are on the girl. 'He said you would come in time. He said no one would get hurt.'

'How long was he here?'

He shrugs. 'I don't know. A while. Long enough.'

'Did he say anything else about me?'

He shakes his head.

I elbow the fire escape door open. The rooftop is empty. The sirens from the street are loud.

'ALEK!' I shout to the wind.

He has gone.

Why did I think he would wait? Why did I think he would want to see me?

I slide down the slick gully onto my bottom, the girl with the wide brown eyes still in my arms, my muscles shaking from the adrenaline comedown.

# CHAPTER 53

They are waiting at the end of the St Pancras Eurostar platform. Viv is smiling. Simon is sniffing. He holds me at arms' length, scanning me.

'You look great,' he says. 'The hair suits you. Elfin.'

He picks up one of my bandaged hands and turns it over, then he lifts my splint, weighing it.

'Are you done?' I say.

He grins through his tears. 'Welcome home,' he says, throwing his arms round me.


It is afternoon by the time we get to the city. A warm afternoon. Bank interchange is swamped with girls in strappy sandals and guys in shirt sleeves.

Reception freeze at the sight of me and then carry on as if they haven't noticed. I picture the word going out.

*She is back, she is back.*

Security are deferential. We clear biometrics in record time. No one has to say it – I take the lift straight up to the top floor.

Control smiles at the sight of me, his number two, a national hero, suspended for manslaughter within twenty-four hours of being appointed.

'Marseille,' I say. 'I need to go back. I want to make it right.'

*A man sways in his chains, his mouth open in a silent scream.*

'OK,' he says, 'in a week or two, if there's still no new contract out on you.'

Control knows what Snow White did in Marseille.

I nod. It is more than I had hoped for.

'Right now, I want you here,' Control says. 'You have a job to do. You are the UK's first line of defence.'

'I will be making some changes to our recruitment policy. No more marines.'

Control raises an eyebrow. 'You have something else in mind?'

I think about a teenager carjacking a Renault.

'Yes,' I say. 'I want people who will do what needs to be done.'

'God forbid,' says Control.


I lean up against the wall, looking out through the circular clock window. 'How's it going with the French prosecutor?'

Control allows himself a small smile. 'Self-defence,' he says.

I laugh out loud.

'Self-defence.' He says firmly. 'You were unarmed. Frightened. Judgement impaired by days of captivity.'

'Brainwashed by the Prince of Darkness, you mean.'

'Aleksandr Konstantin thinks he is above national boundaries, Winter. He thinks he can make his own laws.'

*He has to make his own laws.*

I stare out at the Bank junction. Pastel shirts wait at the crossing.

They have raided every address he has ever been associated with: a thousand-acre ranch in South Kazakhstan, a townhouse in Astana, a flat in Moscow, a castle in Umbria, an island in the Adriatic. His homes are in smoking ruins, but they haven't found him. Facial recognition software combs the planet, peering out of millions of cameras.

'Looks like we have avoided another contract on you so far – he is too busy running for his life to worry about yours. Langley thought they had him in New Zealand, but it was a red herring. We'll find him. You know that. The world is a very small place once you know who you are looking for and we are seeing unprecedented international cooperation.' He smiles thinly like he finds this funny. 'Kazakhstan are still holding out, but they will come round.'

*No extradition treaty.*

'It is immaterial anyway,' he says. 'No one wants to bring him to trial.'

*Kill squad.*

Things are moving away from me now. Out of my control. I am only a tiny speck in the story. It is unfolding on the diplomatic stage, a global problem that is seeing global cooperation. While I was still in Paris, I gave video evidence to a joint committee – a specially created task force – and they didn't want to know anything about him or how I found him or how he treated me, they wanted to know about his personal security.

I tried to give an objective answer. He had three bodyguards with him the first time I met him. The second time it was an army. The third time, on the island, there was no one. Only Kristophe.

'Low-key protection,' they said, and I shook my head because it wasn't low-key. There was no one and that in itself was so remarkable they stared at me. I could see them discounting my testimony – the testimony of the prisoner – and I couldn't blame them because I would have done the same.

I lean my shoulder against the window. Across the junction, the early edition of the *Evening Standard* is being unloaded on the steps of the Bank of England.

*Now is the time to mention I saw Alek in Paris.*

'Where are we with Firestorm?' I ask.

'Should be down by the end of the week. No one figured Kazakhstan.' A cyber backwater. 'What do they have? Uranium? That's about it. Which is where he got started, incidentally.' Control's attention flicks back to his screen. 'Worst case, we have global support to landlock.'

Landlocking – shutting an area out of the internet. Impossible with a country like Russia. Just about doable with Kazakhstan.

'The NSA have requested your presence, by the way.' Control allows himself another small smile. Clearly the satisfaction at being able to brief the NSA hasn't worn off. 'Apparently they still have plenty of questions. Check in with medical first and then go over there.'

'What about Slashstorm?'

He waves his hands dismissively. 'Finished. It was just the two of them using the kids from the Traynor Trust Orphanages. The other eleven kids have all been identified.'

The Marquise and John J. Traynor. I wonder how they found each other in the first place. And I know the answer to that. What does the internet do? It brings people together. It makes the world small.

The Marquise is dead. John J. Traynor is dead. And two wardens of children's homes founded by John J. Traynor III and administered by his charitable trust are dead. I know it is Alek and I have said nothing. The press is full of outrage at the vigilante justice and my guts twist and turn with an awful kind of understanding. I have put him under a death sentence and he is doing what he can while he is still alive.

Behind Control, the moths flutter their desperate dance against the pheromone trap. There are even more than before.

# CHAPTER 54

Medical is the same as ever. Bright white lighting, disinfectant, fear. The young doctor with a clipboard looks at me.

'Here to have the splint removed?'

I nod. 'Tell me Everard's not here.'

He shakes his head. '*Doctor* Everard is over at the other facility.'

He ushers me into one of the side rooms – medical couch, huge circular lamp, rotating cutters. The minor injuries repair suite. He gestures to the bed and I sit down on the paper, stretching out my arm. Elastic snaps at a wrist and my eyes prick and suddenly I am back in a white room with billowing drapes. Dark eyes flecked with gold stare down at me.

The doctor has finished laying out what he needs. He pushes a plastic bin over to the bed and picks up a tool. The mini rotating drill whirrs into action. I feel a sudden, irrational urge to stop the drill, not to lose this thing he did for me.

*What is the matter with me?*

The drill screeches and squeals as it hits the splint. Disintegrating plaster of Paris falls into the bin. The doctor's short blue fingers pull at the cracks until they are wide open. There is white muslin underneath, wrapped around the arm, protecting it. I was unconscious when it was put on, I missed seeing long fingers expertly bandaging.

He pulls the arm straight. I stare at the ceiling. His breathing catches, sucks in. His heart rate rockets.

'Whoever put this on has left something behind,' he says.

My eyes snap open, my heart thuds, my breathing gulps. There is a raised red square under the skin. The medic hits the panic button as he backs out of the room. The door slams and the seals activate.

*Containment protocol.*

Standard procedure for a suspected biological weapon.

Now I know why there's no new contract. A remote access detonator. Rigged to blow when the splint came off or in response to a remote signal. Delayed gratification.

In no time at all, Simon's anxious face and messy hair is peering through the square glass in the door. The internal phone rings.

I sit up slowly and stand up.

'Yeah?'

'Everard is on his way. He says to keep it still.'

'OK.' I hang up and go back to bed staring down at my forearm. I wipe my cheeks with the back of my other hand. I am not crying in front of Everard.

It is thirty minutes before I hear something outside the door. Then the seals are breaking and the door opens, and in walks Everard tailed by Simon. They are mid-argument.

Everard scowls at Simon. 'It is entirely unnecessary for you to take the risk.'

The door reseals behind them.

'Winter,' Everard says, his blue eyes a bleak Siberian wilderness.

'Doctor,' I sneer the word.

His cold hand lifts my arm. He stares down at the weal. He presses it with his nail. His sculpted lips purse.

'Looks like a tracker.'

He wheels the portable X-ray machine over to the bed, fiddles around setting it up. Tension pours off Simon. Everard, not so much. His hair flops over his face.

'Keep still,' he says.

Then they are out of the room and the containment seals are back up. The X-ray machine does its thing and Simon gives me the thumbs up through the door. They have got what they need. Now comes the waiting, the analysis and then more waiting. I lie back down on the bed and stare at the ceiling. After a while, the strip light burns holes in my retinas. I squeeze my eyes shut against the blobs of black.

It is twenty-five minutes before the door opens and Simon comes in covered in smiles.

'It is nothing,' he says. 'A well-being tracker, monitoring your vitals. Nothing to worry about. Not the sort of thing we use in the Security Services. Developed for the civilian market. They can have it out in ten minutes.' He shakes his head. 'I think Everard's disappointed it's not going to disperse anthrax in your system.' He grins. Simon finds Everard funny. He is too forgiving.

The door opens and Everard walks in. 'Do you know what they call this tracker? The Wife Watcher. The twenty-first century's answer to the chastity belt. It monitors endorphin levels. It rings an alarm for extreme pain or pleasure.'

'Will he know the splint is off and I have found it?'

Simon looks uneasy. 'Probably. Possibly. In theory. Pressure sensitive. It is a reasonable guess. That's if he's still watching. He's got no need to tag you now. Why would he be watching? He is running for his life.'

He was watching in Paris. That's how he knew I would make it in time. I swing off the bed.

'Where are you going? They need to take it out.'

I curve my hand over the tracker protectively.

'No.'

# CHAPTER 55

I kick my jeans into my locker, button up my silk shirt, strap a knife holster to my thigh and pull on some hold-ups. My fingers trace the raised weal under the skin on my wrist. I wriggle into a pencil skirt, shrug on my suit jacket and check my knives. No guns. The NSA take a dim view of weapons in their building.

Security at London's second biggest server farm and the European headquarters of the NSA in Canary Wharf is long and painful and ends with the usual argument about my knives. They have found all my knives and the one on my thigh. I don't know why I bother trying. They put the tagged plastic bag under the counter and watch me like I am some kind of urban legend, something that might blow at any moment. I turn my back on them and wait.

The lift doors open and my escort appears. It isn't the usual flunky deputised to escort VIPs.

'Hi, Brad,' I smile, my mood lifting fractionally.

'It is so good to see you, Winter,' he says, enveloping me in Chanel Bleu. I kiss him gently on each cheek.

Security watch disapprovingly. Brad's face is pink. We get in the lift and he presses one of the basement levels. I lean my shoulders against the wall.

'I still can't believe it about John J. Traynor,' he says.

'Yeah.'

The details that are emerging about his predilections have shocked an unshockable generation.

'Sometimes it is hard to know who the good guys are in this business. I can't believe he had a Nobel Peace prize.' Brad shakes his head.

'How long is this going to take?' I say. I feel like I have already answered every question there is about the Prince of Darkness.

Brad doesn't answer.

The lift doors open and I realise where we are. We are on the incident floor, the NSA equivalent of the GCHQ incident room. This is where they run live ops from. My breath hisses out through my teeth.

'Why are we down here?'

'I had to get you here somehow,' he says. 'You need to see this. We've found him.'

My heart thuds a single painful beat.

He opens the door.

The room is full of analysts manning terminals. Screen after screen shows a fortress in a desert. Another shows a Chinook interior full of men – a dark ops squad. On the big screen, the Langley incident room. I recognise the man in the corner of the picture, James McKellen, the Director of the CIA.

'Where?' I ask.

'Turkmenistan.'

Eight hours ahead. It is 4 a.m., in Turkmenistan, exactly the time to strike.

'Operation objectives?' My mouth is dry, my voice a long way off.

'Shoot to kill.'

'Estimated time of arrival?'

He gestures at the screens. The Chinook has nine minutes and fifty-six seconds to destination. I squeeze my eyes tight against the burning. In the Chinook they are pulling on gas masks.

'What are they using?'

He tells me. 'Three-mile dispersal radius. We're taking no chances. It was dropped an hour ago. Just reaching maximum dispersal.'

*Is he asleep?* Vulnerable in the dark.

I look round the room at the intent faces. I am finally going to get to watch him die.

And I don't want to.

I stare down at the tracker in my arm, my brain slow. The gas may not have made it into the building.

The tracker will ring an alarm if I experience pain.

I need a knife, fast.

I pick up a fountain pen from the desk and flick the lid off. Seven minutes, forty-six seconds to destination. I brace myself against the desk and jam it hard under my arm.

The axillary nerve.

My knees buckle, the room swims, the nausea rises. I close my mouth on the scream. Pain is going to make me black out. I fall back against the desk, but I keep the pressure up. The pain goes on and on while I watch the seconds tick down.

Beside me Brad hasn't noticed. He is fixing on a headset, taking a call. An internal call.

'Yes, she's here.' He nods in understanding. 'Send it down. She can't leave the room right now.' He hangs up. 'There's an urgent parcel for you here from GCHQ,' he says without taking his eyes from the screens.

The door opens, a flunky stands on the threshold, a white GCHQ internal envelope in his hand. I take it and a small gold shape falls onto the floor.

A single Hershey's Kiss.

My vision is blurred. My legs are weak. I stare at the chocolate. Then I am backing out through the door, bypassing the lifts and staggering up the fire escape concrete stairs. Security gape as I hurtle through, not stopping for my knives. I vault the turnstiles and screech to a halt beside Reception.

'Who delivered this envelope?'

She shrugs. 'Some guy.'

'Where is he?' I slap the envelope down and snap the words out.

'I don't know,' she says, holding her hands up like I have pulled a weapon.

I slam out through the weighbridge onto the street. It is still light. The evening chorus of songbirds shriek their heads off. Plane trees line the street, their leaves a thick canopy overhead. There is no one here. I spin on the spot.

A taxi is idling up the street. I sprint up the road and hammer on his window. He lowers it questioningly.

'Did you deliver this?' I hold up the packet.

He nods.

I sag. My forehead touches the glass. I slide onto the back seat and he pulls off. I rub the tracker reflectively. 'Where are you taking me?'

'I don't know,' he says. His voice is all South London taxi. 'I just follow the satnav. You have to give me your earring.'

I unhook my GCHQ locator and pass it through the little window in the glass. He unscrews his cigarette lighter, pops it in and screws it up again.

We take the slip road down to the A12 going north. Not the Blackwall Tunnel. That rules out everywhere south of London. We pass the ArcelorMittal Orbit, the Olympic stadium, the arc of the velodrome.

The traffic is light and I peer out into the evening wondering if anyone has noticed the taxi, if anyone has noticed me being carted away by organised crime. Who else knew about the Hershey's? I feel the belt round my left thigh, missing its blade. I wish I'd had a chance to pick up my knives. Unarmed and off-grid.

Dual carriageway, knackered tarmac, a sign for Kelvedon. The A12, north of Chelmsford. There is absolutely nothing but East Anglia this way, miles and miles of sugar beet.

I tap on the window. 'Where are we going?'

His shoulder lifts but he doesn't answer.

South of Ipswich we turn off onto the A14 and pass bleak industrial wasteland and now I can make a good guess. Container lorries keep pace with us.

The road skirts Felixstowe town centre, funnelling the traffic round through the marshy wasteland onto the flat, man-made dock of Felixstowe harbour, the UK's biggest container port.

We stop at lights, and then more lights, as we funnel forward into queues. I knew Felixstowe was a big port, but I had no idea. Mile upon mile of container parks and quayside filled with loading cranes like giant blue Meccano. Corridors of rusty painted boxes, yellow, orange, blue. Cosco. Maersk.

The smell of sea and shipping seeps into the cab. We drive through the queues and through the loading bay and come to a stop beside a ship the size of several icebergs. She looks loaded and ready.

The cab door opens.

'Where do I go?' I demand.

He shrugs.

I climb out of the cab and close the door and he drives off.

I swing round. There is no one here. A forklift stands abandoned, reminding me of the quayside in Marseille. It has to be the ship. I stare up at it, rising high above the dock.

A gangplank leads to the front deck. I take it in long strides.

The containers are so tightly packed there is barely room to walk down the side between the high wall of metal and the edge. The deck shifts beneath me like it was just waiting for my arrival.

There is nothing to see, rusty container after rusty container, no one around. I swing round the end of the ship. Twenty-four containers end-on, eight high. I step back, scanning the wall of locked doors. One hundred and ninety-two locked doors. My eyes sweep left and right.

Something jars, a discordant note, and my eyes snap back along the sweep they have just made. In the middle, one row from the top, a yellow container has its door ajar. My heart starts to race.

I walk to the side of the ship and scale the corner. Hand over hand, hitching my skirt up until I am right on the top of all the containers. I straighten up. We are several hundred yards out to sea. I hadn't even noticed us cast off. The lights of the port twinkle behind me. *No going back now.*

I pick my way across the container roofs until the yellow one is below me, slide down the top layer, push the open door wide with my boot and drop down.

It is empty except for a figure leaning against the far wall. The most wanted man in the world.

# CHAPTER 56

'Hello, Winter.'

This man has every reason to hate me, this man who beat twelve men to death with his bare fists. Tiger eyes glitter. Behind me the boom of Felixstowe harbour echoes out into the night. The stained metal creaks. We may have been on the same side against Slashstorm, but this man is still the enemy.

'Why am I here, Alek?'

'You are here to surrender.'

*This guy does not give up.*

'What do I have to do? I've choked you, axed you, knifed you and made you the most wanted man on the planet.'

He folds his arms.

'Why did you keep the tracker, Winter?'

'So you could find me.'

'So you could lure me into a trap?'

'Obviously.' I fold my arms back at him.

'How do you explain what happened at 7.55 p.m. this evening?'

The tracker alarm.

'You experienced intense physical pain,' he continues. 'Self-administered intense physical pain. Five minutes to touch down. Cutting it a bit fine, I thought.' Triumph blazes on his face. 'It blew all the lights on your tracker. Why was that, Winter?'

I walk into the container, back him up against the end wall and catch a wrist in each hand. I slam them against the metal. I can feel his heart beating. 'Maybe it's malfunctioning.'

'You'll have to do better than that,' he says.

*Fight it or fuck it?*

Desire slices through me, pooling heavy in my blood, aching in my lower stomach, pounding in my ears. Hot and heavy and needy.

I let go of his wrists and pull his face to me, kissing him hard, grazing him with my teeth. His arms lock around me, his hands grip my hair. The skin round my mouth buzzes. I want to climb up his long hard body and bruise him.

He lifts his head. 'I am mad at you. I want you to know.'

'Likewise.'

'And you are going to admit what you did to the tracker.'

'You've got this all planned out, haven't you?'

'Yes.'

He scythes my legs, dropping me on the metal and holding me in place with a knee to the shoulder. 'We are going to do this real slow,' he says. 'I want to hear you beg.'

Firm hands unbuckle my thigh holster. He traces a long finger down my chest. My back arches, my shoulder blades press the metal. One fingertip.

*Have a little self-control, woman.*

'I never beg,' I say. 'I held out five hours against Everard during interrogation training.'


After a while we lie on our backs, dragging air into our lungs. My heart pounds like I have run a marathon. I feel boneless, spatchcocked, flattened, fucked. I think about his brother's description – 'women just fall at his feet'.

*No fucking wonder.*

'Five hours?' he says. 'I don't think you lasted five minutes.'

*He's not wrong.*

I slam an arm down on his smug face; it's all I can manage.

He grunts. 'If you want to fight, you'll have to give me a minute.'

'Why do they think you are in Turkmenistan?'

'I didn't want to be disturbed.'

'You set this whole thing up just to wring some kind of admission out of me?'

'Yes.'

I roll my eyes. 'I don't know why I'm surprised.'

'I've got something for you,' he says, sitting up and reaching across into his pile of clothes.

A clink of metal, smooth as silk and heavy, falls onto my bare stomach.

The knuckledusters are a perfect fit. I stretch my hand out admiring them like another type of woman might admire a ring.

'They're perfect,' I say. 'How did you get the fit?'

'I took the mould while you were with me.'

I jump up and hit the wall. One, two. Left jab, right hook. The metal clangs. It leaves a dent in the container a mile wide.

'Oh my God. Look at that. I am Superman.' I go again harder, then I clutch my chest. 'I'm going to need to put a bra on to really go for this.'

I look down at him. He is laughing.

'I think I've died and gone to heaven,' he says.

'It can be arranged,' I say. 'Although I doubt you're going to heaven.' I boot him in the ribs. 'Get up. Now I've got these I am going to kick your butt.'

I square up to him and then he is behind me, my wrist across my throat, his arms around my body.

*Dammit. How does he do that so quick?*

'I'm going to kick your butt as soon as I can stop you putting your arms around me.'

'How's that working out for you?' he says, his lips against my ear.

I swing my hips, grinding against him.

'Hey,' he says. I feel his concentration waver. I dip and shift and he goes over my right shoulder and hits the metal with an almighty clang. I kick him again. 'In. Your. Face.'

He takes me out at the knee and I collapse on top of him.

'So, what's next?' he says, checking them off on his fingers, 'You've strangled me, knifed me and axed me.'

'I don't know. How long have I got?'

'Five hours. This ship is going to Rotterdam.'

I push him back, straddle his ankles and he looks down his long hard body at me, his eyes laughing. Slowly I lower onto him, teasing him with my mouth, moving down inch by inch, grazing with my teeth, pulling back again and again until his whole body is an iron hard mass of roped tendons and the thick veins stand out on his neck. He's not laughing now.

'Jesus, Winter, what are you doing?'

'I'm gonna assume that was rhetorical,' I say, my mouth full.

'Please,' he groans.

'What do you say?'

'Please, Winter.'

'Not that.'

'I'm begging.'

'You can do better than that.' My mouth curves in a smile.

He hisses out a long breath. 'No way.'

I hollow my cheeks sucking hard and rhythmic. I take him to the edge and stop. He pushes at my shoulders weakly. I swirl my tongue. I do it again, hard and fast, to the edge and stop. His head thrashes. Hard and fast, to the edge and stop.

'Never.'

'I can keep this up all night,' I say.

He groans. 'Please, Winter.'

Hard and fast, to the edge and stop.

'Say it.'

'I surrender.' The words burst out of him.

\*

I lie with my head against his chest listening to his heart rate slow.

'You know the child that was kidnapped? Was that your brother?'

'My kid brother. Who you are never going to meet, by the way. And not because you are the long arm of the law.'

*Ah.*

'I sent him after you, but he couldn't get near. Which is just as well. He is way cuter than I am.'

'I wouldn't say that.'

His smile fades.

I raise my head and look back at him steadily.

'Tell me you haven't…' His voice is ominously calm.

'Yeah.' I do that shrug that Léon and the Marquise do. 'Better to get it out there.'

He is on his feet in a single move.

The dent he puts in the container is far bigger than mine and that is without knuckledusters. He stands looking at it for a while then he goes again. Unreconstructed alpha male. Like Attila the Hun. Or King Kong on the Empire State building.

'I'm sorry,' I say when there is a pause. 'I didn't even know you. It was nothing.'

'So, like a one time?'

'Five, if we're counting. You know what twenty-two-year-olds are like.'

The container rings with the sound of fists on metal.

I let the storm rage around me.

'I am going to kill him,' he says. 'No wonder he kept telling me we needed to recruit you.' He glares at me. 'I think I should probably just kill you right now. I am obviously not going to be good at handling jealousy.'

'You think?'

\*

We sit in the open doorway of the container, my legs dangling. The edge is sharp against my bare thighs. The sea winds gust, cold against my teeth, against the damp of my bare skin. He pulls his black long-sleeved T-shirt over my head. It is like a tent. His teeth graze my neck. My bare legs kick. Waves crash around us, the rise and fall. I will always associate him with the sound of the sea.

'I like you in my T-shirts and nothing else,' he says. 'Not that there isn't a lot to be said for a suit and hold-ups.' He picks up my left wrist and examines it, turning it this way and that in the dim light. He curls each finger under one by one.

'How is it?'

'I will always have a weakness.'

He puts his arm around me and kisses the top of my head, then my neck, then my face, then he is lowering me onto my back, his body weight on top of me. He pushes inside me, pinning me to the metal, supporting himself on his elbows. His hands are in my hair, his thumbs rest on my cheeks. His thrusts are hard and slow and vehement and I know it is goodbye.

'Say it,' his voice is soft.

I turn my head away from the look in his eyes. His hands jerk my face upright.

'Say it.'

'I surrender.' I whisper the words.

He stands up and dresses quickly, methodically. He leaves me the T-shirt, pulling the body harness over his bare chest. He pulls the straps tight.

Overhead, distant at first and getting closer, I can make out the whirr of a helicopter. He goes to the door and signals to them. He braces himself for the winch.

'First and last time of asking, Winter. Come with me?' He holds out his hand, his face dark against the dawn.

I shake my head.

'Start running, Alek.'

He laughs and then he is gone, the harness winching him up and away into the helicopter.

As day breaks, I sit in the doorway of the shipping container shivering in the sea air and watching the dock lights of Rotterdam get closer. I tuck my knees up to my chest and pull the T-shirt over them. Wind whips my short hair.

*My name is Winter and I am the UK's first line of defence.*

# EPILOGUE

Hôtel de Police. The words are carved into the stone. It is a modern block, but built in the pale sandstone of Marseille so it looks OK. An arch cuts through the building. An orange checkpoint arm blocks the way. A massive *tricolore* flag hangs limp from a flagpole. I take a deep breath and climb the steps.

It is bedlam. The Hôtel de Police is also an ordinary police station. I have to wade through the daily detritus of lost phones, street fights and missing cats to get to the front desk. The duty sergeant picks up the internal phone.

'There's a woman here to see you,' he says to Detective Fresson. 'She won't give her name.' His voice leers.

I picture Fresson putting the phone down and hurling himself at the door. Four floors up. Will he wait for the lift? I lean up against the wall and check the burner location. It still hasn't moved. They are waiting for the dust to settle. I am surprised the battery has lasted this long.

A second later, Fresson comes hurtling down the stairwell, taking the stairs three at a time, spinning round the bend, his hand braced.

I lever myself off the wall by my shoulder blades. His expression falls at the sight of me, a woman in a suit. It is not Snow White.

'Detective,' I hold out my hand. 'Take a walk with me.'

He hesitates for a moment then follows me out through the double doors and down the steps.

I put my sunglasses on.

'Everything I have to tell you is classified,' I say.


After I have left Detective Fresson, I cross town on foot to the old port. It is a beautiful day. I walk slowly across the main square towards the café. The heat is blistering, the air full of roasting meat, Gauloises, bins, coffee. Streets just need a bit of heat to release their sticky, sweaty smells. I pass the fountain, a group of kids hang over the ledge laughing, a dog scratches, its back leg rotating. I shrug my jacket off and pull at my blouse – the silk sticks to my back. It is too hot for a suit.

Café tables spill across the pavement, the tablecloths red and white, the chairs wicker. I duck as I go under the awning. A teenager is working the bar, his back to me.

'Hello, lover,' I say in Snow White's Russian accent.

He spins round at the speed of hope.

His face falls.

'Sorry,' he says, 'sorry. I thought you were someone else.'

I give him a look.

'You can do better than that, Léon.'

He stares and stares and his forehead creases.

I smile, more pleased to see him than I expected. 'You would recognise me if I took my clothes off.'

He always did catch on quick. He charges for the end of the bar, rounds the corner and throws himself on my neck.

'What? How?' he splutters. He pulls back. 'What has *happened* to your face?'

'You don't approve?'

'No.'

I grin. 'This is what I normally look like.'

His mouth drops open.

I put my sunglasses back on. 'Walk with me.'

He tucks his tea towel into his waistband and follows me out under the awning and into the square. I take his arm like we are just having a stroll.

'I waited and waited…' His eyes are full of tears. 'Then the police were there and all hell kicked off.'

He wipes his nose on the back of his sleeve.

'Did they pull you in?'

He nods. 'They were looking for you and Marcel. They saw you arrive but then you vanished.'

'Yeah.'

'They put me in the back of a van and questioned me.'

'Did they do any damage?'

He shakes his head. 'Not really. A few bruises.'

*Amateurs.*

'I didn't tell them jack,' he says fiercely.

I pat his arm. 'Good.'

We sit on the fountain and watch the glittering, sparkling waterfall. It reminds me of a square in Italy.

'Where is Marcel?' he says.

I watch the light dancing on the water. 'He didn't make it.'

He nods like it was what he thought. 'Can I see you again?' he asks.

'Yes.'

His face lights up with disbelief.

I shake my head, smiling. 'Not like that.'

'You don't want to go out with me?'

I put my arm around his shoulders.

'Better than that – I want to offer you a job.'


I have one last place to visit. The pavement is all grey concrete and dried chewing gum, dusty in the heat. Madame Jo Jo's is closed for a siesta, the Tabac is open, but I walk past. The 7-Eleven is empty. The green cross of the *Pharmacie* glows across the street. The grill door is shut. I press the bell.

The door buzzes.

I walk down the corridor and into Reception. He perches on his stool, still slightly awkward. He looks up and his eyes widen at the sight of me. A woman in a suit is not what he was expecting.

'Hello, Henri.'

I put my hands in my pockets and when they come out they are encased in metal.

He stares.

'Shall we?' I say.

# A LETTER FROM ALEX

I hope you enjoyed *Winter Dark* – and that you'll look out for the next book in the series, *Winter Rising*, which carries straight on. If you'd like to keep up to date with all of my latest releases, you can sign up at the following link. Your email address will never be shared, and you can unsubscribe at any time.

www.bookouture.com/alex-callister

If you have time, I'd love it if you were able to write a review of *Winter Dark*. Reader reviews on Amazon, Goodreads or anywhere else are so important to an author and can spread the word to new readers.

Back in 2016 I was sitting looking at a version of Firestorm on the dark web.

The city analyst in me was thinking: *Not very well organised, not very well laid out, no customer complaints process.* And it made me think, *What if you had an amazing version of this site? What if it was as appealing and well run as Amazon or eBay? Up on the main web? Freely available (and untraceable)? Would it be popular? Would anyone use it?*

I sat and thought for a long time and came to the conclusion it could change the world. Everyone has someone they are afraid for, someone they don't want hurt – 'if you care, your enemies have all the leverage they need.' The potential for coercive intimidation and control would be immense. This is where Winter's world comes from.

And Winter herself?

I love action movies (you may have got that from the one liners) and was mulling the idea of a female James Bond. What would she be like in our surveillance age? Winter is the result, but I have tried to stay faithful to the original idea of Bond with his louche, promiscuous ways. It is interesting to write this kind of female hero today. I hope I have found a way without crossing too many lines. Maybe true equality is discovering a small element of toxic femininity.

I would love to know what you think! Contact me directly on *alex@acallister.com* or via my website, *www.acallister.com*.

Best wishes,
Alex

 www.acallister.com
@CallisterAuthor

Lightning Source UK Ltd.
Milton Keynes UK
UKHW011926060120
356461UK00002B/153/P

9 781838 881085